BREAD and CIRCUS

Other books by Morris Renek

LAS VEGAS STRIP
HECK
SIAM MIAMI
THE BIG HELLO

Morris Renek

BREAD
and
CIRCUS

WEIDENFELD & NICOLSON
New York

Published by Weidenfeld & Nicolson, New York
A Division of Wheatland Corporation
10 East 53rd Street
New York, NY 10022

Library of Congress Cataloging-in-Publication Data

Renek, Morris.
    Bread and circus.

    1. Tweed, William Marcy, 1823-1878—Fiction.
    I. Title.
    PS3564.E58B7 1987   813'.54   86-26652
    ISBN 1-55584-070-1

Manufactured in the United States of America
Designed by Irving Perkins Associates, Inc.
First Edition
10 9 8 7 6 5 4 3 2 1

This book is lovingly dedicated to
NAOMI

Part One

THE
DRAFT
RIOTS

ONE

"I did their dirty work. Now Fifth Avenue wants someone clean." This vengeful utterance came from Tweed's friendly face rising up for air from a plate of oysters. His face, which could charm birds from a tree, was shining with confidence. He was tickled at the combat ahead, relishing victory because right was on his side. How he despised the coldness of Fifth Avenue, the party's big money contributors tossing him away after he served their purpose. Yet, how he admired their practical organization! No wonder they ruled stronger, smarter men who are burdened with illusions. He took pleasure wiping his lips with a small flag of a Delmonico's linen napkin. Wasn't he trembling inside that his secret thought escaped from his lips, and didn't this prove he had no control over himself when he had to get to the top? Success glowed on his face. He was almost mindlessly happy, and this mindless quality evoked envy from canny political professionals.

Only a prehistoric appetite could pile up so many shiny, licked oyster shells. At a Delmonico's table glossy iridescent half shells are jammed down the long throats of dessert glasses. Gleaming shells overflow gold-wreathed whiskey tumblers. Half shells lie belly-up in finger bowls. Shells float in the shallows of delicate vichyssoise. Stacked shells are capsized and tossing in pitchers of ice water. Shells dress the silver lip of a spice bowl. Shells lit from within with their rainbow glow of primitive Indian money clog the matching Waterford crystal.

Tweed lets fly from his stout bagpipe of a belly a ripping belch into his monogrammed napkin. Shells blow off finger bowls, ice chatters in the crystal decanter, hidden ashtrays stand revealed, shells sink to their watery bottom. Tweed's ox shoulders bump contentedly back against the banquette. His claw marks of feasting staining the snowy linen of the littered table.

Tweed's gargantuan appetite conveys that the world *is* your oyster. His men bask in his gorging, which whets them for success. Tweed is an eating behemoth. His hunger makes men merry. He's a force of nature fired up to eat the green of this world. His eating reveals the voraciousness needed to succeed.

Tweed's high expectations give him ruddy cheeks. His six feet of whale shape is his outer protection. His inner protection is his experience. His face, extraordinary for a public man, lacks armor. Somewhere behind his sunny, unbridled ways of outrageous corruption is a decent upbringing.

His longish face is egg-shaped. He'd be homely if not for his exuberance and those good-humored eyes twinkling with animal alertness. His high, domed forehead would be called a thinker's forehead except that it doesn't have that effect due to his natural friendliness. His nose is Roman in stature but not in dignity. His fine brown hair has a reddish glint and grows in uncared tufts about his cabbage ears.

He waves his thick arms to show there's nothing up his custom-tailored sleeves. "I'm a magician! One minute you saw a dummy. Abracadabra, siss, boom, blah! I elected Horatio Seymour governor!"

Applause from the boozers with their sleek rosiness of a high-priced rubdown. Their expensive suits can't hide their smell of dog lying too near a warm stove. Only Brains Sweeny, pale as frost, shied from Tweed chasing his appetite. Sweeny's dour look implied celebrations are for the blind. His shrewd, lizard stillness gave off a foreboding that Tweed's victory would turn to ashes in his full mouth.

"Did you hear," Tweed beamed, "of the mayor who resembled Governor Seymour?"

"No, no." His cronies begged Tweed to go on.

Tweed gave the marvelous illusion his experience had not spoiled his innocence. "This mayor is not saluting the flag at the playing of the National Anthem." Tweed's face rounded with delight. "A reporter sidles up and asks the mayor why he isn't saluting the flag? The mayor tips him off that it's too early to commit himself."

The crystal- and silver-laden table trembled with their laughter. They reveled in Tweed's candor, which proved they were superior to the men around them.

No sooner had the laughter chuckled down when Tweed hoo-hooed. "When I served my one term in Washington, Senator Vest said this about his fellow congressmen. When they speak, they are lying. When they are silent, they are stealing."

The explosion of laughter tumbled crystal, bolted men to their feet, dislodged Tweed from his encampment. Waiters, water boys quickly wiped away the mess while Tweed sang out, "Braves, since we're up, off to the Wigwam to celebrate turning Seymour into our governor." Standing up expanded his full belly and gave him a buzz of euphoria. His belly had become his triumph of indulgence. A rosy proof his dreams had come true. Out of shape, no longer muscular to race to fires and rescue victims as he did as a volunteer fire captain with breath enough to blow a silver horn clearing traffic, yet his belly bespoke his success.

Only Sweeny lagged as they were let out by a respectful door-man, their rowdy walk proclaiming they owned the streets and more than a few gentlemen on it.

Tweed inhaled the city as an elixir. His father's stories in his blood. Indians could not read from nature more than Tweed from city skylines. The higher the church steeples, the more pious the men felt whose money built them. The gloomier the prison walls darkening the marketplace, the more frighteningly they lectured the poor. Miles of new commercial buildings would soon be hiding steeples and prisons, as steeples and prisons had taken over the landscape from forts and gibbets. Steeples and gibbets had welcomed traders from all over the world. Now traders would see a commercial skyline of astonishing triumphs and promise. This horizon no longer offered salvation, but success without any signs of punishment.

Tweed knew, no matter how often the government was praised in the press, the only government the poor could trust to provide for them was himself. Too many took spiritual comfort that being poor was punishment from God and therefore deserved. The poor felt important in his company. He greeted them by name. He *asked* about their welfare. His big hello was a boost as well as a greeting. He connected people into their city. Connection was all the justice they needed. He was on an eye-winking confidence with them. They believed he knew the real right, not the right you swallowed to keep from being slammed. Yet no one was more aware than Tweed of their coarse trespassing, ready to rip the guts out of anyone they worshiped and leave him nothing for himself but their devotion.

A worn woman shoved her runty boy at him. "Touch me, sonny, on the conk, please, sir, Mr. Alderman Tweed. I swear he has no cooties. Smell the fresh turpentine on his hair. The boy is an empty drain. If he finds his desk, the teacher gives him a star."

Amid the smiles and laughter of the people who had formed around them, Tweed seriously lay his hand on the boy's gritty scalp.

"Mind you," the vexed mother warned her pod, "Alderman Tweed has put sense in your drain."

The boy popped a mucky finger up his nose for security and as a comment on his elders. "I'm no drain." His voice nasal.

"Teachers is right, you snot." She smacked his noggin to hear his ripeness. The whack popped out a shiny clean finger from his nose. "If you could stick everything up your nose, you'd be the cleanest boy in school. Touch him again, Mr. Alderman Tweed, sir. The frost is deep."

Tweed knighted the youngster with a thumb press.

"Please, Mr. Tweed, sir, tell the runny egg any boy can grow up to be President of the United States."

"President?" Tweed was indignant, taking the measure of the boy corkscrewing a finger back into his nose. "Of the U.S.A.?"

"I'm sorry, Mr. Tweed, sir. The boy needs boosting."

"He'll never be president of anything. And if he should be, whatever he'll be president of won't work."

"Och, don't curse him with honest judgment. He came when I wasn't looking."

The crowd laughed and Tweed was touched.

"The runt," Tweed backtracked, "can certainly be a mayor. If he knows who his friends are, he can be a district attorney. As long as he's regular."

"He's regular as chicken droppings." The mother swore for his loyalty in spite of the finger up his nose.

She had no sooner dragged her boy away when a nudgy woman

threw herself at Tweed. "Do you have an opening for a gray-haired man who can run to fetch your cigars?"

Tweed was tickled. "You know I don't smoke. And I'm Temperance, as my father before me."

"A saint." She roughly wiped her lips that had given voice to such an evil as smoking. "My man opens doors so fast, you'll believe you're royalty. His corns predict the weather. He's a hundred-and-ten-percent regular. You want a sunburn? He'll give you a tan."

"Perfect man." Tweed was impressed. "Does he ever lie?"

"Only," she said proudly, "when a lie is the right answer."

"Send him 'round."

She slapped her knobby hands in ecstasy against her graying temples. "I'll send the lifer over. Bless you, Mr. Tweed. Without you, the farts would've taken over the city to do what they pleased."

When the smiling gathering parted to let her by, Tweed saw through this opening the socialite beauty Mrs. Augusta Cordell sitting in her open barouche. *My God, why is she here?* He dare not face her. *How could she be so thoughtless? Anyone could see her.* She could ruin him. But the more heedless Augusta was, the more he knew passion was ruling her. Thus he worshiped a daring woman who could ruin him at her whim. One wrong twitch by her and his political brightness would be darkened forever.

His father warned him business came first, and he listened, but as he gained power he attracted extraordinary women—only they wanted to come first.

The flagrantly independent Mrs. Cordell was as vital to him as a crown to a king. He could never send her away. He took for granted the lawlessness of politics, but with Augusta he experienced the thrill of being lawless. He patted his neck to ward off her pressure, but the wetness on his fingers proved he was defenseless.

"Tweed's last meal is in his belly and his next meal is in his eyes," said Samuel Tilden, gazing down from the president's window of the Broadway National Bank. Tilden was matinee-idol handsome. His business suit was so white, it was defying. His perfection was in being righteous without being impassable. It was Tilden's superiority that caused him to be baffled by Tweed's good cheer with the crowd around him. "Are you sure Tweed knows Fifth Avenue is dumping him?"

"Quite." The Buddha-shaped Elijah Purdy, president of the bank, nodded. The wrinkled political war-horse was merry the way men are who suddenly catch themselves from falling down stairs.

"Tweed promises them anything."

"Tweed has enough ambition to make the sun rise." Elijah Purdy's eyes were two black seeds refusing to take root in the rest of his noncommittal face. His eyes gleamed like bottle blacking, reflecting back to office-seekers their humbled image. He concentrated only on the detail that interested him, like a barber.

Prominently displayed behind Purdy were citations, medals and pictures of Tammany chiefs gazing down in their resolute Sunday-best faces. A group photograph over his head showed Purdy being sworn in as the Grand Sachem of Sachems of Tammany. One-third of Tammany directors were directors of banks. The city's money was kept at favored banks with a low return of interest. Above this photograph was a formidable sampler: AS THE CURRENCY EXPANDS, THE LOAF CONTRACTS.

This wisdom hanging in a bank was due to the 1837 Panic. Banks were rightly blamed for easy lending, which led to wild speculations—a stock investor needed only a ten-percent down payment —and the ruin of decent hardworking families, companies and stockholders. The more money issued, the cheaper money became. The cheaper the money, the higher the prices. Money became a religious force overriding religious beliefs. Inflation taught the more puritan it was better to spend than to save. Cheapening money cheapened beliefs.

The most powerful party symbol was not on Purdy's wall, but stood behind him in a corner: a statue of the mythical Indian Tammany, a fabulous warrior who fought the demonic anger of *the* Evil Spirit with wisdom, courage and heroic hard labor. The political organization begun about 1798 turned Indian rituals into gobbledygook. Party officials had Indian titles, including the door-man. Their headquarters was a Wigwam and the party's first Wigwam was in a tavern. The Indian Tammany and his fight against evil became such a powerful symbol, he was raised to sainthood by the party. Saint Tammany proved to have short coattails. The record shows that the periods when the organization was free of corruption generally coincided with the party being out of office.

Tilden worried himself away from the window; ordinarily he

viewed the world as though playing scales on a piano. Street life was an alien scene. He couldn't enjoy it and he didn't understand it. He thrived in an office where he ruled the roost as a highly connected railroad lawyer. An office gave him organization—solid, dependable, controllable—no matter how office operations contradicted his beliefs. "If Tweed is so ambitious, why doesn't he know enough to keep on the right side of Fifth Avenue? Any dummy would know that."

Purdy was careful with Tilden. He knew reformers have a fatal way of listening with their vanity. "Show me the man who improved his character by being a leader. Ambition is best when blind. Know nothing about the odds. Know everything else clearly. Leaders destroy themselves before they destroy others."

"Bizarre," said Tilden.

"Only if you lack experience. *How* we arrive shapes us."

"Tweed courts the lowest common denominator." Tilden was uneasy.

Purdy knew how to nick knuckles without drawing blood. "The lower he stoops, the longer his reach. Success takes most of us away from our roots that made us."

"Shouldn't we be at the celebration to cut down Tweed?"

Purdy was amused. "It'll take us only a minute. No one will stop *us* on the street."

Tammany Hall was over a tavern near City Hall Park, and its modest entrance reeked of dog. Tweed knew he must not let his hidden thoughts surface, yet he felt his face stiffen as he approached the Wigwam. When the garrulous thug Red Rooster moseyed up to him, Tweed shooed him away. But Red Rooster, with his shock of brick-red hair, instinctively knew when Tweed needed a jester. "Did you hear about the gentleman who took a lady to bed?"

Tweed's eyes opened wide for Red Rooster to scoot. Tweed and his beefy cronies climbed the worn stairs through the backslapping crush.

Red Rooster persisted. "A gentleman took a lady to bed and asked her if she smoked after sexual intercourse?"

Tweed gave a slight signal with his chin, and a heeler threw a stranglehold around Red Rooster, who by force of character continued telling his joke into Tweed's ear while being choked. "A gentleman took a lady to bed and asked her if she smoked after sexual intercourse? The lady says, 'I don't know. I never looked.' "

Tweed's hearty laugh boomed out, and he entered the pandemonium of the Long Room, king of all he surveyed. The packed arena was ablaze with light shining on the star-spangled bunting. A beaming Tweed rapped the smiling Red Rooster on the back of the head in thanks.

The noisiest furor came along the sides where formally dressed Shiny Hats madly gestured. Their jeweled fingers in the air glittering like fireworks. Their future swam before their eyes as they hollered themselves hoarse, like traders in a grain-exchange pit. Shiny Hats were in the grip of auction bidding for public offices.

Bids became embroiled with those nearby, yet so fierce was the concentration, no one was confused. Booing erupted from sore losers who had to drop out. Their stylish formal dress took some of the sting off their humiliation, though their street origin would not allow them to yield quietly.

A jeweled pinky ring sparkled in the bright lights. "Five thousand dollars for Office of Encumbrances!"

"Booooooooo!"

"No booing, gentlemen."

"Do I hear six thousand for Encumbrances?"

An overlapping shout from a neighboring auction. "Fourteen and a half for Inspector of City Manure!"

"Fifteen thousand!"

"Sixteen thousand!"

"Do I hear sixteen and a half for city manure?"

Frog-croaking desperation. "Who got Department of Street Openings?"

"Ten thousand for Chief Sprinkler."

"Ten thousand, one hundred."

"Ten thousand, one hundred and five."

A throaty craving. "Who got Docks?"

"Thirty-five thousand for Commissioner of Docks."

"Forty thousand!"

"Booooo!"

"Fifty thousand!"

A cry from the gut. "Fifty-five thousand for Assistant to the Tax Commissioner."

"Booooo!"

"That's higher than City Inspector!"

The crowing Shiny Hats who wore high silk toppers bought jobs they did not work at. Their profits came from salaries and fees connected with the office. Only faithful party workers won the right to bid. Inspector of City Manure went for sixteen thousand dollars. The inspector sold the manure collected off the streets for thirty thousand. Sheriffs kept all fees due their office, including bribes from deputies for their jobs.

A shiny hat was a badge of honor, and for that honor the owner supplied the party with a commodity always in short supply—cash. This tower of party loyalty was extremely exposed. He could be tapped for funds without notice. To prove his loyalty he gave. Shiny Hats were spawned by the amount of offices for sale. Thus they were a true measure of a leader's muscle.

A half exception was in the public schools. Teachers had to toe the line of a rigid code of conduct inside and outside the school while kicking back a part of their first year's wage.

At the head of the ballroom-size Long Room, Tweed presided on a commodious throne. On his right, Elijah Purdy. On his left, Brains Sweeny—friend and foe, insecure in his company.

Braves waited in line to get Tweed's attention. Hearing about Tweed and being in his presence was the difference between having fire described and touching it. Their fealty was in their patiently waiting for a moment's notice. In line were the crudest roughs who were the indispensable foot soldiers. They anxiously sought Tweed's grip of congratulations. None could take Tweed's large mitt quick enough. His bracing handshake. The jolt of energy charging them with confidence. The optimistic paw shaking them out of their routine self. He had a politician's vibrancy, freewheeling and personal, yet impersonal in his quickness.

The coarse roughs doubled as shoulder hitters. They invaded opposing parties to spy and disrupt. The brawnier roughs with leather lungs became Shouters. Shouters drummed enthusiasm into rallies. At rallies of the opposition they shouted the most scurrilous accusations to poison the air. Should that fail, they bloodied noses to end the rally in a fight.

While Tweed glowed in their loyalty, he choked on the bad news Purdy gave him with ice-water agreeableness. "I did Fifth Avenue's dirty work. Now they want reform?"

"You've no kick." Purdy evinced surprise at his reaction. "Fifth Avenue made you rich."

"With a dirty name." Tweed burned that he had coddled the

high-handed madness of these men only to be curtly dismissed.

"You don't come first. Think like a party man."

"I don't need boosting." Tweed scorned the advice of a man he admired. "*I* bribed aldermen for your big-money contributors on Fifth Avenue. *I* got them franchises for streetcars, ferries, railroads, markets. Each franchise a license to print your own money."

"Your bribing put reform in the air. For the good of the party, Fifth Avenue wants you out."

"I bribed with *their* money." *Didn't the all-seeing Purdy see?* "My wards elected Seymour, who can't button his fly, governor."

"We didn't want a governor who is self-sufficient. You go through Fifth Avenue or you go through hell."

Tweed threw his ace. "I go through my wards."

"Bill, you've a right to be upset. But the first Republican mayor has been elected in this city. We need to push reform or we'll lose what offices we have."

"*I'm* the only real reform you have. I get immigrants jobs."

"There's your trouble," Purdy said as a favor. "You've become too ambitious to take orders."

Tweed's smile conveyed that a man's success, no matter how crooked and vile, is often a triumph of justice over the injustice done to him on the way up. "Fifth Avenue fears *me?* I beg them for patronage they knew is due me."

"You're turning patronage into a highly efficient army. Look how the street people worship you, and their landlords, and the merchants. You cross all lines and, some say, even party lines."

"I fought the ignorant bigotry. Did you ever read those poisonous school textbooks your high-minded Fifth Avenue friends never protested?"

Purdy went opaque when facts went against him. Then he outflanked the facts triumphantly without having to face them. "You've been around long enough to take hypocrisy for granted."

He yearned for Purdy to turn that stubborn corner. See things his way. Thirteen years ago he'd come up fresh from the seventh ward with Purdy's backing. Now, at forty, with his skills sharper, surer, and yes, more successful, defeats became intolerable. Sure, he was popular, organized, ambitious and money-hungry. Was he to pay for his virtues? He tried to reason with Purdy the way a boy takes castor oil. "How can I be more loyal than by doing the dirty work?"

Purdy pressed him to be fair. "Dirty work is duty."

This ABC lesson thrown into his face, he was about to explode when saved by a rowdy pushing match at the door. A flying wedge of roughs, sleeves rolled up in the street sign for a muss, shoved and whacked Shiny Hats out of their way.

Tammany's guard against invaders were the Dead Rabbits and Bowery Boys, and they furiously hooted and razzed. Their street wars of the fifties were legends. Now, united under Tammany's cloak, they maintained their separate forms of violence to restore order.

The high-fashion Bowery Boys sported toppers crammed with bricks. Their trousers were amply cut as Oxford bags to hide iron-tipped shoes for shin cracking. Deep pockets of frock coats held sappers and iron knuckles. They set their hair in bear grease with a dipping soap lock curled across their forehead. Dead Rabbits were short on style. They charged into combat with a rabbit skewered on a pike as an example of the mercy their enemies could expect. Both gangs strained for Tweed's sign.

The invader's ringleader was the feared and fearless Francis Boole. A pistol riding his beer-barrel pot. Curses of traitor were loudly heaped on his unkempt head.

Purdy was alarmed enough to order Tweed to close the Hall before the newspapers smeared them with another brawl.

The leashed gangs were catcalling themselves into a frenzy. Under their curses swaggered Boole, as a furred beast through a shorn thicket. Boole was pure street. He was not a middle-class roughneck with a picked-up accent hiding behind nervous toughness. Boole's fuse was continually lit. Tweed's very proper Temperance upbringing—no drinking, no tobacco, no gambling—was foreign and even distasteful to him.

Boole was certain he could muscle out Tweed, except that the higher councils of the party didn't want his saliva image up front. Boole took pride in the image no one wanted. Only Captain Isaiah Rynders of Tweed's seventh ward raised the hackles quicker. No matter how many repeaters his gang dragged to the polls, nor how many enemies they kept from voting, the party could not trust him to eat with style at Delmonico's, though Boole had an imperial sense of his worth.

When the game threatened to become brutal, Tweed's status was enhanced. Purdy deferred to him. Under the uproar Tweed played the gracious host. "Let Francis Boole advance."

Purdy thought Tweed lost his keen senses. "Boole is out for revenge. You froze him out of jobs."

The danger lit up Tweed's face. "Fifth Avenue forgot the troubles I took off their shoulders. They think politics comes out of a checkbook."

Purdy wasn't listening. He was watching Boole arrogantly advance, pushing Shiny Hats out of his way and smelling his callused hands as if they had touched unclean things.

Boole stopped within accurate pistol range of Tweed.

Sweeny hissed for a muss. Brains had no respect for the strong unless they were demented, and no sentiment for the weak unless he suddenly became one of them.

Boole addressed Tweed with a directness that drew curses. "The Wigwam must not favor men whose personal ambition is placed above the party."

Fire came into Tweed's eyes at this ruffian daring to tell him his place.

A Dead Rabbit staff rose aloft.

Boole began again. This time with the hungry grumbling of a dog worrying a bone. "Ambition above the party is against our laws and the traitor must be punished."

What was it? Tweed racked his brain. Both ends of the party falling on him. He glanced at Purdy to test the waters and saw him leaning away, expecting the worst and knowing the worst was not to be stopped. Sweeny's nostrils dilated with fright. Brains was physically separating himself as far as possible without it showing to his detriment. Boole's bulging eyes exposed that not everything in him was tied down. This gave his bravest foes pause.

Purdy marveled at Tweed standing his ground as a robin breasting spring.

The howling was at a pitch just before battle.

Boole, knowing what he must do to get back in the good graces of the party and ride the gravy train of jobs for his followers, shouted, "I regret my errors!"

Confusion. Suspicion. A pall. Everyone disarmed. Many hung on Boole pulling out his pistol, but no one knew whether he would shoot Tweed or himself.

Tweed's note of surprise covered his gratefulness. His accepting Boole had a calming effect.

Boole struggled to cleanse himself. "I regret the errors of my ways in leaving the victorious chief, Sachem Tweed."

Those who cursed Boole now applauded his good sense.

"Political death," Boole scourged himself, "is justice to traitors." He lowered his grizzled head.

Tweed opened his arms to welcome a prodigal's return, though Boole was born more than a decade earlier.

Braves heartily cheered as a contrite Boole grasped Tweed's hand and bowed his scarred head three times, each time lower than the last, and every time with a frightening devoutness.

Tweed silenced the ovation. "I welcome back all braves and their warrior chiefs who return to smoke the pipe of peace."

Boole and his toughs appreciated not being humiliated. They withdrew backward, bobbing their heads in thanks.

The applause was aburptly halted as Boole's space was taken by solemn men in black suits moving with defiant slowness. These militantly plain men had not half the numbers of Boole's followers, nor bore any outward signs of violence except for their rigid purity of purpose. Yet Dead Rabbits and Bowery Boys fell silent as dogs before a taskmaster.

Confidence steamed off their sullen leader, Richard Connolly, like an engine riding into a station. He came forward on the deliberate white horse of his ego. A man with chest out in public but never his heart. Everyone admired Connolly with a touch of fear. They knew he shared their rigorous detachment from principles. His realism crushed all learning into the pulp of one word —*bullying*. He had a square jaw and cheap blue eyes that resisted intelligence.

Connolly was holier-than-thou to make up for his lack of formal education. "Alderman Tweed, we are in your debt for not yielding to Know-Nothing bigotry."

A rousing cheer.

"Here, in the summer of 1863, in the midst of a murderous Civil War, we call upon you to defeat the infamous and prejudiced Conscription Bill allowing any man with three hundred dollars to buy himself out of the draft. We are lucky to earn twelve and a half dollars a week. We feed our families butcher's soup from the scraps off his counter." Connolly's upraised arm acknowledged the applause seconds before he received it.

Brains hissed to Tweed. "Slippery Dick is your friend only until a better offer comes along." Sweeny's thinking scorched his cheeks. He lacked a public mask and smarted at Connolly's shameless piety, which didn't stop at leading his own applause. A gold chain with gold Greek letters hung across his tight vest, certifying Sweeny's academic excellence. No one needed proof. All agreed he had a deathlike clarity. Normally he was so pale, he appeared a man without a heart. He despised Connolly, whose face lacked all introspection like a boy waving his hand to go to the bathroom. Yet the uneducated, obvious Connolly had a mastery in public that riled the smarter man.

Tweed treaded his way between these two valuable men as he whispered back to Sweeny. "Your strength is that you see conspiracies where none exist. Connolly controls the Sunday vote. We don't care how pious that vote is, as long as we can buy it."

Sweeny wanted to fuel Tweed with his resentment. "Not a word of regret for deserting us because we wouldn't run him for comptroller. Now he's back telling us what to do."

Tweed tried to pipe Sweeny down. "We can live without trust but not votes." He knew it was now his turn to answer Connolly. He could never forget when coming up from the ranks how awkwardly he spoke in public. Now he didn't have to search for words to express himself. He had only to rouse crowds. "I will wage war against the Conscription Bill." The challenge forced on him.

His words set off whistles, cheers, foot stomping.

Connolly's stiff followers turned satisfied and moved to the rear. Their place was taken by intelligent, neatly dressed men grouped around the white banner of the Citizens Association. Their leader, the immaculate Tilden, set Tweed on edge.

"Silky Sammy," Tweed needled Purdy, "stands in public like he's crossing the Delaware."

How accurate the observation, and though he thoroughly enjoyed it, Purdy nevertheless pulled Tweed up short. "That's envy."

"I'd never envy Silky."

"Envy means Tilden has something you lack. Respect means he has something you'll never have."

"I envy him." The damn Purdy forced this out of him. "A politician like Tilden dies last in the face, and that's what makes him such a good liar for so long."

Tilden had a boardroom voice. The timbre bought at a fine men's shop selling English imports. A voice full of its own resonance like a shopkeeper's bell. Tilden's formality was thinly separated from aggression. "The Citizens Association wants to know why we have higher taxes and poorer services."

"Take the pipe!" cried a Shouter.

"More men on the Street Commissioner's pay and dirtier streets?"

A burst of hissing as they would a villain.

"The selling of public offices and a bankrupt party treasury?" Tilden excelled in facing jeers, as if rubbed by balm. "What are you going to do about it, Mr. Tweed?"

Tweed was at home playing to the crowd rather than the argument. He had faith in people believing opinions were facts. "Mr. Tilden, pet of the press, honored member of restrictive clubs, tribune of reform, where were you hiding when immigrants needed a champion against bigotry?"

Catcalls at the poised Tilden.

"Why aren't you protesting the Conscription Bill instead of trying to split the party?"

Bitter laughing at Tilden.

"The Conscription Bill favors the rich against the poor. The educated who got us into the war against the uneducated who sacrifice their lives for the mistakes of their betters."

A wave of intense booing at Tilden.

Tweed enjoyed calming his roughs and Shouters. "Let Mr. Tilden reply."

Tilden stoutly replied, "You haven't answered my questions. Your wasteful, inefficient, corrupt patronage is the answer."

"Jobs for the jobless is not waste, Mr. Tilden. Your exclusive social set jokes that the poor have nowhere to go but potter's field or Tammany."

"I demand an apology for that mindless slur on honest people."

"And I demand the truth, Mr. Tilden. We are not lawyers, sir. We are humble folk. We do not know how to win arguments while losing obedience to the truth."

A thundering approval of foot stomping for Tweed.

"Mr. Chairman," Tilden roared with dignity above the foot stomping, "the more than one thousand five hundred strong of the Citizens Association—"

An uproar builds against Tilden as he speaks.

"—declare their lack of support in you, your corrupt methods and your bankrupt results. You are a mockery to our great party. A travesty of democratic leadership. A tragedy to our wondrous city."

"Give Sammy the hook!" boomed a Shouter.

"Mr. Chairman"—the dignified Tilden stood steadfast against the storm of abusive catcalls—"we turn our backs and are marching out. We won't return until honesty is restored to our noble party." Tilden handsomely turned his back.

Tweed roared his defiance. "Reformers are queen hornets. They sting you once and die."

Cheers for Tweed while Purdy condemned him. "You just lost the decency vote."

Tweed raised his arm in a toast:

> *"Here's to Sammy Tilden,*
> *Our lean reformer.*
> *May he never get fat*
> *While wearing two faces*
> *Under one hat. "*

Tweed sparked the roughs to sing out boisterously to march Tilden and his association to the door:

> *"I thank my God the sun and moon*
> *Are both stuck up so high*
> *That no presumptuous ass can stretch*
> *And pluck them from the sky.*
> *If they were not, I do believe*
> *That some reforming ass*
> *Would pass a law to take them down*
> *And light the world with gas. "*

Under the roar, "Tweed, Tweed, solid for Tweed," Purdy was vehement. "We don't need you anymore. We can get what we want with reform."

"I can be trusted. I never go back on my word."

"Comptroller gives you over five hundred jobs. Street Department more. You elected the district attorney. He quashes indictments and gets important men in your debt. You appointed three judges who are in your pocket. You control the Board of Supervisors, which controls the city purse strings. Everyone billing the city has to go through you. And you take your cut. And you keep asking for more."

"You don't fear the poor anymore, now that this cursed war has put them to work."

Purdy's lips wrinkled prunishly in appreciation of Tweed's breathtaking confidence. He wondered where Tweed got it. He only knew Tweed's remarkable father, as did almost everyone else in trade. An honest, upright, dedicated man who worked alone in his dark shop, slowly and painstakingly crafting Windsor chairs of museum quality. Out of the shadows of this marvelous father emerged a son who'd dare anything and feared nothing. That's why he wasn't going higher, and that's what Purdy bluntly told him.

Sweeny tried to pry Tweed away before he destroyed himself. Purdy saved him the trouble by his banker's walk to the exit, but Purdy's self-assured gait fired the injustice seething in Tweed and forced him to rant to keep himself together. "I'm not going to be an errand boy! You're so strong?" Tweed spit. "Pick that up."

The Long Room quickly emptied. Tweed sickened at how easily he was trumped after all his experience. He needed to embrace his public again and feel the upper hand. He hurried outside, and what he saw brought him to his knees. *My God, she's still here!*

Augusta, in her open barouche, glanced at men as if they were gross bedding needing airing. To a beautiful, intelligent woman the trouble begins with being admired. She knew too much imagination shone in her eyes. This attracted shallow men who saw imagination as a weakness making her easier for conquest. Her paleness appeared to stem from her reserve. Her vitality was fascinating in being distant, only appearing when her complete self was appreciated wholeheartedly. Her finely boned cheeks, her moralizing chin—yet how to explain a natural paradox?—her sensual chin, too; her receiving-line posture was part of her distance against the hordes. What Augusta was helpless to do was dull the unguarded sea light in her eyes. She achieved the next best. To protect her inner life she took the life out of her face.

Her spontaneous smile retained an innocent embrace of the world. Men never recovered from it. The smile was so suddenly pitched at what she believed was their discovery of her complete self. She never wanted to be simplified by her surface beauty. Men never got over her mistaken smile in praise of them, and they didn't get a second chance.

Augusta's marriage was a success, in the prevailing view of her society. Marriage being the nearest avenue for a woman to succeed as men do in professions. Augusta married old New York blood. Her husband's family went back to the days when the right to vote was withheld even from many property owners. A voter had to be free of debt. This left many soldiers of the American Revolution unqualified to vote.

Seeing how she stunned Tweed lifted her spirit. She was reigning!

He had to get her on her way, but how to appease her while doing it? His progress across busy Nassau Street was slowed by crossing sweeper children.

Scrawny, ragged girls, bunched together like scraps in the wind, swept the muddy streets in front of gentlemen and women. Their little fists fastened on the stub of a frowzy broom. On bare, bruised, dirty feet they diligently tried to keep the mud off wide trousers and long skirts in hope of a tip. They constantly risked being maimed for life by horses and wagons. Tweed promptly tipped them on sight. One crossing sweeper had the resisting frown of a child not wanting to sweep yet sweeping more vigorously than the others. She stared to her right while blindly sweeping to her left. Tweed tucked a double tip into her blackened hand, stiff from sweeping, which could only be closed over the coins by his gentle pressure. He stopped a polite distance from Augusta's barouche.

Augusta's floating voice challenged his courage. "Come closer."

"Please think of me," he pleaded.

"Why else would I ask you to come closer?" Her frank eyes graded him.

He froze though he was sweating. He glanced up and down the busy thoroughfare. Passersby could single them out. He knew he was in her hands. "Mrs. Cordell, will you please return to your country home in Cos Cob?"

Her floating voice, so faint, was the opposite of her will. "Touch me."

He closed his eyes, shocked yet undeniably happy. "Augusta." *My God, she changed his voice.* He sounded so forgiving. He dare not quarrel with her. He could only suggest, barely, politely. "A politician can steal anything except another man's wife."

"These are hard times." She pitied him. "I like you," she admitted, "when you're superstitious."

"Thank you." He was grateful for any crumb from her table.

"And unbalanced," she added to show her goodwill.

He was so nervously happy, he cared less about who was on the street.

"Come closer, scaredy-cat, if you want me to go away."

He rubbed his Santa Claus belly for luck. "Where's your husband?"

"You're making Courtlandt rich, letting him in on the street openings."

"Courtlandt pays like everyone else."

Augusta's dipping into herself before she could speak sent an intimate quiver through him. "Climb in my barouche. We can ride where there's less city."

He had to say something worldly or she'd have him around her pinky. "How's the sailing at Cos Cob?"

"That reminds me, how is your wife?" She got him back for bringing up her husband.

He nobly defended his wife. "Mary Jane is fine, thanks."

"She's gloomy."

"You're jealous." He didn't mean it.

"Of a Puritan?"

He turned away to hide his merriment of her wickedness, only to get the willies at seeing a butcher leading a steer and tooting a horn to call attention to his splendid meat on the hoof. The names of his customers were marked off on the parts of the steer they had contracted to buy. "Prime parts. Prime! Last chance."

"When I asked for help building a museum, you found me interesting." She gave it little importance.

He was happy she remembered. "You're not conceited today."

"I'm conceited only when I'm unsure of myself."

He delighted in her candor.

"Touch me," she demanded, the float gone from her voice.

"Are you loony?" He desired to touch her.

"You've no worry. I told Courtlandt to meet us here."

His delight vanished.

"Since you insist on looking respectable, I invited my husband to ride with us to the Fifth Avenue Hotel."

Her audacity drove him crazy. Why did he have to meet her on a day like this? "I don't want you as a bribe."

"You think I'm immoral?" She was unconcerned.

"No, you're just rich."

"What about well-bred?"

"I want you to be with me for *myself.* Not for any use I can be to Courtlandt." How it galled him to be one-percent unsure of her.

"Dummy, you're so insecure. You couldn't take what I don't want to give."

"I know." Her independence kept him off-balance, and his "I know" came out as an apology.

Her thoughtful smile taunted him. "You don't know whether you're being adored or milked?"

"I know you could never be a hooker."

"Prostitution is one way to meet a man of property."

He could die.

"You're such a big man, yet you can't be sure a society woman likes you for yourself or your favors?"

"*Please,* don't give me *your* answer."

She warmed to his distress. "You know you couldn't have what I don't want to give."

"Last time you said you disliked me."

Augusta didn't blink. "I said it and I meant it. I dislike your coarse energy. Your determined willpower. Your being generous with gifts but not with your time. Now reach in and put your hand on me or I'll scream."

"I must go, Augusta." Her frankness made him feel inferior though he adored this quality of hers.

"Come closer, swine."

He grinned stupidly as a respectable disguise and glanced up and down the street before stepping toward her as he would to a firing squad.

"Touch." She was well-mannered.

"I'm married." He defended himself.

Oh. She raised her eyebrows conveying a ladylike sensitivity. "We've something in common."

He was helpless before her freedom.

"A woman you claim is beautiful is inviting you to bed and you're worried about losing your popularity?"

"These are strict times." He tried rubbing her logic off his face.

"I'll tell Mary Jane you're sleeping with me."

He slipped his hand over the side of her barouche, alert for onlookers on the busy street.

"That's the doorknob you're squeezing."

"Sorry."

"You want me to touch *you?*" she asked, bored.

"No." He was paralyzed.

"I know where the parts are."

She was so wicked, he was spellbound. His hand slipped over. Augusta bolted upright. "That's my knee." She was as surprised as he.

"Augusta," he pleaded to withdraw.

"Higher," she coaxed.

"Mrs. Cordell." *For God's sake* was on his face. "If only you knew the day I had."

"Your hand is medicinal." She pressed his paw against her thigh as a hackney drew up.

Tweed wrenched his hand from her just in time. A lean and fastidious gentleman emerged. The hollows of his eyes held his diffidence like a hereditary cold.

"Courtlandt, you're just in time. Ride with us to make Bill respectable." Augusta's eyes declared she'd never be caught in a net, and her husband's courteous arrogance showed she had.

"Augusta is ungovernable." Courtlandt greeted Tweed and held the barouche door open for him.

"Look," Augusta decried the sight, "the new wealth from the war. Her gold hair-dusting costs twenty-five dollars."

The barouche was passing City Hall. A copy of the Hôtel de Monaco in Paris whose elegance contrasted with the rough-and-tumble city yet represented the spirit of a free city as no other building. City Hall was open, accessible, unguarded. The architecture had none of the fortress quality of civic buildings proudly portraying a government within and the people without. New Yorkers are spared having a pile of faceless gravestone. There's less magisterial weight in City Hall than an opera house. A government building devoid of temple fever. A free people's City Hall lacking authority, save in its graceful sweep astride the heart of a thriving city.

Advertisements blazed everywhere: across painted office windows, awnings, fences, wagons, the faces of steps going up and the tops of steps going down. Huge and striking banners of Barnum's Museum showing the nightmare creations of nature loomed over the City Hall area. Posters of every size are pasted, nailed and hung: SULPHUR BITTERS WILL MAKE YOU LOVE ONE ANOTHER AGAIN. BACO-CURIO, THE ONLY SCIENTIFIC CURE FOR THE TOBACCO HABIT, SOLD WITH WRITTEN GUARANTEE. ENGLISH JELLY SALVE FOR INVALIDS. VEGE-

TINE, THE GREAT BLOOD PURIFIER. FLORAPLEXION FOR FEMALE AND LIVER
COMPLAINTS.

Augusta brought up a disturbing sight she saw on Blackwell's
Island in the East River. Women let out in the sun tied forty to a
rope.

Tweed told her they were roped together for humane reasons.
A section of Blackwell's was used as a charity home for women
broken under their domestic burdens. If a woman plunged into the
river, the others could pull her out.

Courtlandt, lighting his pipe, sent a tiger pacing through
Tweed. Courtlandt didn't care. Sucking on his pipe, he took the
world for granted. Courtlandt was content while Tweed was
humiliated by getting the power to sell Courtlandt his opportuni-
ties. He suddenly felt temporary, seeing Courtlandt and his bunch
as the permanent ones reaping the benefits of his power. They'd
be around long after he was gone or discarded.

"That gold-dusted woman." Courtlandt remembered. "The fun
these days is watching the new rich Shoddy. Every Shoddy believes he is imitating the old gentry when he's only imitating the
Shoddy who just climbed up before him. You should see the
Shoddy strutting at the opera with their jeweled walking sticks.
Their women are always trying to remember not to say those
awful you-was-iz, I-done-its, sawrs. All the while they parade instead of walk in their expensive silks. Yet with all their nervy push,
they hide their large farmer's hands and thick wrists in the folds
of their costly dresses."

Augusta hinted for Courtlandt to take another tack. "You're
making the Shoddy sympathetic."

"No one can do that. They are so insolent about every little
thing they get in their head. The Shoddy steps on those beneath
him, shoves aside those on his level, kneels to anyone far above
him. All the while Shoddy is twisting, pulling, beating his children
to behave like ladies and gentlemen."

Tweed agreed. "What is hard to forgive the Shoddy is that he's
rarely guilty of innocent pleasures."

Augusta's smile complimented Tweed. He adored her smile,
which unearthed her for him without a thought. Augusta's affection went right through Courtlandt like light waves leaving no
mark.

The barouche drew up before the gleaming marble facade of the
Fifth Avenue Hotel off Madison Square Park. A luxury hotel

crowned by the prewar visit of Edward, Prince of Wales, who admired its superiority to royal castles. The hotel housed the first vertical railway to lift guests from floor to floor and pioneered the luxury of a bathroom in each suite.

Courtlandt was impressed by the heavy swells in the lobby. Augusta took them in briefly and impatiently said, "If no one will envy the work they do, they'll make us envy the clothes their work bought."

Courtlandt rode up in the vertical railway with them. This liberal attitude toward his wife's activities made Tweed uneasy. Courtlandt acted tactfully. Stepping off on the fifth floor, he handed Augusta the keys as he would a leash to a dog he wanted walking and took the back stairs.

Before he could embrace her, she dropped on the bed to sulk. "I wanted us to come here to humiliate Courtlandt."

"I'm glad you had nothing dirty on your mind." He clapped his hands to bid her a fond farewell. A comic regret on his face as he beheld the luxurious bed. "I looked forward to taking off my tight shoes."

"Don't you dare go." She commanded him with tears in her eyes. "How can you humiliate someone who has no scruples as a point of honor?"

"Divorce him."

Her resentment rose like steam off her. She shook her head no. "Divorce is not as good as revenge."

He lowered his head to show he had no more answers.

"Kiss me," she said, troubled.

"You don't have your heart in it."

She gave him credit for more sense. "You want everything?"

She began to undress. Though he longed to see her surprisingly coltish legs because they revealed her true self under her sophistication, though he adored her sad smile when naked, as it revealed how awkwardly she felt connected to her lean and shapely body, he protested her undressing. "You're going to make our coming together no more than a handshake."

"We have to start somewhere." She continued undressing. "It's like measles, only the fever goes down faster."

My God, who'd have a woman like this? He became crazed. "You want me to touch you, squeeze you, sleep with you, feel yourself getting sweaty, but you want to be independent. I want the hot, hysterical sex of a spinster going to bed with the devil!" He didn't know what he was howling about. "And you're concentrating on street openings! Revenge! I like you better when you're shy."

"No, you don't. Then you have to be sensitive and loving to draw me out."

"You're right. My power to run a city—that attracts you— becomes worthless. I want to go to bed with a woman the way they do in the scandal sheets. Steamy. Sex is criminal. A horror. No one talks. The man and woman know they're going down in a flame of passion, and if they enjoy it, my God, they're cursed for life. They can't get jobs. No money. They can't talk of street openings before going to bed."

She quietly said, "Courtlandt caves in to everyone for his dealings, but he keeps the upper hand over me."

He gave in and sat down on the bed beside her. His bulk rolled over her trim body. She became fragile under his weight, shapeless, gasping as though drowning. By his rolling over on her, she experienced in sex the helplessness she did in life. "I'm not yielding." She made sure he knew that. "I'm giving up hope."

Her squirming, thrashing, fighting to breathe made her delicate under him. Her yearning for an all-embracing, deeper feeling through sex went beyond him. It was too late.

Courtlandt sat in the darkest corner of the hotel bar leaning over his street openings map. Fever to get in on new Manhattan streets was matched only by California gold prospecting. Courtlandt spread apart the map revealing juicy openings. His fingers tenderly coaxing out the folds and pleasurably smoothing them down. An angry couple driven from their suite by a disgraceful couple ended his reverie. Their walls were being battered by a bed in Suite 525. His suite.

Courtlandt sneaked up the back stairs. To protect his reputation he had to remain in his suite hearing the skidding bed, Augusta's intimate hoarseness. Courtlandt lit his pipe and unfolded his street map with a victorious gleam, encircling the undeveloped parcels he desired to own. Guttural moaning caused Courtlandt to snip corners off his map even as he studied it. When he heard them expire, he was tortured by their silence.

Hurrying down the back stairs, Courtlandt overheard maids and bellboys giggling about the randy couple in his suite. Waiting outside for Tweed to leave, Courtlandt saw a frantic young man drive up, shouting to the doorman, "Have you seen Alderman Tweed?"

"No, Shamus," the doorman said respectfully.

"The alderman is wanted at Henry Street. His father is dying."

In spite of their physical appearance sprawled across the bed, Tweed was disturbed by his lack of closeness with Augusta. He traced this emptiness to his fanatic ambition to run the city, which spilled over into his affairs with women. A mysterious alchemy was robbing him of a vital personal exchange. Justice was working where he least expected. He knew it was the justice in the original cord of life because it came forcefully through without regard to his defenses and lay heavily in his heart even when he knew himself to be most successful. Women brought out the secret of what he had done to himself.

He gained power and lost the closeness he once enjoyed with his wife, Mary Jane. What no will in the world can recreate is the pleasure of being so deeply in love, you are defenseless.

Losing his closeness, having to imitate consciously his own best self because he couldn't recover it, didn't seem to matter to anyone but himself—except for Mary Jane. With his wife he had an unbridgeable trouble. "I've lost my closeness with Mary Jane."

"And you have it with me?" she asked, pleased.

He mumbled fitfully. "Power grows a terrifying muscle, detaching you from those pleasures that power gets for you."

She beat on his bulk to drive out his devils. The harder she beat, the more helpless she felt.

He was afraid that one day what he felt eroding in him would rise to his surface and expose his secret for all the public to see. Ideally public life should be a man's dead skin. What was dead in him served to protect him.

Urgent knocking startled them.

Courtlandt carefully called, "Bill?"

The interruption touched off Augusta. "Get away from that door, you disgraceful man. He never wants to see me enjoy myself."

"Bill"—Courtlandt was humbly hesitant—"your father is dying in Henry Street."

They bolted from bed. Augusta instinctively covering her face, knowing the sorrow Tweed must feel. He ran into the bathroom to wash. Augusta rounded up his clothes.

This was the last place he wanted to hear about his father dying.

He couldn't look at himself in the mirror. A terrifying thought ate in him about what had died in *himself.*

"Bill"—Augusta couldn't understand—"why are you washing? You love your father so. Go to him while he can see you."

He was stunned into mumbling. "I can't see my father ever being gone." He was too upset to hold the soap. He splashed cold water against his face.

Augusta dried his head with a towel while he dressed. He was pulling himself into clothes tailored too smartly for an emergency.

"Augusta, I need to see you. The next time we'll have days together. The Morrissey-Heenan bare-knuckle fight for the championship of America."

"I hate fights."

"Don't watch. Stay in the hotel. I must find out if Morrissey can be my strong-arm leader and protect the polls on election day with my gangs."

"I'd like to be with you after you're excited by a fight."

They kissed, impatient for more.

Courtlandt waited by the door to tell him to take his carriage parked at the entrance. After Tweed raced down the hall Courtlandt viewed the untidy room and ordered Augusta to dress. When she stalled, he threw her clothes at her.

The vertical railway operator greeted Courtlandt with unusual camaraderie. Augusta couldn't understand this unspoken man's talk, although Courtlandt evidently did. Courtlandt took her off on the landing above the crowded lobby, and Augusta was grateful. She sickened at what she saw was in store for her. Courtlandt was forcing her to walk down the grand staircase where the heavy swells could see them.

"Please. Don't degrade me."

Her begging pleased him.

"I'm paying for your cowardly weakness," she said, disgusted. "Whore."

"It's easy to be a whore. Too many men put you out of touch with your body."

Courtlandt escorted her down the marble stairs under the glowing chandelier. He was scandalous. She shrunk headlong into herself. Courtlandt kept a tight grip high on her arm.

The swells and bellboys smiled slyly. She could believe anything about Courtlandt, but she couldn't believe what was happening to her. Courtlandt was turning his disgrace into a feat he could boast about. He was taking credit for her sexually puffed face.

Tweed saw torches spitting flames into the night. He heard the muffled bumping of padded wheels over cobblestones. Long, wavering lines of grieving mothers and fathers headed for the yawning hold of the charity commissioner's boat. This boat snuck into an East River dock every two weeks in the dead of night to keep the city from seeing how their commission prospered. Parents filled the boat until the deck was walled with flowerbox-size coffins of children who had died since the last docking.

Saddened neighbors had gathered outside his father's dark workshop. Bill was their hero in spite of helping newcomers who were moving up Cherry Hill and ruining their neighborhood.

Inside the door was his old desk, dusty and forgotten. The freshly curled wood shavings wafted a forest-floor aroma out the open door while street noises and smells poured in. In this aromatic darkness he had started his career as a bookkeeper. His squeaking pens rained down black and red numbers in the ledgers, building a world without sentiment.

His father lay across his workbench like his own durable hardwoods. Raw Windsor chairs in unfinished stages lay jumbled atop one another. His father's dedication could be seen in the handgrips fluted so finely as though a sitter's comfort was in their fingers. The Windsor, a particularly revered American chair. The chair sat on by the great Founding Fathers in Philadelphia.

How many times out of mind had he beseeched his patient father that he didn't have to build the perfect chair every time? His father replying each perfect chair brings its own pleasure.

His father's eyes were surprisingly wide open. No pain, only a shadow of remorse, and that caused Bill to bite his lip.

"I took a few hours off." His father sounded healthy enough.

"How many times have I asked you to retire?" When there was no answer, Bill praised the old man as much as he could get away with. "Can you tell the sun not to shine?"

A mortal pain different than the fatal pain appeared. A father's pain that Bill recognized even when his father was healthy. "I didn't raise you to be an errand boy."

Bill lowered his head under the weight of this accusation. He knew he had to be positive, not argue with his father anymore. Let there be rest from honest differences. "Let's concentrate on what's wonderful."

"If you believe everything is wonderful, you've no ideals."

He couldn't help a smile at the old man who, when dying, was stronger than most men alive, and this made it easier for a son to defend himself. "When I delivered your first set of Windsor chairs to Fifth Avenue, I saw their world and was never the same. Fifth Avenue taught me the first commandment: To be poor is to be ignorant." His father could be listening for a distant train. "Ambition gives you a taste of your true self. How will I know what I am if I don't try? And if I don't try? That's what I am. I grew up ambitious to sell your chairs. I was so proud to sell the best."

"Now"—he made every word count to his son—"you are dying with a dirty name."

His father's gaze of reproach compelled him to confess. "It's impossible for a man in office to know if he's maturing or losing himself. I've become as a success the man I never wanted to be."

His father rested in himself, reviving on sheer fatherly devotion to help an erring son.

Bill had to clear himself. "I saw the charity commissioner's boat. Fresh air can save thousands of sick children, but windows cost too much to put in. If an alderman fought for ventilating tenements, he'd be fighting the powers running his party."

"It's *you* the newspapers call a thief."

"Dad, they called the Board of Aldermen forty thieves long before I arrived, and they'll be called that long after I've left." His sigh showed he wished it was different. "The people are too hopelessly split into factions of races and religions to govern except by bribery and corruption. If people loved their city, they wouldn't let bribery and corruption become the efficient way to run government."

"Fight the good fight. Get windows put in."

"Fresh air is free every place but in politics. You can only do as much good as your backers let you get away with."

"There are laws you could write."

Bill agreed. "There are laws for everyone on the books. Those with connections and those without connections. Only the sentencing is different."

His father lowered into himself to impress on his son. "Your grandfather came here from the River Tweed in Scotland as a blacksmith. He built a trustworthy name and made certain that I could be apprenticed to a superior trade than his own. I was apprenticed to the chairmaster Thomas Ashe. I made certain you'd work with your brains. You learned how business works by being a bookkeeper. Three generations of improvement."

"Dad," he treaded cautiously, "the city is faster now. Building a Windsor chair is a slow trade. Yes, three generations of improvement. But immigrants are making fortunes overnight."

"In opium, selling women, stealing and drink." Worms riddled his father's face.

Bill held his breath.

The storm passed over his father. "I'm going to say something wonderful."

His father's humor, while stricken, made Bill a son again.

"People believed in you, Bill. Orders came in all the way from Harlem where people were running away from the immigrants. In my father's day we ran from immigrants by moving up to Greenwich Village." He held out his strong hand as a token of peace.

Hands like his father's, with their unassuming strength and the ghostly fever of a lifetime's labor in them, were not seen as often anymore. His hands had an honest directness that good men take for granted in themselves. His father wouldn't think of hammering a nail into his chairs. He good-humoredly said that he hugged his chairs together. This was the truth. They lasted solidly for generations, as children might with the same care. Suddenly he experienced time ticking away in his own heart. His father's dying exposing his son as mortal.

He finally held his father's hand just as his father became childless, concerned with himself for a change. Had his father ever been such a man who thought of himself first? So impossible to imagine now. Maybe he thought first of himself before he'd married and had children. He made marriage look so easy to last. Think of the family first.

His father opened his mouth unsteadily—an invalid taking food. He spoke without tears or farewell. The Book was open. He had read it, found the words fair and truthful, though painfully inexorable. Whatever weaves an independent child into a giving parent also gave him words. He could swear this wasn't in his father, yet somewhere he had learned to talk about himself. Could this other man be hidden all his life in his father? He was breathing peacefully, as if he would last forever, when he said, "Death fits us back into nature."

Tweed's legs and arms trembled with emotion as he drove home. He thought of the wood drying out in the shed for hardness. Letting nature do your work by living in its grain. The raw wood turning into comfortable chairs. The patience of time itself in his father. His life the work he wanted most.

Good parents are miraculous, like trees. They inhale the poisonous air of their times and breathe the air back out around their children, cleansed by their insides.

A good father sees two weaknesses: your own and the one he unknowingly gave you that haunts him and he hopes you will outgrow by your strength of character. And a third. The third weakness is the unforgivable one. The goodness he happened to give you that you somehow spoiled. How he wished his father could have seen him not as a dirty success but as a decent man taking things as they are.

Fathers are notorious for substituting authority for learning. They spend a lifetime saluting men who crippled, cheated and narrowed their outlook. Is that the life they want for you?

A hateful father prepares you for the world in record time. He makes you a child prodigy. Your conscience burnt out at an early age. You become free as a maniac. The igniting guts of a murderer are in you. You have to take care your biggest victim isn't yourself. Running away with vengeance on your soul is a lucky break. Vengeance can be used on the world to succeed. His father was impractical. He believed a son betters himself by becoming a better man. But the dumbest son learns more from a good father's blindness than from the most honored schools of learning.

At his own modest house he saw his bedroom window a crack open, as it was in all weather. A memento of his fire fighting days as a volunteer chief jumping to the tolling of fire bells. He fingered his gold watch on his belly, inscribed in honor of his daredevil run that made him popular with the public.

He opened the door, and Mary Jane read the lines on his face. He no longer knew how to approach his wife of a lifetime. Mary Jane withdrew herself to kiss him. The hasty touch made her anxious. Her intimacy was in her defense. He knew how difficult it was for her to break out of her routine self, where she felt safe.

He couldn't be more gentle with Mary Jane, yet he could not be gentle enough to allay her awkwardness at a physical encounter. His strength, even at rest, in mourning, was more than she could absorb. Her withholding came from her decent upbringing. He longed for a kiss, even a kiss of sorrow. He needed to feel warm, sympathetic flesh that was alive. He could cry that the standoffish virtue trained into Mary Jane had made her so attractive to marry. Yet when Mary Jane was near, he was in contact with his true center.

She kissed his cheek as if it were a loan repaid. "Did you make up with your father?"

"He called me an errand boy."

"I'm sorry." She lowered her head. Her private face just below her amenable surface might be seen by others as a trifle hard, even slightly uncaring, but it was very easy to like and respect his wife and call these qualities her reserve.

"Dad was right. Forty years and I remain an errand boy."

His weakness, if she dare call his conquering ambition that, was all too human. She leaned forward and pecked him on the cheek.

He was frightened of more bad news. "Why're you kissing me?"

"Elijah Purdy was here."

Tweed was surprised.

"Mr. Purdy wants to take you to his club." She was honored.

Tweed was at a loss and suspicious. "You can bet it has nothing to do with improving us socially."

"It's about the Conscription Bill. Mr. Purdy is worried about what he's just heard from the wards. The wards may rise up and riot against it."

He confided in his wife though he knew she wouldn't understand. "I never want to see anarchy. What's done in the name of law is horrifying enough."

Purdy bullied the larger Tweed, who stood admiring the Greek Revival architecture of the club. The temple style the Greeks had used to house their gods was now used to house private clubs and banks. The livery and equipage waiting at the curb was spotless and shiny. No roughs, no secondhand pants, no white cravat spoiled by a drop of gravy and handed down to the groom was to be seen. The livery was English coats for form. Paris hats for affectation. Inside the club the waiters and footmen clapped along the dream-white marble floor; billiard balls clicked, drinks poured, rich cigar smoke lingered in the air. Tweed appreciated Fifth Avenue's accomplishment. They excluded the unfashionable while living off them.

Purdy advised the tourist in Tweed. "When you enter a private club, you must do it uncritically—or else why the fuss?"

Purdy led him through a carpeted portrait gallery where the holy look of repressed men was the success look. Eyes lying in wait. Mouths embalmed in silence. The clenched jaw a mirror into their soul. Tweed worried aloud that he didn't have the right face.

A fishbowl light filtering in from Fifth Avenue gave the club's library a cathedral largeness, groined vaults and lofty ceiling decorated in gold leaf. An oak table displayed eighty newspapers and forty weeklies. A portrait of Myndert van Schaick hung from the ceiling. Purdy said that on birthdays the club hangs the member's portrait and prepares a feast, if he's important.

Identical overstuffed chairs and brass ashtrays were placed in identical squares around the library, but the main part of the room was occupied by van Schaick and friends. Two kinds of men were asleep in the library. Men so arrogant, they slept upright, as though on guard duty. White-haired men sleeping peacefully, and their complete relaxation revealed their weaker drives. The warrior sleepers were apt to be new money and not as highly prized. The restful sleepers were inherited wealth, generally less money but highly prized. Tweed gathered they were old wealth. Old wealth was worn so offhandedly, it is difficult to detect whether their assurance is sufficient to their wealth.

"I'll go in first and pave the way." Purdy broke through his reverie. "When you enter, don't be impressed."

Purdy's confidence infected Tweed until he noticed no one rose to greet the banker. No one pretended to rise. They hid their motives for the same reason a bank never keeps money outside its doors. Purdy was their equal in that he ignored their arrogant reticence, which they wore like scarecrows in the field.

Purdy strongly pleaded his case. "If Republican reform comes to power, it's our advantage to have Tweed's popular base with the immigrants. His wards are pocket votes. Every election, another ward is overrun by immigrants and falls to us. If there's trouble in the wards, Tweed is there to settle it."

"Give the dregs what they want," said van Schaick, "and they'll think you're afraid of them."

"If the wards explode, the blame will fall on us. We'll have a Civil War in the South and another behind the lines in New York. No nation can win a war that way. Tweed has done us many services, loyally and with dedication."

"To his profit," said van Schaick.

"True." Purdy pacified them, which meant he didn't fully agree. "Tweed is not the best man for the best of times, but he's the best man for the worst of times."

Tweed heard their laughter, which was more of a tribal honk than wholehearted merriment. He stood fascinated before the portraits in the gallery of the men from the Panic of 1857. A Panic that need not have happened. Bankers lost trust in their system and set off the Panic even while more funds were going into banks than were being drawn out. The '57 Panic gave Tweed another chance to rise up. He owed a debt to the men honored here: De Peyster Ogden, Bleecker Street Savings Bank; John Oothout, Bank of New York; George Opdyke, Opdyke and Sons, who fought the idea of saving banks; John Stevens, Bank of Commerce; John Jay Cisco, Empire City Bank and a Tammany power.

To Tweed's surprise, right after the laughter a grave Purdy emerged. "They don't want to see you. They're grooming old Waterbury for the city and Sam Tilden for state. Waterbury and Tilden will be built up as independents."

"Independent"—Tweed didn't blink—"as a fireplug to a dog's raised leg."

A rare grin crossed Purdy as he escorted Tweed out with haste.

Tweed took in the moneyed silence of the club. He felt the opposing tides of old and new. New wanted their rights. Old had the permanent land grants. This fortress challenged Tweed. He was impressed by the club, even as it handed him a defeat. "Good architecture is priceless," he said on his way out. "It gives the impression those inside know what they're doing."

TWO

$\mathcal{T}$he rising July sun was clinging to roofs and steeples like scalded batter pouring down into the trenches of the city. The wards appear to have lost a siege to an invisible enemy. Heat ticks in dark tenements. Heads sleep on windowsills. Families camp on roofs under lopsided tents of bed sheets. Icemen, seeing their investment melting in the gutter, sing coolly, "Iiiiicccccceeeee!"

Sleepers wrecked from the heat, their vanity and modesty thrown aside, come out to buy a penny's worth of ice. They rub the ice over their most private parts, shrieking and gasping for breath.

In nearby Printing House Square the news boards are being changed. The old board celebrating a glorious victory is going down: LEE DEFEATED AT GETTYSBURG! The board going up reads: CITY'S WAR DEAD, WOUNDED AND MISSING AT GETTYSBURG. A horrendously long list for a victory, especially for one city.

Street moss see the bulletin first. They can't read, but the lettering is squinched so tightly, they are frightened. Row upon row, line upon line of small letters pinched into every space, resembling how these dead might have lived. Soldiers made faceless even in their great sacrifice.

Early birds on their way to work fall silent and helpless at the news. A crowd gathers under the board. An old-timer points to the bottom of the long list and wants to know what has been added. A clerk reads to him, "To be continued."

Those ready to surrender anything for a piece of ice now stand uncomplaining under the sun. They can't understand the strange fate dealt to familiar names. Yesterday's victory becoming today's mourning.

The educated, on their way to work, oblige the unschooled by reading the names out loud. Men, women, schoolchildren take up the reading aloud. This terrible news brings a unity to people. Soon three and four readers of different columns of the list are reading names. Eyes of bystanders fill with tears. The sheer toll of names is more than many can bear who bear a tireless city patiently. Familiar names cause moaning and sobbing, and this mourning sends shivers through people. Shivers meant for living with the justice of this world. Names keep cascading out, conjuring up a world where reason has vanished. The dirge in Printing House Square makes it easy to believe the city itself is in grief. The grieving draws other bystanders until the Square over-flows. The city's thriving morning energy—usually so inspiring to live with—gradually takes over the streets and covers up the mourning.

A rising sun glazes windows orange with heat, and not a cry from an iceman is heard this morning.

Roughs casually mingle and move out of the shadows of the Lower East Side. They wander across the island. Along the way they are joined by women who appear to have thrown on any dress at hand to get out of the house. They meander up Eighth and Ninth Avenues in loosely forming, silent groups, certain they've gone undetected by the police. The city largely sleeps. Streets empty. Those who labor with their hands are the ones most likely to be up, and they saunter into the group.

From the moment the roughs took to the street their course is charted by the ultramodern police headquarters at 300 Mulberry Street. The prize of this police center is a telegraph network throughout the city. News from the farthest streets flashes into Mulberry within seconds. Mulberry also recruits lifers as inform-ers. Coppers are sent out disguised as laborers and bums. Plants everywhere and all out on the streets.

Superintendent Kennedy runs Mulberry. Incorruptible

Kennedy was the hope of a new breed of coppers promoted to raise the profoundly low level of the force that defies human scrutiny. New York coppers are so shamelessly corrupt, they're the butt of stories and jokes in the Wild West.

Kennedy routinely reports for work at dawn. His first order is for the report sheets of the night before. The usual brawls. A sergeant routinely asks if there's going to be any special orders for the new shift. Kennedy replies, "All assignments routine."

At six a.m. half the police went off duty.

Telegraph sets in the modern communication room click at a faster tempo. The sole unusual report is of men wandering peacefully up the West Side with large amounts of women.

Kennedy neatly stacks his reports by precincts. At a glance he can see which precincts are active. The reports causing Kennedy concern are of whites not joining the shape-up at the docks. The docks are a continuing trouble spot since the hiring of ten percent blacks to keep whites in line from striking and with the further threat of filling all their jobs with blacks.

No policeman takes strikes more seriously than Kennedy. A long and bitter strike at Brooks Brothers had the police on the side of the clothier. Then the Brooks Brothers scandal erupted about their selling shoddy uniforms to the War Department.

Many laborers building the new Croton Reservoir in Central Park are not showing up for work. The gang boss says that his men often dry out after a weekend.

Fewer white domestics are seen going to work. This is attributed to the Monday morning blues and the heat.

The entire crew of a street contractor is missing.

Paving stones were dug out of the ninth ward at night. A common occurrence, though the amount is high.

Except for election days when roughs are the hired muscle of politicians, roughs seldom move out of their neighborhoods unless to muss.

Kennedy, hard as a cop's locust stinger, was sensitive to one fact. He had only two thousand men to spread across twenty-two precincts.

A lifer ran in to report that the United States Arsenal at Seventh Avenue and Thirty-fifth Street had been captured. The enormity of this defeat startled the Kennedy reserve. He dispatched a sergeant and fifteen men by streetcar.

A milling crowd outside the arsenal dispersed at the sight of the police. An easy assignment, but it left fifteen less police to guard the draft office at 677 Third Avenue at Forty-sixth Street.

Forty-sixth Street was a fantasy terrain of craters, rocks, and barren hills. Isolated three-story houses stood here and there among undeveloped acres. At nine a.m. the draft office for the upper part of the island would open.

The handful of wandering men and women were joined in an amazingly short time by hundreds. They moved through the hot streets of the wards picking up baling hooks, pitchforks, crowbars, clubs and paving stones out of nowhere. The hundreds swelled into a thousand, and the thousand began chanting at the top of their lungs, "No draft!"

Laborers ran off their jobs to join them. A foundry owner closed his heavy iron gates to keep in his workers. The crowd battered the gates, bending and wrenching them off their massive hinges. The owner was confronted by a neighbor, Tom Fitzsimmons, while the crowd noised behind him, threatening and jawing with those inside who would not join.

"We're not out to harm you or your foundry," said the friendly Fitzsimmons. "We only want to make a big show of resisting this unjust draft so someone will listen to us. We're not here to wreck anything but this draft against poor men who don't have the three hundred dollars to buy themselves out of the war."

The owner stepped aside, allowing his workmen to rush into the crowd cheering them. Fitzsimmons shook the owner's hand and promised to get the men back for a good day's work.

The thickening crowd leisurely wended their way up the West Side. People who came out wondering what the excitement was about were pulled in and swallowed up. Those hanging back were hooted, bullied and beaten into the crowd to stick up for their rights. Most men and women needed no encouragement.

Speakers walked alongside, drumming up grievances and keeping spirits high. Boldly printed placards began rising above their heads reading NO DRAFT!

The crowd took the shape of an uncoiling serpent gorging on humans in its path and fattening until it filled Eighth and Ninth Avenues. The head turned east along Central Park and south on Fifth Avenue. The body grown so long, those on Fifth Avenue could see across the vacant lots to the double tail winding up the West Side.

Fifth Avenue was a world apart—the prize staring everyone in the face. The fabled wealthy of the nation lived here to authenticate their success in the eyes of the greatest city. A breed of volatile individuals conforming to a single idea. A Fifth Avenue mansion is their knighthood. They also served as an invaluable inspiration that being your own boss could give the lowliest a chance.

Yet Fifth Avenue bore warnings from the very drive that made its residents famous. The commercial invasion up the avenue was as high as Fourteenth Street. The stolid Grinnel mansion, once the jewel of the avenue, was now a restaurant in the Delmonico chain.

While sheltered residents of Fifth Avenue sat down to breakfast the crowd roared, "A rich man's war and a poor man's fight! No draft!"

Red-shirted volunteer firemen fed the excitement by heading east on Forty-seventh Street toward the draft office. The roar took on the rage of fever. The crowd's intensity became a magnet pulling thousands. They clogged morning traffic in and out of the city. Streetcars, wagons, carts were backed up into the heart of the business district.

Men climbed on the roofs of stalled streetcars to see what was going on. All they saw were undulating waves of humanity in a crush they couldn't understand. Clerks and supervisors climbed to the roofs of downtown office buildings. To those waiting below for an answer to the tumultuous roaring, they could only raise their arms in despair.

Streetcars emptied. Stalled wagons were abandoned. Merchants unhitched horses and fled.

The front of the crowd reached the draft office to be thrilled by the store being unguarded. This quickly fanned a rumor that the draft was called off.

Sixty policemen advanced on the double ready for action and became dumbfounded by the jubilant crowd. While the crowd sang, danced and cheered, Captain Porter lined his men in front of the draft office with locust stingers in hand.

The sight of the police spread another rumor. The draft quota was raised. Tripled. Quadrupled. No one poor was safe from the costly war. Groaning curses rose and fell. The crowd was subjected to doomsday tirades.

Sightseers on stalled cars and wagons were dragged off and pressed into the crowd that kept filling in from Fifth Avenue, hooting and cursing the latest inflaming rumor. They overflowed

Third Avenue for a half dozen blocks in both directions. No one went untouched by their bone-trembling roars.

The front line of the crowd kept a no-man's-land between the police. Pressure from the howling newcomers edged the resisting front toward the police.

Joyous shouts took over the roaring. "Ten o'clock!" The blinds of the draft office remained down an hour after the scheduled opening. Counter-rumors of the last rumor spread through the crowd. "We won!" "They're not drafting!" "They called off the draft!"

This rumor brought a chorus of singing and impromptu dancing. Those in the business district, who had just heard a tumultuous roar of protest roll downtown, now heard a torrential cheering.

To celebrate the victory a grogshop was smashed into. Kegs of beer were spiked open and given free to all.

Inside the little draft office, Provost Marshal Jenkins, who ruled by the book, placed the wheel drum on the table and ordered his clerks to line up neatly. He asked the anxious telegraph operator if they had a line to police headquarters. He was told the line was dead. The roughs must have cut the wire.

The human rumbling outside caused the windows to chatter and the closed office to hum like the ocean inside a shell. Jenkins addressed the clerks, telegrapher and two disabled war veterans from the Invalid Corps. He told them that they take their chances behind the line as soldiers do at the front. If they didn't pick men for the draft, then they'd be the ones breaking the law.

"Noooooooo draft!"

"Clerk, raise the blinds." The neat, white-shirted man did.

The blinds rolling up ignited a storm of protest.

Jenkins motioned to the telegrapher to desist, as they had to maintain a calm front.

"Clerk, open the door."

The roar exploded upon them. "Nooooooo draft!"

Jenkins climbed atop the table against savage yelling. "We're humans, not pigs!" "The poor go in and the rich stay out!" "Three-hundred-dollar blood money!" "Don't spin the wheel against us!"

Jenkins could not be heard even by his clerks as he read the laws from his manual authorizing him to select draftees. He motioned a clerk to stand atop the table, and Jenkins blindfolded him.

"Freed slaves take our jobs!" "Don't spin the wheel!"

The police could not see the outer limits of the crowd. Sixty police against ten thousand.

Jenkins whirled the drum as a maddened roar spread through the streets, mounting and carried by voices joining the crowd until the upper half of the city appeared to be in an uproar.

The clerk reached into the drum and brought up a tightly rolled-up slip of paper. Jenkins slowly unrolled the slip and announced, "James W. Hart, West Forty-second Street."

A wall of booing.

Jenkins handed down the slip to be registered. He spun the drum again. Nothing stopped the roar, not even to hear the names. "Cashel Boatwright. Joseph Fergus." He called slightly faster.

The police stood stone-faced.

"Michael Forrest. Alvin Whitehouse." Jenkins quit spinning the wheel. To save time the clerk was ordered to grab up the names by the handful. "Caswell Hawks. William Dunne."

Jenkins hollered down to the registering clerk as he would to a man miles away. "How many more names to go?"

"Less than five hundred, sir."

A distant shouting was speeding to the front of the crowd. "Here they come!" "Here they come!"

The police could only see the parting of a cheering crowd.

The fear on the faces of those in the draft office was that their time had run out. Jenkins continued to call the names. "Francis Corrigan. Alfred Hastings."

A hose cart from the fire station piled with paving stones stopped several yards from the police. A stone was hurled, and the draft office window crashed around the police, who stood their ground.

A rock hit the blindfolded clerk in the forehead. His knees buckled and he bravely maintained his poise. Jenkins held him up to grab a handful of more names as the clerk's blindfold turned red with blood.

The crowd bulled into the police, who clubbed them down. The sight of their own blood from men and women clubbed underfoot and groaning helplessly had them dazed. Captain Porter seized his chance and ordered his men to charge and drive the crowd back. Sixty clubbing policemen dived into the ten thousand and vanished.

Jenkins ordered his clerks to take the draft list and run out the back. All the lists could not be gathered up in time. The crowd swarmed in, demolishing everything in sight.

Bleeding police were clubbing their way back into the draft office that was being torn apart. The police were clawed, kicked, punched as they beat their way to the rear, pursued by deadly rock throwers who potted the police on the run.

The draft lists were torn into bits and thrown in the air. The confetti covered the rioters as at a wedding. The drum was stomped into pulp.

The office safe would not open. A volunteer fireman poured turpentine on it and threw a match. The office blew into flames. A wild rush to get out pushed against the mob blindly pressing to get in.

"Fire!" "Fire!"

Burning men and women climbed over the mob. They fell outside to see the crowd dancing and singing to celebrate the burning draft office.

The mob, having vanquished the police, destroyed the draft office. Knowing they were in control, they began chopping down telegraph poles for butting rams. The Harlem Railroad tracks were torn up. Nearby houses were set on fire. Hardware stores were rammed open and raided for rifles, ammo, knives, axes, pitchforks.

At Mulberry a bloodied policeman reported to Kennedy. The chief knew he had to deploy his men with the utmost caution yet attack with reckless speed. The intelligent Kennedy was not a leader to piddle away his force. He knew striking boldly with the largest numbers was half the victory. Kennedy was the right man in the right place at the right time, and none knew this better than his men.

A telegraph report told Kennedy that it took twenty-five minutes to clock the crowd passing a single point. He sent an emergency call to all precincts to call in their reserves. He ordered Captain Speight to take seventy men to guard the draft office for the lower half of the island at Broadway and Twenty-first Street. This left Mulberry grieviously shorthanded should the rioting spread.

Kennedy and his assistants, Mellen Murphy and Bill Kimball, jumped into a buggy and raced uptown. A half mile from the clouds of black smoke, Kennedy came upon the outer ring of the crowd and was astounded at their overwhelming number. While the center of the crowd rioted, the edge was sitting under shade trees as though on a picnic.

Kennedy went unarmed. He wore civilian clothes and carried a bamboo walking stick. Murphy feared no man, and his walk conveyed it. He hopped out to guard his chief while Kimball minded the buggy. A burly loafer barked to his mates. "Hey, there's the chief in civvies."

Kennedy took no notice of the buzzing around him.

"Get the chief," came the cry.

Murphy knew the brawler and hard-nosed up to him. "Cusick, what's an old policeman doing here?"

"Ex-policeman. Too good for Kennedy. He wants angels on his force."

Kennedy came up. "You want to be run in?"

Cusick sassed the chief. "By who?"

A rough pushed Kennedy violently from behind. Kennedy whipped around. His fleetness gave him an opening to smash the man. Seeing his attacker was a soldier, he held his blow. "What's that for, soldier?"

The soldier replied by punching Kennedy's face.

A second rough sneakily tripped the stunned Kennedy and sent him sprawling. Murphy jumped in, swinging at the soldier and the tripper, and Cusick clubbed him down from behind.

Kennedy stumbled up groggily to help Murphy. A rough clubbed Kennedy on the ear, forcing the chief to lose his footing and roll down an embankment.

Hearing maniacal yelling behind him, Kennedy slipped, stumbled, crawled over sharp rocks while skillfully evading a heavily outnumbered attack.

Kennedy raced west across empty lots baking in the sun. His eyes glowing as hot pins in his buzzing head. His ear a mash of flesh and blood. He reached the opposite embankment and had only to climb up to Lexington Avenue and he'd have a chance to get away. Kennedy staggered up to the top, only to be met by a gang blocking fire companies from going to the fires. They spotted the injured Kennedy. A paving stone was flung, and it hit Kennedy in the chest, tumbling him back down the embankment.

Kennedy raised himself on wobbly legs and ran blindly back toward Third Avenue. He stopped before a crazed brute swinging a nailed club at his head. He dodged the blow, feeling the air rush by his hot, pulsing ear. The mob formed a circle around them so that there was no escape for Kennedy.

The mob cheered the loony on while tightening their circle. Wherever Kennedy moved, the circle moved to keep him dead-center. Kennedy moved lopsidedly and in a crouch to keep away from the raised club while trying to clear his head. He made sure the sun was in his attacker's eyes whenever he gave him a target. The attacker swung and missed. The jeering drove the attacker mad. He went wild, swinging at Kennedy, whose face was fogged with pain. The crazed swinging widened the circle and gave Kennedy room to maneuver. The circle was forced to break when Kennedy backed into a deepening mud hole that ran the width of the block. Trying to blink away his pain, Kennedy was slipping on the muddy bottom until his feet sank in and stuck.

The madman charged into the mud hole and swung. Kennedy dived into the water. The splash in the sunlight was streaked with Kennedy's blood. Kennedy didn't come up. The mob cheered the lunatic, who beamed at winning their respect.

No Kennedy broke the surface. Kennedy swam underwater until his lungs were about to burst. His head bobbed up for air and his blood trailed in the water.

The mob splashed through the mud hole. Kennedy was too out of breath to flee and was caught. The mob punched and kicked his helpless body, tossing him into the air where he twisted dumbly before dropping headfirst into the mud hole. Strings of bubbles showed Kennedy was alive. He was kicked and punched underwater, the blows sliding him along the bottom. The more vicious the blows, the farther he slid out of their reach. The blows coming less often with the water deepening and the mob churning up the bottom and losing sight of him.

Kennedy floated up in deep water. He did not know where he was until he felt the hot sun on his bruised face. The mob, seeing Kennedy's muddy head, went berserk and howled as they ran around the wide hole to get at him.

Kennedy waded toward Lexington Avenue, crawled up the embankment. This drained all his strength, and at the top he had none left to call for help. If he could call, he wouldn't have been heard. Behind him was the howling mob.

With his muddy head in the silt of the embankment, Kennedy spied a lordly and prosperous carter walking his horse with a slow pace for what seemed an eternity until he came close. "Egan," came Kennedy's harsh breath, "it's me."

Egan screwed up his eyes without recognizing the chief. He did see the raving roughs in pursuit and mounted his cart with a dexterity that belied his girth.

"Egan, for the love of God, it's John Kennedy."

Egan smiled faintly at the dirt-caked body. "You're not the chief who I know like my own hand, you scoundrel. Getting your licks for liking the draft?" Eagan took up his reins to slap against his horse's flank.

Kennedy's quivering hand pushed out of the silt and painfully felt for his wounded face. With one stroke he smeared off the mud on his right side from eyebrow to jaw.

"Mary, mother of Jesus!" Egan crossed himself and jumped out of his cart, though frightened sick of the advancing roughs. Lifting Kennedy's limp body, he placed him gently on the straw in his cart.

"Egan," Cusick shouted, "if you don't give him up, we'll burn your damn cart, kill your horse and pull out your fat guts."

Egan, bathing in sweat, turned to face the gang, his prosperous clothes muddied by helping Kennedy. Egan saw his life's rewards about to vanish in a wink. A minute ago he was smugly walking his horse around the riot. His reaching out trapped him. Fear of the unseen brought out Egan's eloquence. "You cannot kill him." Egan reached into his cart as for a sack, raised Kennedy's head by the hair and let the body drop back lifelessly. "He is dead in all but name." Egan mounted his cart and drove off, muttering his prayers.

Egan arrived at Mulberry as Tom Acton, President of the Police Board of Commissioners, was leaving. Acton was a civic-minded Republican belonging to the best clubs. A completely reliable man and imperturbable. "Egan," he scolded, "no drunks. Can't you see we mean business today?"

"Sir," Egan all but wept, "it's Kennedy."

"Are you drunk too?"

Inspector Carpenter came out to see who was bothering the President of the Board. "Egan, take your dirty friend home."

"It's the chief," Egan appealed.

Carpenter glimpsed the truth and bellowed to his men to rush the chief to Bellevue. Then, with remarkable presence of mind, he turned to Acton, who had clapped on his high hat. "Mr. Acton, you'll have to take command."

"Inspector, I'm not a policeman."

"Sir, we've lost the one man we most depend on."

"True, but I'm a civilian."

"The police can't be left without authority."

Acton took off his silk topper and marched in as the police saluted him.

In spite of the burning and looting uptown, business in lower Manhattan went on as usual. Talk was of the heat, which made everyone feel washed in hot molasses. Though fire bells tolled, the draft office for lower Manhattan remained untouched.

The Invalid Corps of fifty wounded soldiers from the Battle of Fredericksburg marched up Third Avenue, led by Lieutenant Reade, who was amazed the mob was a hundred times larger than his troops. Paving stones knocked down several war veterans. At Fortieth Street a rough ran out to grab an officer's sword and was slashed across the chest. The dazed rough watched his blood seep out of his torn clothes, his eyes suddenly sheepish at his ignorance of violence.

Reade lined up the Invalids to block the mob from going down to the business district. The mob tested him with paving stones as they advanced. Reade ordered the Invalids to load blanks and fire overhead. The mob's advance quickened into a charge. Paving stones tumbled soldiers like cannon shot.

Reade ordered his men to load ball and aim at target. At close range Reade gave the order to fire. Women, children and men, so fearless one moment, were shocked to be dying the next, twisting and moaning in the gutter.

The soldiers had no time to reload. Muskets were pulled from their hands. Invalids bayoneted and clubbed with their own weapons. The power the mob felt chasing soldiers down Third Avenue was quickly converted into plundering stores and homes. Looting saved the fleeing soldiers.

Upper Third Avenue was under darkness, rolling black smoke eclipsing the sun. Spectators lined the rooftops and leaned out windows. They heard a roaring that caused even New Yorkers to pause.

"I've a brilliant idea how to stop the riot."

"Your father would approve," said Mary Jane in the mudroom with the cleaning maid. She ushered Tweed into the parlor, thinking the maid might not approve of his ideas. Watching her husband made Mary Jane feel as blind as watching lovers. She couldn't imagine the intensity with which they lived.

"Of course he'd approve." He was grateful to Mary Jane for the thought. The absence of his father when he was about to do a good deed churned him up and he burst out, "Death would be marvelous—"

"What're you saying?"

"If only the bastards were taken and the people who never harmed a soul remained." He was in a deep reverie.

"That's a sweet thought, Bill."

"He worked so hard in his shop at what he wanted to do most that he seemed close to nature, and time itself didn't want to touch him."

"That's no reason to be sad, Bill." She was grateful he was sharing his memories with her. Too many times in recent years she had only to appear silently and he took her presence as a hostile question. "You should take him as a standard to emulate."

"He was sorry to see me."

"No." She bit her lips.

"Yes. The only time he thought I said something worthwhile to him was when he told me he wished Grandfather had stayed home on the banks of the River Tweed in Scotland and never come to New York. I'd have grown up among trees and a river and known about the earth from whence everything grows. I told him that the people are the earth of the cities."

She was so touched, she said what would have been unthinkable to her a few minutes before. "Why don't you go out and talk to the rioters? They'll listen to you if they'll listen to anyone." No matter how intensely she wanted him to leave politics, she knew there was no one who was his grass-roots equal. His knowledge of New York was like knowing fate. When he was slow to respond, she said strongly, "You'll have the satisfaction of knowing you tried."

"Tried and failed. They have their steam up. It would be shouting in the wind until I had something to offer. It's like a general in battle. If you saw the bleeding wounded, you might think twice about ever fighting again, and if the bleeding didn't affect you, you might think twice about yourself."

Then, like a sudden storm, her old husband was hovering over her, only with elation.

"I'm going to pass a bond that'll give three hundred dollars to any poor man who wants to buy himself out of the war."

She recoiled. "You're rewarding killing and looting."

"It's my big chance." He wanted her to see the light.

"How can you be happy about a riot?" She could choke him.

"Can I speak to you as an adult?"

"How do you speak to me?"

"Like a husband."

"I don't know why you think you're dumber as a husband."

He was startled by her sense of humor. "Whoever controls the riot will control the city. Fifth Avenue wants to strip my patronage."

"After all your work?" She was on his side for a change.

"The city is blowing up, and Fifth Avenue is worried about appearances."

"Don't you see you're playing into the hands of your enemies? The new mayor will veto your bond and become a hero."

"No, the city will be grateful not to be living with violence. The more violence, the more they'll think they need me to control the rabble. I'm counting on their ignorance."

His exhilaration infuriated her. "How can you think that?"

"Did I make the rules that work? Why should a stranger to the wards like Mayor Opdyke rule the city? Does he know the people?" He knew he had Mary Jane because he counted on the purity of her honesty. She'd never be loyal to a party no matter what they did. "Did the mayor feed the poor when they were hungry? Did he give them jobs when they were down-and-out?" In the midst of his titanic energy his arms hung down to plead.

Mary Jane had no defense against his surge of optimism. She ran from the parlor as if pursued by the furies and shut the door against him.

He was compelled to run after her and clear himself. When he opened the door into the kitchen, he found her trembling. That his strong wife could not take him caused him to shout out: "These are my streets. My city. My home. Why should strangers take it over?"

He dashed out of the house to a rummy theater over a stable called Walhalla. There he asked the manager if any of his whips were in the theater. He had to whip up a quorum fast. The manager wasn't sure, as some of his whips could lie about for hours in the darkness. He went down the aisle to the front row where they were usually unburdening themselves from politics.

A fiddler scraped music as a faded green curtain jerked up, revealing Susannah in her bath. A hardened woman had a gauze rag draped over her shoulders. Walhalla featured a French import from Victorian England entitled *Tableaux Vivants*. Naked women posed as famous characters from biblical and classical antiquity. The audience applauded. The curtain with an iron bar sewn in the hem banged down. The curtain flew up to reveal the gauze rag gone and three coarse elders from skid row stooping over her in lecherous agony. The curtain banged down to whistling appreciation.

After finding no one he was looking for, Tweed ran over to the Franklin Museum, much haunted by aldermen. The curator told him the riot had scared them into hiding. At the museum live women posed as historical figures—Marie Antoinette, Good Queen Bess, Bloody Mary, Catherine the Great—in the nude. He spoke to Photo Egan, the bookie who never forgot a bet, and told him to send any aldermen he'd see to City Hall. Booster Kelly and Red Rocks Farrell of the notorious Farrell brothers and Dirty Dollar Dolan of the lush cribs spoke about the prosperity. The riot would bring with it tons of stuff to be fenced. They loudly went for Tweed's idea of the bond, but there were no whips around at City Hall.

He was disappointed going down the steps facing City Hall Park when a cold, bony hand clutched his wrist. He hadn't felt that desperation since giving out food in the '57 Panic. "Garvey!" He embraced the skeleton.

Garvey licked his chops at Tweed's friendliness.

"Where you been since we chased fires?"

The forlorn figure bowed his head. "I heard about your sainted father."

The humble tone touched Tweed. "Come to my office at 95 Duane Street for a job." He took a bill from his choking roll and slapped it into Garvey's limp hand. "What line are you in?"

Tweed's concern made Garvey feel the rags melting off his back. "A poor plasterer, Bill."

"Perfect." Tweed patted the derelict, as a doctor spanks life into the newborn. "You'll work on the new courthouse."

An aide came out to tell Tweed he was wanted by the mayor. He went to the mayor, groping for a favor he could throw him. The affable banker, industrialist, real estate mayor had no dark side. Whatever Mayor Opdyke did in the open was dark enough with self-interest. Though he was a reform mayor elected to chase out the crooks, he was so respectful of Tweed that he was nervous. Shaking the mayor's hand gave him the pleasant surprise of a shiny fruit bruised within. He took the mayor's nervous respect as having the same function as octopus ink.

Though the mayor had the magic wand of money, he knew how to pose reasonable requests. "This insurrection, riot, disturbance" —he kept downgrading the violence until it was in harmony with Tweed—"it has to be stopped."

Tweed snapped his fingers before the worried mayor. "Back my bill and it's stopped. The bond will cost no more than three million. It'll pay three hundred dollars to any man who can't pay the exemption."

"I don't bargain with murderers."

Tweed knew the mayor was floundering, when all he had to fall back on was principles.

The mayor began reaching. All eye contact off. "My black servants are hiding in the cellar. My wife, children, house on Fifth Avenue."

He was delighted to have the favor. "I'll send Judge Barnard around."

"Barnard is shady."

Tweed chided him. "Barnard is only accused of taking gratuities for opinions he already holds. You won't find that honor in large supply." He knew he had nailed down a part of the bargain.

"We stopped the draft!" the mob roared against the tolling bells. Hordes broke off in every direction, swarming into streets, sweeping everyone before them. They cheered the rumor that the draft office for lower Manhattan had shut down. A mob raced down Broadway to see for themselves. On their way they shouted to spectators lining the rooftops and filling windows, "We stopped the draft!"

The restless mob was united by the revelation that they could get away with almost anything. They had passed from protesting their just grievance to tasting the heady privileges of being above the law. This violence had no political odor. They felt pure. They had accidentally fallen through a hole and plunged out the privileged side of the city. A dream come true.

One arm of the mob came upon the lawns and gardens of the Half-Colored Orphan Asylum, a pastoral silence shaded by lofty trees on Fifth Avenue from Forty-second to Forty-third Streets. The sunlit white building with white picket fence was a pride of New York philanthropy.

The mob overran the grounds, knocking down the fence, trampling the garden, kicking up the vegetable patch. An unassuming guardian stepped out and locked the front door behind him. He put the key in his pocket when even the strongest men might be thinking of running for their life.

"Davis," a rioter yelled at the thin, white man in a starched white shirt with jacket and tie in the July heat, "hand over your tar babies and no harm will come to you."

The bigotry of the drunken rioters repelled the quiet Davis. He calmly blocked the door with his unimposing body. "Go away before you're arrested for trespassing."

The mob hooted. The defiance of Davis only pointed up his helplessness. They encouraged Davis to stand there so they could trample him to death.

Davis warned them. "I've sent for the police."

"It's going to be a long wait. We cut the wires."

The mob leader raised his arm, let out a war cry, and they charged.

The cool Davis stood his ground and saw the mob halt in a peculiar fashion. He had no idea what was prolonging his life. He glanced up at the windows that caught the mob's attention. Tan and brown children gazed down as if the mob had come out of a storybook.

Davis vented his disgust. "You can't be so low as to harm children?"

Davis's outrage connected with their anger. In the heat of the moment opposites found kinship. They were both scorched by injuries done to them. The mob backed off to parley. An astonishing victory for the courage of Davis that left him shaken. His educated face, which vanished and became deformed in his defense of the children, returned to glow with hope.

"Davis!" the leader shouted. "You won!"

Davis didn't know what to say. He stepped out to shake hands with the leader of these misguided rioters who had justice on their side but violence in their hearts. Before he got too near, he was told, "You've five minutes to clear everyone out. Take nothing with you."

Davis turned without a sign. Stepping inside, he locked the door again and rang the hand bell to save the children. "Fire drill! Five minutes to go out the back!" He raced upstairs with his anxious staff. Children cried only after being taken from the windows. A frightened boy wet his pants and hid under his bed in shame.

The mob outside was counting. "Four, four, four, four . . . three, three, three . . ."

The orphans lined up, holding their toys and teddy bears. Bigger children carried smaller ones. Sick children were carried by the staff. Several hand bells were rung to hurry the children.

"One, one, one . . .!"

The door was battered down as the children rushed out the back. Rioters fought over the rugs and furniture and chopped with axes what was hotly disputed.

A drunk stuck his head out of a top-floor window. Seeing the children sheltered by Davis and his staff irritated him. He cursed the children and stirred up his mates to get them.

Davis heard them running through the house. When they ran out on the lawn, Davis ran to meet them. "You dumb beasts, come to your senses before you become murderers."

The mob came at Davis and punched him down as he cried out, "Don't touch the children!"

A fireman's trumpet turned their heads. Pulling its pumper onto the grounds was a volunteer fire company, set to hold off the mob with hooks and axes.

"Burn the orphanage," yelled a drunk. "That'll keep them busy."

Whiskey was thrown against the building and then matches lit. The firemen were jeered at to save the building. The firemen protected the children and had to watch the flames.

The children recognized a call for help behind the flames. They howled and jumped and flung themselves on the ground as the staff called the roll. A floor crashed through and the cry stopped.

The mob cheered and overflowed back onto Fifth Avenue.

"We're marching to tame a beast." Inspector Carpenter fired up his men outside Mulberry. "They've murdered, lynched, looted, burned, destroyed an orphanage with a child inside. Feed them cold steel. Strike quick. Strike hard. Take no prisoners. Shoulder arms, hup! Left face, hup! Marrrch!"

The police stepped off and neighbors cheered.

Carpenter shouted, "Cadence, count!"

Voices blasted out. "One, two, three, four!"

"I can't hear you!" Carpenter scowled.

They erupted. "One, two, three, four!"

"Let them hear you coming!"

"One, two, three, four!"

"Louder!"

Eardrum-splitting. "One, two, three, four!"

Families came to open windows to cheer and wave handkerchiefs.

Their support brought out a deafening response. "One, two, three, four!"

"Let the beasts hear you coming!" Carpenter yelled.

"One! Two! Three! Four!"

This brought families out to the curb cheering.

Marching with an emphatic beat up Broadway and shouting their cadence at the top of their lungs, the police drowned out every noise in their path and cleared New York traffic. Their militant exuberance was infectious.

Then the police heard an ominous thunder effortlessly overwhelm their shouting, as a tidal wave sweeps pebbles under. In a city where tourists never forget the spectacular sound, this tumultuous thunder was not in the scope of human effort. The roar rolled down Broadway, walling up the city.

There was no sight of this colossus. Who? What? How was it able to create this sound that put fired-up police in awe? The roar was inhuman. Not a moment's pause, not a moment's lowering, not a moment's hush. The roar did not breathe. It had no cadence, no rhythm, no center, no edge, no end.

The police marched into this roar that was swallowing them up, their shouted cadence a mere ticking of high grass in a squall. To feel the tremor of the roar was to become disembodied. Insides stolen. The roar so encompassing, it appeared to be coming out of their own imagination.

The police marched uptown past Bleecker Street, past once fashionable Bond, past Great Jones, Fourth Street, Washington Plaza, Waverly, Clinton Place—going under the roar.

The source of the roar was coming toward them around the bend of Broadway at Tenth Street. A moving horizon of humanity, people armed with pitchforks, rifles, clubs, telegraph poles—all packed into a summer skyline.

An American flag was held high. Handmade signs with a coarse scrawl bobbed over their heads: NO DRAFT! Their protesting cries against the draft that made the body hum were lost in the undertow of their own roaring. Women, children and men formed the proud front ranks.

Carpenter shouted to his men. "Fix bayonets!"

The Battle of Broadway had begun.

The mob, seeing the police ready to run them through, slowly came to a halt in front and gradually began to draw back. It was as impossible for them to pull back as a whale trying to shrivel into its fin.

The mob was packed into Broadway for over a half mile. Those a block away had no idea what was happening up front. The rear of the mob kept coming, pressing the front ranks forward. The rioters were helpless to keep from being pushed into the police. The front of the mob wanted to withdraw, while the rear was aggressively booming, "No draft!"

At point-blank range the mob was trying to shoulder itself backward but all too slowly. Carpenter gave the order. "Fire!"

Screams and groans of the wounded and dying didn't keep the rear from blindly pushing forward. The front ranks were pushed over bodies begging for help. The wounded with a chance to live saw themselves about to be trampled to death by their own.

The police kept firing. The slaughter of those screaming for help was taking place under the triumphant roar from the rear.

Carpenter ordered a charge over the dead and wounded. The mob chaotically splintered down side streets, bodies and weapons left behind. Taking no prisoners, giving no quarter, the police cornered men and women and clubbed them.

Horrifying cries mixed with victory cheers.

New signs appeared. New chants were heard.

"Abolish slavery! Support the war! Union Forever!"

Carpenter, flying a captured American flag, paraded his men toward Mulberry. Hotels emptied, families dashed out of their homes, white-shirted businessmen and office workers came out to cheer and wave the police home as they celebrated the victory of the Battle of Broadway.

Heartbreaking cries expressing the lack of pity in the world shrieked over Broadway. Women keening in the middle of the street, hugging bloodied heads. Hundreds of kneeling and bent women grieving soulfully with blood in their voices. Their keening caught the ears of the retreating mob. One second the mob was running for their lives, and the next they were shouting for vengeance. "We need guns! To the armory!" In the magic of mobs they regrouped into one pulse. Fresh yells celebrated their new purpose. "Guns!" On their way they overturned stalled and emptied streetcars from the morning traffic jam. Commercial wagons were set on fire where they were abandoned. "We need guns!"

Rioting embroiled all New Yorkers except Dutch Hill squatters. They lived on Forty-second Street overlooking the Hudson River in sow shacks worse than what they had left in Ireland and Germany. Tourists drove by Dutch Hill at a gallop to observe life at the bottom. What they rarely observed was that the Dutch Hill squatters had nothing to show that they were industrious. They were constantly carrying empty gunnysacks or lugging full ones or pushing jerry-built carts down Tenth Avenue, skirting the river to Beach Street where on the docks they took wing like birds, leaping down to the garbage scows. The heavier men and women shinnied down the coarse hemp rope, burning and scarring their thighs and ankles. Their unfinished faces turned up at the slightest creaking, like chicks in a nest waiting to be fed. The black smoke and tolling bells could not distract them from their livelihood.

Horses trundled onto the piers, pulling dump wagons. Garbage rained down on them. They scrambled up this mound, squirreling into their gunnysacks the pick of it. While sunk waist-deep in the mounds, they heard laughing and singing.

Looking up, they saw men, women, children dancing by with gold watches swinging and trinkets glittering. Women wore feathers in gold-dusted hair and silk dresses twisted and hiked on them. Unkempt boys whirled swagger sticks. Men had high hats popped on their beans and, with a fireman's carry, lugged gorgeous rugs.

Whatever wealth could buy and commercial art could produce was lavished on the palatial St. Nicholas Hotel. A decade before the war's inflation cheapened money, the hotel cost over one million dollars. One thousand guests a day walked beneath its tall Corinthian columns to the elegant appointments inside. This interior drew sophisticated people to admire it. New York materialism so grandiose, it is spiritual. The divinity in man himself. One look at the St. Nicholas and the observer knew the future belonged to New York.

Three steps off calamitous Broadway and Spring Streets, a guest no longer heard his own footsteps, so creative were the artisans. They created the lush amenities of silence in the face of the city's din.

Every inch of the St. Nicholas lay deep in carpets. Candelabra placed at breathtakingly short intervals gave the halls the impression of being aflame with light. Walking up the grand staircase toward the crystal chandelier's spectacular light, a guest could feel he was ascending to his own immortality.

A hand had only to be raised and one of five hundred bellboys and waiters, one for every other guest, would answer. But of all the tapestried rooms it was the St. Nicholas bar where a man with money reigned. If there was a service known to man that money could buy, it could be bought at the St. Nicholas bar.

The bar housed one of the finest telegraph offices in the city. Here the three military generals of the area and their aides met. The mayor moved his office out of the vulnerable City Hall to the more easily guarded hotel.

Tweed was on edge in this bar, and it had nothing to do with his being Temperance. The luxuries of the hotel taunted him dreadfully with the achievements of men who had gone before. He couldn't even do the right thing in getting a bond passed without paying a fortune.

How could the people he backed burn down an orphanage? Kill a child? Put Kennedy in Bellevue? Fire at war veterans? What he believed could never happen was happening before his eyes. His future was being taken from him. Being a politician, he judged acts as they would appear in a newspaper. Everyone of importance in this bar had already read in his mind the newspapers that had not yet come out.

Mayor Opdyke was weaseling with him while trying to become a hero with a military solution, but as luck sometimes comes with humor, the military was squabbling over which general was responsible for defending New York. General Wool had troops but is too senile to act. General Brown is eager to act but has no troops. General Sandford commands the state militia and can put down any riot, but his rigid sense of duty compels him to protect state property first and not the city's. The mayor tried to go around them by getting men from the forts sitting in the harbor, the Brooklyn Navy Yard, West Point, but all reserves that could be spared were sent to Gettysburg to turn back Lee.

Tweed deliberately picked his nose as a comment on the goings-on. This, as he knew, only served to highlight that he was becoming helpless. To give himself the influence he felt he was losing, he went up to the mayor and asked him if he had telegraphed the War Department and warned them the city wants no trigger-happy troops here. The mayor told him not to worry, as a storm had cut the lines to Washington.

He was given the high sign by the bell captain that he had a private message. Tweed excused himself to the mayor, who was glad to be rid of him. Tweed was hoping for a bit of good news when the bell captain told him he was wanted at the Fifth Avenue Hotel. Tweed said that his answer was to glance out the window and see why he can't come. The captain said that he was told to say that if Alderman Tweed doesn't arrive soon, he'll be paged.

"Tell your source that she's won the battle but not the war."

"My source said that if you mentioned winning the war, you've yielded."

He itched to get his hands on Augusta.

She opened the door and he cornered her in her lavish suite before she could properly greet him. His exuberance wasn't what she wanted at present, even though she was the cause of it.

"Go away, Bill."

"You called." He wedged his big nose under her chin as if shucking an oyster.

She pressed her stern jaw down to squeeze him out and inadvertently conveyed intimacy by her pressure. "Not now." She warded off encouraging him.

He mumbled into her scented neck. "The sexiest women are those who don't want it."

"You're wrong and I'm proof." She hit him.

He spoke into her aromatic armpit, which he was trying to pry open with his nose. He raised his nose as a rabbit scenting prey.

"Horrible man." She hit him again.

He began to unbutton her dress.

"Bill, no. I've a backache."

"Backaches," he praised her, "means you're a sexual volcano." He chewed on her ear as she struggled to get out of his grasp. "A sign of lecherous tension." He released her, and she leaned into him and began to undress him. "What're you doing?" He despaired.

"Isn't this what you call making love?"

"Something is on your mind."

She knocked her head against his chest for help. "Do you know what Courtlandt did to me after you left?"

"You risk ruining me with a message at the St. Nicholas to tell me humdrum." Her outrageous license exhilarated him.

"Courtlandt paraded me about the hotel."

"All you think about is yourself." He was disappointed.

"He carried on like *he* was the one who satisfied me."

His eyes opened wide in disbelief.

"He puffed himself up on his own ignominy."

He embraced her to hug out her distress. "I'll set you free."

She kissed him with a shiver.

"I like you"—his eyes lit up with enjoyment—"when you're on the lip of hysteria. You gave me a real kiss."

"Sometimes," she confessed, "one slips out."

"I'll give Courtlandt two hundred thousand dollars for your freedom," he said proudly.

"I hate you." She flung herself away from him.

"Is that too high? I always pay the Tweed price."

"I don't want you to buy me." She raged. "I want you to run away with me."

He was astonished. "I'm a loyal husband."

"Am I more beautiful than Mary Jane?"

"Yes."

"More intelligent?"

"Yes."

"Younger?"

"Yes."

"More passionate for your career?"

"Beans."

"Every time I see Mary Jane, she looks like she's been over-charged."

"You and I are so ambitious, we take the world as it is." He brought her back to why she called, and he was hurting. "I don't want to be your revenge on Courtlandt."

Her beauty—he dare not tell her—was in her being unsatisfied. This was eating into her reserve, leaving her bereft of will, bringing out a woman of passion.

She must have read his sympathy because she was at him again.

"Is bare-knuckle fighting savage?"

"Yes."

"Do you become excited?"

"Yes."

"Very?"

"Yes."

"We must see each other after the fight." Her afterthought: "What does sports have to do with politics?"

"A popular champ will be in my corner. Morrissey's bloody victory will spill onto me and make me acceptable to more people."

"All from a savage boxer?" She smiled at his innocence while half believing him.

"Everyone helps." He kissed her with a rough passion that reddened her. "I must be getting back. Idiots are killing me."

"The cure for idiocy is election day."

He smiled fondly at her optimism.

A mob spread so far and wide, no eye could take them in. They formed around the armory on Twenty-first Street and Second Avenue under a hot, late-afternoon sun.

The show horses of the police force were the popular Broadway squad. The biggest, brawniest coppers, posted at the busiest crossings for tourists to take comfort in their beefeaters' presence. They were inside guarding the armory. All thirty-four of them. The mob was over ten thousand.

The police with rifles were lined up behind fortress doors and barred windows. The ground floor was a gun factory. The munitions maker leased out the top three floors as an armory.

A brazen horseback rider was haranguing the mob with a Dixie accent, revealing that Mayor Opdyke owned the armory and that his son-in-law ran the gun factory. He recalled the forty thousand signatures the Chamber of Commerce collected, calling for compromise with slaveholders. He spoke of New York bankers who had an understanding not to take another dollar of government loans unless the demands of the slave states were met. He read from a copy of a letter Elijah Purdy sent to the President: "I can assure Mr. Lincoln that so long as he conducts this war for the suppression of the rebellion and the supremacy of the law, he will always find a cordial response from Tammany Hall. But if this war is to be prosecuted for the dishonest purpose of emancipating the Negroes of the South, he cannot expect the support of the Democrats."

Seconds later a hail of rocks and paving stones rattled against the armory, crashing through windows and forcing the police to dive for cover. Under this hailstorm the rioters charged the door with a telegraph pole for a battering ram and used sledgehammers to break the hinges. The collision thundered through the armory, visibly shaking the police behind the door, who saw the heavy iron hinges bend from the wall and let in sunlight.

Sergeant Burdick ordered his men to shoot at the rioters as they ran back. A policeman took his life in his hands to peek out against the uncannily accurate stone throwers. Police appeared in the windows, and a hail of stones destroyed the frames.

A rousing cheer and fresh rammers charged with stones and rocks flying before them to pin down the police. Rifle shots came through the splintered door. Roughs fell away from the battering ram. Those who were left crashed through the door with the mob right behind them. The police were chased out the back under a barrage of rocks. Gangs followed police taking refuge at the nearest precinct and burned the station house down.

At Mulberry the officers fumed at not being able to control the mob. The victory of the Battle of Broadway vanished with the defeat at the armory. The mob appeared everywhere. A defeat in one battle meant nothing to a part of the mob in another neighborhood.

Smarting from their armory defeat, the police decided to sneak back and catch the mob by surprise. A boy playing behind the armory spotted them. He ran upstairs to alert those in the drilling room on the third floor who were seriously practicing military discipline and rifle inspection. They had nailed their door shut to keep out the boozers. Not being able to open the door, the boy pounded on it, but the drillers were shouting cadence and were too caught up in their disciplined marching.

A drunk, seeing the police clubbing their way through to the battered fortress door, hanging off its hinges, threw a lit match on crates marked for the Union Army.

The oil-soaked factory floor blew into flames. The fire ravenously chewing up walls, stairways, ceilings. Oil drums exploded, blowing out walls. The armory rumbled as in the fit of an earthquake. The building's facade cracked, stairs caved in, crumbling ceilings showered fire on those running and screaming below. Geysers of suffocating black smoke streaked with fire mopped the armory in a whirlwind from top to bottom and boomed out of windows like cannon shot. The only direction in the darkness came from the screams of those blocked by the flaming doorway. Human torches hurtled out of windows. The anguished shrieking reached the drill room where fire blew across their windows.

The drillers stampeded toward the door they had nailed shut. The floor began swaying, fire licking through the cracks opening up. They couldn't go near the door, warping in flames. When the door split open, the drillers rushed out as the black smoke and flames blasted in. The collapsing floor pitched bodies back and forth, tossing them into the flames below as the armory caved in, bombarding the streets with bodies and debris. The armory burned in a cloud of ash against the setting sun. For miles the taste of burnt flesh stuck to lips.

Through the day and into the night, no matter where he went, from the Franklin Museum to City Hall, to homes and love nests, merchant stores and offices, Tweed could not get or even find aldermen for a quorum on his bond. The price to change minds had not skyrocketed; worse, it was nonexistent. The rioting was out of everyone's hands. Yet he couldn't help feeling jubilant. Violent events played into his muscle. He thrived on hopeless situations.

He had the one positive idea: the bond to bail out the poor. The killings and the destruction of property made it an untouchable subject. Yet it wouldn't be untouchable if Fifth Avenue had to depend on him as the voice of sanity and affirmation to control the mob.

He rode through the midnight streets in his buggy. Bonfires of surplus loot lit the street crossings. The summer's heat thick with smoldering fires. Men and boys continued to lug costly furniture down muddy streets while weeping women and children carted home their dead. Through the haze, red scars of lightning flared across the humid sky, pulsing with a storm yet unseen.

When the storm broke, he drove under his noisy canvas roof. A torrential rain beat against the wilderness of signs. The downpour rent huge holes in the night among the fires. The wind threw open hovels stocked with gilded chairs and tables, oil paintings and tasseled carpets. At Canal Street, where the city was extended into the Hudson River by landfill, he looked down open cellars where looted steaks were being cooked over mickey holes in unfinished floors. The drumming rain could be heard softening their walls so soppy ears of refuse could slowly unfurl through the wet walls and slide down against them as they ate undisturbed.

In a deserted doorway he saw a woman struggling with a man beating her. He jumped from his buggy into the rain to break them up and thankfully stopped in time. They were kissing and hugging.

He jumped back in his buggy, wiping a mysterious sweat from his face. It wasn't a summer sweat. It was a viscous sweat, gluey and up from the gut. It had the alarm of a cold awakening. What had drained out of him that he, of all men, should be so mistaken about lovers?

THREE

The New York sun is without style in July. It
bakes on contact. In the tropics the night's thick moisture must
first wear off before the day becomes unbearable. There is that
refreshing dawn illusion of escaping the heat. New York's hot
mornings come without illusions.

Inspector Carpenter, with two hundred and fifty men, toured
the silent city to learn if the riot had ended. They headed toward
the Upper East Side where the destruction began. Steam from
puddles wafted past shuttered stores and mansions. The draft
office for lower Manhattan had burned down. Idle factories and
boarded-up office buildings stood blackened in the sun. Ghostly
ashes floated in the muggy dawn. The rain doused the bonfires but
thickened the bitter smoke. Children scavenged among the ruins.
Men were nailing up notices of Governor Seymour speaking from
the steps of City Hall today. The homeless waited on street corners
resembling specters. Carpenter sent a runner to Mulberry to say
that all was quiet and that he saw no signs of the riot being
renewed.

The police proceeded up-island when a runner dispatched from
Mulberry caught up with Carpenter to report that a mob greater
than at the Battle of Broadway was forming outside the Union
Steam Works.

                    *   *   *

Tweed was certain that the bastards had a magnet to speed up his heart. He knew from experience that a politician is to human nature what a hummingbird is to gravity. He defies it. He was on his way to City Hall to hear the governor.

The Battery bore no scars from the riot. Gunboats rode ashore. Clippers lay anchored in the bay. Ferries carried whites and blacks out of the city. The gunboat *Tulip* had her cannons trained on Wall Street should the rioters attack. Bullion from the Sub-Treasury was taken to Governor's Island. Custom House windows held bombs with forty-second fuses to throw down. The top-floor offices of the Bank Note Company had tanks of sulfuric acid to pour down on the mob.

Orderly, neatly dressed citizens waited in front of City Hall to hear the governor. Sharpshooters were on the roof, and two howitzers guarded the building. Newsboys ran through the park shouting, "Civil war erupts in city! Read about the Battle of Broadway! Third Avenue Massacre! Draft offices and police stations burning down!" Black smoke curled into the sky behind the governor as he spoke.

The governor was overly cautious and not about to drop his winning style. He had a high-domed head that looked quizzical on him. He was without chin whiskers but sported fulsome muttonchops that gave him the face a mother might keep scrubbing clean, and at age fifty he still wore the grimace.

Governor Seymour first put his listeners in his debt. "Hearing there was difficulty in the city, I left the quiet of the country to do what I can to preserve the public peace."

No listeners were more solemn than Tweed and his nuts-and-bolts man, Sweeny. Those knowing Tweed knew his solemnity was contempt.

"I beg you," the governor addressed his audience, "listen to me *as a friend. I am your friend.*"

Insulting groans from the people that had Tweed and his cronies smirking. The governor was mistaking these respectable citizens for the rioters they hated.

The governor was blown up with his importance. "I have sent my adjutant general to Washington, urging the draft's postponement."

Tweed paled at the ground being taken out from under him.

"I pledge myself," Seymour said triumphantly, "that money

shall be raised for the purpose of *helping* those unable to protect their own interests."

The governor was boldly jumping out with his bond idea and making it legitimate. A flushed Tweed grabbed dapper Judge McCunn and hustled him aside. "I want you to declare the Conscription Act unconstitutional now."

"Here?"

"In your office, dummy. Write your decision and make sure the papers print it tomorrow. We're going to lead the fight against the draft."

"You stuck me in the Court of Sessions. I've no power to declare a Federal Law unconstitutional."

"Are you going to give me your loyalty or your legal opinion?" Tweed had contempt for the latter. "The wards have to know we're fighting for them." He shoved the judge on his way and collared Sweeny. "Get that bond passed today, no matter how much their honor costs. Tell the aldermen the governor is stealing our thunder and will take all the credit."

The mob could level the city in any direction. They were jammed shoulder-to-shoulder from Twenty-second to Thirty-second Streets on Second Avenue. But they stood immobile before the steam works. They boasted of extorting money from shopkeepers to leave their stores alone. They showed off their trinkets and top hats, puffing on Havana cigars and acting the instant gentleman to perfection.

When the sorely outnumbered police came upon the huge mob, Carpenter began the foolhardy task of pushing the mob back from the steam works. Carpenter was so confident in his commands, the mob gave ground. Not a rioter raised his rifle, though it was apparent the police would be overwhelmed.

It was the women, cursing, chanting, spitting at the men, who gave this sea of humanity a life. "Die at home!" the women shouted, herding their sheep. "It's better to die at home!"

Carpenter skillfully did not rush the mob, yet could not pursue them at their own pace. They gave ground to Twenty-third, Twenty-fourth, Twenty-fifth Street. He had to keep a delicate, even fragile, pressure to show he meant business, yet not enough pressure to arouse their violence.

The women screamed with loathing, "Die at home!"

The mob drew back to Twenty-sixth, Twenty-seventh, Twenty-eighth Street. Falling back grew on itself to discourage the mob: Twenty-ninth, Thirtieth, Thirty-first Street.

The women were distracted out of mind. Their shrieking chants filled Second Avenue. To brand the men where they lived, some women took off their drawers in public to loud hooting and waved their drawers at the men's cowardice.

The mob's humiliation was cushioned by retreating loot fat. Second Avenue was littered with silverware, drapery, a piano, paintings, books, sheet music.

Carpenter and his men realized they had won the most amazing victory in the annals of the police. They were greatly outnumbered and rolled back an armed mob without firing a shot.

But at Thirty-second Street, a paving stone out of nowhere felled a policeman, and then another and another rapidly opened holes in their ranks. The stone throwers were on the roofs, and they stirred the mob to charge. It was one of the strangest charges of citizens upon their police; some charged, while others held their peace. The police fired on those who charged and those who were peaceful.

Carpenter dispatched police to clear the roofs, and within minutes the mob saw rioters falling like kites through the sky.

The mob was astonished at the citizen soldiers suddenly appearing on their flank at Thirty-fifth Street.

Colonel O'Brien was leading the newly formed Eleventh New York Volunteers. While many in the mob were frightened, those who knew the colonel, on horseback, grinned at the sight. "O'Brien, you lush, you must be in the tank to fight against your neighbors." Many of his volunteers were greeted by nicknames.

Two howitzers were pulled up as the mob hooted the colonel for playing at soldiers. O'Brien gave the order, and the howitzers fired into the mob. Carpenter attacked head-on, and the streets cleared as though a hurricane had passed through.

O'Brien returned his volunteers to their barracks where he was told his home had been sacked. He rode home to learn his family had disappeared. His house was in shambles and his family possessions strewn over his yard. While standing shocked at the sight he heard a cry go up: "There's the traitor!"

O'Brien had no time to think of his family, his house, his loss. If he thought of running, it was too late. He fought off a gang with his sword until a stone opened a gash above his eye and blinded him. He escaped into von Briesen's drugstore. The pharmacist locked his door and took O'Brien inside to treat his wound. A brick smashed von Briesen's window. O'Brien stepped out to confront the roughs as his attackers knew he would. The colonel was clubbed from behind and left for dead.

Children came over to kick O'Brien for amusement and found him alive. The kids stuffed paper in the colonel's uniform and set him on fire. O'Brien crawled through the mud to put it out. Grown-ups returned to claim their neighbor. They dragged O'Brien by the legs up and down the street as a trophy for their neighbors to cheer.

Von Briesen came out with a cup of water for O'Brien, and the druggist was beaten senseless, his pharmacy looted and demolished.

O'Brien remained alive, eyelids twitching, mouth gasping for air. Von Briesen's drugstore was set on fire and O'Brien tossed into the flames. The house next door caught fire. In minutes the entire street was burning. Those cheering now screamed in horror as they ran from their burning homes.

In the same slow manner as before, the mob formed outside the Union Steam Works. Their humiliation put steel in their backbone, and they didn't want to prove their women right. They were astounded the defense plant was unguarded and broke in and captured crates of guns and ammunition earmarked for the Army in the field.

When news of this catastrophe reached Mulberry, the remaining police felt demoralized.

St. John's Park is a haven for contemplation where the rages of men are not seen and seldom heard. The idyllic walks of the park are bordered with exotic flowers shaded by cottonwood, silver birch and the voluminous headdress of weeping willows. The park is on Hudson Square just below Canal, and the riot might be on another planet.

Slow, painful, dragging footsteps can be heard on the gravel walk while bold, heavy, footsteps approach it. The unsteady footsteps belong to a dignified, burned-out dignitary of imposing bearing with a large hook nose protruding under a skullcap. His neck is rendered shapeless by age and cranes forward out of stooped shoulders. His eyes cloud with a mustard sting. They have lost their vision without losing their accusing character. The eyes are sunk into the folds of a stormy face so lacking in blood, the flesh is more silver than pale. Age has kneaded his stark profile. He is prisoner to the pains of his Mother Hubbard body. At rest, his mouth stays open. His humility is not officious but lies in his battlefield weariness. He leans heavily and infirmed on his ornately carved shepherd's staff, sumptously robed on this hot day. His realistic face shaped by the acid hate of enemies. He wears his victories over their intolerance as a badge of honor. He is John Hughes, Roman Catholic archbishop and the highest officer of his faith in the city. He is genuinely pleased to see Tweed approaching, and the warm feeling is mutual.

They begin their exchange like old warriors going over the long battles they've fought, particularly the bigotry in public school textbooks. The archbishop thanks Tweed for coming and quietly comments that St. John's Park is as rare as Vauxhall Gardens that Astor destroyed to build dreary row houses. That old, flinty Commodore Vanderbilt is buying St. John's Park from Trinity Church to turn into a freight terminal.

Tweed is delighted to see the old warrior in fine fettle and acknowledges that beautiful St. John's Park will make way for Vanderbilt's freight terminal.

The archbishop says forcefully, "Greeley's *Tribune* calls the rioters scum and claims they are not loyal Americans."

Tweed sought to cheer up his old comrade-at-arms by telling him the *Daily News* is rightfully blaming the Conscription Act.

Hughes hands him a letter. "I had this written over my signature. Bennett will print this in his *Herald* tomorrow."

Tweed read with interest. " 'In spite of Mr. Greeley's assault, in the present disturbed condition of the city, I will appeal to all persons who love God to respect the laws of man and the peace of society to retire to their homes with as little delay as possible and disconnect themselves from the seemingly deliberate intention to disturb the peace and society rights of New Yorkers. If they are Catholics, or of such of them as are Catholics, I ask, for God's sake —for the sake of their holy religion—for my own sake, if they have any respect for the episcopal authority—to dissolve their bad associations with reckless men, who have little regard either for Divine or human laws.' "

Tweed handed back the letter and said quite mildly, "There should've been an apology to the blacks for hanging them from lampposts."

Hughes was exhausted. "This letter will not do?"

"It is sympathetic. It is right-minded. It is the best one can do under terrible circumstance. The tragedy of the blacks is that the savagery against them will never be fully understood until they are driven to become narrow-minded, hateful and destructive to their friends and enemies." Tweed sagged with reality. "And then their actions will forfeit any desire to give them their long-overdue justice."

"That's disagreeable enough to be the truth."

Tweed eyed his admired friend frankly. "Look at your great patriarchs of religion, the Jews. They opened their stores like a bomb exploded their inventory over the sidewalks. Clothes are flung over pipe racks, signs, everywhere you look. Chatham Street in the morning looks like a caravan that can never repack. On this crowded, noisy street, Jews take care to educate their young and keep the peace."

"There's no more than ten thousand Jews in New York." A weary smile from Hughes as he took Tweed's example one giant step forward. "Jay Cooke sells war bonds at a profit to himself of three million dollars. J. P. Morgan sells defective rifles to an Army fighting the war. Commodore Vanderbilt sells the Navy a rotting hulk. But General Grant singles out the Jews as unworthy to do business with the army and forbids them. Please, spare me the honor of taking on the ancient burden of the Jews."

Tweed raised his palms in surrender.

"The press will murder us again," said Hughes.

"Why not? The power of the press is printing their prejudices as objective reporting."

Hughes shook his head with a fatigue that made despair secondary. "How can we trust Mayor Opdyke on the war when he's making money out of it?"

"The mayor has dog-collared the Irish with a loyalty oath for city employees. If you're against the war, you're against the Constitution and disloyal. Bang! You're dismissed. A loyalty oath is the perfect dog collar. It keeps the Irish on a tight leash. Every morning they have to wake up and prove they're Americans all over again. Best of all, you don't have to improve their lot. You've scared the sympathy vote away from them. But don't worry, I'll stop this protest and bring them justice."

"God's will," Hughes said hopefully.

"I wish," said Tweed, "His will didn't come with such deep pockets."

They heard footsteps racing toward them. It was Tweed's young aide Shamus, soberly dressed, decent to a fault, whom he had rescued from a Know-Nothing rally that was a bigoted plague of New York a decade earlier. "The Germans have armed! They are marching out of Tompkins Square to hunt down Irish! You must stop them!"

He knew everyone was losing their grip on the city. He kept an ace in the hole everyone could trust, just for such emergencies. "I'll send Judge Hoffman. The judge is respected across the board."

Inspector Dilks took pains to sneak back unseen with his force to the Union Steam Works. What Dilks couldn't see in his successful effort was the other side of the steam works where there was a mob of over ten thousand to face his two hundred. When Dilks wheeled his men around to the front in a surprise attack, they were surprised. They saw an endless field of humanity. What's worse, the mob had finally found a leader; a one-armed giant who went berserk at the sight of police. Dilks ordered a hasty retreat as the mob jeered without chasing them.

Dilks had noted a bigger surprise. The mob was no better armed. Too confident? The ammo didn't fit? Carloads of ammo sent by munition makers to Union soldiers proved useless. Dilks was inspired to attack again. To neutralize the mob's superior numbers, his men rushed around to the front firing. Lounging rioters fell over like struck pins. The barrage shocked the mob into paralysis, as Dilks knew it would. But out of their ranks rose the one-armed giant wielding a club. At his side was a young, delicate-featured man armed with club and sword. The daring of this unlikely pair lit a fire under the mob for action.

They locked the police in hand-to-hand combat. The raging giant clubbed police caught reloading and those holding fire in fear of hitting fellow coppers around him. The young man slashed and clouted his way through the police ranks. Their wrath was clearing a wide swath when a policeman slipped around to the side where the giant had no arm and shot him through the head. The police shot the young man and impaled him on an iron picket fence as an example to the rioters, who were then easily subdued. They abandoned the steam works.

A doctor passing by raised the impaled man off the fence. Curious about his appearance, the doctor opened his dirty shirt to uncover an expensive vest, linen shirt and cassimere pants. The police took it for granted he was a Southern agitator as they easily infiltrated a cosmopolitan city with its share of Copperheads.

A message from Mulberry urged Dilks to turn his attention to a fire threatening to burn down the entire Upper West Side. His men, exhausted at dispersing an army, were disheartened. The mob was everywhere and their end nowhere in sight. The tide was turning against the police, even as they scored victory after victory.

Dilks saw the fire on the horizon. He concluded it was best to let the arsonists spread the fire over the Upper West Side than to leave Mulberry undermanned. The fire could be a trap to divert police from Mulberry and leave police headquarters an easier target to destroy. Dilks returned his men on the double to Mulberry where he was sure the last stand had to be taken.

Captain Walling raced his men into the smoke hiding Eleventh Avenue. He soon felt their courage had helped to ambush themselves. He could barely see his men, and finding the arsonists was out of the question. Then he shuddered at a subhuman sobbing under the smoke. It wasn't actually sobbing. It wasn't altogether subhuman. At breaking moments the pain expressed was all too human. Insides spilling out. Yet the sobbing was too unearthly to be human. The barbaric catch in the breathing left no connection. The sob was so close to the supernatural, the police glanced toward the black sky. They couldn't identify the trembling sobbing with anything on earth.

Hotel Allerton was a torch in the sky for hours and now collapsed. The burning debris showering through the smoke fell across the City Cattle Market yards. The crowded pens caught fire.

Walling and his men lost their outlines in the smoke as the earth began shivering under them. The hides of the blinded cattle were catching licks of fire. The cattle reared madly against their barriers. The sobbing was coming from the trapped cattle.

Walling and his men saw the rioters sitting like crows atop the burning pens. When Walling shouted they were under arrest, the roughs opened the pens and the panicked steers charged the police. Earth pelted them. Smashed and splintered fences came flying at them through the smoke. Thunder rumbled in their ears. Walling shouted into the smoke and dust swallowing up his men. "Run to the river! The river! River!"

The rioters atop the fences released pen after pen of the sobbing beasts along the path of the escaping police, who dived for cover.

The charging cattle thundered by demolishing shacks, booming through frame houses, knocking over water pumps, crashing through ash bins, toppling signs and poles. People ran for the nearest strong buildings and cowered as the buildings trembled and darkened in the dust. The cattle stampeded to the downtown business district.

In the St. Nicholas bar the mayor was seeking action from the generals. Mulberry couldn't hold off the mob if attacked. Repeated calls to the War Department in Washington produced no results. General Wool chided the mayor for not being able to get in touch with his own administration.

"It doesn't matter whose administration is in office," Opdyke told him. "Getting help from a bureaucrat is like trying to play a flute with the wind from an elephant's behind. If Mulberry falls . . ." The mayor couldn't finish.

A rumbling was heard through the thick walls of the St. Nicholas bar, as though the street had come inside the bar. Windows trembled, tumblers danced off the bar, waiters dived under tables with their patrons. Cattle careened off buildings, smashing plate glass, bending lampposts.

Tweed glanced out City Hall windows at the billowing dust turning the middle of the city into a prairie crossroad.

Sweeny was emphatic. "The city is falling apart. Your job is to be the indispensable man."

Tweed scratched the back of his neck though the irritation was in his mind. "I'm falling apart, myself, trying to be indispensable."

"You must play on Fifth Avenue's ignorance," said Sweeny.

"Do you have the iron arguments for passing the bond?"

Sweeny tapped his wallet with assurance.

"You pocket the aldermen. I'll see what Tom Acton wants from me."

Sweeny wasn't shy. "Acton wants to put the blame for the riots on you."

"That's the kind of status I need. Maybe Fifth Avenue will come through with my patronage if they think I can stop the riots." Tweed became worried. "It eats my heart out. I'm feeling pleasure these days only when I'm thinking of revenge."

* * *

Police stations throughout the city were sheltering black families. When Tweed walked into frantic Mulberry, hundreds of blacks from Thompson Street's Little Africa were bedded down with their worldly belongings. He watched policemen shed their uniforms before venturing out on the streets.

It was evident to Tweed the police couldn't hold Mulberry. The police knew it and so did Acton. Yet Acton's quiet resolve gave his men confidence. Tweed walked into the chief's room, sincerely praising him. "Splendid job, Tom."

Acton possessed the wall of a social club man. "Then don't blackjack me."

Tweed recognized Acton was not an unfriendly man as long as friendship wasn't wanted from him.

"Since your governor called these murderers my friends, the roads are jammed with people leaving the city with their possessions. You can't buy a cart or wagon at any price. Those who can leave become prey to thieves on the road, and I've no police to spare for them." Acton picked up a fistful of telegraph messages piled on his desk. "Blacks hanging from lampposts. The mob warns St. Luke's Hospital to carry patients into the street before they burn it down for treating a wounded policeman. Servants are pointing out the homes of abolitionists to be burned. The mob attacked Greeley's *Tribune* building."

"Your outrage does you credit, Mr. Acton. You should have been outraged by an unjust law that incites riots. You elect a mayor ignorant of the people. You want to rule the people but not serve them. You make these heartless mistakes, then lay the blame on our doorstep."

Acton took the dose without emotion. "I know the masterful politician you've become. And I know your future is at stake. I also know the long, hard climb you made to get where you are."

Tweed admired Acton's calm eye.

"I was at the club when you waited in the portrait gallery to be approved and Fifth Avenue wouldn't see you. I'm going to flush out every rioter, and I'm offering you the chance to help me."

"I don't like to be on the losing side."

Acton gave him a grudging smile. "You have nerve."

"You'll find the wards have a will, even when they have no direction."

Acton also didn't care for his nerve. "It's no excuse for you to say you must buy aldermen before your enemies do."

"I learned that from your exclusive clubs." Tweed stung him. "When I was their errand boy."

Acton was tough, not because he had climbed up from the bottom. He was tough because he never wasted struggling at the bottom. He was born into privilege that magically gave him Tweed's hard-won experience with his mother's milk. Acton was bred on that milk. His second nature was to be charitable without being friendly, and friendly without being charitable. "The gentlemen at the club were right in not wanting to see you. When you chose to be a politician, you chose to be an errand boy."

Whores were a constant friction to family neighborhoods. From cheap waterfront hookers from Corlears Hook on the East River to expensive Prince Street tarts, they roamed the streets in silks and rags, spreading disease, recruiting children, using their police protection to flaunt their short-lived life. Today some of the neighborhood women became part of the mob women and took this opportunity to run out the whores. They attacked Sue the Turtle on Broome Street and went on to the flash houses of Baxter Street. Flushed with victory a rallying cry went up: "On to Sisters Row!"

The rows made a strange city less forbidding to newcomers. There was London Row and Scottish Row in Chelsea. A row for clerks and secretaries off St. John's Park. New England farm girls gravitated to Sisters Row. Familiar faces brought a sense of security. The farm girls had worked in the mills of Lowell and Lawrence until Irish immigrants threw many out of work. In Lowell the former farm girls earned two dollars a week plus seventeen cents a day for room and board in factory dormitories. Mill owners saw they could replace the native farm girls with immigrant Irishmen and save the cost of dormitories.

A leader of Sisters Row came out to meet the mob women. She told them how their lives had become entwined with immigrants. How they lost their mill jobs. How they journeyed to New York to find work. How some fell into whoring and now lived elsewhere. How they didn't want to fight anyone, they didn't want to pay with their blood in New York as they had already paid with their youth on farms and mills. This simple plea to leave them in peace didn't penetrate the mob women, who fell on the New Englanders and bloodied them.

* * *

The night retained the muggy heat of the day. The bitter taste of ashes seeped through the tightest doors and windows. Entire blocks were aflame or in smoldering ruins. Under the cover of night, opposing forces hunted and ran. The violence was breaking out everywhere, and Tweed remained home to protect his family, even though he needed this violence to gain the upper hand against the party men who would cut off the jobs he had to give out.

Mary Jane poured tea. The younger children played on the carpet while the older ones sewed or played piano, four hands. Tweed read Tammany's own newspaper, *The New York Leader*, without concentration, getting up from time to time to part the heavy drapes and see the darkness lit by bowls of fire. Dogs deserted by owners whined and tearfully barked while sadly silent dogs curled up on the front steps of all that remained of their master's homes.

The ebb and flow of the mob's ceaseless tramping, threatening to come to their door and departing, kept the Tweed household on edge. The gut-splitting grief of the keening women left no one untouched by their rage, seeking to give sight to a world gone blind.

Billy Junior asked, "Why are we keeping our door lights on?"

"In sympathy with the protestors," said Tweed.

His children were not in sympathy and grumbled.

Billy Junior rushed in to save his father's face. "Seeing the lights, they won't harm our house."

Mary Jane dismissed that thought. "Won't the rioters see almost everyone has their lights on?"

"We won't worry," Tweed assured his family. "A few hours ago the aldermen passed a bill to pay three hundred dollars to any poor man who wants to buy himself out of the draft. Soon as the mayor signs the bill, there'll be no cause to riot." He gratefully watched his family breathe easier. He tried to be a good father in the accepted ways. He didn't drink, smoke or gamble. His children could only disapprove of him as they knew the world, but not as the world actually is. His habit of not touching the demon evils of drink, tobacco and cards gave him a strong sense of virtue.

A call-to-arms outcry: "Save us!" In the second it took him to open the door, Henry Street was silent. A sign was scraped in the street: KN ORGANIZE!

Mary Jane quickly herded her children inside. "The Know-Nothings are back."

Tweed himself began to despair. "If the Know-Nothings organize, this rioting has only begun."

The murderous tramping of the mob swerved toward them.

Tweed hurriedly locked their door without easing the helplessness of his children, who were trying not to cry as the tramping came closer. A howl went up above the loud tramping of the mob. "On to Brooks Brothers!"

Now, Tweed knew, the mob and everyone else would have the threat of Know-Nothings hanging over them. Know-Nothings had been hatched by the secret Order of the Star-Spangled Banner, cloaking their bigotry in a defense of liberty. When asked about their organization, they were instructed to reply, "I know nothing." This lie became the basis of their secretive public greeting of rapidly pointing to their eye (I), nose (know), curling forefinger and thumb into a zero (nothing).

Their biggest outdoor successes had come in the early fifties at the height of the Irish immigration. Know-Nothings skillfully staged extravaganzas around City Hall starring escaped nuns, a runaway priest, a bugler dressed as Angel Gabriel and white-robed women holding an enormous American flag. Speakers whipped up the crowd that America was for Americans and that the Irish Catholic was not an American when he took his orders from Rome. They quoted Washington, Hamilton, John Adams for their distorted propaganda; they quoted the Archbishop of St. Louis, who extolled Spain and Italy, "where the Catholic religion was an essential part of the law of the land" and where heresy and disbelief was "punished" as a crime. And a surefire roar came from quoting the *Boston Pilot:* "No good government can exist without religion—and there can be no religion without an Inquisition."

Know-Nothings revived popular books of the thirties. Though the books bore the imprint of respectable religious houses, some carried illustrations of sexual activities in convents that outstripped the penny thrillers in forbidden areas.

Fog off the river covered the opulent display windows of Brooks Brothers on Catherine Street. A salesman slept in the store. A porter was finishing up his work when he heard the heavy tramping coming closer. The porter fled. The salesman awoke and secured the door with a bar across it. When he heard the immense depth of the tramping, he, too, fled.

The mob's anger suddenly vanished at the sight of the store in the haze. The dream of shopping for nothing gave them a momentary awe, and then they rushed the door and broke it down. The men and women were soon swinging away and dancing on the display tables as they were made merry and genteel by the softness of opera shawls, soaped leather, silk cravats, morning robes. They began undressing in front of mirrors and trying on whatever took their fancy. Mirrors became hotly contested zones. Within a short time the meanest resembled the stylish. The store a bobbing sea of men in shiny hats and overflowing cravats flirting and butting with proper airs the gloved and shawled women.

Bolts of English cloth sailed out of second-story windows and draped like streamers over the street. Underwear and garters were thrown down on those who couldn't push into the store.

Women rushed into fitting rooms where amateur tailors took delight in closely measuring and fitting them.

In the darkness outside, Inspector Carpenter and his troops silently came up and lay in wait with fixed bayonets. Every light in the store was turned on, and the halo of haze made it difficult to see inside. Carpenter ordered a patrol to extinguish every street- and house-light surrounding the store. As the lights went out one by one, Brooks Brothers became a glowing stage throwing the happy rioters into bold relief. Police watched them carousing as in a drunken opera. The women becoming pregnant with loot and the men growing potbellies.

Carpenter gave the order to charge.

Those left out on the sidewalk ran away. The jubilant mob inside, goosey with style, was so densely packed in and good-natured, the clubbing police could make no headway. Women invited police to try on clothes and become gentlemen. Without effort the mob pushed the police back on the sidewalk and ignored their presence.

A drunk leaned out the second-floor window and ordered the police not to loiter about. When they didn't move, he shot at them.

The police charged into Brooks Brothers. The looters, staring into the guns about to kill them, dropped their loot in surrender but couldn't drop the fancy clothes they wore. They ripped their stolen clothes off to prove their innocence and dropped to their knees pleading not to be shot. This was the first time the rioters asked for mercy. Carpenter took his first prisoners. The spine went out of the mob after tasting the grand life.

*　*　*

In the middle of the night the city was awake. Terror ready to leap out of every shadow kept them awake. Shamus, the bright young aide in the sober dark suit, was running from the St. Nicholas at such headlong speed, it was difficult to tell whether he carried good news or bad. His frenzied knocking sprung Tweed to the door. "The mayor will veto the bond."

"I kept my word." Tweed's only ventilation was his fingers drumming on his belly. "I protected the mayor's home. Save me. Save my house, my servants, my dirty laundry. How could I forget that holy looks make lying foolproof?" He leaned against the door, down in the dumps with his defeat.

"The mayor is issuing a proclamation tomorrow that all is normal."

Tweed shot up straight. His eyes brightened at the folly.

"Merchants are to open their stores."

Tweed clapped his hands joyfully. "What's wrong with me that I overestimate these lunatics and let them get to me?"

"Five regiments are pulling out of the war to come here."

Tweed sunk inside himself at this military solution. The news sloshing painfully inside him. The glow of fires on his defeated face. The harsh smoke in his nostrils. The bitter taste his own.

"The mayor said the rioters dictated his veto. He couldn't appease a mob with soldiers dying at the front."

Official reasons darkened his heart. "Men in office must make their insanity logical. Failing that, they make it patriotic." He said it but it wasn't important to him. He took it for granted. He had to express something. He couldn't express what he thought about himself. He became, as a success, the man he didn't want to be, and his ambition fights to be this man!

FOUR

The day dawned hot. Thickly overcast. No breeze. Oppressive mugginess. No fresh air to breathe. Between the stagnant clouds and the cracked mud streets, New York was an oven.

Streets lay deserted. No rioters. No police. No soldiers. No merchants. New fires gutting the landscape. Going up in flames unattended was the St. George Episcopal Church on Stuyvesant Square, the Baptist Church on Fifth Avenue, the huge lumberyard on Fourteenth Street and several Protestant missions.

Those remaining in the smoking city could squint through their ash-covered windows and see a great city paralyzed. Institutions defenseless. Law-abiding citizens angry, confused, demoralized. Government helpless.

A Brooklyn ferry pulling into a slip was quickly overloaded with blacks who had run out of their hiding places.

One dawn ritual didn't change. The back alleys of the finest hotels filled with the hungry. When a service door opened, the alley crowd smelled the sweet and spicy fragrance of a morning kitchen. Slop-coated men rolled out rattling barrels. Behind them, to set the juices running at high tide, were the aromas of sweet rolls, bread baking, smoked ham and bacon sizzling with eggs, freshly ground coffee, warm syrup, sugar-powdered pastry, almond coffee rings. The slop-coated men hurried inside, slamming and bolting the service door. Over the noises of a busy kitchen they heard the thick door trembling with the beating of bodies against it as the barrels of bones were feverishly fought over.

On Bloomingdale Road, the extension of Broadway above Twenty-third Street, families who happily escaped the city in the night found themselves at dawn in a traffic jam miles long. Armed thieves, picking and choosing, swooped down on the families stuck on the road to steal the wagons and carts piled with possessions.

Mulberry prayed for rain, rain being more effective than weary police at stopping rioters. Thunder puffed through the low-lying morning clouds. The sticky heat sucking up the air in competition with the people.

Imperturbable Acton was finally, inevitably losing his grip on himself. The lauded, modern telegraph system was easily sabotaged. His men were worn down by the sheer numbers of the rioters. When the storm broke, Mulberry's police and the families they sheltered cheered.

Grand Street opened its doors.

Far uptown were the unsung heroes of the force, Crowley and Polhamus, repairmen for the telegraph system. Disguised as laborers, they worked under the noses of the violent mob, tracing and splicing miles of wire over backyards, down gutters, through burned-out houses and across exposed lots. They were tracking a break when they heard the one cry these brave men dreaded.

"There's the spies!"

Crowley jovially greeted the mob, explaining they weren't fixing wires. They were cutting them. To prove it, Crowley snipped wires they had tirelessly worked on through the night. The rioters cheered and left.

Crowley and Polhamus went right back to work scanning doorways, windows, roofs for snipers before daring to splice wires out in the open. They reconnoitered every burnt house, stringing wire overhead wherever possible to keep it from shorting out. Rain improved their safety without lessening their fear. The wires they spliced began clicking messages to Mulberry.

The better-off blacks hiding in the basement of their own homes were dragged out, stripped naked and sent running up and down their streets. Degrading nude victims affirmed the respectability of the rioters.

One message pushed Acton to the brink. A black shoemaker, Costello, whom he knew, was lynched by a mob led by a white shoemaker. This unprovoked horror starting a day the mayor proclaimed peaceful had Acton exhorting his exhausted men, "Chase these beasts up trees where they belong. Quail on toast for every man who gets a dozen scalps. Quail on toast, men!"

On the heels of this news a report came to Acton that a mob as large as any seen during the riots was slowly forming on First Avenue and Eighteenth Street. Rumors of the terrors to be multiplied: Croton water supply will be cut; Union League Club destroyed; Dry Dock Savings Bank attacked because its president was a former Know-Nothing.

Mayor Opdyke couldn't believe the helpless situation he had fallen into. No returning soldiers. The mob could easily put the city to the torch before any soldier arrived from the front. The soldiers themselves would be fatigued, while the rioters were fresh for blood. They will be shooting at the heroes of Gettysburg. Just then Provost Marshall Nugent entered the bar to speak to the governor. The mayor intercepted him. "Do you have orders from Washington halting the draft?"

Nugent said that he did indeed have the order, and though this was the answer to the mayor's prayers, he was struck dumb hearing it.

Governor Seymour hurried over to speak to the tight-lipped Nugent as he would to a dog who had buried a diamond and needed kindness to prod his memory. "What exactly are in your orders?"

"Suspend the draft. New York is a battleground behind the lines."

Seymour was versed in Washington craft. "In writing?"

"A telegraph from Colonel Fry."

Seymour was heartened. "You must publish the order at once." *What are you waiting for?* was on the governor's face.

"I have no authority, Governor."

Governor and mayor stared at a ghost. *Did they hear right?*

"I have an order I cannot publish without an order from Colonel Fry."

Seymour saw the light. "Announce you cannot publish the order. I'll inform the press of the contents you can't publish."

"I cannot announce I'm not publishing what I have no authorization to publish."

Seymour was not governor for nothing. "In what form could you announce the order without an authorization?"

"None."

Seymour and Opdyke were deflated.

Nugent added, *"You* can announce it."

Seymour and Opdyke smelled a rat. Liberating the city would make them heroes. A wrong move could whistle them to oblivion. They ached to be heroes but without the risk of being fools.

Seymour, though mired in caution, came up with the right thrust. "I've no authority to suspend the draft. That is federal law. If I made an unofficial announcement, I could be accused of treason."

Nugent knew how to butter up civilians and have his cake too. "I can publish an unofficial announcement without my signature."

"I would say"—Seymour richly baited the hook for him to bite —"that your thinking saved the city from further damage and bloodshed."

Nugent briskly walked away.

Seymour and Opdyke pursued him, surprised the governor may

have said anything wrong. "Where are you going?" Seymour made it an order to stop.

Nugent replied, "To get the order published."

A brainstorm seized Seymour. He began to write a proclamation:

To the Citizens of New York:

I declare this city to be in a state of insurrection. Anyone resisting efforts to quell unlawful acts after the publication of this proclamation will be liable to the full penalties prescribed by law.

—Horatio Seymour
GOVERNOR OF NEW YORK
July 14, 1863

Opdyke thought he was being helpful by pointing out that Seymour had put down yesterday's date. Seymour was not grateful—the fourteenth being the day he arrived and saw the riots were an insurrection.

Opdyke speared him. "Then your 'my friends' speech at City Hall is wrongly taken?"

"My friends," Seymour tried to harmonize his words with his deeds, "are the peaceful citizens of New York who were listening. While Tweed fed the mob, I stood for law and order.'

Opdyke shrewdly accepted the transparent lie, knowing the hypocrisy was so blatant, it would get Seymour in political hot water. "The riot has done the city more good than anyone knows." The mayor counted himself a big winner. "The rabble is without a leader. No one will want to smell of that honor for a while."

Tweed knew his last chance was in the jaws of his enemies. He dashed to the club where he was contemptuously ignored. He was drained by sleepless nights and events going against him, plus the hot sun took the shine off his appearance. On his way he noticed the Fifth Avenue Hotel was guarded by soldiers and sandbags while the Webb shipyard where the ironclads are built was left unguarded.

He waited in the upstairs gallery where the portraits no longer frightened him. He now saw their faces could be formed by the same experience he was having.

Purdy was pleased to usher Tweed into the great room he had

been denied. Men were still sleeping with more importance than many of those awake.

Tweed thought how difficult it was for a newcomer to be disagreeable while sunk into these soft leather chairs.

Purdy ordered bourbon for himself and sarsparilla for Tweed, who upgraded his order to a sherry cobbler. "You can't be serious about this bond for the rioters?"

"How can bringing justice to an unjust law be wrong?"

"You're giving Opdyke an out. The mayor has done nothing in every direction. This riot will ruin Opdyke because he hasn't asserted himself."

"Except to save his own property."

"Do you know Washington is suspending the draft?"

Tweed calmly shook off Purdy's apparent mistake. "If it was official, I'd have heard. Millions of rumors are flying around."

"This is official, unofficially. The mayor gets credit for stopping the bloodshed through his influence in Washington, while you'll be condemned for supporting the rioters with a bond."

The leather chair's deep-seated comfort got in the way of Tweed's desperation. "Elijah, I need your backing. I'm going to ram that bond through over the mayor's veto."

Stupidity, said Purdy's tightened lips. "You're letting murderers go free when they should be going on trial. You'll be convicted because your bond is late, meaningless, suicidal." He saw Tweed was unimpressed. "I see. Your district attorney, Oakey Hall, will free the rioters or let them off with a tap on the wrist. That'll inflame the press and you'll be the voice for murder."

"That's why your backing is important. The bond will prove I stand for equal justice to all."

Purdy had only a professional sadness and it was unemotional. "The bond will kill you. If Oakey frees the rioters, you'll make our enemies unbeatable."

"Blindness made the conscription law. Ignorance forced it on us. Now the men whose stupidity incited the riots are going to be heroes for riots that wouldn't have happened without them. Is that just?"

"It doesn't matter and you know it. What's just is what fits the prejudice of the day."

Unbearable knowledge working against him gave Tweed an indigestible pain that lodged within him like shrapnel made up of all his past mistakes. In the midst of being changed with titanic energy, his arms hung down lifelessly. "I wouldn't have chosen a riot to become needed. Fifth Avenue sets the standards that will move their conscience."

That broke no ice with Purdy. "General Sandford has released his troops."

Tweed's hoarse exhale signified he was aware of his ending. "When the lions depart, the jackals come to feed."

No bad feelings, Purdy implied, shaking Tweed's hand to end their meeting. "Until a bigger catastrophe appears you're not an indispensable man to Fifth Avenue."

Tweed accepted the rebuff, but it didn't stop his agony. Walking out of the great room, he saw an imperious footman and rattled club members running to a commotion at the entrance. Members were crying out for their carriages while not daring to step outside. There were not enough attendants to handle the crush. He shouldered his way through the doorway. Cries warned him not to go out. "The city is burning down!" He had to see. The avenue was peaceful. On a clear summer's day Manhattan takes on its true island light, reflecting the waters around it. This was the light he saw and abruptly couldn't believe his eyes!

Huge bursts of fire scattering like pollen over the city. Fire whipping through the air from First Avenue where the mob was massed. The fire landings on roofs and setting houses ablaze. He rubbed the back of his hand across his mouth. This latest taste of the riots was too bitter even for him.

A headlong horse rider raced up to the club. When the members saw how gratified the major was to find Tweed, Tweed took on new importance. The rider's urgent message was from the governor. Tweed was to use all his powers to stop the rioting before the city burned down.

Tweed told him he couldn't stop what he hadn't started. The intelligent major asked if the governor would know how to interpret his answer. Tweed replied that he assumed the governor would be reminded of the patronage owed for electing him.

When the major galloped off at top speed, Purdy clapped him on his broad shoulder. "You're the best bluffer I ever saw." He motioned for his carriage.

"Where're you going?" Tweed needed his help.

"Back to Newport." Purdy thought Tweed's disappointment

merited an explanation. "I wouldn't coddle this mob. If they're the dupes of their enemies as you claim, we all have paid that same price along the line."

"I also have Judge Hoffman to try them."

"Hoffman has a fine reputation. He'll give the rioters their due. His popularity will then allow you to promote him for higher office." Purdy let Tweed know he saw through his machinations of virtue.

"Where's the fault in running an excellent man like Hoffman with the rest?"

Tweed's bravado intelligence stirred the old mentor's memory. "When I remember the brilliant, ambitious men who came up around the same time as you and were far better connected? Lorenzo Shepard, with the natural charm of a born leader. Nothing could stop him. He was killed in an accident. Postmaster Fowler was intimate with high society and the people in the street and loyal to both. Old Buck Buchanan, who had as few gifts as Fowler had many, became president and railroaded Fowler. That sure thing, Dan Sickles. Shot his wife's lover and killed his chances for office. To be honest, Bill, no one could have guessed you'd survive those brilliant men. But there was something right, instinctively right, about you even when you were going the wrong way. You're at home in these violent times the way poor Lorenzo, Fowler and Sickles were fated not to be."

An embarrassed Tweed scratched his ear. "I, too, was not brought up for these times. I never thought of sinking, so I swam."

Purdy stared down the avenue and saw Tweed's game was up. "You should have done the governor a favor. Your end is coming with music."

The sight was out of the *Arabian Nights*. Flamboyant Zouaves marching up Fifth Avenue in glittering pantaloons. Angelic bells tinkling time for soldiers carrying fixed bayonets and pulling two howitzers.

Tweed was lost taking in the exotically dressed soldiers.

"This is no time to travel." Purdy turned back to the club. "If you need me, I'll be here." Purdy understood without being sympathetic. Tweed had played one card too many.

An avalanching roar came from First Avenue where the mob controlled the streets around a large gun foundry. They had stolen every conceivable wagon in every conceivable condition and loaded the wagons with hay stolen from stables. Inside the gun foundry the mayor's new civilian volunteers were shooting at the mob whenever they advanced into range.

A torch was flicked across the hay, and flaming wagons were pushed toward the gun foundry door. The wagons bumped over cobblestones to fall on their sides, or collapse after a wheel rolled off. No wagon reached the foundry, but every wagon had burning hay sucked out by the wind. The burning hay blew over houses and into windows opened in the heat.

The mob was distracted by the tinkling bells and happily moved out to greet what they believed was a parade. They couldn't take the circus-uniformed Zouaves seriously. They clapped at their appearance as they would at a show and imitated their precision marching.

The Zouaves did not lose a beat. They were confident these rough sightseers would give way. When the mob stood their ground, the Zouaves marked time, not knowing what to make of these high-spirited ruffians. A sniper poked a rifle from a shuttered window and shot a soldier. A sniper from the other side of the street shot a second soldier as the crowd cheered.

Colonel Jardine ordered his soldiers to return sniper fire. The shuttered windows were thrown open, and a woman and child popped up. The Zouaves held fire. The mother and child dropped down, and the sniper fired to drop another soldier. When the Zouaves took aim, the mother and child came back in the window.

A hail of paving stones from the roofs felled Zouaves standing with no target to shoot at. The colonel ordered the attackers to desist on pain of death. A heavier barrage of paving stones opened a wider hole among his fallen soldiers. Seeing he had marched into an ambush, he ordered the howitzers to fire into the crowd.

Moments before the howitzer fired, the mob fell flat on the street. The shot whizzed over them. The mob was ecstatic. Their triumphant roar could be heard by merchants opening their stores. The howitzers fired again. The mob fell flat and the harmless shot passed overhead.

Before the artillerymen could reload, a hair-raising cry went up. "Shoot the officers!"

Zouaves fired at the chaotic mob advancing higgledy-piggledy but in pairs with one in back of another, the man in back firing a rifle on the shoulder of the other for a steadier aim. Colonel

Jardine was felled, shot through the thigh. Officers dropped around him.

The mob overran the howitzers and trained them on the retreating Zouaves. Their first shot sent the ball straight up into the air. Friends and foes alike ran for cover. The explosion sprayed more of the mob than the Zouaves.

Exotic Zouave uniforms became prize booty. They were torn from fallen soldiers and changed the street from a battlefield to a carnival.

Inside the St. Nicholas Hotel soldiers ran on the double to reinforce entrances. Bombs were handed out to soldiers stationed on the roof. The governor hovered over the telegraph operators. His message finally was clicking in. Seymour called, "Get me Tweed's boy. The Zouaves have been routed. The mob can't be contained. Fifth Avenue is going with Tweed." He turned to console Waterbury, who had been primed for Tweed's spot.

"They're romancing the mob." Waterbury was outraged. "They swore never to do it."

Seymour placed an arm around the loyal party man. "We're doing it for party unity."

"Unity in destroying a city?" Waterbury was hot under the collar.

"To save it. We need a man the rabble can trust."

"Who can trust the rabble?"

"Nelson, don't make this harder for yourself."

"You're splitting us into factions and you call it unity."

"Tweed can be used by everyone." Seymour recalled Tweed's checkered past in the best light.

"Tweed is the biggest thief in office this country has seen."

"Don't dig your grave, Nelson. Tweed ran many franchises through the Board of Aldermen. Some say Tweed helped Dan Sickles kill the land-grant bill against Trinity Church. That bill would've had Trinity share its vast city land holdings she was given under English charters."

"If some say Tweed helped save Trinity's land, why didn't they say it before?"

"Now they want to believe it. Tweed will look after our interests by giving the rabble bread and circus."

"I despise him, fought him—"

"That's why you've been chosen to welcome Tweed as leader. No one can make our unity look more solid than you. Smile, here comes Tweed's boy." Seymour told Shamus, "Tell Alderman Tweed we have an answer to his patronage."

Shamus found a brooding Tweed leaving Tammany Hall and gave him the message. He also told him the Zouaves have been routed and their cannon captured. Tweed's eyes twinkled as he headed away from the St. Nicholas. "Where're you going?"

"To my office, brave lad." Tweed was feeling his oats, tapping his tummy for luck. "I'm owed humility. I want to be sought after. I want to cock-a-doodle-do. The perfect weather is when bastards are shivering. There's no meaning in the English language they haven't cleaned their muddy boots on."

The retreating Zouaves were running toward them.

Tweed pulled Shamus out of their way. "When are the regiments arriving?"

"The Seventy-fourth from Gettysburg is due at Canal Street at midnight."

"Seventy-fourth are German troops. When's the Fighting Sixty-ninth due?"

"Thursday. If they arrive at night, the mayor will hold them over in Jersey City. The Sixty-ninth must enter in daylight when they can be seen."

Tweed grew uneasy, all too aware he stood to lose it all if fighting broke out against the soldiers.

Midnight. Tweed woke and dressed, his heart beating faster than it should, hope pulling his insides like a crazed bell ringer. He was a stranger to this new rhythm. He was up and dressing so early, even Mary Jane was curious. She urged him not to go out. He told her he must see if the German heroes of Gettysburg were attacked. The rioters would be finished and so would he. He took a long, deep, hopeful breath without steadying himself.

Opening the door, he heard the far-off tramping of the mob. Canal Street was abandoned. Stores barricaded. Homes dark. A ghostly, smoking night. Ashes floating in the air. At the river's edge a string of lanterns guided the troop ferries in. The waterfront was deserted. No sounds floated across from the packed ferries; the darkness might have them imagining they were going ashore in enemy territory.

Tweed waited in the shadows, knowing anything could happen.

When the ferries creaked against the pilings, he heard the whooping of an attacking party running down Canal Street. His heart sunk and then was startled.

Blacks!

Who would have thought so many blacks remained in the city?

They were wildly cheering the soldiers, who had been pulled so quickly from the line that blood and mud still stuck to their tunics. They marched smartly until they neared the rim of fires and had to move around the wagons and furniture in the crossings and see the jagged walls of cratered homes in the moonlight.

Tweed went home and couldn't sleep. He woke Mary Jane with his tossing. She asked if he was having a nightmare. He answered, "A nightmare is the world we already live in, only without the sympathy."

Thursday. Dawn. Breezes are breaking up the heat. A sea sky brightens New York. He opened his window wide and smelled smoke and heard sniper fire uptown. He had no doubt a mob still existed. He dressed hurriedly to see what effect the 69th would have.

People were standing around marveling at the destruction, saddened by personal belongings scattered everywhere in the muddy streets. A streetcar started a run with soldiers riding shotgun. People were so starved for a normal sight, they waved and applauded. Cavalry was stationed along the route with flashing sabers drawn.

The crack Fighting 69th heroes marched straight off the ferries, their rousing band first off. Pipes and brass and drums blasting forth. Tears rose in the eyes of men and women while injustice rankled in their hearts. Seeing their tears, Tweed knew the riot was finished. He sped off in his buggy to Purdy. At the barren edge of the city below Central Park he saw refugees plodding back with their mounds of jumbled possessions.

Purdy hailed Tweed outside his club in the vacation clothes of a Newport yachtsman. "Is it over?"

"I got the patronage." Tweed raised his arm in victory.

"The riots?"

"They're over too." The contrast between Purdy's suspicious face and his carefree retirement clothes was disturbing. He found it scary to say, "You look retired."

"I am, Bill." Purdy responded with rare spark.

Tweed didn't want to see this spark, as if it undermined the man he respected—enthusiasm somehow marred his character. Those blacking-bottle stares gave Purdy the upper hand because whatever you told him, he put it in a questionable light. Now Purdy's experience lined his face like makeup from a play recently closed. His work face showed everyone what his life of retirement may want to hide.

At this moment of victory a tremor ran through Tweed. Purdy's appearance was a terrifying tribute to New York, where the strongest men throw their best selves in as casually as a stoker shoveling coal into a furnace. "Elijah"—he became exhilarated—"for the first time I feel a part of the prosperity. I love the world on its own terms."

Part Two

THE
WORLD
OF
BOSS
TWEED

FIVE

*T*weed's modest Duane Street office was in complete darkness, full of beefy ward captains, one balancing on the windowsill cutting a small hole in the shade where he guessed the sun was hitting.

Sweeny was pressing Tweed not to keep Commodore Vanderbilt waiting. Tweed whispered back that wanting favors makes men patient. Just to show he had all the time in the world, he began to tell a joke to the men in the dark. "Did you hear," Tweed was off and running, "the last health report said congressmen were in excellent condition? Only two percent had piles. The other ninety-eight percent were perfect assholes."

Laughter burst out of the men in the dark.

Sweeny hissed to Tweed. "You don't know the commodore."

"I know he's the raw sewage of success. He's no time for family, friends, sports, books or anything but moneymaking."

"That's why you should be on time. He has the money to get us to the White House. He has no scruples," Sweeny warned.

"They're the easiest to deal with. You've only to know their self-interest."

"Ready?" called the captain on the windowsill.

"Let there be light!" rang out from Prince Garvey.

Sunlight burst through the hole and lit Tweed's brilliant planet diamond on his shirtfront. Tweed's face became a rich pudding reflecting the rippling diamond light. A discreet wetness shone across his lower lip. "The biggest planet diamond in New York."

The men couldn't clap away their envy. Liquid blue light swam in waves across their eager faces. Slivers of rainbow shimmied like phosphorescent plankton without gravity along ceiling, walls and furnishings, settling on faces where it drew out the innards of men turned to envious slugs in the diamond light.

Tweed's eyes twinkled at the churning his planet diamond brought out. "Are you ready to dance the Whore Hysteria?" He sprayed the sparkling light on their heads. "I piss my blessings on you all."

Sweeny urgently whispered, "This is no time to show off. Just when you want to clip their wings."

"Push and energy does it." Tweed socked them with assurance. "A heeler told me he wanted to be Commissioner of Parks because he had push and energy. I asked him how he could prove he had push and energy. The heeler said that his father gave him ten thousand dollars to start life with. He went out West and lost it all. 'How,' I asked him, 'does that prove you have push and energy?' The heeler replied, 'I walked all the way back.' "

In the roar of laughter Tweed nodded for the shade to pop up. Though the planet diamond lay subdued on Tweed's chest in the everyday light, it retained the attraction of a shark patrolling underwater.

He took his quiet aide Shamus around the shoulders. "Want to see me, lad?"

"It's personal." Shamus wanted to put off his request, seeing Sweeny breathing down Tweed's neck.

"I always have time for the personal."

"Kathleen—"

"That woman is trouble." He scolded him, cutting him off, wanting to hear no more.

"Kathleen says the Industrial Home for Boys is a firetrap."

"You tell me that while we're celebrating?" He felt badly at showing his temper and turned proudly to the captains. "Remember the Know-Nothing rallies around City Hall? This lad ran right into those crowds giving out leaflets against their scurrilous bigotry."

Clapping from the hardened captains.

"I'd do anything for this loyal lad."

Louder clapping.

"Except run him for office."

Laughter.

"I want to keep him honest."

Louder laughter.

Tweed's ward captains were cutting smart except for the clothes advertising their blind side. They dressed to imitate club members who rejected them. They were too confident to see expensive clothes can bring out the poverty of the wearer.

Tweed draped an arm around his old fire-fighting crony he had rescued from the gutter. "What good deeds today, Prince? The courthouse is progressing?"

"Does a diamond shine? Fifteen more jobs on the payroll."

"I hear the plaster is crumbling."

"We may be short of plaster but we're not short of jobs."

"No better progress than that." Tweed clapped his prince of plasterers on the back, knowing how to praise a subordinate to dismiss him.

Now Tweed had to face the fireworks of his captains. To face them he had to confront himself. An elemental force was driving him that had no name. Getting what he wanted had made him feel pure, no matter what he did. Without him there'd be no efficient organization. The pie would be smaller. He didn't mind carrying people as long as they didn't tell him which direction to go.

The more powerful he felt, the better he felt, and the colder his blood ran, thus the more keenly he felt the encroachment on his power. His captains saw themselves as kings of the wards. He saw them as underlings. Their infighting to get ahead kept him animal-alert. To live on Fifth Avenue as he wanted meant being embroiled in the gutter.

"For the coming election campaign," he told the captains, "City Chamberlain Sweeny will hand you one thousand dollars each."

Groans at the absurdly small amount.

Tweed smiled at their grousing. "Increase the amount with assessments in your wards."

Moans of disbelief.

A captain called out, "Landlords are howling now."

"They'll howl louder if they have to make repairs."

"Voters are getting smarter. They won't take a shot of whiskey to repeat. Even our loyal backers are up in arms."

"They don't want city business?" Tweed thought them daft.

"They want a bigger bite."

"From where?" Tweed rubbed his behind.

The captains had to laugh, and one replied. "The fifteen percent the merchants raise their prices to the city. The city keeps the fifteen percent."

"Selling to the city is a privilege and not a right."

Captains murmured approvingly.

Tweed knew he was throwing a bombshell. "Assess the saloons."

Abrupt silence warned Tweed he was trespassing.

Connolly, whose manner implied life is a guarded mystery and whose blunt eyes asserted he had the answer, spoke ominously. "The saloons are beating the war drums. You're taking patronage away from the saloons and giving it to the new clubhouses."

The murmurings backed Connolly.

Sweeny's dry lips thinned in distaste that Connolly had loyalty to anyone. He explained the change of bases in the wards from saloons to clubhouses. "Do you know public schools were once decentralized?"

No one dared answer Brains, not that they didn't know the answer; they rightly feared the question was to catch them in his web.

"Decentralized schools were inefficient," Sweeny lectured the captains who didn't take orders well. "Each ward became an education empire. No one knew where all the money went. Public schools were centralized to make them efficient and accountable."

A captain sang out, "No one knows where the money goes now."

Sweeny rapped their knuckles with his lesson. "The city does not progress from bad to good but from change to change."

Tweed came in pleasantly. "Saloons are decentralized and inefficient. They must change with the times like everything else or be left behind."

Connolly was not one to be put off by the truth. He asked questions and condemned at the same time. "What kind of trust is that? Saloons are loyal to the party."

"The clubhouses will replace saloons. You want a favor, you go to a clubhouse."

"You want votes, you go to a saloon." Connolly was applauded.

"I want no self-appointed saloon kings going their own way.

Organization comes first. Clubhouses are more efficiently organized."

"Saloon keepers only want to imitate your great example. Everyone wants to come up as you did. Work for the party, be loyal, get rewarded." Connolly was so self-centered, no one valued his praise. He had his own bombshell. "There's talk in the archdiocese."

A poisoned silence. The religious truncheon was not used lightly and rarely openly. Everyone braced for a storm.

Tweed was humiliated his planet diamond so quickly lost its power, but Sweeny flaunted his gold Greek letters of excellence at Connolly as a crucifix against vampires. Sweeny's rasp bore into the stomach. "Don't climb the cross every time you want to win an argument." Sweeny had Connolly's fat over the flame.

Connolly ignored Brains as he would a ticking bomb and faced Tweed. "You're not placing *ould* countrymen high on the ticket, and we do most of the work to get out the votes."

The charge in the air could light a match.

Tweed asked consolingly, "Does that include yourself, *Comptroller* Connolly?"

The captains grinned, knowing a hit when they heard one.

"No argument there." Though Connolly was caught with his pants down, he knew how to accuse others for looking. "The ticket is Hoffman, Hall and Barnard."

Tweed was deftly curious. "Judge Hoffman is not sufficiently honest?"

"Hoffman can't be touched," Connolly admitted without retreating, in fact growing bolder. Tweed was falling in his lap.

Sweeny understood this, too, and was uncomfortable.

Tweed sparred again. "Oakey Hall is a bad choice for district attorney? He belongs to a blue-chip law firm, exclusive clubs, and is a popular journalist in his spare time."

"Oakey is a fool but he's smart enough to take orders. I honor him for freeing as many draft protesters as came before him."

Now Tweed knew the blow was coming.

"Judge Hoffman threw as many as came before him in the Tombs."

"Boss, listen to Connolly, please," a determined captain spoke up.

Tweed could not do enough for captains who spoke with that special resonance of loyalty.

"You're taking power from the saloons," said the captain, "because they don't take orders quick enough. Hoffman won't take any orders."

Loud agreement.

The earnest captain knew he had Tweed's sympathetic ear. "Hoffman will be mayor, and we won't get favors from our own mayor. Our word in the wards will sink fast."

Louder agreement.

Tweed was his satisfied self. "Hoffman is our mayor even if he doesn't do us one favor."

"No, no!"

Connolly rode in on this tide. "Kelly can carry the wards as mayor."

Tweed twinkled. "Bad News Kelly?"

"Honest John Kelly," Connolly corrected the slur.

Tweed smiled. "A *rose* by either name." He held his nose.

"Honest John takes orders."

Tweed agreed. "I told him to stay out of the race and he is."

Connolly was eager to force the issue. "Hoffman can't be trusted with our plans."

Tweed assured them, "Hoffman won't know. I want to keep him clean for higher office."

Grumbling dissent. Thumbs down.

"We will elect Hoffman mayor and then governor," said Tweed.

"No, no!" Shouts and murmurings at the abhorrent idea.

Connolly came out with his sour-stomach voice. "You'll never get Hoffman governor even if you gave hundred-thousand-dollar envelopes, even if you got the champ Morrissey to stand watch on every polling place to keep the enemy out. Republicans own this state from the city line to Canada. They've only to hear the amount with which we bury them in the city and they make up whatever amount they need to beat us in the state."

Dissent grew louder. "Stick to the city." "The city is our meat."

Tweed hit strongly. "Albany feasts on us. Drains us. Milks us of taxes for their upstate benefits and then spits on us. We're not only going to elect Hoffman governor, we're going to elect Hoffman president of the United States."

Agonizing shouts. "No, no!"

Tweed hammered them down with his fist on the table. "You couldn't get a Kelly in the White House except to empty spittoons."

Connolly dashed cold water. "President, governor, that's ducking the issue. We're concerned about a mayor we elect but can't control."

The captains backed Connolly to the hilt.

Tweed enjoyed putting their resentment to the torch. "We're going to raise Hoffman up so high—"

"Terrible! Awful! Disgusting!"

"Hoffman will do anything not to fall back down."

Laughter congratulating Tweed's horse sense. The captains knew Tweed was more than their leader. He was nourishment. They lived off his optimism. His candor was their fearless education.

Tweed leveled Connolly without malice. "If Archbishop Hughes was alive, there'd be no *talk*. We fought the good uphill fight against the bigots."

"Grand battles they were," an old-timer hailed.

Connolly wouldn't give Tweed an inch. "Raking up the past doesn't change the present. We want a mayor or district attorney." A touch of the boot in Connolly's demand.

Tweed casually turned to Sweeny. "How much did we give to worthy charitable causes this year?"

No gun had the muzzle velocity of Sweeny. "We gave to all races and religions, but to the archdiocese we gave the most," said Sweeny, as if holding the head of John the Baptist on a plate and thinking what dance would be in order. "Over one million dollars."

Applause for Tweed's generosity, which he good-naturedly accepted.

Friction developed against Connolly. A captain called out. "Comptroller, splitting the party keeps us out of office."

Connolly chewed his bitter cud.

Tweed, always the first to let bygones be bygones in a manly way, graciously saved Connolly's face while knowing good deeds only went skin-deep with the comptroller. His arm fell across Connolly's rigid shoulders. How much was to muscle him and how much to befriend him was a sore point. "Did I tell you"— Tweed took in the captains, too—"the time the state was investigating the money Tammany gave to the poor? In those dark ages they gave out figures by religion, and the archbishop complained the figures for Catholics was much too high. The archbishop sent his assistant over to check the figures. One glance at the books and the assistant tells the investigators in his grand brogue, 'I see where you made your mistakes. You counted Italians.' "

The roaring laughter softened even Connolly.

Tweed sped them hopefully on their way. "Remember the assessments. I'm running for state senator. I want to win *big.*"

Sweeny burned after Connolly and the captains departed. "Slippery doesn't control enough votes to be comptroller."

"We need the Sunday vote."

Sweeny warned, "Comptroller keeps the money records."

Tweed exhaled as though going out into a storm. "You can't look cleaner than having the leader of the Sunday vote keep your books."

"You gave him the office without taking a cent and he still threatens you? Where's the loyalty he's always preaching?"

Nothing's perfect, Tweed's closed eyes expressed. "I need Connolly. He's a yea-sayer. Yea-sayers cover up the crimes."

Seeing Sweeny was irritated, Tweed said no more. Sweeny had no blocs of votes, couldn't make a speech, scared more people than he attracted, yet Tweed needed him more than he did Connolly. Sweeny wrote the laws, pounded out the platforms, worked the backrooms, was the nuts-and-bolts man who kept the machinery oiled and wanted to be a U.S. senator. Competition with the oily-tongued Connolly brought out his homicidal streak.

"You don't need Slippery." Sweeny wouldn't let go. "We've given the archdiocese a ninety-nine-year lease on city property between Eighty-first and Eighty-second Streets, bounded by Madison and Fourth Avenues. Free."

Tweed steamed. "Why didn't you say that when Slippery was twisting our arm? Eighty-first and Madison?" Tweed blew out his cheeks at the enormous value and wished he owned it.

"Charity is a loaded gun. You can aim that bullet at him anytime." Sweeny digested the tasty morsel.

"How can we go against the archdiocese? Do you know what Trinity owns through English land grants? Both sides of Broadway from the Battery to Central Park and whole blocks in between. What Trinity and Dutch Reform don't own of this city we're now giving away. We won't have a johnny pump to tax if this keeps up. Am I the only one around here who cares about the Constitution of the United States?"

Sweeny didn't need lessons.

Tweed relaxed. "Mayor Fernando Wood dropped his pants for

the archdiocese. How else could that crook get elected mayor three times? Fernando Wood got results." Tweed brayed out what was eating him. "Fernando should've been in jail, not in City Hall. What a mayor! Fernando cheated his partner out of his business, was an embezzler, forger, briber, seller of city land and offices for his own good, had the police kick back part of their salary, forced teachers to hand over one third of their first year's wages, illegally naturalized citizens for money and votes. Fernando didn't get guff. I get abuse, threats, orders." He calmed himself with a deep breath. "Where's the silver lining?"

Sweeny gave it to him. "When no one's satisfied, everyone is equal."

Tweed bucked that red flag. "When there are Irish lords and ladies, and I pray there will be; when their sons and daughters go to college, and I'll fight to get them through the quotas; when their offspring become higher than High Episcopalians, and I'll give them the stepladder—they'll have forgotten me. The Good Samaritan who opened the police force, city jobs, issued licenses for grogshops, quickly made them citizens and a first leg up from the muck."

"You're late for Vanderbilt."

SIX

*W*all Street began as a wall, the outermost Dutch stockade. When the English captured the stockade, they permitted former black slaves of the Dutch East Indies Trading Company to own property—outside the wall. If New York was attacked at night, the cries of the blacks being slaughtered would alert the settlers inside. The street has physically changed since the wall. The stockade mentality remains.

When the street became the nation's financial heart, New Yorkers noted a graveyard was at one end and a river at the other. This boundary marked the arena where fiercely ambitious men entered to prove their worth.

Commodore Vanderbilt doted on fast rides through heavy city traffic in an open carriage. The commodore was in his sea-hearty seventies. His title was the only false ring about him, and even that was half true: Vanderbilt was a commodore of city ferries whose franchises he stole by bribing aldermen without prejudice to their political opinions. Riding with his white head bent, he didn't see the people his carriage splashed with mud. He was not concerned about their opinion on land or sea or before the U.S. Senate.

The commodore's right eye squinted into foul weather. His turnip nose lacked bravura vanity. His was a base-born nose shaped by centuries of crude laboring ancestors and landing on his face to spread light on his origin. Distrust wrinkled his mouth. No matter what he said, his lips moved as if he were counting change. His ache of a smile was only to ward off bad luck. There appeared to be not a thought in his head, only desire. Vanderbilt had an economical face. He didn't have to say anything disagreeable to convey it.

The commodore acquired his monumental fortune late in life, surpassing the older fortune of Astor, who was now the largest private landowner in the city. Vanderbilt was into railroads. Railroad franchises meant he printed his own money in watered stocks and bonds the public bought for profit and security.

Vanderbilt had advanced ideas for railroads but not for their upkeep. His desire was to control every line into New York so he could charge the highest prices for food and fuel that the traffic could bear. One newcomer stood in the formidable commodore's way, and he had fewer ideals—the Skunk of Wall Street, Jay Gould. On the street the nickname was also one of praise.

The Skunk accomplished the impossible. He stole the commodore's Erie Railroad from under his bloodhound nose.

The commodore's carriage was slowing. "Faster!" The commodore cawed at this insult to his dignity. "Faster, idjit!" he scolded his scared driver. At the side of the commodore was his youthful factotum, Chauncey Depew, whose polite smile had nothing to do with politeness or smiling but was a primordial gum the unwary became stuck in, to their detriment.

A hive of ragged children blocked the crossing. For mysterious reasons one or two children hanging around a crossing would attract others as bees to honey. Nothing drew them except the lure of shared aimlessness. No matter how many blocks the spreading hive of children covered, it represented only a fraction of the children who made the streets their home.

Coppers, dock wallopers, roughs gave the kids a wide berth. The children were seen as a volatile force of nature capable of darkening the city as a biblical plague. Their presence also had the fascination of a fault running through rockbed, capable of swallowing up the city's glory in a moment.

"Yuh kin't cross a black cat's path. Git 'round."

The driver was relieved. "Yes, sir, Commodore. I'll get us to Delmonico's twice as fast."

There was more than one Delmonico's. Each luxurious restaurant served a different purpose. Delmonico's uptown, Fifth Avenue and Fourteenth Street, catered to high society. The lure of a fashionable restaurant is seldom its kitchen. Seeing that high prices could not keep out the Shoddies, Delmonico's uptown served as society's watchdog. With the exactitude of a book of peerage they kept out women chasers, mistresses and divorcées. Those permitted to pass inside the velvet rope dined in the security of a restaurant chain that authenticated their good breeding.

Delmonico's downtown, on Chambers Street, was a chicken house of politicians, judges, lawyers. Here the lathe of politics polished justice.

Delmonico's Citadel served bankers and brokers. Here the Yankees of the fabled China trade, which included opium, ventured down from New England with spiritual and temporal disgust for the city while longing for the overnight fortunes to be made in its bedlam. At the Citadel counter stood young men eager to gaze at the new celebrity of the age—the financier. In less than one incredible generation the financier amassed fortunes worthy of ancient kingdoms. The young men studied financiers as if ambition were an oyster whose profound irritation produced pearls. These aggressive young men had the tension without the prize of talent. Their protective glares warded off intruders from squeezing into a place at the counter, while everyone knew that standing at the counter meant you were unimportant.

This noon, Citadel patrons were ready to wet themselves like puppies. The uncrowned beauty of New York society entered. She was on the devoted arm of her short, stocky, scarred and warrior-limping husband, who lacked every quality to attract beauty, save fire. Delmonico's rare silence at the lunch hour was homage to her beauty. Her shining, idealistic face had a spark of daring, as if she were flinging her husband in the face of a snooty society of restrictions.

Her silken hair was brushed back from her face. White orchids were entwined around a long strand of hair curling down the back of her bare neck. She wore the latest French styles as a caprice. Across her daringly naked chest lay ropes of diamonds whose worth shortened the breath.

She was the daughter of a famous and true commodore, Commodore Perry. The niece of Oliver Hazard Perry, hero of Lake Erie, who defeated the invincible British Navy in a decisive battle of the War of 1812: "We have met the enemy and they are ours." Yet at New York's social ball of the century honoring the visit of Edward, Prince of Wales, she was not invited to dance with the prince. Mrs. Kernochan, who weighed more than ten pounds for each year of the teenage prince, danced with the future King Edward VII. The taciturn Mrs. Goold Hoyt and other dowagers trod the Academy of Music ballroom with the prince, but this beauty of breeding and spirit, whose maiden name was Caroline Slidell Perry, was not invited. Miss Perry had refused the most eligible bachelors of New York to marry a Jew—a German-born, Spanish-transplanted, Frenchified Jew with a limp received in a duel to protect a woman's honor.

August Belmont was a Jew to Christians. For himself, he attended elegant Grace Church. If Jesus, so the intemperate say, came down to Grace Church, He would be told that to be admitted He had to live above Bleecker Street. August Belmont would have approved. He had the manner of embracing more than he accepted. A natural prey for religious conversion.

Belmont came up through the House of Rothschild. He was presently the highly regarded and respected chairman of the Democratic national party and their worthy chief fund-raiser. His friends included important Republicans. He was at home in exclusive clubs. He was a banker whose faith in the future of the United States, in spite of its horrible and periodic panics, compelled him to risk stupendous loans more conservative bankers, though no less patriotic, were unwilling to risk.

The boundless Belmont had not a moment of *weltschmerz*. The difference between the real world and the ideal world was no concern to him, not because the worlds were impossible to bridge but because they were all too easy for him.

Belmont's horses were legendary. His carriages were imported from Paris. Servants in his Fifth Avenue mansion had the terrifying reputation of being better dressed than the guests. His wine bill was second to none in a city where the wealthiest lived. A cosmopolitan, he knew a converted Jew is to Christians as mice to an old barn. There's no way to keep them out.

No sooner had the Belmonts vanished upstairs and the dining room resumed its noisy chatter than Chauncey Depew ushered in the commodore. Where moments before, patrons gazed at beauty and felt enhanced, now they glanced at Vanderbilt, who had the personality of a shotgun blast, and felt inspired, awed. Citadel diners reacted as though the figures they feared were more important than those giving them joy.

Who did the commodore come to see?

The lordly maître d' at the upstairs private chambers gave Vanderbilt a low bow. "Sir, Mr. Tweed will arrive momentarily."

The commodore blazed, "Hain't dat dog here?"

The maître d' boiled lobster red. "Perhaps, sir, you'd like to read the menu?"

Depew winced at the maître d's gaffe.

Vanderbilt tore the menu from his hand and *read* it, up and down, so fast that it was hilarious. He smacked the menu back into the maître d's chest. No one smiled. The commodore had *read* the menu upside down. The illiteracy of the richest man in the country terrified the maître d', whose lordly air became a ludicrous imitation in his own mind and evaporated.

Vanderbilt's words came with spit flying. "I want dat slimy fat barstid Tweed to climb up here."

"Yes, sir."

"To wait here like lime in a outhouse."

"Yes, sir."

"Not told I came."

"Yes, sir."

"When de barstid iz waitin' so long hiz fat iz meltin' off'n hiz carcass, y' say d' commodore iz expectorin' momentarily."

The Belmonts were descending as Tweed was huffing up the steps. Lint on Mrs. Belmont's sleeve received more attention from her. Her mortifying indifference knotted Tweed's stomach. She opened wounds he hadn't felt since the old days when he was coming up and losing elections. August Belmont's cordiality widened the gap. Belmont extended a greeting warm enough to be friendly, yet not so friendly that Tweed wouldn't know his place. Tweed understood. Belmont represented the party at the highest national level. Tweed was considered the necessary thug. Yet Belmont expected the thug to be sensitive enough to catch his slight. In that friendly exchange Tweed knew he had been bruised.

Bruised before meeting the commodore! How Mary Jane would have rejoiced to be invited to a Belmont dinner. The menu in French. Not knowing what she had ordered. One Belmont invitation, just one, would have conferred class on Tweed. Not being invited kept him sharp.

Tweed addressed the introspective maître d' after pinching out his gold watch and seeing how long he had waited. He couldn't stand a third straight snub. "Will you go downstairs and see if the commodore has arrived?"

The maître d' morbidly answered, "Commodore Vanderbilt was here, Alderman Tweed, and left."

"Why wasn't I told that downstairs?" He would have been spared the insufferable snub by the Belmonts.

The maître d' wished for a thicker shell than his morbidity. "The commodore wanted you to climb the stairs as he did."

Tweed accepted the commodore's revenge as more sporting than Belmont's snub. He sped to Vanderbilt's home at 10 Washington Place. Riding to meet the richest man in the nation is exhausting. No man simply goes to meet a financial titan. He goes to nose out their secret, the mystery of how legendary wealth is acquired. Yet the rich are not idolized solely for their untold fortune. In acquiring their colossal wealth there is the belief that they have found the secret of the country.

Yet nothing about Vanderbilt frightened Tweed: not the commodore's vengeful coldness; contempt for law; pleasure at being heartless; committing his wife to a lunatic asylum for disagreeing with him; cheating his son to teach him lessons in finance. All this in Tweed's eyes proved Vanderbilt's genius.

Tweed was not frightened of the man until he was shown into his parlor. He entered a stale and musty room. The shadowy light couldn't hide the holes in the torn rug and served to bring out the room's poverty. If Vanderbilt had entered at that moment, Tweed would have had no voice to greet him, so overawed was he. Vanderbilt's rug fanned his idolatry. Tweed knew the sweat around his eyes rose from his soul. He was in on the unexpected secret.

Torn rug. Worn linen. Chairs and tables bearing the teeth marks of repossession. This glorious dedication. Money for its own pure sake. He, himself, who hungered for possessions, was humbled by the master's ratty furnishings. The commodore's original fire was burning as freshly in old age as on the morning young Vanderbilt had stepped out in the world to make his fortune. The wretched room inspired Tweed by revealing the commodore's concentration. How logical that this purity of will should rage behind the greatest fortune.

Squeaking floorboards heralded Vanderbilt's coming. Though the commodore wore serviceable clothes, his feet were richly shod, four silver buckles on the shoes of his ungainly feet. Those buckles calling attention so guests first looked down at his feet, and this suited the half-playful side of the commodore's ego.

Tweed glanced up at the testy old man carrying chipped mugs of green tea and hardtack that he presented as tea cakes. "I'm sorry I'm late, Commodore. Election campaigns take endless attention."

The commodore bared his junky teeth. "Dangle dat excuse afore yer fartin' asshole t' see which smells worsen."

"You seem mighty happy, Commodore." Tweed ribbed him.

The commodore accepted happiness as a convenient lie to make conversation. No one would suspect happiness was in him as a scent in a hound. "Any man I wants to be m'friend 'comes m'friend. I got the hundred-percent personality—money."

Tweed grinned. He saw why Vanderbilt triumphed. The wisdom of his old age was the same as the ignorance of his youth. Tweed sensed the favor Vanderbilt wanted was all the protection he had against the old man.

"D' Skunk has a bullet hole for a heart. But he hain't bin in a fight yet by a long shot. I cornered Harlem Railroad stock. I paid Albany t' pass my railroad bill. Albany is slicker'n shit on a rainy day 'n dey trickered me. Took m' money. Voted m' down. Den— lissen to dis what d' barstids did—wid m' own money dey trickered me. Albany wid m' own money sold m' stock short, knownin' d' price on Harlem wud drop on dere rejecting m' bill. How's dat?"

"An itch everywhere else is a venereal disease in Albany."

"D' commodore smells Albany barstids quicker'n a bloodhoun' gets wind of an outhouse. How? Spies come cheaper den friends. I bought all d' Harlem stock I cud find." The commodore's show of warmth exposed his cold-bloodedness. "Albany barstids made d' stock cheap as compost. I drove Harlem's price through d'roof 'n caught dem barstids wid dere pants down. Dey had to buy m' stock back at m' price to cover their shorts. I chokered dem. I bleddered dem. I left dem for dead. Den I kickered dere ass. When dey were down, I pissed on dere new shoes. When dey wuz out, I made a fortune out of dere trickern me wid m' own money. No one breaks a Vanderbilt corner."

Tweed was elated at the commodore's boasting while knowing why the commodore was doing it. He wanted to make his request for a favor appear easy pudding. What could that favor be? Tweed trembled to think. The commodore was bigger than life, and he inadvertently admitted the Skunk was bigger. How could anyone be bigger than Vanderbilt? He had to believe the commodore, who hadn't a drop of modesty. "You sure outwitted those lawmakers."

"What do I care about d' law, hain't I got money?"

Tweed knew his own price would be chiseled down if he let Vanderbilt think Albany came cheap. "In New York you need a permit to walk on water."

Vanderbilt gloated so enthusiastically, his teeth showed down to his jaw hinge. "I turned water into cash. Forty-four million dollars watered stock sold."

Tweed's own infinite mind about money was but a kitchen garden compared to Vanderbilt's.

"Skunk 'n' hiz whoremaster, Jubilee Jim Fisk, stole m' railroad. Stole m' books t' Jersey City. Took m' cash t' pass a bill legalizin' their stealin' from me."

Even Tweed's eyebrows raised at such mastery. "Jersey City is only across the river. Why don't you ferry—"

"I ferried an army over. M' snot is cleaner den the men who run Jersey City. Skunk promised every ass-licker a job. Why, dey protected d' Skunk with state militia." The commodore's mistake came tumbling out with his distaste for the vileness of men. "It never pays tuh kick a skunk. I wants yuh tuh stop d' Skunk 'n' Albany. I need yer Judge Barnard to writ out injunctions against d' Skunk."

"You can bet Gould will be stopped." If Tweed drank, he would take his own words as whiskey bravery, since everything he heard about Jay Gould caused him to think him more devil than human. How else could a younger generation of financiers scare the dickens out of men like Vanderbilt?

Vanderbilt soured on expressions of loyalty. "I bin tuh Albany afore. Y'need freight cars of money." His crusty face peeled to an unguarded level. "Y'll git five hundred thousand in cash." The commodore wiped his nose on his forefinger for emphasis. "Ten percent is your'n when yuh win. Y'go tuh Albany only if yer 'lected senator."

Tweed was sunning himself in a future of fifty thousand dollars in commissions and a White House backer when he abruptly woke to the price he had to pay.

The commodore coarsely dismissed him by picking up the platters of tack and green tea and leaving him to find his way out. He didn't want Tweed to think he was in his debt for needing him.

The arrogant insult told Tweed he had arrived on a national

level. The commodore's backing was a shortcut through Belmont's circle. Future victories were burning off Tweed. He needed the run of the streets to catch his breath and get his feet solidly on the ground. The Battle for Erie! This could go down in history along with the commodore's legendary corner of Harlem stock.

His cheeks puffed as he blew out nervous breath. He passed Civil War veterans perched, without arms or legs, outside luxury hotels. A tray of shoelaces hung off their necks. They wore Union uniforms yet were as forgotten as park memorials. He dropped a dime into their trays, conforming to the unwritten code of not taking a shoelace. The donation supplied a needed amount of caring.

SEVEN

*E*veryone knew O'Brien was sheriff. His face was ready to blow into a tuba. No matter what people thought, no one sold Tweed's bagman short. He was sheriff for his weakness. Thus he was capable of any deed to prove no one could step on him. His ass kissing was a fault Tweed raised to a prized virtue. Yet O'Brien's character was not perfect for an organization. Ass kissing gave him delusions of grandeur. While he dutifully shoveled money into a satchel embossed with the city's seal and frantically checked vouchers, he knew he was risking his neck and wanted bigger rewards for being weak enough to do this dirty work.

Tweed was holding forth in City Hall with the powerful city watchdogs, the Board of Supervisors. The bipartisan board had to examine by law every bill the city had to pay. Tweed was at his best with starched men whose depths he had plumbed. He told them, "My experience shows it's cheaper to buy men than to elect them."

"Bill, you tempt fate," Henry Smith frowned. "You awarded a butcher a contract to build a bridge."

"We need to encourage his kind of push."

It ate into him that cautious men shared the spoils of his daring. He beckoned to Sheriff O'Brien, who had entered humbly. "Here's my bagman."

"I wish you'd call me sheriff, Boss."

"Everyone has push." Tweed motioned for the sheriff to pass out bloated envelopes before each supervisor as a butler might serve a meal. Tweed donned his spectacles and glanced down his nose, looking every bit the bookkeeper he had been. "Before you is a token from our Subcommittee on Armories. We purchased used benches for five dollars apiece and sold them to the city armories for fifty." Tweed glanced over the courteous men of the board. Silence except for the riffling of money being counted. The money weighed them down with sobriety. "Any questions? Objections? Ayes have it."

Tweed stuck his envelope in his ample pocket. "New bills for the courthouse. Andrew Garvey, plaster, $464,229.73. Rufus Jones, royal house of stationery, $111,331.29. Compton & Son, furniture makers to the quality trade, $604,446.21. James H. Ingersoll, chairs for the elite taste, $396,411.10. G. S. Miller, skilled carpentry at modest prices, $360,751.61."

"How can the city be charged a fortune for wood," asked the meticulous Briggs, "when the courthouse is mainly marble and iron?"

"A very good question," Tweed remarked. That was also his answer. "James A. Smith, carpets and shades for the discriminating, $511,685.78."

Sheriff O'Brien accidentally whistled at the amount, and Tweed shot him a jaundiced look.

Briggs asked, "Didn't we just pay Jimmy Smith almost a quarter of a million dollars for carpets and shades in the new courthouse?"

"Are you objecting or inquiring?"

"There's not that much carpeting in all Turkey."

"It's the public's fault." Tweed bore no grudge. "Carpets in public buildings wear out fast."

"But the courthouse hasn't opened yet." Fox reminded him.

"Do you have a carpet?" asked Tweed. "Do I have a carpet? Does Briggs, Smith, Roche or Hayes here have a carpet? None of us have carpets. Invite reformers to your office. Show them our Spartan life. Carpets are purchased at the request of judges. Judges know the full extent of the law. The New York bench is celebrated for their verdicts on carpets and shades." Tweed gave them courage by taking away their logic. "R. J. Hennessey, quality plaster, $626,482.97."

"More plastering?" asked Briggs patiently.

"I never heard of Hennessey," said Hayes without wanting to solve the mystery.

"Prince Garvey is a model of considerate behavior. He's taken a second name for billing purposes. John Keyser, plumbing $876,124.99."

Roche walked on eggs. "We just paid Keyser a half million."

"This," Tweed enlightened them, "is for plumbing *repair.*"

"I wouldn't ask," asked Roche, "but who is using the plumbing when the courthouse has no tenants?"

"Keyser is a conscientious contractor. He's repairing the plumbing he installed."

"Even without us asking," Roche murmured, not to Keyser's credit.

"John McBride Davidson, burglar protection, $251,679.23. James W. Smith, 318 awnings, $102,342.33."

"Jimmy Smith again?" Briggs wondered out loud. "Wouldn't reformers see we have a hundred times more awnings than windows in the new courthouse?"

"You don't want the sun shining in the eyes of our judges and blinding justice?" Tweed returned to business. "Archibald Hall, Jr., paint, $176,781.18."

"Isn't that Garvey's name too?" Roche asked.

"Prince Garvey has only one more alias. Cashman." Tweed waved the bills for the sheriff to take them. "The ayes have it. Get Comptroller Connolly and District Attorney Oakey Hall to sign their approval as required by law." He took in the board. "New business?"

Briggs warned, "There's complaints about the higher taxes."

"How else can we pay for running the government?" said Tweed. "You raise taxes to give tax relief."

"Tilden says you're using tax favors to keep powerful men in your debt." Briggs treaded carefully. "Reformers say you have Astor in your pocket."

"I should hope so. Astor is a great example to us all. Before the Civil War, Astor was the richest man in America. His wealth equaled one fifteenth of the country's investment in cotton, wool, iron, ships, wagons, sugar, leather, furniture, silks, paper, candles, glass and soap. Now immigrants add to his boon by living in his tenements. Better to win over Astor than reformers."

"Best to have both," Briggs suggested.

"Boss," O'Brien reminded Tweed, "the Ludlow Street jail?"

"All those in favor of constructing the Ludlow Street jail say aye." Before anyone opened their mouth, Tweed rolled on. "The ayes have it. Ludlow Street jail will be constructed to relieve the overcrowding of city prisons."

EIGHT

*N*ight came to the Industrial Home for Boys, and Nipper's day was about to begin. Nothing of a boy was in his eight-year-old face. Kindness might have once illumined the boy beneath the hardness like breathing on embers, but neglect bred iron in his scrawny body and self. Nipper slept in the home's white flannel nightgown, with his clothes on underneath. To be undressed was too scary, making him feel unguarded. Beneath his tick mattress a burlap sack was wrapped around a yard-long iron tong. Both were his nightly tools on the river marshes.

The home darkened slowly, the overhead lamps keeping their heat like fireflies dying. City noises came alive in the dark. He never felt alone, only lonely. Loneliness was muscle. The more he could stand loneliness, like swimming in ice-cold water, the stronger he was.

Laundry lye in his fresh pillowcase kept him awake yearning for a better life. The cots on the drafty floor were of untreated pine. The soft wood was alive in the darkness with the smell of the outdoors.

The home, in spite of the white nightgowns, was miles better than the Children's Cell at the Tombs. There battered boys lay with their faces against bars like fish coming up for air. Boys roasted over the spit of their wild energy. They were caught because they couldn't stand loneliness. They had to brag, show off, team up. Not wanting to be lonely, they end in solitary, taking the count painfully.

The home's workshop teacher said that when they scraped the streets off him, they found an old man. So? Who wants to be a kid? Helpless. You want to be a man. The fastest way to be a man is to steal. But that leads to the Children's Cell. Next best is making a living on his own as he was doing now. The quicker you're not a boy, the less is lost. Being a boy is for rich kids. Who's a grown-up to say who's who? Grown-ups are pies out on the counter too long, their filling going out from under them. They're always on display for what they're not inside.

The dumb shop teacher called him tough because he fought to stay dumb. He was tough, all right, but not the way they thought. He slept soaked in his nightmares; because of this fright he faced the next day with the kick of a mule.

If only nightmares were about monsters, he'd feel safe. But they were about himself. Stuck fast. Never knowing the pitch that held him in its pulse. Everyone believing him a street animal. He fought to be at peace with himself. To grow up, not be helpless, not be gripped by what the beating of the heart meant.

He never felt safe sleeping. If he cried out, frightened, no one listened. Only deaf people were in his nightmares. They boasted being deaf and dumb. One night in his life, just one night, he wished to be in a dream—and safe! His soul no longer his enemy.

When the other kids dropped off, he hid his nightgown in his pillowcase and snuck off. His hunting tong was over his shoulder, and the burlap sack trailed behind.

No sooner was he on the street when a ground-shaking run trembled up his spindly legs from the cattle herds being driven to the slaughterhouses. The rampaging beasts thundered to the slaughter, leaving behind their exhilarating energy.

Hookers roamed night streets with candy-striped parasols. The toughest hookers came out of Corlears Hook along the waterfront he was passing. Hookers painted their faces white to be spotted in the dim light as being available. No man went by, however lifeless, who wasn't fished for as prize sturgeon. "How do you do, m'dear? Come, won't you go home with me?"

Hard as hookers were with their mackerel nearby, their parasols used as lances, their hat pins sharp as pig stickers, they feared boys of his trade. Hookers froze at his sight, pressing against walls out of the profitable lamplight to give him the sidewalk. His outline against the moonlit sky was half beast, half insect—no boy. His hunting tong was an antenna sticking up from his head, his burlap sack a beaver's tail. Hookers were in such superstitious fear of his trade that some spoke to him only to ward off evil. "Good luck to you, rat-catcher boy."

Children crawled in everywhere to sleep. Kids not as ambitious as he lay crumpled in doorways, twisted in open cellars, curled across bakery grates, bodies spit out of a battlefield. The city night charged with absent crowds.

He walked off the street onto the lumpy landfill along the marshes. The fishermen upriver could barely be seen in the mist. They resembled thieves in the night, fishing for squid while holding a lantern off the bow, their still bodies arched over the river, their nose into the current and frozen in that position until the flash to strike.

A fog bell-ringer on a crow's nest high over the docks has a ghostly penetration in his plaintive warning. "Fog on the river!"

Fog is sky let loose and drifting and dangerous to catcher boys. Nipper raced over the marsh under the steaming moon. The palest moon would do for light. Garbage hills lay smoking outside the shacks of trimmers. Trimmers are the worker ants of the city. They earn their living stealing garbage. Sunrise to sunset, industrious trimmer families cart off debris dumped for the scows. Wheeling their prizes to their shacks, they rake their mounds for valuables. Sundown finds them locked in their shacks as wild dogs ferret for the leftovers.

When Nipper arrived, there were boys staked out who cursed at him to stay clear of their mound. Nipper razzed them. He knew their cursing was a cover-up for their cowardice. Their hill had no wild dogs. To get the biggest catch and earn the most money a boy had to follow wild dogs. Dogs know the mounds to ferret. A catcher boy's courage earned him the respect of blacksmiths who traditionally charge a token penny for luck to hammer out their tongs.

Ahead is a wild pack ferociously digging into a mound. Two boys are up to their knees on the other side of the dog pack. It's easier for two boys to establish ground. They give each other courage. The dogs have ignored the boys, and this proves the mound is a rich one. No matter how tough the boys, they are forced to live by the rules of the dogs.

Nipper's legs are protected by rags wound around his torn black cotton knee stockings. He must climb the mound without hesitation lest the dogs smell his fear and attack. After a giant step into the mound his head is sweating. Nipper knows stories of boys running for safety and never living to run again; or taking a step in what the dogs sense is the wrong direction, and that step is their last. A boy must not run before a maniacal dog. He has to, must, brave it out. If praying, the prayer must be so well hidden, it scorches his heart.

Nipper was as skillful as any hunter in darkest Africa. He hunted by moonlight, at times in fog, against wild dogs possessing every advantage. He had to catch a tiny, fleet animal in the blink of an eye—and catch it alive!

Bruised, the catch is worthless. They must be unmarked to sell to the entertainment world. No entertainment rivals sports. No sport except bare knuckles draws like the bull pits. Without boys like him there'd be no pits raking in the money. He worked a seller's market, though dive owners break any boy whose price goes out of line.

The best protection is not to let the dogs know you are alive. Dogs have a fifth sense about territory, some keep this sense dormant while others carry it with their heartbeat. Animals they are, but they can read a boy's thoughts before he can express them.

His spine went cold as the boys nodded a courtesy warning. They were leaving the mound to him, backing down slowly. He saw they believed him more crazy than brave to hunt alone, especially with a fog settling in the marshes.

The gnashing, gnawing, growling dogs were so near, he was sprayed with their debris flying over the top from the other side. The dogs kept him maddeningly alert.

Yet he had to be silent without a breath to spear his catch. Hot and cold waiting. If he was not crazed by concentration, he'd swear—God himself would swear!—nothing happened. In between a swift ripple and stillness he had to strike.

Strike! Miss. Strike! Miss. Strike! Got 'im! All gut ears. No eyes. Delirious. Caught life tingling up his arm. Frightening him. He flicked his catch into his sack as a smoker tapping away ash. Damn animals! Their human squeaking for life just before being flicked into the sack. How could they turn—at the last second—to reveal a higher source of being?

He was raging alertness, catching even as his arms became

leaden. He struck with one hand and jumbled the sack with the other hand to tumble his catch and keep it from gnawing holes in the burlap. The catches came faster as the dogs came closer, driving the game before them. In his fury he smelled a dog too near —hairy, muggy, sour beast. He looked up into maniacal eyes drawn to the squeaking in the sack he was jiggling.

He shrunk into himself at the dog's crazed power. There was absolutely nothing behind the dog's eyes. The horror drained him. Instinct told him not to run, and his muscles burned to run. He was forced to taunt the dog by jiggling his sack to keep his catch from escaping. Pointed eyes in the dog's teeth.

The dog had shrunk him to nothing. Liquid. Humiliation. The stupid beast's raving barks. Madly treating him lower than an animal. His tong was blunted so as not to bruise. It would be suicide to try to stop the pitiless barking and baring of sharp teeth. In the dark the wild dog took on the outline of the entire night!

The tense dog was rocked by madness. He didn't know why the dumb beast hadn't sprung. Nipper's body flamed at the expected leap. He had a mysterious feeling that the catch was saving his life even as it was baiting the dog. The steady jiggling of the sack might be a display of insane power to the maddened dog.

The barking ate through Nipper in shock waves. There was no winning way to fight back. He couldn't leave his catch. His nerve endings were popping. He was more whimpering than brave, caved in yet standing his ground. Strength from another world kept steadily jiggling his sack. His bridge to the dog told him this is what the dumb beast sensed. The barking lost its belly and became watchdog barking rather than out-of-his-mind barking. He read the dog's undertone clearer than he could English.

Nipper was dazed at snapping free from the brutal connection. He couldn't retreat while the dog stared, and he couldn't tempt fate by hunting.

The dog dived for a catch. Nipper slowly backed down, the arm holding the tong shivering slightly less than the arm jiggling the sack. Getting off the mound did nothing to steady him. His blood surged back with a king-of-the-hill victory.

He was surprised to see a thread of dawn. He had to walk down the middle of the street. Gangs might be lying in wait to jump him and sell his catch as their own.

The last humans out at night are bill-stickers. He was glad to see company. Bill-stickers worked with their pockets inside out to show thieves they carried no money. They are weighed down by a bed of paper over one arm and a paste bucket in their hand. They slap up shiny paper in seconds and vanish. By morning they've redecorated the city with advertisements from opera to politics.

The first sign of dawn along the East River is not the sun. It is little girls outlined against the moonlit river, trudging up island to harvest the largest bog remaining on Manhattan. An edge-of-the-world bog running along Ninety-second Street, inland to Third Avenue. Five freshwater brooks feed the bog. Blackberries and blueberries are had for the picking, as are the first violets of the season and blankets of wild iris. The little girls carry the berries and flowers back to sell them on the street.

Nipper hurried through the long line of pickers to Big Nose Bunker to sell his catch. Big Nose was named for constantly eyeing women. He might have slept, but his face didn't. A sloppy, fat man as wrinkled as bagged wash. He was brutally realistic without being honest. He was too all-business not to be a bit crazy. Those who could like Bunker also hated him, none more so than the catcher boys. Bunker asked no quarter, gave no quarter and taught by his actions that life on the landfill with wild dogs had more honor than dealing with him.

Big Nose bought his catch but wouldn't pay until after the show. This protected Big Nose against boys loading up on the more easily trapped sewer rats who were poison to pit bulls. Handlers weaned bulls from pups to pits with cold and cruel calculating discipline and were not about to lose valuable property. A celebrity bull was a prize draw on the circuit.

At the waterfront sporting dive, Nipper knocked on the iron door at the rear of the saloon. A Judas window opened, and Bunker let him in. The first sight down into the dazzling white pit always thrilled him. Early arrivals stood pressed against a waist-high fence. Skye and English terriers aching for combat moaned while being cunningly held in their handler's arms. The bulls scented the excitement of the men as the men were stirred by the unquenchable crying of the bulls.

Pits attracted drastic extremes. Fanatics gave Water and South Streets a reputation for mayhem unmatched in Singapore, Marseilles or Liverpool. One of the Wild West's notorious gunslingers came out of these New York ranks, Billy the Kid. The airless arena clouding up with tobacco smoke smelled of dog and man and the stale air from bygone matches. The smell whetted the betting and lashed the spectators with the pleasure of being there.

Bunker handed Nipper a punk stick to light the pit. Nipper skipped down the tiers of worn benches, jumped the barrier and lit the eight-armed lamp.

A batlike chittering from caged rats in the pit aroused the pit bulls to squeaking. Their air passages clogged with their intense desire, pit bulls sensed the terror of the caged. The more frightened the rats, the sharper was their high-pitched chittering. The tension between attackers and prey produced a howling of dogs barely above a quiet weeping, and over these animal sounds the spectators yelled their bets.

The huddled rodents were a dust ball in a corner of the cage. Nipper opened the wire top and heard the pings of their rapid breathing. They clung together, as a pile beating with one heart. Pulling them apart Nipper felt a buzzing through their tails. He dropped them one by one onto the white pit floor while loudly counting.

When they would not separate without bruising, Nipper stuck in his hand as leisurely as stirring a pond. The captive bodies had the same stitched breathing as blind, newborn kittens. Bets were screamed over Nipper's head as he yanked the ticking bodies of fear off one another.

"Silly Billy, forty-five kills a minute. Lord Jeffrey, thirty-five kills."

When Nipper spilled the fiftieth and last unwilling one into the pit, they magnetized into one palpitating pile against the white barrier.

Nipper was fascinated by the gross vamping of the shrewd handlers. Matinee idols could learn from handlers about inflaming pulses. How masterfully a handler placed a hot-blooded hand lightly on the fierce bull's sorrowful brow or a heavy, bloodless hand skillfully against the bull's tense chest to keep his edge. How he would whisper forcefully into the bull's sprig of an ear one moment or coo the next to fan the bull into exploding at the instant of leaping into the pit.

Nipper vaulted back over the barrier, climbed the benches to the top tier where Big Nose and the other catcher boys held forth near the door.

"Silly Billy will lead off," Big Nose announced. "Mr. Piker Ryan will umpire the kills. Weeper Molloy will sound the kills. Only Molloy's count will carry."

Applause to get the action started.

"No one will hurry the count or molest the animals or they'll get a speedy hike, personally, by me. For your enjoyment I bring you the popular idol of the New England circuit, who I booked sparing no expense, Silly Billy."

The rats understood. They fizzed against one another. They felt the body heat from the marble-eyed Silly Billy, held over the barrier to whet his appetite.

The pit bull shrieked in agony to leap. His bettors pounded against the staves of the barrier with their blood up. "Silly Billy! Silly Billy! Silly Billy!"

To fire up the bull the handler's bite-scarred hand pumped against the dog's beating chest, pressing the bull back into himself until the bull's eyes bulged madly and he bucked out of the grasp onto the white pit with the senseless thud of cement.

The fizzing rats startled him. Silly Billy hunched his back with the instinct of a cat. Silly Billy rooters took bets fearlessly to the last second. That last second took faith. Nervous Silly Billy was up on spiky legs, muscles rippling under tight butcher-paper skin, grape-clustered paws squeezing tight, mashed snout running wet. Silly Billy froze in a ballet pose.

"Five seconds," called Bunker with gold watch in hand. Big Nose started counting with the cement-bag thud of the bull.

The bettors for high kills began sweating.

Silly Billy would not move. Countless bites from other pits were rashed over his body. Earlier these bites were seen as favorable signs the bull was unafraid. Now they appeared as stitches leaking out his courage.

Silly Billy's clear eyes pleaded to return to the comforting arms of his handler, who stared back venomously. Silly Billy would not attack. The fizzing rats would not scatter.

Frenzied Silly Billy bettors screamed at the men standing against the barrier. "Blow on the rats!"

The ringside men leaned into the pit and blew on the pulsing dust ball until their faces turned red. Not one on the lumpy pile moved. The biggest ballooned cheeks with the most ferocious exhale could not make a dent. The dust ball only quivered as if an internal storm were going through it.

"Harder!" shouted desperate Silly Billy bettors. "Get your noses into it!"

Steaming red men puffing like bellows into the pit finally caused the rats to break like billiards to every part of the white circle.

Silly Billy feared he was being cornered. Biting, slashing, clouting, snapping, he speckled the circle red. The havoc was unbearable to the bettors against Silly Billy, while his backers went berserk pounding the wooden barrier to cheer him on.

"Ten! Twelve! Thirteen! Fourteen!" Silly Billy bettors eagerly called the kills.

Weeper Molloy called, "Nine."

Nipper jumped up and down, clapping and groaning with the bettors. He was one hundred percent for Silly Billy, who slid headlong and crashed into the barrier. The bull yelped when bitten back, a funny yelp, as if the bull were claiming a foul.

"Twenty seconds," Bunker called.

The "for" bettors sunk into a moan; even by their inflated count they were going down the drain. They pointed around the pit. "Twenty-two! Twenty-three! Twenty-four, *five and six!*"

The officious Weeper called, "Nineteen."

The eyes of the bettors became bright as the bull's. They argued kills, and well they might. The rub was that kills were not always dead. Kills could be slashed, bitten, quivering on their sides out of action but not out of breath. Once up, it would be impossible to subtract a kill without causing bloodshed among the bettors. No counter, even one as astute as Weeper, could prove which one in the hurly-burly got up after being counted out. This never to be fairly decided point was part of the game. White cheating. Thoroughly respectable. You got what you could.

A class gentleman was always on hand to settle disputes. Piker Ryan was the wise man for this tribe. His very nickname of being tight with money proved his probity. Piker was called on and sided with Weeper.

Silly Billy raged on to the pounding furor of his bettors. Nipper was caught up in the excitement of this unlikely champion. He noticed the bull kept shortening the odds against him. Weeper began counting as fast as the "for" bettors. Bettors *against* were groaning at the bull's devastation.

The bull stopped as abruptly as he'd begun!

His furious handler pounded the staves. "Yi! Yi! Yi!"

Silly Billy simply believed he had killed enough.

Nipper wildly cheered the bull's independence.

The bull was astounded by the kills his frenzy piled up.

He daintily lifted his ballet legs to step around the bloodshed while his backers were cursing their lungs out.

"Thirty seconds," called Bunker.

Silly Billy's bettors heard their doom in Bunker's call.

Nipper kept cheering though he knew this moment is so dreaded, no handler dares think about it. The murderous hysteria of the pit takes over the dog. The killing fit is over and the pit bull discovers, to his astonishment, that he has broken through his iron discipline. He has reverted to his true untrained self. He has broken free.

Nipper marveled at this lifesaving resource in a dog and was tickled at how lovable the dog looked when reaching into its natural self.

Silly Billy was pleading through his marble eyes, pepper reddened by his savagery, to return to the arms of his handler. The bettors against the bull in an uproar, cheering the crack in the dog's shell.

Nipper's hidden boyishness finally emerged in a broad grin at the gentle dog under the ferociously trained disguise. Silly Billy's eyes were saying he was only a Silly Billy dog at heart. In his bones he didn't want to kill. But he had to eat and wanted to sleep where it was warm. He was horrified at being a killer dog.

The handler's unforgiving eyes glazed over. He pounded the barrier, screaming until his voice cracked, "Kill! Kill! Kill!" Silly Billy wincing at each command.

The commands painfully went through Nipper, and he wildly waved his arms for the dog not to listen. Then Nipper's face lined to the edge of crying as something tipped over in the bull who struck again with renewed ferocity. The care the dog received in training might have left him too lonely to stand on his own. Slipping, sliding, crashing into the barrier turned Silly Billy into an arousing attraction. A startling individual though not his own master. The mayhem count was above forty, even with Weeper.

Silly Billy bettors applauded his madness. In the midst of the bull's fury bettors for and against groaned. Silly Billy let out a telltale yowl at being bitten and withdrew.

Bunker himself barked in pain. In his own fit Big Nose could strangle the lot of the catcher boys around him waiting for their pay.

The alarmed handler was shouting, "Sewer rat!"

The count stopped. The clocking went off. The bettors moaned in disgust.

The handler scooped Silly Billy out of the pit. He uncorked a long-necked bottle of peppermint water. Swig after swig was spewed against the liverish folds of the bull's snout.

The funny dog brought Nipper alive, and not just animal alive, as sports are wont to do. A warmth was driving feelings openly to his eyes.

His cheerful face set Bunker off. Bunker had little use for honest emotions except as they covered up what was false. "Nipper," he hollered, "it's *you!*"

Nipper didn't want to dirty his warm cheerfulness by defending himself against a lump like Bunker. "If you don't know by this time I'd never hurt a pit bull, then you'll never know anything."

Bunker grabbed Nipper's marker out of his hand and tore it into bits. "You're getting zero."

Nipper slowly took off, chalking up this hard day's loss to experience. He felt better, braver, less lonely than Bunker could ever dream about.

Bunker went after Nipper in his tobacco-fogged saloon and called to a rough three sheets in the wind from slogging whiskey thrashers. "Get the thief!"

Nipper easily eluded the drunken rough, but Bunker kidney-punched him from behind and clapped iron cuffs on Nipper's skinny wrists.

"Trying to act like a man?" Bunker discouraged him. "Swindling. Poisoning. Ready to take money not owed you. You're not going back to your fancy hotel in the industrial school. You're going straight to the Children's Cell at the Tombs, and not having no pull, you're never getting out. But I got pull with Tweed's captains, and I'll get you thrown into the swamp cell."

At the mention of the swamp cell Nipper kicked and struggled to get free, and even the drunken rough blanched at Bunker's murderous threat.

"You won't come back from there," Bunker swore, "to practice your cruelty to animals." Bunker was choking him in a stranglehold. "Nipper, you'll be breathing swamp gas tonight. By tomorrow you'll be gone to your just desserts. Take a last look around at what you'll be missing."

NINE

Seeing Kathleen Doyle running through Duane Street, her poppy-red hair flying, her long legs taking a yard at a stride in a homemade dress, made Shiny Hats scatter. One ran up to Tweed's office to warn Shamus, who could hear Shiny Hats hooting her arrival. The Shiny Hat reminded Shamus how she hated the Ring yet came to them for help. She was a natural troublemaker. If she took care of number one, so strikingly attractive a young woman would be in silks and furs. That she didn't care for silks and furs is what also put Shamus in Kathleen's power.

The mere mention of the troublemaker caused Shamus to doubt himself and feel certain he wasn't worthy of her. Trying to improve on his decent, clean-cut looks in the mirror did nothing to restore his confidence. She disarmed him long before she confronted him.

Kathleen's paleness was mysterious because it appeared rooted in her shyness, which he had yet to behold. He longed for the briefest glimpses of her yet dreaded being in her presence. He was certain his strengths were thrown down before her like a losing hand.

The Shiny Hat warned Shamus to lock the door. He made excuses that the office was open to everyone as Tweed wanted. "But not to her!" cried the Shiny Hat, and flew down the stairs to keep from meeting a tantalizing, attractive young woman.

Shamus felt at home in the simple arithmetic of politics. You gave favors and you called in your markers when needed. A reassuring life. Kathleen's arithmetic was a mystery to him. She'd help anyone without politics, creed or cash. She also excited him without her knowing she gave him anything. She didn't even look at him as a man because he was in politics, tied up to a closed system, and gave away his rights to do anything on his own. He gave her devotion without her taking it. If he gave her a thousand favors, he'd feel he had not done enough for her.

Kathleen had lived through the hunger. She had been a little girl watching first her mother, then her father and her older and younger sisters and brothers, die away from her in starvation. This family she loved did not just die. They slowly wasted away looking for food, helping each other, sticking together after being thrown out of their home and forced to wander down dirt roads with hundreds, thousands of other families looking for food.

He could not conceive of a million people dying of hunger so near to the great cities of Great Britain and Europe. Why, under the most corrupt administration in New York this would be impossible. Ireland was cursed with age upon age of violent invaders, yet none was more destructive than the absentee landlords. So much violence, houses were built without front doors to keep out attackers. A million starving to death with so little protest. Irish tragedy should have been everyone's tragedy.

He heard her leaping up the stairs two and three steps at a time in a long dress. He hurried to sit in Tweed's commodious chair to impress her.

She dashed in, her poppy-red hair wild as flames, and unceremoniously yanked him up by the arm. "The coppers have thrown Nipper into the swamp cell at the Tombs to die." She spoke as if the city were swallowing her up.

He only saw her green eyes. They always reduced him to the inaction of worship. He was also hurt she didn't notice him, was using him, taking him for granted. "There goes your bleeding heart." He didn't know where he got the nerve to speak to her like that. He must be going crazy. Except that he knew it came from resenting her not seeing him as an eligible, steady young man with a good job.

"Bleeding hearts"—she hit him between the eyes—"were the

only ones trying to help us in the hunger. You think practical men like yourself did?"

Her character spoke to the dreams in him. "Kathleen . . . you're beautiful."

"I want you to be stronger than that." She was discouraged.

"What did Nipper do?" He was ready to do anything for her.

"Bunker claims Nipper stole from him, poisoned a bull and wrecked his saloon. That's impossible."

"Yes." He stoutly agreed, only to have his weakness pour out as a dike is opened. "Bunker is a big party contributor."

She pulled him out of the office, down the stairs, without wanting to hear his petty reasons. She was dragging him through the streets yet couldn't believe his embarrassment. "Why do you look so confused?"

He thought he would put himself in her good graces by admitting, "My confused look and my look of certainty are the same look."

"A born politician." She pulled him through the streets though she valued his honest reply.

He defended politicians. "Do you enjoy Central Park?"

"The lungs of the city," she answered robustly.

"If not for politics, Central Park would be half of what it is today or nothing at all."

"Doesn't anything hurry you?" she asked, though they were going as fast as the crowded streets allowed.

"Real-estate contributors didn't want Central Park because it would take too much property off the market. Taxpayers didn't want Central Park because it would raise taxes. The Association for Improving the Conditions of the Poor didn't want Central Park because the park took away land needed to house the poor. Church leaders wanted the park closed on Sunday. The one day working people had off."

"Morris Pease," said Kathleen, "says the park was delayed because politicians had to be bribed."

The sad cry of the soap-fat man pushing a heavy cart expressed Shamus's feeling. "Sooooaaappp-fat man!" His long-held note of grief pictured his trade as one of sorrow. Housewives and maids beckoned his shabby figure into dark doorways and service alleys. He emerged bent with buckets of slopping fat, scraping and pouring the fat into his own buckets while keeping up his cry as if the fat were being wrung out of his own hide. His sadness impressed women with his honesty. The soap-fat man lived off their thrift as the housewives and maids lived off his pennies.

Shamus cautiously tried to change the subject with well-meant advice. "The heelers say if only you'd dress right, you'd be so respectable-looking, you'd get whatever you wanted."

"Heelers?" She couldn't believe his source for respectability. "No men are more truly named. Always at the heel of a master. If I dressed right, you'd want me to meet your parents?"

"Oh, no. Da is on the police force because he's solid for Tweed. Da wants none of your views."

"Your da is a worm who worships a crook."

"Holy Mother."

"Tweed breaks the law hundreds of times a day just by selling citizenships to the immigrants and teaching them by it that anything can be bought. The poor immigrants vote for Americans they think are building a strong country while these crooks are helping to destroy their liberty and education. Poor, poor immigrants. The more run-down their street, the more loyal they are to it."

He knew he was a goner, for every look she had vanished off her face too fast for him. "Kathleen, if ever my life is held by a string, I'd return by remembering your eyes."

Though she was touched, she replied, "How morbid. Do you think I've so many suitors you must declare yourself first?"

He shot back with a boldness she hadn't expected, "Yes."

"You think so little of yourself?"

"Only with you."

His openness was getting to her and slowed her pace. "In your moaning way you're romantic."

"Oh, no," he protested, "I'm not romantic. Fright makes me say what I do."

"You never hinted at kissing me or even holding my hand."

His voice, for being unsteady, came out all the more honest. "I don't know the different woman you'll be after kissing." He quickly changed the subject with a prophecy. "Your goodness will be my ruin."

The massive Tombs loomed over them as they walked under its somber walls. The prison was New York's spectacular copy of an Egyptian tomb. At high noon the grandeur of the entrance kept it in deep shadow. Tourists stood on Centre Street to gaze into the monumental emptiness of the entrance that narrowed into a dark throat, out of which came hollow echoes of shoes scraping aimlessly against stone.

Entering the dark throat, Kathleen and Shamus felt the cold clinging to them like a sickness. A chilling wind whipped up grit and soot.

A cheerful keeper met them. He was the pipeline of the Tombs' profit back to the party coffers: selling the best cells, auctioning the right to practice medicine, getting so high a price for the food service that the food had to be bad to be profitable. To calm their fears the keeper took them to the swamp cells to show Nipper wasn't there. They had to cover their noses against swamp gas. The Tombs was built over the Lispenard meadow. Underground springs could be heard running beneath Leonard Street houses. There was an enormous crack in the thick wall where the prison was sinking. When a vicious prisoner needed hanging yet had not done enough to be hung, he was thrown into a sinking cell of swamp gas and was soon gone to his reward, saving an eventual walk over the Bridge of Sighs to the gallows.

They passed through a narrow cell block where cells rose tier upon tier on either side above a passageway. A dirty skylight filtered down the light over prisoners hanging against their bars like hides. Clothes lay on damp cell stones. No hooks were allowed. The eyes of some prisoners were glazed back to another time less imperfect than the present. Many men lay curled in their position before birth.

Kathleen turned her bright face away from the raw outbursts of prisoners. She understood helpless people who spoke directly out of their heads. They sensed that a falling-off of outrage is the beginning of paralysis. She had felt the same in the hunger.

The Children's Cell was a huge cage. At the sight of the bloodied Nipper, Kathleen clapped her hands over her mouth to keep her scream from waking him. As soon as her fingertips touched his bony body, she knew she should have left well enough alone. In comforting him she had touched a deeper bruise than any she saw on him. His flesh had been thinned from the agitation inside him.

Nipper bolted up, as if his sleep were on fire.

Kathleen maintained the calm vital before a chaotic kid. She introduced Nipper to Shamus. Nipper's matchstick legs kicked through the cage at him. Shamus looked unsure about releasing him, but Kathleen nodded she wanted Nipper freed. The keeper shook his head no.

To Shamus, Nipper was an incendiary bomb off to an early grave. Nothing would change the course. Kids who are truly tough are out of their minds with violence. They must act threateningly, as their brutality tells them they're nothing. No one wants to know their nothing. Their only trump is the violence that will kill them. This frightened Shamus. He suddenly was in contact with the murderous helplessness of a tough kid, and anything could happen.

Seeing Nipper reminded Shamus of when he himself lived in Blindman's Alley, where he slept against a buckling tenement wall. Winter seeped through that wall. He heard the frozen wall cracking like a tent. At night he reached out to it as he would to a dangerous stranger he didn't want to meet. Next to his pillow was this smooth sheet of ice, so cold that his fingertips burned. There are no lake countries for poor city kids. They drop into nature against tenement walls.

Against his better judgment Shamus turned to the scowling keeper and told him to release Nipper. He flew out, kicking at Shamus. Kathleen caught him by the collar. Nipper howled that if Shamus sprung him, he was also friends with those who threw him in.

The keeper saluted false gold. "How bright the vermin is. And he, schooled only by the strap."

"I'm not going back," Nipper raged. "You said the home is a firetrap."

"It is," she told Shamus.

"Can we talk later?" Shamus pleaded.

"He's yellow." Nipper choked himself to demonstrate he was as good as dead if he went back to the industrial school.

"Let's go to Barnum's Museum for a treat." Kathleen tugged Nipper away. "You can hug the tank with the big white whale."

A brightened Nipper tugged her forward. "I wish the whale to swallow the grown-ups."

"I'm glad you're feeling better." Kathleen squeezed his hand.

TEN

*N*o man worth his salt wanted to be left in the city today. But not every sport fan could afford the illegal ride to an unknown destination. At the last and only stop a bare-knuckle fight would take place for the United States championship. Bare knucks was outlawed in the state. Those who went were gamblers, promoters, pimps, bookies, politicians, reporters, illustrators for the new and popular mass magazines, visiting Englishmen who idolized their own great champs, rabid fans from the wards, and the beau monde.

A fight train chugging north along the Hudson River and then west through New York State found homes and stores shut. Women out of sight. Men peering from afar. Horses hidden. Streets deserted. A New York City fight crowd was viewed as savages. The unusually long passenger train of twenty-six cars was looked on with wary silence as it rolled by. What was most difficult for country people to swallow was that many of this murderous horde were more formally dressed than their own bankers and leaders. Those along the route saw a contradiction where none existed and thus missed the import of their age.

The river valley, so short a distance from the city, was an Eden come to life. The shore lay deep in the storybook shade of water poplars. Centuries-old trees were down at angles to the river, as if they were dying of thirst and fell just short of their mark. Visitors to the valley could easily believe they were the first humans on earth.

A mystic violet tinted deep inside the bowled-out gorges. Mountain shadows sprawled like giant drunks. Game ran wild. Red and white grapes hung down for the picking. Fields of wheat and corn gave the valley a Midwestern landscape. When the ocean's salt thinned in the Hudson, porpoises vanished and sturgeon appeared. New York was the world's largest exporter of caviar. Sloops with shallow drafts skated the tricky tides and capricious valley winds while being dwarfed by the modern floating palaces powered by steam.

West Point was high atop a cliff, the focus of everyone going up and down the river. On the cliff's prominent face were mammoth advertisements extolling GARGLING OIL TO KEEP FROM SPITTING, SAPOLIO FOR CLEANING POTS, SOZODOUT TOOTH POWDER FOR THE SMILE OF SUCCESS.

The men inside the train viewed stereopticon French postcards and fell to playing cards and eating and drinking out of the picnic hampers they brought along. Suddenly the train ground to a crawl up an incline. They had entered a forest of flaming red oak and granite-gray beech with leaves hanging like shards of tobacco. A heeler ran through the cars shouting, "Thieves! We're going to be robbed! Hide your money!"

Tweed peered out the window and his buoyant face fell. Sports who saw the sight stashed their wallets in the trapdoor of their underwear. Tweed muttered, "Did any man ever look this uncivilized? Don't ever say anything against the city." Tweed threatened them.

Along the track were men bundled in horse cloth with puttees of burlap and birch bark tied around their legs with string to keep out the boggy damp. The dumb rudeness in their eyes penetrated sophisticated defenses. Their weathered faces had the finality of a brain growing back as old trees do.

A conductor ran through the cars. "Put away your guns! They want food. Toss them coins."

"Who are they?" asked Tweed.

"Tenant farmers of the Patroons," answered the conductor, and left.

"You're going to see the endless estates of the Patroons," said a reporter, "and you'll know who runs this state. The van Rensselaer duchy is an empire. A city ward has a hundred times, a thousand times more people and little of its power in Albany. Patroons didn't get this enormous amount of land for being brave or adventurous. Van Rensselaer was a diamond merchant who never left Amsterdam. For every fifty men he settled here, the Dutch gave him sixteen miles of river land stretching inland until you don't know there is a river. This is what Southerners were talking about to justify slavery. Patroons had it better than slave owners. Slaves are property. An investment. Slaves have to be fed, clothed, doctored, kept out of jail. A dirt hand tenant farmer is forgotten in jail because he's worth nothing to the Patroon."

Tweed nodded a thanks to the reporter. "I'll always remember your view of this valley and not mine." Tweed opened the window and pitched out a thin slice of ham. An unshaven farmer lunged at the slice and missed. A native dropped to his knees and picked the ham off the ground and swallowed it in one gulp before anyone could grapple with him.

"They're harmless." A Shiny Hat cheered. "They're only hungry."

His observation opened the floodgates of generosity.

A cigar butt sailed out to the rural natives who leapt to catch the butt before it sizzled in the bog. Ashtrays were cleaned out the window.

Tweed heaved scraps from his plate, which were dived for and fought over.

Favorites were chosen and cheered by the color of their puttees. "Blacklegs, catch this. Whitelegs, here's your chance. Bowlegs, let's see a one-hander."

The sports complained when the train picked up speed. The natives trotted alongside, eagerly waiting for the next morsels to fly out the windows. The mad scramble of the rurals, their deftness catching food, their diving for scraps drew hearty applause from the appreciative fans. A spectacular catch was greeted by a fresh barrage of food. A Shiny Hat went overboard. After an elaborate windup and shout—"Take that!"—he flung a five-layered cake and hit a native flush on the chest. The hit drew cheers from inside the train. When a lethal drumstick whizzed by a native, a groan went up. The drumstick ricocheted off a branch with such force it sprayed grease on those below. A stuffed duck was thrown into a group of heads, and on impact the stuffing showered over the thankful.

The locomotive reached the top of the incline and chugged faster. The natives were eating and licking their food off their clothes, faces, necks, on the run and begging for more. A leg of lamb was pitched with diabolic force, hit a rural in the head and knocked him flat. A rousing cheer and bets exchanged at the knockdown. The lamb was snatched from the woozy victim.

An uncorked whiskey bottle tumbled through the air, raining whiskey over trees and men. The ferocious barrage of food and drink did not stop the rurals, who ran faster and bunched closer to become more inviting targets pleading to be pummeled. "More, more!" Ashtrays, spittoons, mugs bounced off them. The train picked up speed as every car was splattering the countryside with food from the city.

The next morning the train pulled into the lake port city of Buffalo, which to New Yorkers was the North Pole. Trains from other parts of the country had arrived and were hissing and popping. The fight crowd had taken over the hotels and saloons, and a wild variety of men and women stalked the streets.

Talk was about the great mill they had come to see. California prospectors came with the dirt of their state on their clothes as a badge of honor. Cowboys, cattle barons, Chicago grain speculators were thrown in with red-coated British officers down from Canada. The largest, toughest delegation was champ Morrissey's. The sniggering highlight were the dandies who curled their hair, wore long leather gloves and unwalkable narrow boots trimmed with sable.

Tweed hurried to the grandest hotel to see if Augusta had checked in. The lobby was one big bar. Drinkers jammed in, living on rumors, seeking denials and expecting anything. The Benicia Boy Heenan was laid up with a game leg! Was it rumor? Fact? Another trick to drive up the odds on the favorite Morrissey? No, no! The Boy has not been in Buffalo and is not to be seen! Where's the Boy training? That's it, the Boy has not been seen training! Here's an eyewitness. He's seen Heenan. Spectators pushed Tweed out of the way to press around the little man.

"The Boy has lain abed five days." Groans. "His leg is game." Groans and cheers.

The eyewitness could be a Heenan man jacking up the odds. Who but a Heenan man could see Heenan since no one else has? A punch is thrown at the solid eyewitness, who ducks into the crowd.

If Heenan has a game leg, the mill has to be postponed. No! Heenan needs the money. Money on the Boy would dry up if not for California gold plunging recklessly on their hero.

Tweed wedged his way to the front desk where a letter awaited him. He recognized Augusta's crimson stationery: "Dearest Bill, I've snuck out of this noisy zoo to nearby Niagara Falls. Meet you among the honeymooners. I need their inspiration. Your heart, the Scarlet A."

A hand clutched Tweed's arm with deference, yet imposing pressure as if directing a servant. Tweed was about to elbow his nasty touch away when he handed Tweed a card bearing a gold ceremonial seal. "I am Commodore Vanderbilt's lawyer, Chauncey Depew. The commodore wishes you to have a lifetime pass on his railroad."

"Thanks to the commodore." Tweed knew Depew to be the image of the new lawyer. Depew had little to do with the law simple soldiers die for. Depew was a tireless lobbyist. Jewelry resting on velvet could not present wealth more quietly, nor stir the depths of promise more turbulently.

"If I can be of help to you in Albany, don't hesitate to call."

A cry went up, turning the fight crowd into a herd. "The steamers are going!" Steamers in the harbor were tooting. "We're going to Lake Point Island. The Canadian side of Lake Erie."

Lake Erie creates an isolation one only expects to find in the middle of the great prairies. After riding for hours a cry went up as the boat neared the cold-water air of the island. "Follow the stakes-and-rope man!" A man shouldering stakes and ropes went over the side into a lighter. The fans scrambled after him for ringside positions.

By the time Tweed and his cronies arrived, the square had been set up, and Heenan's backers were rightly in an uproar. The square was on sand when it should be on sod. Morrissey the champ had the right to choose the site. He chose sand, knowing a big man with a game leg was goners. Heenan's bettors shouted for postponement, a different site. They raised the cry that only sod was legal. All agreed sand would destroy a game-leg pugilist.

The champ's happy backers taunted the Californians with being sore losers. Their Boy from outside San Francisco couldn't win. Anger from the Boy's backers turned to cheers when they sighted their unassuming giant modestly approaching between his seconds.

There were two good reasons not a boo was heard. Boy Heenan was a colossus of a man. The second reason contradicted the first. The Boy's good nature shone from his face. Heenan was not called the Boy for nothing. He was taller, thicker, harder in body and softer in face than anyone could have imagined.

Heenan was a good giant whose parts did not go together. His towering physique gave him his chance at a jackpot. Unfortunately this jackpot was in a bloody trade alien to his nature. Every man of honest heart could feel kinship with the Boy. Heenan, as sport hero, was invaluable. He touched the honesty in men.

Tweed was impressed by the calm Heenan, who resembled a tribal chief. The Boy bore the simple pride of a dead game mug. His face appeared soft in contrast to his body and was suprisingly handsome. His fists were darkly stained from pickling to toughen his skin and keep cuts from flaring open. His handsome face was also stained from pickling and gave him a savage nobility.

The Boy walked stripped to the waist and wearing a tall beaver hat. To announce he had come to fight, he threw his hat in the ring. He did it without bravado or defiance and earned a loud cheer for his poise.

The keen-eyed British promoters were quick to remark how perfect a foe the Boy would be against their own artful champion, Sayers.

Heenan climbed through the ropes and sat in his corner, a good-natured giant dropping in for tea.

Before a fight the fans feel part of one big, loud, invincible family. This spirit gave Tweed a satisfying glow. The optimism underlying sports made him think of Vanderbilt's backing. Every goal he dreamed about was burning a hole in his pocket.

Fans hovered about Heenan's corner, bandying remarks on his chances. Bettors against the Boy aimed their shafts at disturbing him. The Boy paid no heed. His quiet face showed he enjoyed attentive fans without worshiping them.

Tweed's height allowed him to look over the heads of the crowd. He admired the giant's character, taking the coarsest barb without a quibble when weaker men would have killed for half of what was said within earshot. The Boy's keeping an inner eye on the main prize was an element of the true champ already in him.

"Boss, ever see a bare-knuckle fight?" asked a reporter.

"Never been my pleasure."

"The fight is to exhaustion. The rules are against a quick knock-out. Strength must be saved for the long run. The madman is one who comes in to slog from the start. Yet the slogger wins the hearts of the fans if not the fight. He's remembered for his fire long after careful champs are forgotten."

"Heenan is monstrous," observed Tweed, "yet not rock-hard."

"A big man can't be rock-hard. He couldn't move."

"The champ is shrewd by not showing up."

"Right, Boss. The Boy has been sitting too long."

A raucous cheering. Morrissey is spotted strutting. He doffs his hat with a bravado flourish and waves both arms to ignite his cheering boosters. When the applause threatens to ease, Morrissey shies his castor into the ring and receives a loud ovation as he plays to his fans.

The champ's hat skidded to a halt before Heenan's tree-trunk legs to taunt him with the challenge. This increased the applause for Morrissey. The champ kept waving his arms triumphantly as he climbed through the ropes and strutted over to shake Heenan's hands. The cruel and handsome champ was everything he pretended: thug for hire, mackerel, gambler, thief, strongman, policy dealer, saloon keeper and Tammany pride.

A gentlemen climbed into the ring to announce: "Mr. Francis McCabe will be the umpire on behalf of the Boy. Mr. William Mulligan on behalf of the champion John Morrissey. There will be a short delay."

"Boooooooo!"

"Morrissey and Heenan can't agree on a referee."

Umpires and seconds huddled in the center of the ring to chose a referee from one of the prestigious gentlemen present.

"Heenan," a spectator protested, "shouldn't fight with a game leg. He can't pack steam behind his punch."

A bystander butted in. "Heenan needs the leg to hit off. But the Britisher Hammer Lane went thirteen rounds against Molyneux with a game hand."

"That," said a third, "is because Hammer Lane stupidly slogged in there with all his might. You can't fight bare knucks that way."

The fans were silenced by another announcement.

"Professor Page of Boston will be the referee." Halfhearted applause. Morrissey bolts from his stool complaining. "My umpire agreed, but I didn't." Impatient rumble from the crowd. Heenan surprises by getting into the act. "I don't want Professor Page."

"How," asks the announcer, "can you refuse your own nominee?"

The Boy strolls to his corner, ignoring the question. Smart money believes Heenan is simply countering the champ's pesky tactics.

Morrissey addresses the strained crowd, which has been through this rigmarole before. "It appears to me from so many persons having been proposed and rejected by the Boy's party that the Boy hasn't come to fight."

Boos and catcalls. "Damn right the Boy shouldn't fight. Who picked the sand? Boooo! The match has to be on sod or it's off!"

Morrissey, stung by his courage being questioned, could have emptied a pistol into the crowd. "I came here to fight."

Four referees meet to iron out the trouble, and finally their plan is announced. "The well-known and highly respected New Yorker, Mr. Louis Beiral, will commence as the first referee." A sassy burst of mock applause. The timekeeper glanced at the heatless red sun setting in the sky and gave the signal to start. It was twenty-seven minutes to four.

The referee called the fighters to the scratch in the center of the ring and spoke without emotion. "A pugilist who is bleeding profusely or losing his sight or consciousness and can no longer protect himself can end the round by dropping to one knee. His seconds have thirty seconds to carry him back to his corner and minister to him. If after thirty seconds the pugilist has not regained control of his faculties, he must come out to the scratch. The pugilist can then, without being hit, fall to one knee to end the round. He now has an additional thirty seconds to regain his faculties and rest. The pugilist may continue this procedure round after round until he regains full control of his faculties or has his bleeding stopped. In the interest of the sport you are not to abuse this rule. Do not take the fall in order to coast. Is that clear? All agreed?"

Both fighters and their seconds nod.

"If the fallen pugilist cannot be brought to his corner in thirty seconds, he is deemed a beaten man. No champion is deemed beaten unless he fails to come up to the scratch in the required time or if his second declares him beaten.

"The purse shall be publicly divided in the ring among the pugilists, notwithstanding any private agreement to the contrary.

"No pugilist is to hit his opponent when opponent is down, or seize him by the hair, or the breeches, or any part below the waist.

"A man on his knees is reckoned down.

"Shake hands like gentlemen. Return to your corners. Come out when I order you to the scratch. Good luck to the both of you."

Heenan returned to his corner while Morrissey harangued the crowd from the ring. "A thousand dollars to seven hundred I beat the Benecia Boy!" Loud boos. "A thousand to seven hundred fifty I beat the Boy within an hour." The champ's roughs roar their approval, but no takers.

Morrissey peacocked over to Heenan's corner to badger the quiet giant. "A thousand to six hundred I'm the champ after this fight." Raising the odds brought applause without bringing bets. To the dismay of Heenan's backers and the surprise of all the fans, the Boy does not stand up to stare down Morrissey. Heenan instead confesses, "I don't have the money."

Morrissey is infuriated by this artless confession. He shouts at the Boy, "Three hundred I'll gain the first knockdown."

The Boy ignores him without rancor.

Morrissey bettors scatter through the crowd boldly hawking bets. "First knockdown by the champ! Five to three." They flush out a few Heenan bets. Morrissey works himself up shouting at the placid giant. "Five hundred dollars to three hundred I'll draw first blood." The Boy remains silent, patient, waiting for the fight to begin.

Morrissey gazes down on the giant, who takes no notice. "Five hundred to three hundred I win first fall!" Heenan remains quietly to himself without being critical of the swaggering champ. The fans chant for the fight to begin. Morrissey boastfully waves his arms in victory and returns to his corner.

The referee orders the fighters to the scratch. The Boy toes the mark first. His stance for so big a man is not without skill. His left is extended and bent. His right is up and ready. His arms and legs are prepared to go on offense or defense. The Boy is a statue with signs he can move.

Morrissey is an engine of a fighter. He's strong, durable, loose-limbed and aroused. He's gone in the stomach though it's flat. A wall of muscles is not to be seen. The champ is as light on his feet as the challenger is heavy.

"Their windpipes are cleared." A fan thought it an excellent sign for a ripping long fight. "They don't spit. They were fed crackers before going to bed to absorb the night's saliva."

The fight crowd, at last, goes silent. In the soft orange light of an autumn afternoon the fighters circle each other. The brutish circling for a weakness is a slow dance of tension, showing they are becoming less human. The flapping of the birds wheeling overhead is all that can be heard.

Morrissey throws sharp feints to scare out an opening. Though the Boy does not favor his game leg, he has no footwork to speak of, and that bodes ill. Without footwork Heenan needs raw, hammering power. He can't hammer unless he has two strong legs. The Boy's flaw is painfully evident from the start, so that his backers can almost feel the blows before they land on him.

Morrissey's lightning left ignites a roar that flushes the birds away. A more astonished roar follows. The giant has artfully parried the blow. The Heenan parry rightfully causes uneasiness in the Morrissey ranks. That fine a skill from so raw a galoot does not add up. Worse, the parry generates dark suspicions. Is the Boy's game leg a hoax? Is Heenan biding his time to powder the cocky champ? Whatever the answer, Morrissey has to test for it.

The champ lands a stinging left on the Boy's face. The first clap of knuckles against bone, the grill marks punched into flesh bring cheers. The crowd relaxes out of their anxiousness. The mill has begun.

Amazing how Heenan skillfully parries one moment and how defenseless he is the next. Morrissey comes at him with the air of a man putting away his dessert. He hits Heenan another wicked facer. The cheers die aborning.

Heenan socks a counter to Morrissey's left eye. A doubly demoralizing blow in that it easily plows through Morrissey's defense. The Boy's strength has the Californians shouting, "Hammer! Hammer! Hammer!"

Morrissey skillfully clouts the Boy another facer. The Boy drives a counter facer. Suddenly the champ's nose is bleeding.

"First blood! First blood!" Heenan's jubilant bettors jump up and down. Bookies pay off on first blood as the mill goes on.

The reporter scribbling away at Tweed's elbow sees as fast as anyone the pattern the fight is taking. "Puncher against counterpuncher. Let's see if puncher Morrissey can hit rib roasters after taking the Boy's rattling counters in return."

The clapping of knuckles against body tingles through the spectators. The cool lake air is forgotten. Morrissey and Heenan fall into a clinch and there's no letup. Each fighter works the stomach and their breathing bursts out in grunts. They break by shoving off against each other, only the champ does it with a stiff hand on the Boy's jaw.

They cautiously feel each other out while moving closer. Heenan is wary of the champ's quickness, and Morrissey is alert to the Boy's devastator.

Heenan confidently goes on the attack with a straight-arrow left high on Morrissey's head. Morrissey is forced into counterpunching, and he desperately wants to get out of this role. He buries a fist into Heenan's billboard stomach. Counterpunching means taking the Boy's devastator and finding strength to punch back. Heenan begins to destroy Morrissey with lead punches. The Boy's tremblers leave Morrissey too weak to counter.

The reporter tells Tweed, who is disappointed in the champ. "Morrissey is forced to give up the attack that made him champ. Heenan's counterpunching is too murderous to take. The champ is trapped between styles. Taking the first blow will leave Morrissey weak, and giving the lead blow will leave him open to Heenan's devastator. But there's a bad sign for both. They already appear eaten up by the blows buzzing in them."

"The champ is lost?" Tweed didn't want to be bewildered.

"No. The sand is bringing out the Boy's game leg."

Though Heenan is a target as big as a wall, he keeps throwing straight-arrow lefts through Morrissey's guard with an ease that dazzles the crowd. No one is more silent than the Morrissey backers who had eagerly panned the crowd for bets. Heenan keeps moving in, hooking left and right to the champ's head. Left and right to Morrissey's ribs. Morrissey can't believe what is happening to him.

Heenan drums lefts and rights up and down the bobbing Morrissey. Morrissey's counters flick harmlessly off the giant moving in. The clap of Heenan's fists against Morrissey are short bursts of applause leaving red-grilled knuckle prints. Heenan's fans are hollering themselves hoarse.

Morrissey takes his desperate stand near the ropes, the top of his head bending toward Heenan to ward off the devastators. Heenan's lefts and rights have Morrissey back on his heels like a punching toy that keeps righting itself. Morrissey covers up in expectation of the tremblers. The Boy's sock to the stomach immediately shows up in the redness of Morrissey's eyes. Heenan's huge, cutting fists rap paralyzing stingers down Morrissey's neck, shoulders, stomach. Morrissey counters to the ribs, but his blows don't roast.

Heenan bulls in with the fury of a finisher. Morrissey meets him head-on. Both men drub the body at a frenzied pace. Morrissey's muscled shoulders sag from a devastator to his chest.

In this overpowering attack California money doesn't like what it sees! The Boy has forgotten. The Boy is slogging. Bare knuckles is a test of endurance. Morrissey is iron. Yet the Boy smells the kill this early, and the crowd smells that the Boy smells the kill and it is bedlam. The Boy must win before his leg gives out.

Game leg and all, Heenan steps in without fear, driving lefts and rights, wilder lefts and rights. Morrissey is pounded against the ropes. Morrissey is bobbing, covering up, desperate to survive. The Boy has pinned Morrissey to the ropes like putty. Heenan's fans are leaping up and down. "Hammer! Hammer! Hammer!"

Lefts and rights smash into Morrissey's cheeks, bloody his mouth. Morrissey is rocked. Morrissey is swaying. Morrissey's eyes are clouding with soup. Morrissey shoots out a weak counter. The pounding has taken the snap out of the champ. He is wobbling under the devastators. He is defenseless.

Heenan moves in for the kill, smashing through the champ's guard. Morrissey won't punch first and leave himself open for a counterpunch. He is doomed if he does and doomed if he doesn't. The Boy lets fly a straight-arrow paralyzer at the helpless champ. Morrissey woozily ducks. The giant's devastator strikes the ring pole!

The Boy winces. The Boy doubles up. The Boy is in pain. His bettors are groaning. The Boy stands lost in the ring, swallowing pain. His broken, swelling fist hangs lifelessly at his side.

Morrissey bobs in. Heenan falls into a clinch to give himself time to recover. Morrissey shoves him off. Heenan's busted fist is swelling pink through the dark brine. Morrissey throws a left and right at the Boy covering up. Morrissey pummels the Boy and gets no counter. Heenan, dazed and in pain, will not give ground. Morrissey forces the fight, sinking left and rights deep into the giant's stomach.

The Boy's backers stand dumb at this unexpected reversal.

Morrissey's bettors are jumping up and down.

The Boy's hurt face cannot be seen in the toe-to-toe barrage. Heenan is punching with one hand. The fighters clinch. They are struggling for a fall. The crowd is wild.

Morrissey slips his leg into the crook of the Boy's game leg to throw him. Morrissey is cracking Heenan's leg back. Heenan's face is distorted by pain. His injured leg will not bend. Morrissey is crushing it. Heenan's eyes are popping. The Boy is gasping for air. He's off-balance. He must throw Morrissey before he falls. Morrissey himself needs a breath of air for strength to throw the giant. Morrissey pauses an instant for that breath, and Heenan throws him to the sand. Heenan jumps on the fallen Morrissey with all his weight. Morrissey's breath groans out of him.

The Boy's backers go wild. "First fall! First fall!"

The bookies are paying off on first fall. The Boy's bettors are kissing their winnings, waving their winnings, pocketing their winnings with Indian war whoops.

Morrissey's bettors are stunned. The Boy has come back from a game leg and busted hand.

No fan can recall such ferocity so early in a mill. Everyone's pulse is racing at being in on a kill.

Tweed is downcast. He tells the reporter if Morrissey doesn't come through, the champ will not have the reputation to terrorize the polls at election time, stop enemy votes.

Heenan's seconds are outwardly elated and inwardly troubled. The pickled fists are swelling and losing their cutting edge. The Boy's wrists are also swelling. Wrists are more important than fists. Sensitive wrists reduce the steam behind the blows.

The first round has lasted five minutes and left Heenan breathing hard.

In Morrissey's corner the seconds have less time. They had to lug the champ back to his stool. Morrissey's ribs are purpled. His seconds are massaging life back into him and sucking the bleeding cuts on his fists until they close.

"Time!" The referee calls the fighters to the scratch. "Round two."

"Look at the legs," the reporter advises Tweed. "That'll tell you which fighter is more fatigued."

Both fighters are prompt to the scratch. Both fighters are tired. There's no feinting to open this round. Both fighters are tired enough to rely on the desperate solution, the hammer.

Morrissey throws a stinger that is gracefully parried. Heenan is applauded. The giant's skill continues to amaze. Morrissey loops another stinging left, which is countered by an explosive Heenan left to the jaw. Morrissey is stunned. A bullet right to the champ's stomach has him reeling. Guts are all that keeps the champ up. Heenan's fans are screaming.

The Boy moves in, waiting for Morrissey to throw the first

punch. The champ flicks a left to Heenan's ear. Heenan unloads a left and right. Morrissey flicks out a weak left and right to the Boy's ribs. Token blows to show Heenan and his fans he's alive. The Boy powders him with a booming left. The damage of the Boy's earlier devastators can only be surmised. Swollen as his knuckles are now, Heenan almost takes Morrissey's head off. He keeps punching the iron out of Morrissey.

Heenan is using his longer reach to get in and out without taking a blow in return. Morrissey's roughs are shouting at the champ to take the fight to the crippled Boy. While the roughs are shouting, Heenan staggers Morrissey with a straight-arrow paralyzer to the cheek. Morrissey swings wildly. Heenan punishes him for that swing, digging a left into the champ's stomach. Morrissey's shoulders slump. He falls into a clinch, draping his body around Heenan to drag him down. Heenan shoves his hand in Morrissey's face to break the clinch. Roars from Morrissey's roughs: "Foul! Gouging!"

Heenan bear-hugs Morrissey to crush him. Positioning himself to throw Morrissey is a mistake. This gives Morrissey a breather to grasp Heenan's neck. They fall to the sand. Heenan spurts out and jumps up and throws his body high into the air to crash down on Morrissey. The champ is battered senseless. His fans are hooting. "Foul! Call the foul!"

The referee warns the Boy against unnecessary roughing. Heenan ignores the referee. He walks proudly to his corner, his great chest heaving like a bellows.

Morrissey is dragged back to his stool. His fists do not have to be leeched. The champ has to be crisply slapped into alertness. Pain brings signs of life into his eyes. His second whispers into the champ's beet-red, curling ear. "Coast, John." Morrissey's eyes go blank. Consciousness is seeping out of him, and with it the pain.

"Can you hear me, champ?"

Morrissey blubbers confidently through thickened lips, "I'll take Heenan." His head butting forward under his effort to speak. He closes his eyes. Somewhere inside him—having nothing to do with muscles—he has found a world of mercy.

"Open your eyes, champ."

Morrissey opens his eyes. They are crossed.

"Close them, for God's sake." The second lowers the eyelids as he would on a dead man. "Champ?"

No answer.

"Open."

No response.

"Open your eyes slowly."

Morrissey opens his bruised eyelids with effort. His eyes are straight, but it's difficult to tell whether he's laughing or crying.

"Good boy. The purse is yours. Just hang in. You hear me?"

Morrissey nods yes as his eyes close.

"The Boy's wrists are sponges. Champ?"

Morrissey opens his eyes and stares through his seconds.

"You're a cinch to win. Heenan's got to start pulling his punches or he'll cripple his hands for life."

Morrissey closes his eyes. He could be listening to a bedtime story. When he opens his eyes, they are swimming weightlessly. His seconds work doggedly, circulating life into him. "You caught his best. Heenan's carrying too much weight on his game leg. He's exhausted."

The seconds raise Morrissey to his feet with a show of having to hold their fighter down while actually helping him stand.

Heenan is beached upon his stool, unable to move. He is deaf in one mashed ear from blood and contusions. He has to be talked to on his right side. His fists are swollen melons, his knuckles tiny points of meringue.

"Time!" The referee calls. "Third round."

Both fighters breathe through open lips. Character more than muscle prompts them to the scratch.

Morrissey flares out with no preliminaries—a facer that is astonishingly parried. All fans cheer Heenan. Morrissey stands stock still, shaken as much by Heenan's endless reserve as by his blows. The champ, beaten in both his attack and counterpunching, reverts to the attack that brought him the championship. He lashes out a left to Heenan's eye and a hard right to the nose, expecting no tremblers in return from the exhausted giant with a crippled hand and game leg moving on sand.

Heenan counters with a terrific left over the heart. The champ shudders. His tongue rolls out. He doubles up out of breath. Heenan's backers go wild. But the blow is too painful to Heenan to follow up. The Boy himself is jolted by every punch he lands. His injured fist covered by thinning skin, his wrist and arm throbbing. His game leg is not dragging but has no quickness.

Heenan throws a combination. To the horror of Heenan's backers Morrissey walks through the blows. The champ counters with a left that turns the Boy around.

An unexpected, jolly roar. Heenan glimpses down on his bloated wrists to see if he can risk a punch. Morrissey is too surprised by this pause to take advantage of it. Heenan plods forward on the flats of his feet. The fighters become locked in a struggle for the fall. Morrissey gets his legs in the crook of the Boy's game leg and throws him. The giant nose-dives into the sand. Morrissey throws his body on Heenan with all his might. The sand spouts up from Heenan's gasp.

Heenan's seconds haul him to his stool. A sponge is masked over his puffed face. "Coast," his second orders. Heenan's face is still. He can't hear. "Coast" is hissed close to the Boy's good ear. Heenan shakes him off. He can't stand his swollen wrists being touched. His arms hang limp in buckets of ice-cold lake water.

Morrissey's seconds cheer him on as they bathe life into him. "Nothing to be afraid of. You got him where you want him. Don't let him use his weight to tie you up. He needs rest."

No words from Morrissey, who doubles up and vomits.

"That's a good sign." His second wipes his mouth.

"Time, gentlemen. Fourth round."

Both fighters are slow to the scratch. The Boy's tired legs plant themselves to go from offense to defense, but he can't move quickly. Morrissey is a drunken sailor on leave, hiding his condition from a commanding officer.

Heenan throws a woeful left that lacks distance. This try prompts Morrissey to go for the kill. He crowds the Boy, only to be popped by a wild right to the neck and a left and right roundhouse to the jaw and stomach, and the champ is reeling. The fans are berserk. But Heenan lacks the strength to follow through. When he belatedly comes in, he gets caught with a stinger to the stomach and a wicked right uppercut to the chest.

Heenan throws a left that falls short and pumps a right that also lacks distance. Morrissey buries a left and right in his stomach. They clinch to rest yet savage kidney-punching tattoos off them before both shove off with hands in the other's face.

"Gouging! Gouging!"

The Boy lands a left to the stomach that leaves him open for a rib roaster and a clout to the mouth. Fresh blood trickles over Heenan's thickened lips. Morrissey easily throws Heenan and slams the giant to the sand and jumps on him.

Heenan's seconds drag his carcass back to the corner.

A proud Morrissey is on his feet, but he needs to be walked to his corner. The champ's left eye is shut in the shape of a puffed seashell. When Morrissey sits down, he reveals a startling and exciting insight into his condition. He sits down on his own. He doesn't drop or slump. His backers are cheered. Morrissey has caught his second wind. His seconds grin at what Morrissey himself doesn't know.

"Money in the bank," chirps his second. "He can't hurt you no more."

"Time, gentlemen! Fifth round."

Morrissey stands without help. His eyes have miraculously cleared. His breathing is close to normal. The fierce pounding has brought a deadening weight to his muscles so that he moves like an internally injured man to the scratch.

Heenan, in distress, moves slowly and radiates little life.

Morrissey peppers a left and stinging right to the Boy's unguarded jaw. Heenan staggers back as if knifed. The Boy throws a right to protect himself. Morrissey easily blocks it. The champ moves in with right and left and left and right. Heenan can't counter or defend himself. Morrissey bullies the giant, crowds him, shoulders in with combinations and suffers no return.

Heenan's game leg is dragging. His injured hand is used only as a shield. Morrissey's uncontested blows lean Heenan to the right and left. The Boy has become a punching bag.

Out of nowhere, while being pummeled without mercy, Heenan raises the sponge fist connected to his bloated wrist. Is the Boy signaling to quit? To throw in the towel? No one can blame him. His grilled arm raises, painfully slow. He smashes a straight arrow to Morrissey's jaw.

Morrissey is down!

Heenan's bettors go crazy. "First knockdown! First knockdown!"

The Boy, his focus unsure, his sense of distance lacking, gazes out on the money-changing hands while steadying himself on his wobbly legs.

Morrissey's backers are stupefied as the champ is dragged through the sand to his stool. Though Morrissey is out, Heenan can't find his way back to his corner. When his seconds lead him to his stool, Heenan is unable to sit comfortably, though he is dying to rest. His hands hang limply in the buckets.

The champ's hotheads are pacing around his corner with coats open to reveal pistols. They dare anyone to shout abuse at their champ. Abuse is shouted on the sly and can't be caught.

Fans outside New York wonder out loud who could possibly control this rough bunch. The answer is to point to a large, friendly man enjoying the fight. "That's Boss Tweed."

"Time, gentlemen! Sixth round."

The spectators unite in an ovation for the fighters coming round-shouldered to the scratch.

Though Morrissey suffered the knockdown, Heenan plods slowest. At the scratch the fighters stand gazing at each other like beasts in the field.

Morrissey, without ado, socks Heenan in the mouth as easily as hitting a defenseless stranger and draws fresh blood. Heenan counters with a left, easily stopped, and a right, pathetically short. Heenan is too winded to retreat. Morrissey is too tired to advance.

Morrissey plants his right foot forward and hits off it. A left to Heenan's jaw and a right to his head. Though Morrissey's blows come between pauses, there is no counter from the Boy.

Morrissey advances like a toy winding down, left foot firmly planted yet unsure, right foot firmly planted yet unsure.

Heenan loops a feather duster off Morrissey's shoulder and is rocked by a slow-motion combination of rights and lefts to his breadbasket. Heenan gambles on saving himself by locking into a clinch. The now stronger Morrissey grapples with the giant and throws him to the sand, crashing his weight on Heenan's sprawled body.

Both fighters need to be picked up and lugged to their corners. Heenan can no longer place one foot after the other. He is turning to pudding. Morrissey peacocks even as he is walked, as his seconds would a packing case.

The slow sixth round does not bother the fans. On the contrary, as Tweed's reporter informs him, "This is what they've come to watch. Who has the last drop of energy to survive? Who has the will not to be beaten into a numb existence?"

Tweed feels queasy because he understands all too well.

"Time, gentlemen! Seventh round."

A thunderous ovation for the battered fighters walking to the scratch under their own power.

Morrissey has one eye closed. Though both of the Boy's eyes are open, they no longer reflect a soul. His eyes don't belong to him.

Yet he toes the scratch and throws the first blow. A right easily defended.

Every motion from the tired Morrissey is followed by a pause. He moves in, throwing a left that leaves knuckle grills on Heenan's neck. The misplaced blow has the Boy choked for breath, his mouth wide open as they tumble into a clinch and struggle for the fall. The breathless Heenan is thrown and lies lifeless on the sand. Morrissey jumps as high as he can and lands with all his might on Heenan's chest.

"Foul! Foul!"

The referee curtly waves his arms that the foul is not allowed.

Heenan is dragged to his stool. His fists hang down like dead bulbs pulled from the earth.

Morrissey, the winner of the fall, is still down. He is rolling back and forth on his hands and knees in the sand, trying to raise himself. His head drops, and he gets a mouthful of sand that drips out. He waves his seconds off and gets up without their help to an ovation from all. Then he falls and has to be walked back.

The Boy is suffocating under the eye-smarting sponge masking his face. A surprise confronts his seconds when they lift the sponge. Heenan's face holds the radiance of a false dawn. He is quietly tickled. A queer and gassy smile. Heenan has never looked so relaxed. He is tired, out of mind.

"Time, gentlemen! Eighth round."

The hotly partisan fans are now one in cheering both fighters to the scratch. The astute are laying bets in their minds on whether the champ has fallen victim to the phenomenon of regaining his strength, only to lose his will.

Morrissey wanders in with repeated uncontested lefts to the Boy's face. Heenan slides seasickly along the ropes, pursued by the champ. The Boy is cheered for staying on his feet. Morrissey falls on Heenan and throws the giant into the sand. The Boy hugs the sand to relax as the champ jumps on him.

Heenan is cheered. He is trying to raise himself. His seconds can't afford that luxury. They need every moment to work on him. Buckets of cold lake water are dashed against him while he's being suffocated by the astringent sponge that causes him to choke and gag. Heenan is becoming cheerful without being alert.

"Time, gentlemen! Ninth round."

Both men take their first tottering steps to the scratch to an emotional ovation. The unsteady Boy teeters on his game leg, a trace of a smile on his relaxed face. Morrissey stings him with a left to that smile and a right to the ribs.

Summoning strength from God knows where, the Boy clouts the champ on the jaw.

The surprised champ stands flat-footed. The Boy recoils in pain from his own punch. The fans go wild as the Boy lands another left on the champ's unguarded face and recoils in pain, the Boy's last punch burning on his own face. The Boy's rib roaster misses and turns him around.

Morrissey and the crowd are in awe of the Boy, who is exhausted, limping, possessing useless hands and still throwing punches.

The champ stalks Heenan, crowds him into his own corner and clouts him with a right to the midsection and repeated lefts to the mouth and nose. The Boy's lower face is awash in blood.

The champ clutches Heenan about the waist to throw him but does not have the strength though his muscles ripple with his effort. The Boy does not have the strength to break the grip. Morrissey's tenacity dumps the Boy. He falls on him, lacking vengeance.

Both fighters are helped to their corner. Heenan remains conscious through will alone. His strength is nowhere else to be seen. Morrissey has lost his reviving second breath.

The flurry in the Boy's corner comes from the seconds trying to sponge vitality into him, though they know nothing can reach their courageous challenger. They beg him to coast. The Boy shakes his battered head no. A second talks into the side of the Boy's head with the good ear. "Coast till you can breathe."

Heenan opens his mouth to say no, and blood pours out.

"Just drop to one knee."

Heenan shakes his head no, and blood spills over his lower lip.

"Time, gentlemen! Tenth round."

Morrissey's corner cheers in anticipation of the kill.

The sight of both warriors moving to the scratch ignites an uproar. Morrissey can't hear it. He is deaf in one ear, and the other buzzes. One eye is closed, and gashes crisscross his face like war paint. His mouth opens for grunt breathing. His legs move chain-legged for balance.

The Boy kicks forward, believing bees are swarming before him. The two men stare like dumb animals who can't recognize each other. Morrissey shows strong legs by sending home a facer.

The Boy does not go down. Somewhere in him he has flinched, but this doesn't show up on his face.

The Boy catches the champ straight on the forehead like stunning an ox, only the Boy recoils in pain. Heenan keeps coming on unsteady legs. The champ squints unbelievingly at the Boy. Heenan's leg drags heavily, leaving the trail in the sand of a wounded animal. Yet Heenan is going in for the kill!

Heenan's backers are going berserk. The Boy throws lefts and rights to the champ's stomach, the clap gone from his knuckles. Pain shoots through Heenan at each blow he lands. His punching is weaker, shorter, more futile as his fans cheer him on.

The champ measures the Boy coming in, planting his legs to throw a slaughterhouse punch. The defenseless Boy is an open target coming to him. The champ wallops him with a left to the jaw. The Boy is stopped in his tracks, but he won't go down. Morrissey blasts a right to his unguarded stomach. The Boy takes the punch without flinching. He counters with a right that doesn't land, and the crowd cheers his miss.

Morrissey lets fly an uppercut that throws the Boy's head back. Both fighters are throwing punches at the same time. Both are missing. Both are trying desperately to land.

Morrissey stuns the giant with a blow that turns Heenan around. Morrissey clinches, throws the giant and jumps on his chest.

The blood-smeared Morrissey receives an ovation. He gets up and walks unaided, but to the wrong corner. His seconds quickly retrieve him and escort the champ with dignity so as not to tarnish his effort.

The Boy is left hugging the sand. His seconds stand him up like a bag of feed against their shoulders. The fans see blood dripping out of the Boy's ear.

Morrissey's bettors are jubilant. "A concussion! Heenan's out! A concussion!"

The end in sight, the timekeeper signals the referee to begin his ominous count as fair warning: "Five seconds. Ten seconds. Fifteen seconds. Twenty seconds."

No movement from Heenan's corner with ten seconds to go.

Morrissey's fans are starting their cheer.

"Twenty-five seconds."

The entire crowd begins applauding both fighters.

"Twenty-seven seconds."

Heenan's bloodied head hangs forward, jaw pressed into his chest. His once powerful fists are dunked lifelessly into buckets.

"Twenty-eight seconds."

The applause is growing into a thunderclap for both men.

"Twenty-nine seconds."

The fans are cheering their lungs out.

"Thirty seconds."

An abrupt silence to hear the referee.

"Time, gentlemen! Eleventh round."

The crowd is stunned.

The Boy's seconds are climbing out of the ring.

An amazed cry escapes from a fan. "Heenan is coming out! Heenan is coming out!"

The Boy is walking zigzag to the scratch, an ovation to keep him going. It's no longer possible to tell which fighter the crowd is betting on.

The Boy stands alone under a deafening roar.

It is Morrissey who has not come out.

Morrissey staggers from his corner. The ovation doesn't slacken or register on his face. The eleventh round starts under an uproar.

Morrissey can't believe the Boy stands before him. He does not venture forward. He does not know what to expect. He is more cautious than at any time during the fight. His seconds are hollering to keep his good eye away from the Boy.

The unceasing roar flushes birds out of distant trees, swirling into huge, spreading fans wheeling away from the island.

Morrissey push-punches Heenan in the chest and easily dodges a weak return, only the fighters can't hear the deafening roar. Roughs and gentlemen have lost their voices or gone hoarse.

Heenan carries the fight to the champ. He has clearly beaten the advantage of speed and agility out of the champ.

Morrissey plants his feet, waiting for Heenan. The champ needs a few seconds to let his legs grow solid under him. He connects with a roundhouse that turns the Boy about-face. Morrissey plods after him with a facer. A left and right to the grilled welts on the Boy's stomach. Heenan keeps barreling in, throwing wild lefts and rights that fall far short of their mark.

Morrissey catches Heenan with repeated lefts and rights to the face and body. Heenan knows he can't clinch, or Morrissey will throw him.

A fan can't take it any longer. "Coast!" Hardened sports take up the cry. "Coast, Heenan. Coast!"

The Boy will not coast. He wades in with lefts and rights that stop in the air. The champ slips in and slams a right to the stomach, and a left to the throat.

The Boy goes down.

The champ is too weak to fall on him. He knows he would not get up if he fell. He can't finish his victory.

Heenan's seconds quickly haul him to his corner.

The champ is led to his stool spitting blood.

The referee knows he's become the center of attention. Everyone lives months in his gloomy counting of seconds.

Pails of ice-cold water are dashed against the Boy's face. A bucket of cold water is tipped into the front of his breeches.

"Fifteen seconds."

The Boy's ballooned fists hang down at his side. The water has been used to revive him.

"Twenty seconds."

The cruelly astringent sponge is pressed against Heenan's mug. He is slumped inert on his stool.

"Twenty-five seconds."

The sponge reddens the eyes of the seconds, causing them to turn away as they press it on the Boy's face.

"Twenty-nine seconds."

The sponge is slowly raised. The Boy is insensible.

"Thirty seconds."

The crowd, expecting a miracle, is silent.

"Time, gentlemen! Twelfth round."

The sponge is wrung over Heenan's head, and the burning liquid runs down his face. The stare of the Boy doesn't break.

The second heaves the foul-smelling, blood-dripping sponge into the ring.

The fight is over!

The referee goes over to Morrissey. The seconds help the champ to stand. Morrissey is not aware anyone has approached him. The referee raises Morrissey's lifeless right arm in victory. "The fight is stopped after eleven rounds. The winner and still champion, John Morrissey!"

Morrissey lets his head lurch forward as a bow to the fallen giant. He motions dumbly to be helped to Heenan's corner. His seconds hold him under the arms and walk him with dignity.

Heenan does not know the champ.

The champ raises the Boy's bloated fist and kisses it in token of the giant's valor.

Every ear is ringing with the tumultuous ovation except the fighters, whose heads are filled with buzzing. A dumb, unbeatable humanity shines through them.

Tweed's reporter shouts at him over the din. "This is the most savage twenty-one minutes of fighting ever seen."

"We got our man!" Tweed was drunk on the fight. "I'm running Morrissey for Congress!"

ELEVEN

*H*ow was that stupid fight?" Augusta wore a brazenly light wrap.

"Magnificent!" Tweed felt he was the winner. The excitement drained him. Sports gave him all the thrills he needed for the moment. Sex after sports became an indulgence rather than a craving. It wasn't only the fight: He couldn't get Vanderbilt out of his mind. He fingered the pass in his pocket, knowing it was an amulet for better times. A lazy mood was on him of having Augusta as he would a Delmonico oyster. One glance at Augusta and he knew better. Fine women smell abstracted men. They smell distractions as easily as men learn to hide in them.

"What happened to your voice?" She was critical.

"I'm hoarse from cheering."

"Isn't that childish?"

The sensuous laziness he'd felt on entering was gone. A moment in her presence and he brimmed with energy. He knew it would be disastrous to tell her his secret obsession, yet he had to boast, puff up his accomplishment, because she was a prize. "Vanderbilt is falling in my pocket."

She was disappointed. "I thought you came for sex?"

Tweed scratched his neck, embarrassed by her directness.

"You're telling me that knowing Vanderbilt doesn't make me a better lover?"

"Or human being." A petulant breeze ran through her.

"That shows how much you know." He proudly displayed his railway pass, rubbing it between his palms for luck, blowing on it with appreciation, caressing the pass before slipping it back into his inside pocket with a pat of pleasure.

"Remember what you once said that so attracted me to you?"

He waited on tenterhooks.

"You said you had to be careful you don't buy men through their greed when you can win them over more cheaply by their vanity." She smiled, and the pass became an albatross.

"Was I ever that smart?"

"I'm not going to bed with a man who is hoarse. Or who thinks a stupid railway pass is his magic wand when it was given just to soften you up."

"I adore you when you're mad." His face glowed.

"You're purposely putting yourself beneath me. I can't go to bed with a man who lowers himself." Her spark showed she meant it.

"I lower myself out of admiration."

Her voice came on the rise, and he knew it was trouble. "Your happiness seeing me was more like betting on a horse."

He begged for mercy. "Do you know what it means to have the commodore in your corner? The thief means respectability. No one turns away a Vanderbilt man. Once you are bought by Vanderbilt, you have risen in the world. His bribes are a knighthood."

"And you accuse me of letting street openings and deals come into our sex life and ruin it?"

"It's not only a railway pass. It's a passport to the national scene."

"I'm glad something sincerely attracts you." She was drawn to the vitality pouring through his robust candor. His energy touched her intimately though he wasn't paying her attention.

"The commodore cheated the government on mail subsidies. He sold the government troopships in time of war whose planks were ready to fall out on calm seas. The U.S. Senate found him guilty. He wasn't jailed. He wasn't fined. He wasn't asked to return the money. To be judged guilty yet keep what you stole?"

He suddenly caressed an oak table with a strong emotion that startled her.

"My father had more respect for a piece of wood than the commodore has for people. My father died obscure. The commodore is a god of this age. Anyone can be crooked." Energy burned through him as he apologized for himself. "He has only to take things as they are."

His outrageous insights stimulated her more than his hands. He made eminent men look like they had blinkers on. After knowing Tweed she could never go back to her husband. No admirer of her beauty ever respected her more than Tweed in his candor.

The steam in him would not stop. "You want to leave me?" He was hurt and defiant at the same time. "Enjoy your ignorance. Go back to men who swallow garbage with impeccable taste for it."

Augusta covered her mouth to hide her exhilaration. She had waited for him in a sheer wrap to keep herself open. She was proud of her forwardness in promising to be at his hotel. Yet her pride suffered that she could give him such a promise. Sex was her naked self, a privacy not to be shared without being inspired. Being totally surprised and scrambled by intimacy was an experience she craved with frightening zeal.

Tweed's physical form was a barrier. Led by his parade-drum belly, Tweed gave her an unprepared feeling for sex, though she had prepared for weeks. She felt irritable because her expectation was so intense. She secretly, hopefully prayed it was healthy to be irritable before sex, and that it wasn't a sign of buried unhappiness about what she was about to do.

"Let's go out." Tweed patted his Santa Claus belly as though needing to get in touch with nature.

"I didn't come to Niagara Falls to see the town."

"This has been such a marvelous day." He begged to let it stay that way.

Her eyes dared him. "Too good for sex?"

"I didn't say that." He was flustered.

"But you want to dine out." *Clown* was left unsaid.

"Only to settle you down."

"Me? Down? I wasn't this ready on my honeymoon. *Vanderbilt. Railway pass. Hoarse.*"

"See all the obstacles you put up?"

"You put me on a pedestal. Knowing it'll take me hours, if ever, to come down and feel human again."

He said earnestly, "I want you whenever you're ready."

She dropped her wrap. "I'm ready."

"Please, Augusta, I've had such an exciting day. Get dressed. You haven't seen Buffalo." He was on fire with his newly opened path to the White House around Belmont, and here she was being critical of him. He bent with effort to recover her wrap. His eyes, following the lean line of her legs, made her stand awkwardly. His warm face, near her bare legs, brought out a peach tint. The marvel of Augusta was in her peach tint of heat and her intimate body scent even as she looked aristocratic.

Intimacy had a poignant way of first paralyzing her. Her proud eyes shading inward as if searching for shelter in herself. A trembling passed through her shoulders that was so distant, he could not believe it came from a woman so close to him. Augusta's wanting to share herself while remaining aloof was haunting.

In that shared moment as his warm face came closely up the length of her nakedness he felt they exchanged the thought that their successes had made them so willful, they believed anything could be commanded. In her willingness to succeed with him against her temperament by coming here, waiting for him, being at his call, he saw his own coldness. He was right. Without warning they hid their feelings by kissing demonstratively. Kissing this way kept them from looking closely at each other. She suddenly bolted, hollow-cheeked, parched, insulted, and was near tears, fighting herself. "What's the matter?"

"I haven't been truly touched, yet you want sex with me?"

He didn't want to hint he was hurt. He dreaded exposing his increasing lack of connection that came with a leader having his sex serviced, and the more he was driven to recapture a sex of warmth, the colder he was getting.

"To lose your voice about a fight?" She ragged him, going to the closet to dress swiftly but surely, her layers of clothes creating a bell shape though her sensual figure was lean. Her feathered hat shaded her striking eyes. Her crested hairdo distorted, for stylish reasons, the shape of her intelligent head.

"Maybe I did come too satisfied from that great mill."

Augusta was amused at his cheating way of thinking about himself, even when he was trying to be fair. "A show of honesty doesn't balance the books."

"What a whirlwind you are."

"Don't start praising me," she warned.

He knew dark rivers ran in her, but he dare not voice it. What's more, he knew a few bends in those rivers deepened her beauty. Against his better judgment he had to praise her. What excruciating praise! "You're most desirable when you want sex as a battle to avenge yourself."

"That's not true," she said calmly, knowing they were coming together by the uncertainty she unleashed in him. They would not, thank God, come together routinely. Augusta swore to herself there would be passion, or why cheat on her husband? She wanted to experience a revelation of herself she had so far only imagined.

"You're testing me to make sure I deserve you?" He had hit on her secret, and this threw a fever into him. "You're attracted to my political power? But you don't know if I have that power with a woman. If I don't? You think political power is useless."

Augusta connected with the storm in him. Her lively eyes told him he was correct. But—and this was her challenge!—she was helpless to give herself to him. He had to touch the right deep chord in her.

Tweed was ecstatic, though he knew ecstasy was wrong in her presence. This was his own boxing match, exciting and punishing as any he watched. Outwardly he knew her no more than a painting on a wall. Only by her undercurrent running against her outward appearance did he know her behind her poise. He was drunk with her. The more intoxicated he became with her, the less chance he had.

He reached around her waist and held a lifeless woman. A cold sweat started up in him as he held the woman of his dreams. If Augusta was imprisoned to succeed on her own terms, so was he, in ways he never suspected. Did his fierce ambition appear this cold to Mary Jane? Did he make Mary Jane standoffish? He had much in common with Augusta. Their drives had grown a loveless shell inside them, hardened by purpose and disguised as ambition. Yet what they wanted was to be unlocked, and they went about it with the same hard purpose that locked them. "You can at least take your hat off."

"Don't you want to know you're with a lady?"

He was too battered to smile. "I have you to myself just when I like you the least."

"You don't have me." She sassed him, her stiff back making certain he understood.

Stalemated, he bellied her across the suite and crashed onto the bed.

"I want," she said without want, "something more inspiring than bullying."

She was always exposing his shortcomings and, worse, he knew she was right. "I'm no damn lightning shooting out of the sky."

Augusta was pleased with his passionate outburst. "That's the first romantic words you said to me."

He allowed himself an open regret. "I came here feeling so excited. I wanted you, felt you in my back teeth."

She responded under his crushing weight. "How can we have sex when I can't breathe?"

He raised his bulk off her, expecting Augusta to breathe an insulting sigh of relief. When she didn't, he told her he was going out.

She assumed she owned him. "Get my shoes."

He brought them.

"Bring my purse."

He brought her purse.

"Where's my comb."

"Oh, no." He defied her before she had another request. "You're not getting me angry enough to choke you. And win you."

She strongly resented his remark. "I was the one waiting. Willing to please."

"You dare say that? Willing to please?" He caught his breath. "I'm not pleased. You've made a mistake playing with me."

"My worst mistakes come from inspiration."

Her voice suggested they stood a chance of coming together if he was instinctive to her needs, discovered her need of him. But he wouldn't or couldn't take the hint. Something in him, a want, craving, pride at being a success, won out. "With all my money I deserve better than you."

"Climbing the cross?" Augusta gave him the bird.

"You're a waste of time." He knew she had gotten to him.

"Because we don't go to bed? Though I may not need you for bed, you can always count on me for help."

"You sound sweet."

"I tell you to count on me so I can count on you."

He smiled in tribute to her.

"Do you like me without sex?" She was cheerful.

"Only when you're this intelligent." He edged closer. A lioness couldn't command more respect. He plunged in for a kiss, forgetting she was flesh and bone and not a mattress. Augusta bit him.

"I'm not going to be ready when you want me to be ready."

He tasted his lip. "Is that why you bit me?"

"You had me in your arms and you relaxed."

She was right. He was so sure of himself, he did relax. He was about to apologize when stopped by her wrath.

"Did you relax at your stupid sports? No." Her bath-scented hands choked his bull neck. "Ugly! Inhuman!" Her long fingers couldn't encircle his neck, so she frantically kneaded his flesh to choke him. "I don't want the conventional you. I don't want the sex that grows on trees."

He adored her instincts. "You're right."

"Don't say I'm right." She twisted his ears, and when she let go, they didn't spring back at once but look boxed.

"I was having such a marvelous day." He rubbed his cheek as he would a card to change his luck. *What did I do to deserve this?* "All I'm saying. Will you listen? I got a good side too. And you work me up to a sweat. Is that fair?"

Augusta sparkled. "It's not fair, but it's simple."

They fell against each other as if gravity had left the world.

Augusta became demented when physical intimacy gave her the shock of being real. Her heat had a salty tang. An earthy scent buried eons ago in her body. A faint iodine smell of her body cleansing itself.

They dropped off the stormy rim.

Augusta was rarely more desirable than when lying glazed with contentment and her eyes ready for tears.

"Good sex," she bloomed, "makes you feel immortal."

Augusta hadn't gotten her full voice back, and they laughed.

"I may love you," she spoke unsurely into his boiling face, "but I don't think I can go through that again."

"Why?" *Didn't you enjoy it?* was in his eyes.

"Good sex makes me too honest."

"You're so happy, you should get a divorce."

"And get a bad name? Courtlandt will make me mud because he has to live up to his looks. He developed his commanding face in the service of stupid jobs."

Tweed was cavalier. "I'll pay."

"No. Why should Courtlandt get rich on my good fortune? That's like selling a slave her freedom." She swiftly reconsidered. "Would you marry me?"

"God forbid."

"And if He doesn't?"

"There's Mary Jane."

"She doesn't appreciate your accomplishments. An estate in Greenwich. Land in the city. A mansion planned for Fifth Avenue."

"That's scarcely personal." He wanted her intimacy.

"What's wrong?" she asked, tongue-in-cheek. "After sex you need personal care?"

He was too delighted with her to speak. Her body heat had evaporated her bath scent. "If only you weren't so invincible. I'm not praising you. If only you had a flaw to humble you."

"I'm sexy."

He kissed the inside of her wrist. "A bigger flaw than that."

"Stop searching, Bossy Bossy." She might have been calling a cow. "Considering all your money and power, I'm about as loving as anyone you'll ever get." She planted a kiss on his receding hairline. "Let's remain here"—she threw out the suggestion airily but with hope—"for weeks, months, years."

"I have to wire home."

"You didn't get permission to sleep with me?"

"Mary Jane says she has a surprise for me."

"It's probably your anniversary."

TWELVE

$\mathscr{A}$lbany is better praised than seen. In the teeth of prosperity Albany has the smell of a bad luck town. The old stone State Capitol resembled a dead beetle left to petrify with its insides eaten out. The town matched the capitol like a salesman's suit: a trench mouth of boardinghouses. Yet men mortgaged their lives to be here. Albany's prosperity was based on the passing of laws or the killing of them, whichever was more expensive.

Albany merchants had to know how much food, drink, clothing, jewelry and lodging to credit to state senators and assemblymen. The collateral was the legislative process. If congressmen didn't get in on the favors, the merchants were lost.

A man had to learn how to hold out for the highest price without losing everything. How long he held out was his golden chance or ruin. He had no guide. His nerves became his conscience.

Senators and assemblymen lumped together in tiny rooms, their clothes hanging about like an acting troupe on the road. They fought over bread and lived at the mercy of their daily creditor, the landlady, whose mercy did not include providing toilet paper at all times. Thus imposing legislators could be seen carrying rolls under their arms to table.

The Duchess, a ship captain's widow, ran a prized private boardinghouse, though nothing was private from her. She had a kitchen view of Albany, which was the only view that counted with her guests. She had an iron hand to drive bargains and a velvet one to get paid. She waltzed around the table patting her ducks, apologizing for the paleness of her winter butter, boasting her eggs were candled, her sausage pure pork, her bacon lean as pine needles in order to cover her stingy portions.

Senator Miles amassed a tidy nest egg speaking as if he were objecting. "I have my speech ready on the city dregs. Tweed coming up here fronting for Vanderbilt. I will thunder, Duchess. I have stinging quotations from *The Moral Rejection of the Poor.*"

"Ducks," the Duchess pep-talked, "the longer you hold out, the higher your worth."

"Tweed and Gould will not crack our solid front," said Senator Loftus.

"It's all right for you to say," said Senator Baffin, "but it's not realistic. While we're dining here, there are rascals waiting to pass any bill for a fee. While we wait, they charge. Hold out too long and you'll be left out. There are scoundrels this minute feeding from the Erie trough."

The Duchess had a cool reply. "No one has to shut up a man who is already feeding."

"What if"—Baffin sounded the tocsin of discontent again—"Tweed and Gould signed up all they need?"

"Then," boasted Craddock, "I'll attack them from the floor for buying legislation."

"Hear! Hear!" Jubilant raps with knives and spoons.

The bell inside the front door tinkled as in a general store. When the Duchess saw the formidable gentleman, she curtsied. It was A.C. Mattoon, the conscience of the senate. The Duchess led Senator Mattoon to her dining room, which was actually her sitting room, as the dining room was partitioned into a bedroom for four and a cubicle for two and a single that did away with part of the hallway. She unfolded the winged doors and left the gentlemen within. The door was purposely made useless as a sound barrier.

Mattoon clapped right into business. "I head the investigation into Erie. Therefore I know more about Erie than anyone else. I say vote for Gould."

Craddock went on the offensive humbly. "Jay Gould stole the Erie from Vanderbilt. Are we to legalize a steal?"

"I'm not defending Mr. Gould. I'm advancing him. He's the

better man because he's put forward the better proposal for the public good. He'll modernize the Erie Railroad."

"That's prophecy. That's not argument," said Baffin.

Mattoon had many members to see and little time to see them. "You are worth more delivered as a bloc."

"How do we know our price?" Craddock spoke with the integrity of one who didn't want to be cheated. "We've not gone to Tweed."

"I've spoken to Gould. He values you as solid men. Your leadership will lead lesser men into the fold." Mattoon, who was personally severe, did not rap them on the back. "If you wish to clear your conscience, go to Tweed too."

"That's decent." Craddock nodded.

Mattoon hied off to Delevan House where Tweed and Gould, on different floors, were imitating the horn of plenty.

Tweed's suite was awash with visitors eating and swilling drink at the sidebars. A hundred gold canaries in mirrored cages hung from the ceiling twittering away. Belching along with the singing gave a welcoming atmosphere. The conviviality stopped at the inner door guarded by Bowery toughs.

Inside, Sweeny was rolling up money, stuffing small rolls in Tweed's left-hand pocket and large ones in his right. Tweed was a kid in a sand pile. "Whatever you do," said Tweed, "don't let them in as a bloc. We have to cut down on their bargaining power."

The first man Sweeny let in was Senator Herbert, who was sober as Bible covers. Tweed threw a fraternal arm around Herbert's shoulder. "Gopher it," he advised as he slipped him a small roll.

"I have to be honest," said Herbert. "I have to go home and slur the city dregs."

"It's sporting of you to tell me."

"No amount can change my mind."

"I understand. You have to stay in office."

When the door closed, Tweed could barely hold in his exuberance. Next came the most feared man in the senate, Mattoon. Sweeny did not care for him and left, while Tweed found him all in a day's work. He extended a large roll with his genial handshake. Mattoon froze in the posture of dignity remembered. When his value wasn't appreciated, Mattoon looked as if he were about to report a crime.

Tweed praised him. "The others are only getting five hundred dollars down and five hundred after their vote is recorded."

"I'm the head of the investigating committee."

"The facts are simple. Gould and Fisk stole the Erie treasury and took it to New Jersey."

"Let's not quibble about who stole from whom," said the conscience of the senate.

"The commodore doesn't have his railroad. That's a fact."

"Facts alone don't win an argument. You need prejudice to back it up. If I, as the committee head investigating Erie, should go over to your side, everyone will know you're right."

"The prejudice is money." Tweed rubbed his thumb and forefinger together. "The Albany itch is to law what venereal disease is to pleasure."

Mattoon wasted no time on humor. "You need me."

"I'd be the last to deny it."

"Badly."

"Badly is too expensive."

"Send a man to Gould's suite. See his blocs of votes."

Tweed ordered a rough to Gould's suite. "I don't doubt your word, only its price."

The rough returned, confirming that a bloc headed by Craddock was in Gould's pocket. Tweed hiked ten thousand dollars from his pocket and gave half to Mattoon. "Five down and five when you vote."

"Ten now. You have my word."

"I don't have your vote recorded." Tweed was cordial.

Mattoon was sympathetic. "One comes with the other."

Tweed handed over the rest rather than get a stained reputation. Mattoon's bulging pockets resembled a shoplifter's.

Sweeny entered with a flushed face. "The pot has blown. McKinney Glenn of Wayne County cried out in the assembly that wholesale bribery is taking place."

Tweed and Sweeny were impressed by the reassuring Mattoon in his bulging suit. "We have a committee investigating bribes. Alex Frear heads it."

"Alex Frear is the man Glenn accused of trying to bribe him."

"Bad luck for Glenn," said Mattoon severely. "No one can defend the honor of the assembly as Alex Frear can. His investigation will give the assembly a clean bill of health. Then the assembly can censure McKinney Glenn for smearing its members. Glenn will have to resign because he'll be in disgrace. The assembly will be rid of a troublemaker. A big plus, his accusation." Mattoon left.

Chauncey Depew strode in with more good news. The worst disaster in railroad history had just taken place outside Port Jervis. The Buffalo Express lost its last three sleeping cars and plunged off a cliff. The stove in one car burned the passengers alive.

Tweed wondered out loud how this was good news. Depew spelled it out: Erie tracks are lines of rust. This disaster reveals how Gould the Skunk runs a railroad.

Tweed bit his lip to make his thoughts run. He saw the opposite. The disaster proved the Skunk should get his bonds legalized to improve the tracks. Then he dropped the bad news to Depew. The battle was costing more than the commodore was sending. Depew departed with frost on his face. When Sweeny asked what Depew was riled about, Tweed answered cheerily, "A corrupt system makes everyone feel innocent."

The door burst open, letting in the twittering of the canaries and the revelry. A heeler told Tweed he had clobbered the Skunk eighty-three to thirty-two in the assembly. To everyone's surprise Tweed despaired. He had bought a hundred votes.

The senate was a tougher nut to crack. The commodore came through with another hundred thousand dollars that vanished as water in the Sahara. A senator in Tweed's pocket one minute would be in Gould's the next, and back to Tweed to try that pump again in passing. The commodore's flaw was that he remembered his earlier victories when Albany came cheaper. Skunk had no such handicap. He saw today's prices as normal. Tweed kept getting more money and fewer votes. He had to rely on a bought senator's word—the one virtue their action confessed they lacked.

Tweed had every finger in the dike and feared the dam would burst. The Skunk gave five thousand dollars just to keep senators friendly. If the Skunk won legal control of Erie, he could churn millions of dollars of bonds to sell to the public. His reward for stealing would make him a millionaire ten or twenty times over. Tweed slunk off to the senate.

Congratulations had replaced the mechanical smile, so Tweed did not know where he stood until he heard the calling of the roll. When a senator in his pocket voted against him, Tweed let out a groan. "Sir!" This brought a titter in the chamber. When Tweed's "Sir!" came with increasing frequency, an uneasiness stirred the venerable body. Seeing he was doomed, Tweed walked slowly off the floor with the calling of the roll going on behind him. No sooner was he off the floor when a victory shout went up. He was defeated, seventeen to twelve. He caught Craddock and asked, "Why did you vote against me?" Craddock answered, sure of himself, "It's better to be for something than against."

When Tweed returned to Delevan House, he was amazed nothing had changed. He had to wedge his way through the boozing crush to his suite. He was congratulated. He hadn't lost. The bill was returning to the assembly. The battle for Erie was just beginning. He shouldn't have paid out so much on the first round.

Tweed slumped into his chair. He had let the commodore down and needed Vanderbilt for his future. Just when he felt he couldn't feel any worse, he knew the worst had arrived. A sudden silence outside was too ominous to ignore. Telegraphers and messengers were routinely bribed to leak vital news. The door opened on a doomsday silence. Only the canaries twittered. Tweed read the telegraph that was brought in. Vanderbilt, disgusted with Albany greed, had given up.

Tweed went pale. He had lost the fight for Erie. His bright future drained. He had become another scalp for the Skunk. Tweed knew that somehow he had to grapple with a deeper aspect of himself coming out to hinder him. He had lost by being optimistic. The native optimism he needed to survive was loosening his grip on the realistic world he wanted to get ahead in. He was slowly losing his focus between these irreconcilables, and like the battered Heenan he was keeping his drive while losing his ability to judge.

The Skunk had battered him more than he knew. There were still shocks that hadn't reached him, though he was beginning to feel their tremors.

To breathe among friends he threw open his doors, only to see his deserted suite was a looted battlefield. A liveried footman was wending his way around the debris of food and drink. Tweed and Sweeny stared at the man as if he were a prophet of doom. The footman handed Tweed an embossed envelope and was gone without waiting for a reply. Tweed blinked at the sender: Jay Gould.

Sweeny regarded the creamy, thick envelope as a bomb. Gould's note requested the honor of meeting Senator Tweed. Tweed explained to a skeptical Sweeny that this was the gallant victor crossing the ring, like Morrissey kissing Heenan's fist in tribute to a brave foe.

Sweeny, departing in a hurry, gave Tweed a bit of the jitters. Remembering his defeat and Gould's reputation and the commodore himself saying Gould had a bullet hole for a heart, Tweed wiped his palms with his handkerchief as a second man came carefully around the debris—a puny man in a tight suit with dark, wet, plum eyes and a choirboy's face. He looked queerer than the last messenger. To keep the timid man from approaching any closer Tweed asked, "Are you from Mr. Gould?"

"I am," said the tiptoey man in a soft and yielding voice devoid of push and energy. "Jay Gould."

The contrast between the appearance of the man and the havoc of his deeds was too terrifying not to be true.

"Please, Mr. Gould, have a seat." Tweed gave him his own chair. Gould's timidity was hypnotic.

"I hope I'm not taking your seat?"

"Not at all." Tweed was ready to mother him. "Would you care for a drink?"

Gould's neat little head pecked forward politely. "No thank you. I don't drink."

"Would you care for tobacco?"

The question in relation to his habits was so absurd as to draw a wafer-thin smile from Gould. "I don't smoke."

Tweed grinned. "We both have the same good habits, Mr. Gould."

Gould was the picture of a good little boy who would be good even if it caused him pain. His trim black beard, impeccably spaded, hid another alarming revelation. Gould was no older than his early thirties, a decade younger than Tweed.

"Mr. Tweed, you put up a surprisingly good fight, being as you were far outspent."

Tweed eagerly returned the compliment. "You would have won even if you weren't a Republican in Albany."

Gould politely put Tweed straight. "In a Republican district I'm a Republican. In a Democratic district I'm a Democrat. In a doubtful district I'm doubtful. But I'm always for Erie."

Tweed beamed, knowing they would get along famously.

"My railroad goes to New York, but I can't. Because your Judge Barnard has injunctions against me."

When it came to business, Tweed recovered. He said that Barnard always does what's right, and Gould took this to mean pragmatic men are hopelessly corrupt and made an offer of two hundred thousand dollars to suspend the injunctions. Tweed shook his head that Gould misunderstood. "I've my loyalty to the commodore."

"By all means." Gould was only too willing to oblige. "Keep your loyalty. Only tell me its price."

Big numbers gave Tweed courage. "A half million."

Gould thought it high. "That's more than for friendship."

Tweed was sorry he overreached. "I take it you're refusing?"

"No, no," Gould patiently clarified. "My beliefs have nothing to do with my actions."

Tweed alertly stuck out his hand to seal the lavish bargain and grasped a hand so limp, it might turn to water. A sore of uncertainty opened in Tweed. Was he trading in a stingy commodore for an untrustworthy Gould? Gould conquered the giants because he retained his boy's fear of them.

"May I ask, what is your ambition?" Gould apologized.

Tweed saluted the flag. "My own man in the White House."

"Will money help?" Gould asked.

"Does a ship need the North Star?"

THIRTEEN

$\mathscr{G}$reenwich is the South Sea Islands to New York, a village overlooking the Connecticut shore of shaded inlets and coves and tucked away from the city's general madness. Greenwich is the pastoral clearing after hunting in New York. The wood-burning locomotive is painted toy yellow and trimmed with gilt and takes one hour and twenty minutes from Twenty-Seventh Street. Waiting for Tweed was his son, Billy Junior, who had grown into a handsome young man with the bravado assurance of his father. Billy sat in a depot wagon, a two-seater perched high on oversize springs, which were the latest rage. Tweed tilted the wagon precariously as he hoisted himself in. The wagon rocked like a canoe in a storm. Passersby tipped their hats, and Tweed genially returned their greeting. His son basked in the reflected glory of his father. "You're as popular in Greenwich as you are in New York. And why not? You had the telegraph line brought up from Port Chester. You began a steamboat run to the city," Billy continued to boast. "You built one of the biggest resorts on the East Coast. You pay the Tweed price for land, which is higher than anyone else's. You loan money to the natives. You bought the baptistry for the Methodist Church."

The unabashed praise brought father and son together, not because of the praise but in the way the son expressed himself. Billy

Junior proudly drove the checkerboard team of white and black horses uphill to the ridge overlooking the Sound. They passed under the tree-shaded gate of Tweed's estate, Linwood, a spread of forty scenic acres along the heart of Greenwich. A low blue-stone wall ran along Putnam Avenue to a narrow country road dubbed Love Lane, and this was the entrance.

A showplace stable had horses standing on plaited straw. Bright white statuary of gods and goddesses abounded on the green expanse of lawn. The idealized divinities were a gift from Prince Garvey. Mary Jane couldn't wait for her husband to ease himself out of the tipping wagon. To her son's beaming she dragged Tweed inside as though he were a feather while repeating, "You're going to be so proud, Bill."

He bent down to kiss her, but a kiss was not what made Mary Jane happy. Her joyous impatience amused him. When they were in the sun room, she burst out, "Mary Amelia has brought a bonnie lad home. Ambrose Maginnis of *the* Maginnises of New Orleans."

The good news gave him the same exuberance as his wife.

"Oh, Bill, if not for you, Mary Amelia would never have met a Maginnis."

"Come now, Mary Jane, Mary Amelia is a beautiful girl of rare character."

"All the sadder if you weren't her father. You don't know what a bad market it is for young women with character. How handicapped is the best of character without a dowry."

She tendered him a kiss, which was all the more touching for the sincere way she had to break out of herself. He likened her kiss to a delicious Italian nougat with a film of flaky, white-paper sugar that melts on contact with lips and lays bare the underlying sweetness within.

The door burst open in the sun room. "Mary Amelia!" Her mother ran to hug in the assurance that all was still well. Tweed was delighted at his daughter, and Ambrose, barefooted on the beefsteak rug, holding boots and buckets of clams yet arm in arm and carelessly radiant. Mary Amelia dropped her bucket and wet boots to run and hug Tweed. "Father, this is Ambrose Maginnis."

"How do you do, sir?" said Ambrose with a lofty respect that won Tweed's favor.

"Happy indeed, Ambrose. Welcome to Linwood and its pleasures."

Mary Amelia self-consciously beamed.

Ambrose was the paragon his wife described. No man looked better suited for Mary Amelia, especially as she hung on his arm and refrained from giggling.

Mary Amelia wanted their yacht *Mary Jane* to sail Ambrose to Tweed's Island, formerly Finch Island. Mary Jane argued for the smaller yacht *Linwood*, which they could sail by themselves. Tweed happily offered his new steam yacht, the *William M. Tweed.* This yacht was the talk of the harbor. It carried a crew of twelve and could board an orchestra for dinner parties. Though steam yachts were seen on the Sound, the *William M. Tweed* was the first to anchor in Greenwich harbor.

Mary Amelia took the *Mary Jane.* When the young couple left, Tweed bounded into his carriage. He was off to his clubhouse on nearby Indian harbor. In opulence the clubhouse rivaled the grandest hotels. On his birthday a huge floral wreath framed a portrait of the Boss hung from the ceiling. The ornate furnishings were mainly donated. Tweed hurried to his tower suite where he changed into the club uniform of pantaloons, nautical vest and beanie cap. A distress signal couldn't catch quicker attention.

On the terrace, with oyster boats and sailboats in the background, he found the waiting Shamus. He knew the young man wanted a hard favor, and by his face Tweed knew the young man wasn't going to get it. Shamus knew he was out of his element and that this was no place to bring up tenement reform.

Idealistic groups had fought for years for meaningful inspections of schools, factories and tenements with little success. Then came their biggest victory. Sanitary inspectors were appointed. The appointments went through the party in power. Landlords paid to be appointed sanitary inspectors. Not only did these landlord inspectors keep the housing stock from improving, they earned a good living doing it. Sanitary inspectors—born out of years of idealistic struggles of intelligent people believing changing laws changed the party in power—became untouchable no matter who was in power.

Shamus asked cautiously, "Can I talk to you about Morris Pease, who runs the industrial home?"

"Exceptional man." Tweed didn't care for the subject.

"The owner of his building doesn't live up to the fire laws."

Tweed's downcast look told him he was being difficult. "Did you talk to Donny?"

Shamus admired the way Tweed even knew which inspector was on a building. "Donny doesn't talk. He only lies."

Tweed rubbed his nose more in sorrow than in anger. This is the boy his father would have liked him to be. He asked gently, "Do you want an answer?"

"Why not?" He knew he was walking on hot coals.

Tweed cautioned. "To spare you."

"Mr. Pease is a saint. He teaches homeless kids a trade. Gets them jobs. He's almost as valuable as Mr. Loring Brace of the Children's Aid."

"Who gives out the most jobs?"

"You do, by far."

"Then don't speak to me about trades. Saint, indeed?"

"I didn't mean to anger you."

"I'm not angry. Saintly men have no backbone. Anyone can improve one house, one block, one neighborhood. That's stealing your wings. Let me see a saint improve this inferno city. Divided and poisoned by hundreds of groups yawping their ignorance of each other. That would make a saint. If there was no democracy, bigots with flags would be the last to think of it."

Shamus drew in his horns.

"Look lad, we've come a long way. I can tell you that Kathleen is trouble. Why didn't she stay at the Broadway Seminary for Girls that I got her into?"

"After surviving the hunger she didn't want the same kind of education as the privileged."

"Kathleen has no common sense."

"She said the students were educated to protect what made them well off."

"What on earth is wrong with that?" Tweed hummed.

"The hunger is in her mind. No, she doesn't blame the seminary. It's human to educate your children to respect your ways without question. But those unquestioning ways watched the Irish families starve to death before their eyes."

"I'm not holding Kathleen wrong about the hunger. She was there. Good as she is, she'll never get anything done because she's going at it the wrong way. Questioning is wrong. I swear I don't know what's happening to women lately. They filled the Broadway Tabernacle for a convention on the right to vote. Luckily they allowed men in, and the men hooted them down."

Shamus winced, and it reminded him of another injustice.

"Kathleen said it's disgraceful that the first free medical college for women in New York was closed down."

"The medical profession closed it down, saying that women weren't reliable. You want to tell Kathleen something? Tell her what you learned in politics."

"I want her to respect me." Shamus hoped he hadn't said too much.

Tweed wasn't alarmed in the slightest. "It takes time to make good citizens, especially when so many didn't come here for freedom of speech or religion. Jefferson himself thought it would take seven years to make a citizen. The Know-Nothings wanted the law to be twenty-one years. Let Kathleen face facts."

He didn't know whether to laugh or cry. Both emotions stuck in his throat. "I wish I had your confidence."

Tweed leaned his bulk forward to tell his secret and darkened the light from outside. "First you have to get my experience."

Shamus stood up, defeated.

Tweed pulled him down. "Do you know New York was an aristocratic state, one of the last to ratify the Constitution? We've only had free schools since 1834 and then only for boys. In my father's time a poor boy could not attend a public school unless his family signed a pauper's oath. The boys from the best poor families wouldn't go to schools because pride wouldn't let them sign the oath. You want the city in the hands of aristocrats?"

Shamus couldn't reply. He felt right and helpless.

"The first Ring in New York was the Aldermanic Ring run by Hal Genet. Prince Hal had aldermen sit on bills until they were paid. They were like the Albany Cavalry. Once you paid them, they charged. Prince Hal, on his maternal side, goes back to Clinton, seven-term governor, enemy of the people's right to govern themselves, advocate of government by the elite, opponent of ratifying the Constitution of the United States *and father of New York State*. I'm not saying the party is perfect, but we're a lot less exclusive."

Shamus wanted to go. Tweed shook his head; worse was coming. "Do you know about Oscar Sturtevant? One of the truest gentlemen in politics?" Tweed was stirred thinking about him.

"Duncan at the Tombs said he could see his mansion from his jail window."

"Just so." Tweed's emotion nailed Shamus's attention. "Sturtevant was a Whig standing before a Whig judge. We fought the same good fight for streetcars to run on Broadway. The better merchants were against streetcars because it would ruin their carriage trade. In the heat of battle things were said. Sturtevant said no more, nor less, than we. The Whig judge singled out Sturtevant for punishment and sentenced only him. *Sturtevant did not appeal.* Why did a man of principle surrender to injustice? Sturtevant bowed to the court after being sentenced. His bow showed contempt for the judge but not for the law. I felt I would never be sane, secure, intelligent until I discovered why he didn't appeal this injustice that he so clearly recognized." Tweed's voice was of a startled man waking up to reality. "I was in Sturtevant's cell with his select friends. I wanted to know, what was the stranglehold the judge had on him? Was it blackmail? Extortion? What? We would fight it. He had to appeal his unjust sentencing. Had he forgotten his law? Forgotten his judgment of right and wrong? Sturtevant's acceptance wouldn't let me sleep. I couldn't get to the bottom of this mystery, no matter how hard I tried. It was beyond my wit, intelligence, understanding. I knew Sturtevant as the best of men."

Now Shamus wanted to know this mystery Tweed was trying to get at. Tweed himself was perplexed, as if telling the story for the first time. He wanted Shamus to understand, yet he was talking just as much for his own understanding.

"His friends were astonished at my treating Sturtevant to such harsh questioning. I'll never forget his answer. I wish I had never heard it. *He owed it to himself not to fight.* I was in a thicker fog than ever. In spite of our different backgrounds, we vaulted social barriers to find a common ground for friendship. I was proud of this friendship, for all that was needed to cross to get to it. I had to know why he wouldn't fight."

Shamus saw the revelation shook Tweed even now.

"Sturtevant told me with pride, code of honor, call it what you will: 'Didn't I see?' The judge associated with his friends, club men, businessmen, party loyalty; and they, his peers, had pronounced his sentence on him. His upbringing fatally wounded him, yet he didn't wish to go against its code." Tweed was in another world. "I understood the gulf separating me from a well-bred gentlemen. I was still his friend. I could see that in his eyes. But I was also a stranger. Forever."

Shamus shivered at this unbridgeable chasm.

The steam yacht's whistle blew over the harbor and emptied out the clubhouse. Tweed took Shamus back to the city in style on the *John Romer*. The political and business faithful were on board. Garvey was the first to protest for their safety. "No racing. You'll blow us out of the water with your damn steam engine."

Tweed enjoyed their fear. "There's steamboats in the coves waiting to take anyone on. You can't turn tail."

"Keep away from *Seawanhaka*," warned Morrissey.

"Yea." There was unanimous agreement.

The rumble of the steam engine underfoot scared the otherwise calloused men. Tweed gloried in the sensation. They soon passed the *Mary Jane*. Tweed waved to the young couple, arm in arm against the rays of the sun and above the untidy details of life.

Tweed plunked into his capricious chair on the bow while those on deck sat on camp chairs. Below deck a band was playing in the salon and champagne was heard to pop.

"Steam!" shouted Captain White, who stood aft with binoculars trained toward the coves of Long Island.

Pilot Billy Witherwax, at the wheel, rang for steam.

Tweed stiffened to port like a bird dog. The Sunday sailor had a fright, as if the long, idyllic finger of Long Island were the seat of pirates. Tweed halloed to the bridge. "Captain White, what have you sighted?"

"*Seawanhaka*, sir."

The men moaned.

"Why aren't we picking up steam?" Tweed demanded.

"Engineer John Darrah is cautious about driving even such a fine engine as this against such odds, sir. There are too many front-page stories of steamboats exploding."

The passengers on deck backed the engineer.

"Are you certain, Captain, it's the *Seawanhaka*?"

"Nearly, sir."

A ghostly bow cut out of the milky haze. The boat appeared no larger than the *John Romer*. There were sighs of relief at first sighting. But this steamboat kept slipping out of the mist until it hove into full view, twice as large as the *Romer*.

"*Seawanhaka*, sir." The captain was cool. He didn't want to rouse Tweed's competitive spirit.

Tweed shouted, "Take her on!"

His guests moaned.

Witherwax rang for steam.

"It's an ill doing, Boss," groaned Prince Garvey.

"King of the Sound." Tweed trained his glasses on the majestic boat. "She's manned and officered by the best sailors along these waters. She represents the combined wealth and pride of Roslyn and Sea Cliff."

"How do you know"—Garvey paled—"you have the engines to stand her pressure?"

"That's what we're going to test," Tweed maintained stoutly. "We're in the race now. She'll be smelling our arse all the way to Twenty-third Street like a bitch in heat."

Even as Tweed was boasting, the *Seawanhaka* was gaining.

"Steam!" commanded Tweed.

Witherwax rang the bell.

"Never fear, mates," Tweed called. "The engines won't explode. They're the best money can buy."

The *Romer* had Throgg's Neck on her bow with a lead the *Seawanhaka* was rapidly narrowing.

Betting began at once. The *Romer* would win, lose, explode or not. The betting money dried up on the engine surviving every time Tweed ordered more steam.

Darrah the engineer was a Cassandra, loud and clear. *Seawanhaka* was gaining. The faint of heart, as well as the lionhearted, kept folding over the rail, relieving themselves of Tweed's cuisine. The passionate engine throbbed under their feet and up their spines.

Witherwax rang for steam.

Darrah hollered through the tube. "Stop that useless ringing! Throttle's wide open and no more steam to be had."

"Make more steam," Tweed commanded.

Engineer and braves groaned.

Passengers on the quarter deck were madly betting. The latest line was *when* the boiler would explode. To add to their consternation a swarming black cloud of biting gnats lowered on their sweaty flesh. They battered the gnats away in a swirl of arms and improvised dancing steps. Soon their natty uniforms were blotched with gnat slaughter. "A bad omen," said a brave as the furies were blown away.

Under Tweed's maniacal exhortations they managed to come abreast of North Brothers Island with their bow breaking ahead of the formidable *Seawanhaka*. If they could get into the channel between Riker's Island and Barrow's Point first, they could hold the lead the rest of the way.

Seawanhaka was a gleaming terror bearing down on Tweed.

With a superiority worthy of her superior class she let fly four booming blasts of her elephant horn for the *Romer* to lay aside. Tweed ignored the rules of the sea and only considered the source. *Seawanhaka* thought she owned the Sound. Tweed gave her his own four growly blasts back at the *Seawanhaka* hissing over the water and threatening to hove in the *Romer* portside. The scud covered the pale faces of Tweed's braves.

The King of the Sound began to pass the *Romer*. The *Seawanhaka* was slipping by at the rate of ten feet a minute, guard to guard.

Tweed danced out of his mind, calling for more steam.

Witherwax was executing the steering perfectly. One wrong move and the yachts would collide and vanish into a steamy cloud.

Betting, cursing, seasickness intensified on the *Romer*.

The yachts were inches apart, hissing and clumping over the waves. Too close for the scud to clear the rail.

Tweed commanded the band to play loud to drown out the victory cries rising from the *Seawanhaka*. The parade music could not hide the gentlemen and women pouring drinks as they passed. A few had the cheek to raise their glasses to their soon to be defeated foe. Their uniform, when on water, was yellow pantaloon with white stripe down the side and matching yellow beanie.

Tweed's frustration at losing caused him to shout at the passing yachtsmen and women, "If fried eggs could walk, they'd look like you in uniform."

His braves laughed at the sally until they were caught flat-footed by the robust reply.

A gentleman, to the victorious hilarity of his fellow passengers, dropped his pantaloon and bared his hucklebone to the wind with the following caution: "You can smell this in a storm." And farted at the *Romer*.

Tweed dropped his blue pantaloon to the screams of the women, who hid their faces against the bulkhead. He then proceeded to piss onto the gleaming deck of the *Seawanhaka*. His braves were deliriously happy at this bold stroke and Tweed's cry at waving his Excalibur. "This'll rust your fittings."

Just as Tweed and his braves believed they had lost the race but won a social argument, a demure woman came to the rail and dropped her pantaloon to the hilarious roar of the braves, who believed they were being obscenely saluted. Then she dropped her knee-pants underdrawers. Half-squatting, she put the tip of her finger to her orifice and, like a kid at a water fountain, sprayed the braves who dared not open their mouths to protest or marvel.

Word was cried out to Tweed. There was not enough fuel to keep up the pressure. Tweed asked for six heavy volunteers to be thrown into the drink. The captain saved them by shouting, "Hold on, sir. We're throwing lard into the fire."

Tweed's arms raised in victory. "We'll walk by the *Seawanhaka* as the *Pilgrim* passed the *Sarah Thorp.*"

Seawanhaka's passengers razzed the *Romer* as they slid by.

Tweed was maliciously gleeful. "We're throwing in lard!"

The *Seawanhaka*'s passengers fled to the farthest rail from the *Romer.* Black smoke coughed from the *Romer*'s stack as she leapt ahead like a sailboat in a squall. Tweed jumped up and down, cheering along with his rapt crew and braves.

The yachtsmen and women of the *Seawanhaka* proved true sports. They raised their glasses in a toast to push and energy. Tweed was much touched by their class. He had his oyster flag raised. "Delmonico's on me!" They parted, waving to each other while Tweed's band played a jolly salute.

The *Romer* passed along Throgg's Neck, which was part of a jaw, and headed toward Manhattan Island. Throgg's Neck is a breathtaking sea vista that would make any city famous as a seaport. In New York it is a nautical backyard.

Anyone visiting New York and thinking it divorced from nature would be astounded to see the land from the Creator's eye. The waters around the city run with a rich variety of aquatic bird and sea and marsh life with breeding and nesting grounds along winding creeks, kills, tidal basins, fields of wetlands breathing in and out with the tides. Marshes rising fertile and sinking with the stoical tides back into swamps, and everywhere the generous feeder, water. A prehistoric pulse is in these lowland backwaters. One can feel the nebula origin of earth. In the background is the great city, sleepless, watching, encroaching on the breathing wetlands like a strangler who can't help himself.

In Delmonico's the ruddy O'Brien sidled up to the Boss. The sheriff was never more pugnacious than when devious. "Boss"— the sheriff was submissive—"what a palace you have in Greenwich."

Tweed was gobbling oysters the way hygienic zealots take fresh air. "Ummmmm. Slurp."

"No man deserves it more," O'Brien praised him.

Without changing the pace or delight in downing oysters, Tweed knew the inevitable was closing in. He shouldn't parade his wealth, though it was exhilarating. A mark that he had arrived. He wished the evil hadn't surfaced with O'Brien. The sheriff was important to his organization.

"Two steamboats. A yacht. Sailboat." O'Brien admired.

"Ummmm." Tweed swallowed. "See my mirrored stables?"

"Popped my eyes."

Tweed broadcast down the table with a twinkle in his eyes. "All right, sheriff, what's your price?"

The braves roared and hooted O'Brien for having his number taken. O'Brien wiped his nose with his forefinger and knuckles. "Sweeny won't pay the quarter million dollars owed me."

"Ummm." The oyster lodged in Tweed's throat. "Slurp." The oyster went down like a horse pill. "For what?"

"My share, Boss." The sheriff leaned closer to convince Tweed of his honesty by the close proximity of his face. "What's owed me."

"I'm owed a full head of hair."

"I wish Brains had your humor, Boss." O'Brien missed the point. "Brains will listen to you."

"Ummmm." Tweed slurped down another oyster. "Do you recall the terms of your office?" Tweed wiped the jiz from his lips. "A sheriff is entitled to all the fees he can collect. Your sworn duty is to catch crooks. Your fees arise in doing your duty."

"That's not easy, Boss. Big crooks have protection and small ones can't pay."

"Every job is flawed."

"I'm humbly saying, Boss, speak to Brains."

"You speak to him, sheriff."

"No one goes up against Sweeny. He's got the answers."

"There's your answer."

"I don't want answers, Boss. I want my owings. I make the collections. Anything goes wrong, I take the lightning." The sheriff leaned closer. "Sweeny's giving orders all over the place." He called over Mike Norton, a husky young man who knew he'd be a ward captain or die. "Mike, tell the Boss about Brains playing boss."

Norton flared. "Black Brains issues this order to all ward captains. Every bit has to clear him first."

Tweed respected the hotheaded Norton. "That system makes for unity. Makes us stronger together than we'd each be separately."

To Tweed's surprise Norton gave him a hollow laugh. "Boss, unity takes away our freedom. Without it we feel weak."

An understanding smile came to Tweed. "What you boys want, I wanted. Walk down your wards like a king."

"It's not old times." Norton wanted Tweed to see the light. "We're kings unto ourselves, like you said."

"And everyone killed each other," Tweed said calmly.

"Boss," Norton pleaded, "call in Sweeny. Put sense in his loop. You promoted us because we deliver. Me, Tom Creamer, you name it, we walk over hot coals for the party and don't say boo. So why are we questioned? Where does Sweeny come off giving us orders? He's not out on the streets."

O'Brien seconded Norton. "Boss, you can't be everywhere at once when you're in Greenwich and Albany."

Tweed let the dig go. "I'll get Sweeny here." He snapped his finger for a heeler.

Tweed was thanked profusely. He kept eating in order to think without being disturbed.

The sheriff, secure that Tweed was doing his bidding, asked, "Boss, you're going to put the arm on Sweeny for me?"

"Did I ever tell you the story of the poor boy who went to his rich uncle for a loan to start his own business?"

"No," said O'Brien, knowing he had no defense against humor.

"The poor boy repeats to his rich uncle what his mother taught him to say to shake the money loose. 'Uncle,' he says, 'my mother told me to remind you that you have a yacht at Newport, a home on Washington Square, a factory in New York.'

" 'My sister is wrong,' says the rich uncle. 'I have two yachts at Newport, a home on Washington Square and a mansion in Wood Lawn. I have a factory and a foundry and a lumber mill. But did you ever think what it cost to keep your sick grandfather alive in a hospital for three years and specialists brought over from Europe?'

" 'No,' said the chastened boy, 'I never thought of it, Uncle. I'm sorry.'

"The uncle then asks, 'And what about your grandmother who needed new medicines every week and a nurse around the clock?

And care and treatment for your Aunt Hetty, my wife, who was sick with a burning fever that tormented her life and needed expensive medication?'

" 'Uncle, I'm very sorry. Uncle, please, don't tell me any more.'

" 'Or my brother Silas,' says the uncle, 'who was going mad and needed nurses to read to him and bodyguards to protect him from hurting himself and lawyers to keep him from being sent to the asylum on Blackwell's Island?'

" 'Uncle,' cried the poor boy, 'I'm sorry I ever came. Please forgive me.'

" 'Well,' said the uncle, bidding the boy good-bye, 'if I didn't help them, why should I help you?' "

A red O'Brien bolted from the table and rushed out of the restaurant with the laughter chasing after him.

When a grave Sweeny arrived, Tweed said that he wanted O'Brien off the ticket.

Sweeny didn't take the order seriously. "What that idiot do now?"

"Blackmail." Tweed wiped his mouth.

Sweeny conveyed a lack of interest. "That's not enough to throw a sheriff off the ticket."

Tweed finished his sentence. "Against me."

Sweeny turned as a cannon in a turret ready to discharge. "The sheriff is a born idiot, but he's not crazy."

Tweed's thumb poked his chest. "I don't want anyone using my good life against me."

"Let the dummy eat his heart out."

"That's too generous." Tweed burned.

FOURTEEN

$\mathcal{T}$ilden couldn't contain himself. A prize fallen into his lap! Not quite fallen. Coaxed. Shoved. No matter, they were *here* in his gilded library. The bagman O'Brien plus two ward heroes: Norton and Creamer. Their revenge was his stepping-stone to the White House, their revolt a knife in Tweed's back. The opportunity broke unexpectedly.

Tilden knew he had only to open his library door to impress these saloon men. They'd see his indoor splashing fountain in the next room. Tilden knew Tweed's flaw. To protect himself Tweed was killing himself. Tightening his organization, imposing a strict unity over Tammany, and Tweed's discipline had the horses kicking over the cart. No one knew how to hold that nerveless balance between loyalty and discipline.

Tilden was adept at feeding sumptuously over the table of other people's mistakes. He basked in his own shrewd temperament. He could profit from the mistakes of such a tough and daring organizer as Tweed. He knew only greed could have these men waiting in his library. He would not have trusted any other motive.

In the library's stained-glass light, O'Brien blabbered his reformer's credentials. "Slippery Dick has squirreled away a million. It's not in any bank. We searched. Black Brains is worth twice that.

Tweed began without a pot. Now he's building a Fifth Avenue mansion."

"The courthouse," said Norton, "costs twice the price of Alaska, and not finished. Jim Watson, chief auditor of the city's books, is an ex-convict."

Tilden stood in the mystical light while they sat. His white suit gave him the appearance of a shark underwater. He was the picture of the unhurried man wanting nothing. Yet the saloon men knew they were allowed in this luxurious library because the Squire of Gramercy Park wanted everything.

The Squire saw through them as dog smelling dog. He was too ambitious to be honest, too courteous to be kind and was unfeeling when most dutiful. Only his upper lip bore a sign of inner life: internal pressure pointed it at the center.

Tilden spoke with pride. "We must stand as reformers."

"Tweed feeds on reformers," Norton enlightened him. "He made eighteen thousand dollars on the courthouse investigation. He sold the investigating committee stationery from his paper company. He printed their bills and records in his printing plant. He sold advertising space to the committee in his newspaper, the *Transcript*. He found jobs for clerks and recorders on the investigating staff."

Tilden knew he was confronted by magic. What was said as praise should have been accusations. "That's invaluable information."

"But it won't buy a single vote. There's men on every corner waiting for a Tweed job."

"They'll get jobs from us. All of you will get your old powers back." Tilden's talent was to speak as if the job were done by his mention of it.

The moment the street men rode up, they knew they had found the right leader. Gramercy Park was on the evolutionary ladder. A man could be tough while losing the ape look. Though New York has little respect for tradition, Gramercy Park had two tall Mayor's Lamps outside number 4, the home of former Mayor Harper, book publisher with his brother and co-owner of *Harper's Weekly*.

"Through me," said Tilden, "you will connect with the state and national party." He encouraged O'Brien. "Every office will be open to the best qualified."

O'Brien was on needles. "We need a rallying name."

Tilden cautioned. "We mustn't go public too soon. We must first be certain of our power. Then go public when certain of victory."

"Tweed," Norton advised, "can smell a tick in a mattress."

"We'll undermine Tweed silently," said Tilden, "and throw him out with a roar when we go public."

"Tweed won't know what hit him," O'Brien cheered.

The library was charged with optimism. Tilden counted on their greed, and they counted on his ambition.

"Let's call ourselves the Young Democracy," Norton lit up.

"That's positive," Tilden approved.

O'Brien clapped.

Tilden could barely believe his luck as he lectured them. "To be effective, reform must come spontaneously from the grass roots. No big party ties. I will remain in the background until needed."

"That's mighty generous of you, Mr. Tilden," Norton praised.

"It's my duty."

O'Brien admired the stand. "If that was Tweed, he'd be hogging the movement."

The point in Tilden's upper lip vanished. He knew his footing with these raw men was as secure as it could be. The danger was in their brawling among themselves for the spoils and ruining their chances. If Young Democracy collapsed, he didn't want to be connected with it. The prize was worth the danger. The man who toppled Tweed would get national headlines. Within reach would be the Democratic nomination for president of the United States. His goal was to kill Tweed without losing Tweed's enormous following.

FIFTEEN

A tiny fire bell ringing deep in the wards caused the giant bell housed atop City Hall to toll over the city. Families spilled out of their flats to see if their street would escape destruction. Trumpets blew across the wards under the frenzied ringing of bells and the funereal tolling of the big bells. Barefoot hot-corn girls carrying boiling water in cedar buckets tried to avoid being scalded by their own wares in the pandemonium. A watchman ran ahead as a guide, his lantern bobbing off a tall pole. Behind him was the distant rumbling of rival pumpers speeding through narrow, curving streets, lights glancing off them as off sleek animals running down prey through the undergrowth.

Husky haulers and draggers ran with the Big Eight the Eagle Company. The Eagle lay in Ludlow Street and thundered through Grand Street to the Bowery. The shiny tiger-head Big Six raced down East Broadway into Chatham Square on a collision course. Pumpers flew to fires without water, depending on plugs at the site.

Volunteers risked their necks to save lives, yet cared little for the safety of spectators lining their route. The faster a pumper, the less time to skirt unexpected holes. A cracked axle could send men and a one-ton pumper flying through the air. One wrong step in the slippery mud and volunteers fell under the wheels. Children raced back and forth before the oncoming pumper, counting out loud each time they made it from curb to curb. Terrified mothers chasing their children to safety became part of the crowd defying the onrushing pumpers.

Pumper routes were easily traced by the cheering and groans and by captains blowing their silver trumpets to clear the streets. Pumpers took hair's-breadth turns at full tilt, mindless of their own life and those of the spectators, using treacherous wheel ruts as pilots use currents.

Eagle hit Chatham Square first. The breathing of volunteers visible in the mud whizzing off their lips. Spectators who earlier fought for curb position now struggled to get back. Pushing and shoving threw spectators in the street. The fire was raging before them over the wooden roofs less than a quarter of a mile away.

The rival captains blew their trumpets at one another to clear the path. None gave water. The crews threw rocks and leaded saps at each other as the exit out of the square was narrowing, and only one pumper could get through. Eagle was pulling ahead step by step, cutting in front of the speeding Tiger. The challenge brought out the courage of the Tiger's crew. They would do what they would never do when sane.

Eagle's crew was startled. What they began with bravado was going to end in their slaughter. No pumper was getting through. A screaming crowd scattered. Women and men pushing pumpers from behind dived into the mud. The Tiger was not going to be intimidated. Expecting the crash, the Eagle's captain jerked his head to one side. His crew took this for a signal and swerved away. Men of the Eagle tumbled in their traces, let go their ropes to belly whop through the mud. The Tiger shot through the opening and sped out of the square and down the dark slums.

The only semblance of a street were pools of dirty water, though it hadn't rained for days. The poorest shack-row dweller stared down outsiders with murderous confidence, their bruised and scarred faces lined with imagined insults.

The fire raged in a brewery along the old Collect Pond neighborhood where maids once pumped water for their master's tea, so fresh was the water from the underground springs. Breweries moved in to take advantage of the water for their beer. Tanning factories were built on the shore to use the water and polluted the pond. The breweries closed down, their buildings converted into tenements.

The peeling brewery was a torch blowing apart in the wind. An unseen woman on the roof was crying for help. In the street below, her husband and children screamed, out of their minds.

The fireplug was covered by an Eagle barrel, a rough sitting on it to reserve the plug for his company. A fight broke out with a Tiger for the plug. While they fought, the Tiger crew connected their pumper to the plug. They were cheered at being the first ones to send up water. A short spell at the furiously pumped sidebars tired the huskiest volunteer. New hands jumped in at the risk of breaking fingers and arms.

Brewery flats had no walls. Families lived together separated by waist-high barriers, living pell-mell among drug users, prostitutes, thieves who found a sanctuary coppers wouldn't enter. When they were smoked out, the families emerged with their fate on their faces. These dirt poor had a peculiar sleepy stance, as if being wide awake in public would earn them twice as much suspicion.

Eagle's crew arrived screaming for blood. Fighting broke out and the fire was neglected. Pumpers with proud histories—*White Ghost, Black Joke, Dry Bones*—arrived to fight the blaze. A ladder against the burning wall couldn't reach the screaming woman. Seeing a volunteer risking his life to save her, an angry spectator yelled at the distraught husband, "What's she doing on the roof?"

The husband proudly answered, "She lives there!"

"Living on the roof?" The loyal husband was razzed. "A crazy woman is killing a brave fireman."

"My wife's not crazy."

Spectators jeered him and his children.

Unable to stand his wife's screaming, his children crying, the crowd snapping at him, the husband managed to speak with dignity. "The doctor told her to sleep on the roof."

His insane pride in his wife brought louder jeers.

"To cure her tuberculosis." He silenced the crowd.

The volunteer on the ladder threw her a rope, which she tied under her arms. Suddenly she was lost from view in the blaze. Her rope hung slack and was on fire. A burning tent winged open over the roof, terrifying the spectators below. It collapsed into a ball and plunged into a puddle where it sizzled out.

The howling spectators had no time to feel safe. The wife's flaming body was hurtling off the roof at them, the arc of rope a burning tail. Her arms were spread apart. She was falling face-down, staring right into their eyes! A woman just before dying, searching their eyes for hope, and their eyes filled with terror.

Falling through the air put out her fire. The fireman on the burning ladder absorbed the blow of her bundled body, jerking to a halt a few feet above the street. At rest, her dangling body burst back into flames. Her husband and children raced to her screaming and hugged out her fire.

The old brewery's joints shrieked apart, collapsing and spraying burning cinders high into the night like fireworks. When the fire was out, the darkness returned the nightly dangers to the street.

Firemen followed the sparks blowing in the wind, wetting down factories and homes. They were too late for the Industrial Home for Boys. The doorway was in flames, all inside were trapped, yet there was singing behind the fire and it was led by a woman's encouraging voice.

The moment Kathleen smelled the smoke coming up the stairwell, she threw blankets over the boys and told them to start down the stairs singing a rousing song she had taught them. The walls were cracking with fire. The stairs behind them tore away and hung off the landing like a spent accordion.

"Nipper!" she yelled toward the burning landing.

Nipper's sleepy head popped out. "I don't trust you!"

"Jump!" she begged with tears in her eyes. "I'll catch you."

"I told you this would happen!" he accused her.

She understood the resistance in his soul. It was her own. In the hunger she lost faith in the people, with their heartless politicians superior to everything they neglected, their smiling speeches covering up their treachery that doesn't see the hungry as human. She loved Nipper's reckless purity of soul. She must save him. She could almost reach him. "Nipper, please jump!"

Kathleen heard the cheering outside for the boys who had leapt safely through the burning doorway.

She saw a heartbreaking protest in Nipper's eyes. What good was being tough when weak men made the flames you had to jump through to save your life? He wanted to jump. He didn't want to take a stand now—foolish, helpless, hopeless stand. He had to break free and run from it. But something in him had to protest this wrong to him for a minute, a second, a moment, anything. He'd have no soul to call his own.

She smelled that awfully personal smell of a kid's innards

squeezed by fear while fighting to be brave. "Nipper! What's wrong? Jump!"

He idolized her. "You're good and that makes you stupid!" Having shouted that, Nipper took a baby step forward to leap into her arms. He stretched his own arms out to take wing. The landing gave way and the walls caved over him.

Kathleen was thrown down the stairwell, atop the debris, suffocating the fire. The boys outside were screaming her name. She stumbled up, half conscious, her dress on fire. No way out. The back of the building fell away. She ran over the debris through the dust and smoke and lunged headfirst into a puddle, unable to get up.

Shamus dragged her body out of the puddle and bent over her in grief. A compassionate hand touched his shoulder. It was O'Brien, and he said, "Work with us, Shamus. We need the old man's records." Shamus was too stricken to speak. "You owe it to your angel. The books, Shamus. You'll have a higher position with us than you'll ever get with Tweed."

"Have you no feelings?" Shamus's face was hidden.

"That's the only reason I butted in. You can do things with us." O'Brien brazened it out.

Kathleen opened her tear-filled eyes and this was bliss to Shamus. The sight of him pained her and this shamed him. He couldn't believe she was standing up. "Where are you going?"

Unsteadily she headed into the night. Red hair stuck to the mud on her face. Tears ran down her cheeks. Her lips moving silently, upbraiding herself, demanding of herself, despairing of herself. She walked, ran, drawn toward the Battery. "The smell!" she raved.

"What?" Shamus stuck by her side.

She refused to recognize him. She spoke with escaping breath as though possessed. "In the hunger the smell of the morning dead woke you." The torment kept her from walking straight. "Hungry children turning black in the fields, the same as rotting potatoes."

"Let me take you to a hospital, Kathleen."

"Women forgot how to cook because potatoes were so easy to grow." The agony of what was to come was in her voice. "Then, day after day, nothing." Her speech slowed and faded as she hurried on foot, afraid to miss something in the distance. "We had no money. When we missed our rent, we were thrown out. Collectors came from Dublin to tumble our huts and drive us off the land. Ditches along the road became our home. We were dying of hunger while Irish food was shipped to England." She swallowed air as she began to run. "What was so wrong feeding children dying of hunger? England feared we'd grow dependent on government help." She doubled up in agony, her body a part of her speech.

"Kathleen, where can you be going?"

"Nipper is gone." The cruelty blazed in her eyes.

"I'm terribly sorry." He knew how empty he sounded against her sorrow.

She gasped for air. "To know your little sister is dying when her hair falls out of her head and grows on her once red-cheeked face."

"Think on the good, Kathleen."

"Who came to help? Brave doctors. How I cherish those doctors who treated us no matter what our religion or thoughts and died among us. The Society of Friends fed us. Even the great Friends stopped feeding us, thinking they'd open English eyes to the murder going on. What good are the opened eyes of the blind? Families dying together of typhus, scurvy, blacklegs, where blood vessels burst under your skin. Skeleton children swelling monstrously from hunger before dying. The Irish reward for sending her sons to English armies and navies to conquer the world. What was their cure for the hunger? They sent us Queen Victoria on a goodwill tour."

She stood at the dock's edge. Ship bells marked the hour. He felt she was most at home running into the city's darkness to tear at its vitals and bring out some deeply buried saving grace. "Kathleen!" He threw off his jacket to jump in after her.

She stopped, turned, silently gazed at the city from the spot where she had arrived as an immigrant.

He glanced back without finding what entranced her. To him the sleeping city at night was a monstrous Stone Age carcass resting uneasily from the day's tumult.

"Nipper knew." Water slapped at her feet. "Those killing him were the ones telling him to shut up. How I wish I could have made Nipper as strong as he made me."

"You can't help Nipper by dwelling on him."

To Kathleen, life's mystery could be felt as deeply in the city as the country. The fate of so many different people from around the world to be decided on these dirty streets.

Emotion lowered his voice. "I'll do anything for you."

"You could have prevented the fire."

"I tried."

"In the hunger"—she gulped down air as though it were a bitter meal—"politicians said Ireland should be left to the operation of natural causes. Leaving hungry children to natural causes is murder. The gombeen men! They made fortunes selling food at the highest prices to the starving. Fight the gombeen men lest you become one yourself by your silence." She hurried away from him.

SIXTEEN

$\mathcal{T}$he next day, when he couldn't find Kathleen anywhere, Shamus went to Mulberry. They couldn't help him. The day after that the police still knew nothing about her, but they did steer him to the bone boilers. The devil's trade of bone boilers was the authority on the city's lost and missing, human and animal.

Along with everybody but the police, Shamus had not visited the bone boilers in years. He knew them, as did everyone, from afar. Their odor was cause to keep his distance. The devil's trade was a cottage industry above Eighty-sixth Street, the graveyard line. Bodies had to be buried north of Eighty-sixth Street.

No bird, ship or castaway depended on favorable winds more than the devil's trade. When the wind blew into the city, coppers came to shut down the bone boilers.

Their shanties, built from scraps, defied gravity. In their back-yard was a massive black pot no birds flew over. Men and animals avoided this patch. Yet the devil's trade was a shelter to homeless children. No matter how rough or criminal the child, they were hired on sight, no questions asked. A boy or girl had no past in the devil's trade except what showed on them.

Under the cover of night, bands of bone-boiling children combed the dark and deserted streets picking the city clean of its carrion. Coughing out the damp, they scrounged through quays and alleys. What pigs left was poked for value.

The kids were fast, merry, curious and efficient, a mark against the day world that never used their gifts. On this night they uncovered a young woman half buried in the mud and faintly breathing. They picked her up gently and swung her into their dump cart. By first light they had returned to Rotten Riley.

Rotten earned his nickname, it was obvious, not from his outlook but from his trade. He sat on a throne of stacked-up crates, stirring his cauldron with a pitchfork. Bubbles big as melons burst from his boiling properties into his cheerful face. He dressed formally, complete with black tie and topper. In any other man the raspberry scald of his cheeks would be taken for drink. In Rotten it came from hard work, as the bone boilers were prospering since the war.

When Rotten saw the young woman they hauled from the cart, he leapt from his throne and asked why they didn't take her to the police. The youngest answered that she was breathing. Rotten approved and told them to carry her in the shanty. One glance at her and Rotten said, "You can bet she's left a terrible void somewhere, in someone, and the search for her must be going on now."

"What if there's a reward that'll make us kids rich?"

"She still goes in the shanty. We have to see whether her prince is good or bad. Chivalry demands doing good without thought of reward."

"What's chivalry?" asked the youngest.

"Chivalry is dead. Take her legs."

Two days later Rotten heard a barouche creaking up the hill he had purposely steepened to gain time against the police. The live horse was a delight to the kids, who patted it affectionately. Rotten tipped his topper from the throne.

The stench kept Shamus from showing his friendliest face. "Have you seen a lost woman?"

"I've seen nothing but." Rotten reached down his glazed hand to haul up Shamus, who had taken out his handkerchief to cover his nose. "Rotten Riley. Call me Rotten."

"Shamus—" He almost tottered off the crates.

"Like the view? It's not the Crystal Palace."

An unnameable object bobbed by.

"Gettin' ye sea legs, m'hearty?"

Shamus was faint. "Enjoy your work?"

"Found money. Pickings up from the street worth more than Cortez's gold." Rotten deeply inhaled the purities as Shamus winced behind his handkerchief. "Complain for me at City Hall. Factory smoke is ruining my merchandise. I was riddled with acne, sinus, tonsilitis, furuncled ears. All cleared up. I could build a health spa over this cauldron."

"I do think I'll be going, Rotten."

"You'll learn more here than at college."

Shamus was polite. "There's two sides to every question."

"Chemistry, Shamus, is the bloodsteam of the universe. Bone boiling produces glue, self-igniting matches, and who knows the rich future in store for what's rotting now." Rotten poked his pitchfork with the leisure of an angler. "You boil a politician for his lubricating oil. A Tammany judge is a rich source of lard extract in his craneola. Warm him with favors and he turns a liquid base in your hands. Boil orators for their grease. Newspapermen for the worms eating their marrow. Boil the military for combustibles. Mystics for their spray. Boil bureaucrats for sleeping potents. Boil a lawyer for his gall, a tarry substance that sticks to anything and is costly to remove. Boil economists for their fungus, which is a popular item to hookers who've lost their power to please."

Shamus lowered his handkerchief, and his open laughter prompted Rotten to ask, "Does she have red hair?"

When Shamus almost lost his balance, Rotten helped him down and had Kathleen carried out.

"I'll take her to a doctor." Shamus's lower lip trembled.

"That's not the look of a sick woman."

Kathleen opened her eyes. No quarrel was in them. The concern of the children touched her. It hurt Shamus all the more when she glanced away from him and closed her eyes, unable to face the cruelty of the well-meaning.

Shamus sadly and sheepishly walked away.

Rotten followed the forlorn Shamus to his barouche. "You are Boss Tweed's boy?"

"That's right."

Rotten looked over the decent young man and said, "People like you give him a good name."

"If the poor waited for club men to give them a hand, they'd be drowned." This was the first time he said what he knew to be the truth, yet he felt he was demeaning himself.

Rotten agreed. "You wouldn't have come here for the greeting she gave you if you were a villain."

"Maybe I didn't know about it."

"But you think you deserved it."

SEVENTEEN

Sweeny had calming advice for Tweed: "Silky Sammy Tilden would act important in an outhouse."

Tweed was florid with anger, and this was unusual.

"Did you see how Silky ran the presidential convention? All that attention on him. Silky's being groomed. Belmont is in Silky's corner."

"You elected Hoffman governor. You control two powerful state committees in the Albany senate. Jay Gould will outspend ten Belmonts to get what he wants."

"I want Hoffman in the White House."

Sweeny's loyalty to Tweed was loyalty to his own flame of ambition. When Tweed went off the track, Sweeny worried for them both. He was worried now. "Don't muss with Belmont."

"I'm going to get rid of Belmont as the party's national chairman before he blocks every move I make."

"Take on Belmont"—Sweeny's sour-sweet smile assured Tweed defeat—"and you take on the national party. You'll be fighting the men you must win over."

The challenge fueled Tweed. "I need two newspapers whose circulation crawls out of the woodwork."

"Don't hang yourself." Sweeny was disturbed by the thorn in Tweed. "Pockets are stronger than friendship. Belmont has both."

"What newspapers are in our debt for advertising?"

Sweeny saw the noose. *"The New York Citizen."*

"And?" Tweed persisted.

"The New York Atlas."

"Both papers are to demand Belmont's resignation as party chairman."

Tweed scared the stoicism out of Sweeny. "On what grounds? Belmont has an impeccable reputation that even crosses party lines."

"Accuse Belmont of treachery to the party."

"You can't smear a leader of your own party without ironclad proof, or you'll be going down the greasy chute yourself." Sweeny feared Tweed might have stepped over the line of fierce ambition into madness. A thin line to some observers. Who knows? Sweeny had second thoughts. Madness in politics has succeeded before. It was the odds of going against the national party that bothered him, and not Tweed's state of mind.

Accusing Belmont made his pulse beat faster and gave Tweed the sensation of telling the truth even when he knew he wasn't. "Belmont"—Tweed got his focus clear—"is an agent of international money men."

"You sit on the Erie board, thanks to Mr. Gould. A railroad supported by English investors."

Tweed rebounded stronger than ever. "You made my point."

Sweeny was surprised.

"How can anyone accuse the English of being money-mad when everyone wants to imitate their superior manners?"

Sweeny's hint of a smile was as good as an ovation. A man who can smile using so little energy has to be eloquent. Tweed was ignorant of the law and an expert on justice.

Tweed hit Sweeny again. "Belmont is *not* an American citizen. He's only a naturalized citizen."

"So is every immigrant." Sweeny sensed disaster. "How can you accuse the husband of Caroline Perry of not being an American? You're sounding like your enemies the Know-Nothings."

Tweed was back at the jugular. "Did you hear of Belmont being baptized?"

The iciclelike Sweeny was bug-eyed. "You're the last one to hold a man's religion against him."

"When I'm not running for office. Have you ever heard of this convert's baptism?"

Sweeny was forced to admit, "No."

Tweed knew he held a winning hand. "Isn't that what people would say is just like a Jew?"

Sweeny took on a vulpine radiance when he sensed danger, alert to jump ship at the first list. His cherished goal to be senator would be killed by Tweed's foolhardy scheme against the party's chairman. He needed to worry Tweed back to his practical senses. "Wake up. You avoid making enemies. That's what got you here. You befriend Jews. You appointed Judge Cardozo. You dedicated the Hebrew orphanage. Now you're going in over your head." He grunted for emphasis. "And losing it."

"I'm going for president."

"Jews are not that important. They don't have votes. They're packed into Chatham Square and that's it."

"That's why," said Tweed, "we don't have to worry."

EIGHTEEN

The champ Morrissey burst into Sweeny's City Hall office. "Where is he?"

"Who?" Men's rages brought out Sweeny's reserve.

"Tweed, that's who."

"The Boss is not here, Representative Morrissey. Did you try his home?" Sweeny was helpful with the least amount of effort, and that stung the champ.

"The family is in Greenwich." Morrissey perched on Sweeny's desk, sliding papers onto the floor. "Is he at Cos Cob?"

"I don't know where Cos Cob is."

Morrissey dropped off the desk into a chair as though he'd been hit by a straight arrow. "I must find Tweed." Distress forced Morrissey on Sweeny's well-known lack of sympathy. "I'm going to be ruined!"

"Morally or financially?" Either way Sweeny was unmoved.

Morrissey let loose. "Gold!" He could blow it up.

"The Boss doesn't speculate in gold fever."

"Where did he get those maniac friends Skunk and Jubilee? They'll try anything, do anything, think anything."

"Mr. Gould and Mr. James Fisk yacht with President Grant."

"How could the Skunk believe he could corner the gold market?"

"The war made gold scarce. Only fifteen million dollars in circulation."

"All I won in the ring is lost. And more. They were letting me in on gold as a favor, because I was champ."

Fools are incurable, was Sweeny's unspoken diagnosis.

The champ impulsively opened Sweeny's ornate humidor and squeezed a fistful of Havana cigars into dust. "The Shoddy are taking over the country. When I get back to Washington, I'm ordering an investigation."

"Good luck," said Sweeny dryly.

Morrissey's head dropped so low, he could be counted out on his feet. "Where's the rules? Bare knucks is a joyride compared to what's legal. You must get me Tweed."

"I've enough trouble working for the next election. The Republicans have passed a law against repeaters. Federal bayonets are going to guard the city polls."

Morrissey amazingly forgot his own troubles. "No repeaters?"

"Zero."

"That's a good twenty-six thousand votes less. Tweed is crazy to take on Belmont at a time like this."

"You saw Belmont's pack run the convention."

"Reformers are howling for Tweed's blood."

Sweeny's dryness was euphoric. He placed his hands on the thick volume of city ordinances as he would a Bible. "Ten-dollar permit for temporary use of the sidewalk. Ten-dollar tax to move stock to and from a place of business. A tax on awnings. We'll show reformers we respect the law until we make them cry uncle."

"You'll never scare Tom Nast. Did you see Nast's drawing of Belmont as a scapegoat and a Tammany rough kicking the goat?"

"No." Sweeny was defensive, showing he had seen it.

"I'd rather face the Boy than Tom Nast. Did you notice the upper left of that drawing you didn't see?"

"You won't find Tweed here." Sweeny wanted to get rid of him.

"You'll find Tweed in Nast's cartoon for the first time. His likeness is poor. You can barely recognize the Boss. Nast hasn't filled him in. Nast thinks you're the boss because of your brains. But it's just the kind of notice Tweed hates. The Boss is in the background now, but he's walking into a hammer. I don't want to be around when Nast puts Tweed up front. And I don't like the enemies you boys are keeping lately." Morrissey fled City Hall.

NINETEEN

$\mathcal{H}$anging in the mayor's office was a large Matt Brady photograph of Tweed gazing down with disinterest. Stuffed into the mayor's chair beneath the iconic photograph was Tweed himself. The elegant Mayor Oakey Hall sat on a corner of his desk. Comptroller Connolly and Chamberlain Sweeny sat away from each other around the mayor's desk.

Connolly quietly announced, "The city has run out of money."

"Impossible." Sweeny was quick to suspect the worse. "Taxes have shot up like wildfire." Of course, Sweeny knew it was all too possible, even assured. He had to pee a dab on Slippery to mark where the trail began if a scandal arose.

Connolly had a manner of letting the facts accuse those who doubted them. "The city's debt has doubled in two years."

Tweed waved that fact off as time-wasting. "Debt is profitable."

No one cheered up.

"The poorer the financial risk of the city, the higher the interest the banks charge. The banks get their interest and we get their money. That's prosperity, not debt. Everybody gains."

Sweeny was skeptical. "The public may not be smart enough to figure that out."

"Raise taxes to balance the books," Tweed said calmly.

"People are saying politics is their biggest tax." Connolly anxiously paused. "And people vote."

Sweeny offered, "Don't tax. Let people sink into their own muck. They can't blame us for crime and dirty streets if they don't pay taxes to keep up their city, and nobody can point a finger at us. To raise taxes you need voter confidence."

"You want to test voter confidence in us?" Tweed asked heartily. "We'll form an investigating committee of blue ribbons to examine our books."

Distressful coughing and hawking up of phlegm from Connolly. Sweeny and Hall wanted a hole to dive in.

Tweed went through their stop signs. "We'll select the finest investigating committee IOUs can buy."

Smiles and grins.

Tweed asked smartly, "The number-one blue ribbon?"

Connolly frowned on going into the lion's den. "Astor the Second."

"Astor the Second will head the investigation." Tweed shocked them.

"Astor won't act as our mouthpiece." Connolly was out of character by being despondent, although his prudent look and his despondent one were close to the same.

"True," said Tweed, "if Astor's real estate taxes were figured without special favors. Now another trump?"

Hall's cultured voice. "Former Mayor Opdyke, the bastard."

Sweeny declared, "That lizard will never risk his banking reputation approving our books. He'll have to certify a mistake of thirty million dollars or more."

"We need a reputable man," said Tweed.

Connolly coughed his dissent. "We've vouchers made out to . . . you see . . . the boys were so sure of themselves . . . so self-confident . . . a quality you look for in an organization . . . they made out checks to Mr. Dummy."

Tweed brushed it over. "A mistake of overconfidence. Who will notice it if we don't bring it to their attention?"

"There's a legitimate expense of thirty-five thousand dollars," said Connolly.

"Why bother me with honest entries?" Tweed was short with him.

Connolly explained in a neutral voice, "A one was added."

"Where?"

"In front."

"You jumped a check by a hundred thousand dollars?"

Connolly regained confidence at the daring it showed. "It was the right time to do it."

"How do you figure that?" The balm of humor deserted Tweed.

"The thirty-five was small."

"Why," Tweed patiently asked, not to place blame, "when you are devoid of humor do you infect the books with it?"

"It came out of virtue." Connolly felt unjustly attacked.

"Which virtue?" Tweed mildly asked.

"Self-confidence."

"Comptroller"—Tweed broached the question with care so as not to ruffle temperamental feathers—"how much of the city books is cooked?"

A self-assured Connolly answered, "Fifteen million."

Moans, groans and a catcall whistle.

Connolly quietly added, "The first quarter of the year."

Sweeny and Hall sickened.

Tweed came to the rescue. "The best way to cover up a scandal is to investigate it."

TWENTY

*A*ugusta was getting ready for her evening with Tweed by taking an extraordinarily cold bath in her suite at the Fifth Avenue Hotel. She stepped into the tub with the dress on that she would wear that evening to dinner. The cold water that she braved made her lips tremble, sucked in her cheeks and closed her eyes. When her chemise gown was thoroughly soaked against her shivering body, she rose from her bath with purple lips and teeth chattering. No chemist more avidly watched an experiment than she her dripping self in a full-length mirror.

To measure her success Augusta held before her a magazine illustration of Adah Isaacs Menken in her notorious costume for the sold-out production of *Mazeppa*. The popular Menken was billed as The Naked Lady. She wore nothing onstage except pink tights while stretched on her back across a spirited horse, her hands and legs roped to the horse and her wildly attractive head thrown back against the mane.

The scandalous Adah was an international celebrity, a darling of the English literati. She knew five languages, including Latin, Greek and Hebrew. In London she knew Dickens and in the U.S. was idolized by Mark Twain and the miners of the West.

She was married to the ever-popular and still handsome Boy

Heenan. Adah forgot to divorce an earlier husband and kept her bigamy to herself. There is a point of no return in scandals, even when it came to filling theaters.

Adah Isaacs Menken had begun her public life in New York before the Civil War. She belonged to one of the city's unsung glories: the underground poets. They met at Pfaff's beer cellar. The women cut their hair rebelliously short and even smoked. Adah Isaacs Menken read her confessional erotic poetry celebrating her enjoyment of sex with men. But what Adah did as a sideline, far from her scandalous ways that filled theaters and put her face and form in popular magazines, earned her a place in the nation's history. She championed with her considerable intelligence an obscure New Yorker, Walt Whitman.

When Augusta was dry, she was satisfied with the impression she would produce. She flung on an opera cape and went down to the brougham waiting at the curb.

In the Chelsea brownstone where she was headed, Jubilee Jim Fisk was holding forth with Mrs. Josie Mansfield, while Tweed impatiently waited for Augusta to arrive. "I succeeded as a peddler among Vermont Yankees, so I can sell mice to spinsters." Jubilee's bushy red mustache was waxed to a tickle point. A cherry diamond sparkled on his shirtfront. Diamonds adorned his stubby fingers, which were squeezing the padded behind of Mrs. Mansfield. "I peddled every backwoods chicken path. Vermont Yankees talk with their mouths shut and I, little boy Jimmy Fisk, sold them." Jubilee was stout as a tankard. He barked with pathos. "How I love my Yankee wife, Lucy."

"You street dog." Josie tried to free her behind. "Praising your wife but never going back to her."

"Honor keeps me back. I'm not worthy of her. I took my Lucy unstained from a Vermont seminary."

"Oh, lovely," scoffed Josie. "The wife as saint . . . will you get your hands out of my drawers? My cross . . . leave my garters alone. My cross is getting heavier to bear." The neatly gowned Josie was coming apart in his hands. He began to pull down her drawers with his horse teeth. She slapped him away. "You street dog."

Tweed enjoyed their company as he sat in a room stocked with objects of art.

A struggling Josie threw Jubilee off. "I need respect, even if I don't have any success stories."

He pressed his head between her thighs. "Don't interrupt a penitent." His voice bubbled up. "Lucy wants me happy."

"Saint Lucy. The saints rake in the board."

"I bought you this brownstone. Just around the corner from my grand opera house." He took pride in the brownstone, as crammed as an auction warehouse.

"Some grand opera? *The Twelve Temptations* with a chorus of fifty blondes and fifty brunettes. Contains nothing objectionable."

"I bought you a painting by a Dutch master. Where is it?"

"I don't enjoy quiet things."

The door bell had Josie quickly straightening out her drawers.

A ravishing Augusta swept in, whirled off her opera cape and shocked even Jubilee and Josie by her illusion of nudity. Jubilee dropped to his fat knees and crawled to Augusta on all fours with tongue rolled out like a parched dog.

"Bring on your women!" Jubilee barked. "I ain't afraid of measuring my Lucy against them. Don't judge Lucy by her James."

"Street dog." Josie tugged him away by his starched collar.

"Can't a penitent enjoy himself?"

"Dirty dog." Josie kneed him in the ribs.

Jubilee bit Josie's behind, and she jumped out of the way. "I'm Jubilee Jim Fisk. My partner is Jay Gould. Jay is the brains. I'm the executive. I saddle the press for him." He humbly kissed Augusta's hem, then her shoe, before being yanked away by Josie, who pulled him out of the room and slammed the door.

A glowing Tweed asked, "Why'd you do it?"

"In memory of Niagara Falls."

"I want to give you a brownstone like this."

Augusta glanced at him as she would a bale of hay. "Nothing touches the heart in this house except the money it costs."

His laughter rolled in and out like the tide. He wanted Augusta. He needed her independent spirit! "I want to buy you a house, horses, stable, carriage."

"Why?" Augusta was amused.

Her looks made him daring. "The same reason a tradesman joins a club he can't afford. To give me an exalted worth of my success."

She felt his weakness through his generosity and became gentle. In his opening up so completely, she felt his fear. "Something in you is eroding and making you lovable."

"At last."

"And impossible. You can't win happiness back through me."

"Please." He was scared to hear any more. "Sleep on it."

"Sleep is not my restful time of day." She saw he was hurt. "You don't like the way I talk to you?"

"No. Yes." Both answers crisply given.

She was sympathetic and scared. "You and your damn talk of money. I'm not ready anymore." She no more wanted to touch his weakness than he wanted to feel weak. She knew she was unjust, but she couldn't give him anything when he was weak. And the refreshing self he wanted brought out her own weakness. "I can't give what you want. You're not lightning from the sky and I'm not a genie who refreshes. I need one myself."

She was killing him with her honesty. "I can live with unbalanced books."

He had to hold on to her at any cost and found himself saying the worst about his power. "I never want to feel with you what I feel every day in my business. People feeling close to you out of desperation and thinking you share their hatreds. Fear taking the place of closeness. How can you measure success when you're judged by the god you worship rather than the decent children you raise up?" He was sinking as the best of himself was coming out.

She never felt prepared for him, even when she admired him. "I adore you when you're unrehearsed."

A moment ago he'd have given his life to hear her praise. Now he cried out, "I only feel unrehearsed when I'm crazy."

Augusta didn't want him possessing her for qualities she lacked. "Your ambition sticks in you like a knife."

With pride he sunk his teeth into himself as he would a thick steak. "That's the way I always want to be. Hunger for the best sticking in me like a knife."

His honest rough edge coming out thrilled her.

But he showed her a gentler side. "I never want to join that army of men who've lost their drive but not their dreams."

She didn't know how to stop his avalanche that was jumbling her up. She had to stick fast to what she wanted and not be thrown off by his thunderous desires. "You've no time for a woman. You think sex is owed to you."

He was tortured. "You say that to me? I could have any woman I wanted, but I have one who thinks she's owed everything in the world. I didn't have time for you? Me? Who risked everything I worked for just to see you?"

"That shows how dense you are. I was going to bed with a wall."

"I gave you everything and I'm a dense wall?"

Her own insecurities jangled her. "I don't like your fat."

He was stunned and quaking.

"You're not the shape of a man I ever wanted. Is that getting whatever I want?"

He dreaded leaving her yet was compelled to rush away. How could he have been so wrong, so blind? What was worse—wrong, blind, no matter—he needed her. This need agonized him, marked him, told on him by giving him a coarser-grained face that announced he was incomplete. My God, when he remembered how he used to smile without thinking! Did he need this awakening? A minute's refreshment in her company and he paid a price for a lifetime.

"Money made you stupid."

"That's what I thought." He was in a daze at leaving, staying.

"I'm confirming it." She was also railing against herself, and that made her doubly effective. "You thought you could buy everything, and in making money you lost how to enjoy it."

He rushed out, slamming the door, hoping the weakening diseases he carried would be left behind and not follow him with their haunting presence. This break with Augusta came at the worst time. Bad, bad omen. His internal needs had made him powerful, now they weakened him, dropped his guard, made horrendous mistakes out of desire. Unknowingly he slammed the door so fiercely, it popped open and he was hammered with her farewell.

"You stink as the nice man you want to be."

He cried out as he ran from her. "I must see you again!"

"Dirty ticket," she answered his anguished plea. "Open for business. Closed for giving affection."

Street life did not revive him. He must be more deeply troubled than he knew. How could this be happening to him? Losing wife, mistress. No longer sure of his friends. Yet he was on top! The good life is always somewhere else.

TWENTY-ONE

*H*e held an extraordinary note from Mary Jane as the toy-painted train puffed along the scenic wooded shoreline to Greenwich. Mary Jane *demanded* his presence.

Since Mary Jane had left him to his own devices, a demand from her deserved immediate attention. Did she find out about Augusta? He'd never give Augusta up, if he should ever be so fortunate to have her. Augusta was his second wind. How could Mary Jane know? Augusta did live in nearby Cos Cob. But who could look at Augusta and believe she was anyone's mistress? Mary Jane could.

He was prepared for the worst, but the worst was that he had no defense. One look and he'd know whether Mary Jane meant divorce. That would be his ruin then and there. How could she divorce him? A divorced woman carries a stigma.

Mary Jane couldn't have been whiter if she was poisoned. "Bill?" A wife of some years has a shorthand few can capture.

"Yes?" His attentive word let her know her importance.

Color rose in her face only with her effort to speak calmly. "You must stop your anti-Semitic foulness against Mr. Belmont. It dirties us far more than the Jews."

He was ablaze with her insult. "Me, anti-Semitic? Is this a madhouse? I'm the champion of immigrants. Why, Morris Pease, Loring Brace and I are the only three decent men in town. Mr. Pease teaches kids a trade. The Children's Aid Society gives them shelter and care. I give them jobs. If an immigrant was bleeding to death in front of an exclusive club, they'd have him arrested for contempt."

"Bill, the servants."

"Belmont doesn't need your defense. He has an arsenal of Christian friends. They've already quashed any newspaper from following up."

"It's nothing to shout about. The decent thing should be done." She watched him as though he were untrained. "Now lower your voice."

He raised his voice. "I dedicated the Hebrew orphanage."

"That's why you're so awful."

"I race home to take a beating."

"You're the one who told me Jews had to build their own hospitals and train their own doctors because sick and dying Jews are preyed on to convert. They had to build Jews Hospital they now call Mt. Sinai."

In the silence that followed he sensed a truce.

Mary Jane continued on a quieter, more forceful level. "I wish you would stop thinking of people by their religion."

"Do you want to leave me helpless? How else can I know how they vote?" He gazed down through the trees on his green and shaded acres to the sparkling blue Sound. "Anti-Semitism is part of being a success."

She turned away.

"What's got into *you?*" he accused her. "Who can stand being an outsider? Being against Jews shows you want to belong."

Mary Jane tightly closed her eyes.

He tried again, sounding more compatible. "Not liking Jews is like badmouthing your wife to be one of the boys. Okay. Say I'm invited to dinner? I tell the man next to me I'm Tammany. That could make me an enemy. But if I say kike, sheeny or who knows what ignoramus stupidity, we're friends. Anti-Semitism is good table manners. I don't know, Mary Jane, maybe you don't eat out and want to make friends."

Mary Jane opened her eyes to stare sense into him.

"I'm trying," he pleaded, "to make you see reason. Do you expect people to blame themselves for their failings? The easiest way to get a dollar out of a man's pocket is to get him to hate. Be intelligent."

"Sympathy is the best intelligence." She could choke him.

"You're not thinking, Mary Jane. I'm trying to make you see the light, not fairy tales." He turned his palms up to show it wasn't his fault what he knew. "Tolerance to Christians is like pork to rabbis. No matter how beautifully described, they can't develop a taste for it."

Mary Jane couldn't bear to look at him. "You believe you're a success?" She wanted to say more but choked at his coarseness, which he mistook for maturity.

"I know I'm a success. I feel injustice less and less."

Mary Jane left him with a warning: "Do nothing to hurt Mary Amelia's chance to marry." Tears of compassion filled her eyes for her unprotected daughter.

In Mary Jane's distaste for him he saw his drive in a clearer light. His neglect of responsibilities had sadly become part of his strength. But to do away with this fever would be doing away with himself.

TWENTY-TWO

*N*ew York's buildings and monuments are seldom discussed or even noticed. Now the least expected building had become an incendiary monument: the Hall of Justice. In the public's mind it bears the realistic name of Tweed's Courthouse. The Romanesque box is an American-built English copy of a copy Italian in character. No one would have been emotional about this building except for the monumental graft attached to it. Speakers of the Young Democracy reformers had only to mention its popular name in derision to draw applause. To fire up crowds the speakers had only to retell its infamous history, which continued to raise the burdening taxes of the city. The public saw the roof was left for last, and rain and snow fell for weeks on end through this extravagantly costly building as in a sump hole. The courthouse stands in the backyard of graceful City Hall like healthy dog's doo in the sun.

The downstairs was crowded with office-seekers and Shiny Hats who carried on as though nothing were amiss. Inside Tweed's new office it was different. Newsboys from the *Sun* and the *World* were heard hawking their papers: "TWEED MUST WALK THE PLANK. THE RING IS A DEAD DUCK. HONEST MEN FIGHTING TRAITORS."

"Why did we have to move into this courthouse?"

Tweed was offended by Sweeny's lack of appreciation. "The public has to see the courthouse is being used."

"Boilers don't work. Windows won't open. Walls are peeling. Offices are dirty. Department heads complain they have no carpets. Reformers are having a field day."

"The courthouse is our strength."

Sweeny, who was realistic as a toothache, closed his eyes as Tweed chirped away.

"Soon as we control the state, I'm using the courthouse plan on Albany. Let O'Brien and Morrissey howl their heads off. Jobs are loyalty." Tweed rubbed his hands, clapping them over the fires of his ambition, which was visible before him. "I'm going to rip out the center of Albany and rebuild it."

Sweeny's anxiety softened the stone in his face.

Tweed was feeling his oats. "Jobs. Contracts. Every upstate cheese and hayloft leader will be in our debt. We'll be honored for modernizing Albany while strangling reform."

"Reformers are exposing the Board of Supervisors for approving the bills on the courthouse."

The thrill of the game had Tweed's blood up. "I'll do away with the Board of Supervisors. We're going to be the reformers."

That was too much for Sweeny to swallow.

"We'll bring government back to the people."

Sweeny spoke through a built-in damper. "How?"

Tweed slapped his ace. "Home rule."

Sweeny burst Tweed's bubble. "The city had home rule. It was so corruptly run, the reform Republicans turned the city over to the state."

"Which is why people will appreciate having it back."

"How on earth can you convince our enemies to go along with home rule?"

Tweed was amiable. "A new charter."

"What'll that do?" Sweeny wasn't buying.

"It'll do away with the Board of Supervisors."

"That's just what reformers want."

"That's why they'll go along."

Sweeny invoked the age-old curse. "Money?"

"One million should get a new charter passed."

"Is the rural vote that expensive?"

"Rural virtues sell at city prices," Tweed explained. "When you ask in Albany what the legislature passed in this session, they say six months."

Sweeny had to smile, but it didn't stop him from saying, "Giving the reformers what they want is no victory."

"It doesn't matter what the laws are as long as we administer them."

When Albany heard of Tweed's stupendous plan, the boarding-houses hummed.

Tweed was in his senator's office when Sweeny arrived with good news. "I've pocketed the most influential hayloft senator, Woodin from Cayuga and Wayne Counties."

Tweed sang out the top figure. "Twenty-five thousand dollars."

"Woodin is highly regarded. He takes four key senators with him."

"A hundred thousand," Tweed called to be fair on the high side.

Sweeny's solemnity told him his high side was low.

"How respectable is Woodin?" Tweed didn't care to ask.

"Two hundred thousand." Sweeny took pride in his capture.

"That's a fortune to assess city contractors. To get it we'll have to assess dogs peeing against posts."

"You can't get more respectable men than Senator Woodin."

"You're that high on Woodin?"

"I'll stake my life on his reputation," said Sweeny, who was grudging in praise.

"Buy him," said Tweed.

Sweeny dined on suspicions. His day, therefore, was never done. The only weight he ever gained was around his heart. "Can your prince of plasterers stand the reformers' pressure on the court-house?"

"I promoted Garvey because he was the best qualified for the courthouse job. He knows addition, subtraction and silence."

TWENTY-THREE

One moment the reformers had the momentum and were waiting for the prize to drop in their lap, and the next moment Tweed's bombshell charter exploded and sent them scurrying for ways to protect themselves. Norton and Creamer rushed to prospering Albany to stir Tilden into action. They met in a private room at the Bucket O' Blood where the patrons would not know or care about Tilden.

How had Tweed raised another million dollars? Tweed excelled at the squirrel mentality of politics, stashing away favors for a rainy day. He watered everyone without regard to their party or principles professed in public. Men devoid of loyalty were not written off because he never knew when he might need them. Who was going to refill Tweed's public treasury? Tweed's tax levy bill would get the money back from the taxpayers. This latest news put the reformers in a corner. A pall settled over them.

Mike Norton broke from the gate first, leaning across the table to the composed Tilden. "Sam, you must expose the jokers in Tweed's charter."

Caution thinned Tilden's voice and made him remote. His pointed upper lip revealed distress. "What are you questioning? Don't you trust anyone, Norton?"

Creamer came to Norton's defense. "It's that damn Tweed. He

made us this way. He's so friendly, you never know where you stand."

Tilden came off his horse. "I'm with reform all the way."

The men nodded in order not to reveal their doubts. They were glad to see O'Brien arrive, but he had news that shook them. The good gray poet who celebrated country virtues, William Cullen Bryant, had fired Charles Nordhoff from the *New York Post* for fighting the Tweed Ring. O'Brien gave voice to their fears as he hurriedly sat down: "If you don't expose Tweed's charter, we're lost."

Tilden disliked their blunt energy, their thinking by leaps like headlines on a page. They could only be chained for the good of the party. He didn't know how Tweed managed to milk the best of their energies for himself so long. He deftly sidestepped all responsibility that would put him in a corner. "The Astor Committee report will destroy Tweed."

"That report won't be out until just before election," Norton reminded Tilden.

O'Brien's fears boiled out. "Who knows how Tweed also silenced the *Sun?*"

"Tweed's money," said Creamer, "gives him ears everywhere."

"Sam"—Norton wanted to put the screws to the evasive Tilden —"expose Tweed's censoring the press, corrupting legislators, extorting merchants, taking a cut off every city bill that's paid."

To Tilden this bill of criminal particulars only revealed how widely Tweed's power ran. Tilden called for good sense. "We want a winning party, not a divided party."

Norton was at Tilden. "Tweed's new charter will legislate reformers out of office. On a platform of bringing government back to the people, Tweed is going to hang his enemies. You don't know the villainy you're dealing with because he's so optimistic about using you. He always has you saluting the flag. Here you are pussyfooting around with him."

"A head-on attack is not the best policy." Tilden tried to temper their vitality. He knew they weren't safe when thinking for themselves.

"Any attack will do." Norton urged.

Tilden tried to sober them with a matter-of-fact tone. "Tweed sits on powerful committees as senator and gives out plums."

Norton said with pride, "We're the leaders of the biggest wards."

"But Tweed has the people in them." Tilden didn't want to discourage them, only put his foot on their necks.

Norton squared his shoulders and tried to get Tilden to make a move, any move. "Sam, you've the prestige to fight the jokers in Tweed's charter."

"He's giving reform what it wants—a strong mayor. And he's doing away with the old Board of Supervisors." Tilden eyed Norton with an icy disdain they wished he'd use on Tweed.

"To be replaced by his Board of Audit: Tweed, Black Brains, Slippery and Elegant. They'll pass on claims for money and can only be removed by the mayor and judges. All owned by Tweed."

Tilden tossed them the steak. "Tweed stands on feet of clay. The Ring has enormous debts."

"Stealing," said O'Brien.

"This will show up in the Astor report."

"We've got to fight Tweed now," O'Brien urged. "The people are saying you can trust Tweed because he has a full stomach. But the Young Democracy is hungry. Sammy, listen. To decent, intelligent citizens Tweed has made politics the experience of waking up in your own hometown a stranger. Your only protection money and he's just stolen it. He becomes a hero by giving part of his boodle back."

That convinced Tilden his caution was correct.

TWENTY-FOUR

$\mathcal{A}$ news board has gone up in Printing House Square that has not drawn this large a crowd since the list of war dead, missing and wounded at Gettysburg:

ASTOR COMMITTEE APPROVES TWEED RING FINANCES

"Correct and Faithful," Report
Six Distinguished New Yorkers
Investigating Ledgers

From office to home Tweed was congratulated and cheered. He had also had his charter for city reform passed in Albany. Mary Jane greeted him with a smile. Tweed, laden with flowers and cake, read from one of the many newspapers under his arm. "Senator Tweed is in a fair way to distinguish himself as a reformer."

Mary Jane hugged his beefy arm.

A lit pumpkin could not twinkle as warmly as Tweed, who kept reading: "Having gone so far as the champion of the charter, Mr. Tweed seems to have no idea of turning back. He has put the people of Manhattan under great obligation." He beamed. "And *that* from a paper against me."

"Bill, this is one of the happiest days of my life."

He whipped out a letter and proudly waved it under Mary Jane's nose. "Peter Cooper, cream of the cream."

"If only you could have known Mr. Cooper when the Prince of Wales was here. We might have been invited to the ball."

"Mary Jane, please, don't bring up forgotten chitchat. Mr. Cooper has stepped down from his pedestal to write me. Hand-delivered. And you dredge up every social slight. Do you know what Mr. Cooper wants?"

"We're invited to a ball?"

"Mr. Cooper wants a job for a friend." Tweed yawned.

"Is that all?"

"Bigger fish," he said, "have been hooked with smaller bait."

"Even when you're happy, you're discouraging to talk to."

He looked on her tenderly. "Would you enjoy an audience with the Prince of Wales, Mom?"

She didn't know what to make of his enthusiasm, though it did make her happy. "Mr. Cooper knows the queen?"

"Damn that glue-maker Cooper."

In her eyes was the memory of his failure at their not being invited to the ball of the century though he was important.

"We'll soon have money to retire." He crumpled Cooper's letter and tossed it away.

"It'll be so good for you." She inadvertently condemned his work.

"With Jay Gould's backing we'll have Governor Hoffman in the White House. He'll appoint me Ambassador to the Court of St. James's."

Mary Jane's eyes lit up with gratitude for her husband.

"You enjoy that ambition, eh?" Tweed was touched by her affection. "Now, mind you, Mary Jane, when we get to London, you must not be too strict with Queen Victoria."

Part Three

ESCAPE

TWENTY-FIVE

$\mathcal{T}$he modest street door to Tweed's Duane Street office bore a discreet sign: WILLIAM M. TWEED, ATTORNEY-AT-LAW. By virtue of the power vested in Judge Barnard, Senator Tweed was also a lawyer. Behind the door there was a realistic spirit of prosperity. Shiny Hats and favor seekers packed the stairs and foyer leading to Tweed's office. At Tweed's approach the stairway inhabitants squeezed together to make room for his slow and huffing effort up the stairs. A Shiny Hat respectfully jested that it wasn't like the old days when Tweed ran to fires as the chief of the Big Six volunteers. "I'm a living example," Tweed huffed, "to abstain . . . from the . . . good life." That drew laughter up and down the stairs and into his foyer as his reply was repeated and he stopped on a stair to rest.

"You've got a great reputation, Boss," a Shiny Hat boasted.

"Oh, no," said Tweed, wiping his shiny lower lip with his careless hand, "I wish I had the reputation of old Elijah Purdy."

"None better than yours," said a Shiny Hat, and there was an immediate loud murmur of agreement from all within earshot.

"Oh, no." Tweed put his faithful straight. "Elijah Purdy had a sterling reputation for honesty."

"Don't be so hard on yourself, Boss."

"Purdy was known never to take a bribe. He only gave them." Roars of laughter while Tweed finally made the top of the stairs. "You don't have to be an honest politician if you're a level one."

"Congratulations on becoming a lawyer, Boss."

"Do you know how they examine future lawyers before the bar?" Tweed shook hands of congratulations all around. "They question the would-be lawyer if he had a client suing the city for twenty-five thousand dollars, how would he handle the case? The correct answer is, 'I'd go see Senator Tweed.'"

The laughter subsided only when Tweed confessed, "I'd make a better judge because of my objectivity. My prejudices are the prejudices of the many."

The laughter did not fade until Tweed focused his attention on a bantam woman whose dress stuck to her like a burst balloon and blocked his way with a sorrowful reproach in her eyes.

"I'm Mrs. Delaney of Cockroach Row. A dog's pee comes out warmer than me from my flat. I'd like to get into the new Mott Street houses."

Good as done, was in Tweed's friendly eyes. "Where's my boy Shamus?"

By the gun-shy manner in which the Shiny Hats became silent, Tweed knew something important was up. None dared mention a murderous fire to Tweed because his fire inspectors were on the take.

Tweed turned on a Shiny Hat. "Where is he?"

"The boy is with his trouble."

"Was she burned in the fire?" Tweed was aghast.

"The kids from the devil's trade found her, and that's where she is now. The only loss was a rat-catcher boy and that saved him from being thrown into a swamp cell at the Tombs."

Tweed turned. "Give me your name and address, dearie."

"Did you forget, your honor, I said Cockroach Row? You wouldn't if you lived there." She was plainly without jaundice.

He scribbled her name and address on stationery from his rock quarry company.

"You're most kind, your honor, Mr. Tweed." She hugged his arm and left happily.

"The scruddy squash," said Tweed, amused as he moved into his office and was surprised to find three stout and solidly dressed citizens who wasted no time in getting to their point.

"Mayor Hall has canceled the Orange Day Parade."

Tweed plumped down in a stew as the Orangemen stood like a gate in front of him.

"This is the first time in the history of our democratic city that one group has censored the rights of freemen to parade."

"There must be some mistake." Tweed was completely in sympathy with them. "Oakey is not only the mayor but he's a lawyer. He knows it's wrong."

"Does he have the power?"

"He has the power but not the inclination." Tweed hollered for a heeler to fetch him the mayor. He got up and escorted the Orangemen to the door. "Plan to parade. I guarantee you police protection and anything else you might want. Orangemen have an open door with me."

"Thank you, Senator."

He patted each of the Orangemen on the back and confided, "We're riding a crest of popularity, and you know, boys will be boys. Popularity can bring out the worst in them."

They shook hands heartily all around, and the foes he had made friends of repeated their appreciation of him. Tweed moved slowly to his seat. To cheer himself up he opened a jeweler's box holding a pair of diamonds that he quickly snapped shut.

Connolly walked so heavily, it took time to realize he was not profound. This time, as the odds would have it, he was on to something crucial. Connolly came in complaining that Sweeny was reducing everyone to a cog in a political machine.

Tweed amiably likened Connolly to the modern cannon advanced in the Civil War, where for the first time in history you could kill people without having to see them. To lighten Connolly's frown Tweed again pinched open his jeweler's box and a pair of button diamonds drizzled light on him. "For Mary Amelia's wedding shoes."

Connolly felt the pangs of the haves who haven't enough. "I thought she wanted a modest wedding?"

"Look how small they are." The diamonds touched Tweed's self-awareness. "I must be a Shoddy at heart. I make up in display what I lack in taste."

"If you're so worried about being a Shoddy, you can play it down."

"I don't have enough faith in people's sensitivity to play it down. You know how crass they can be?" He returned the jewel box to his pocket, full-chested like a maestro.

Connolly put out his wash. "You and I do ninety percent of the work. Half the budget is spent to raise the other half. The comptroller does most of the collecting from the merchants and landlords doing business with the city."

Tweed iced him. "That goes with your job."

"The biggest job deserves the biggest cut."

"From where?" Tweed reached for his own throat.

"Elegant only signs his name approving the bills. Black Brains oils the machinery without dirtying his hands. I wish I had their racket. I'd be happy with one percent."

Tweed's expressive grimace condemned the thought even as he wanted to know more. "You can't take anyone out."

"I don't want them out. I want them cut. That's only fair."

Tweed resisted the temptation to find out how tough a case Connolly had. "I can't allow it."

"No one keeps track of all the bills pouring in but you and me."

Tweed kept pressing. "Everyone gets his share or they'll be on the warpath."

"They'll get their share. Only twenty percent less on the new bills."

"Forget it. You can't make that steal legal."

"But I can make it foolproof."

"That's legal," Tweed agreed as Sweeny barged in.

Sweeny was so self-satisfied, no one could remain satisfied in his company. He barbed Connolly. "What brings you here?"

Connolly's truculence hid his guilt. "We want to come to terms with O'Brien." He went superior. "Turn the other cheek."

"On which of your faces?" Sweeny asked smoothly.

Tweed hurried to the rescue. "United we're safer."

"Slime," Sweeny uttered a bit too generally.

The pejorative stuck in Connolly's thick eyebrows.

Tweed said with goodwill, "Buying our old sheriff will give us a spy in Tilden's camp."

"Scum," Sweeny retorted.

"True." Tweed agreed, taking for granted Sweeny meant their old sheriff, though not one hundred and ten percent certain he didn't mean them too.

"Gutter fungus," rasped Sweeny. "No backbone. No loyalty. No trust. No work. No contribution. This is what you reward?"

While Tweed and Connolly didn't quail, neither did they reply.

"An illiterate weasel empties your pockets?"

"No one says you don't have a strong case," Tweed conceded. "To be sure, the sheriff is an asshole. But he's our asshole."

"Did the blackmailer raise the ante?"

Tweed sought to be fair. "He added a hundred thousand dollars because he's a reformer now. His word is worth more."

Sweeny wouldn't let them wiggle off the hook. "You must not give in to a low-life ignoramus as a point of honor. You must loathe his lies. The swine doesn't deserve your trust. He will muddy you. I don't see how you can even consider being under the thumb of an illiterate crook."

Tweed tried to reason. "We let him steal to keep him loyal."

"The weasel ran an empire under our roof. Sixty percent of his payroll was a lie."

Tweed soft-pedaled his own defense. "Wasn't I the one who kicked him off the ticket when you wanted him?"

"Best thing you ever did." Sweeny rolled with the hit.

"Now it's time to take the gutter fungus back. We did it with lower forms of life: Francis Boole for one."

Sweeny burdened them with an allusion and fled. "The coward pays many times."

Connolly was so shaken, he sided with Sweeny. "If we give in to the sheriff, he'll raise the ante."

"Why should we go suicides with Brains? The sheriff never harmed a dog. He rankles Sweeny because the slimy devil had no education. We never went to college, either. See how Sweeny talked down to us? We don't glitter with the gold key of Sigma Chisel High. If teachers wanted an answer from us, they had to give us a smart cuff on the bean. We weren't anyone's servant. If Brains wants to be unforgiving, let him be it with his own fat in the fire. We can negotiate with the sheriff without Brains, and it'll be a lot easier. Get Watson, the city auditor. The sheriff knows Watson guards the city books. Thus the sheriff knows Watson has our trust."

The comptroller rose unsteadily. "Did you see Sweeny's eyes? They're graveyards."

"Don't fall in." Tweed didn't guarantee protection. "His heartbeat doesn't tell you he's alive as much as how the rest of him is dead."

The mayor entered and Tweed attacked.

"Dummy, how could you stop the Orangemen from parading?"

Oakey was surprised to see the comptroller had slipped away.

Why blame me? was on his face. "Connolly pressured me into stopping the parade of his enemies from the Old Country."

"He's a dunce and you're a lawyer. Don't you know right from wrong? The Germans are rightly complaining they're being squeezed off the ticket in the wards. The Orangemen are protesting we don't let them parade. The papers will have another hot story against us."

"Not as hot as your burning Harper Brothers textbooks."

"I warned them their school contract would be canceled."

"Burning books to silence Nast is not good business."

"It's splendid business. I've replaced them with my own New York Printing Company."

"Nast has to fall on his face. He champions the Indians' right to vote. The Chinese's right to enter this country. He bites the hands that pin medals on him."

"I can't wait for Nast to dig his own grave. I don't mind what newspapers write. My following can't read. But they understand a Nast cartoon. If Nast keeps drawing me in prison stripes, the public will find it easier to put me in those stripes."

"You won't stop Nast by burning books."

"I'll do it with the iron argument."

"Money can't touch Tom Nast and you know it."

Tweed was on his scent. "I'm refining the argument."

"How refined can a bribe get?"

"A bribe can get to be an honor. A prize. You can't get better tone than awarding a man to shut him up."

Oakey thought Tweed had jumped the rails.

"Nast has to soak up the great museums of Europe. Improve his art by going abroad. See how artists of the past honored their bloody kings."

"Nast won't listen to any of us."

"Of course not. What do we know of art? We're not that sensitive that a woman without arms is beautiful. But I've a banker friend with a sensitive, dark side who thinks a woman having sex with a swan is beautiful."

"It won't work. What kind of an award can you give Nast?"

Tweed smiled beatifically. "We award him for his cartoons."

Elegant was impressed, almost humbled. "I'm sorry about the Orange. I'll retract my order."

"No, you dummy. Your stupidity has done us a great favor. I'll get Hoffman to rescind your order. That'll give Hoffman national

attention for upholding freedom of speech and religion." Tweed
took buoyant steps to the door. "I have to make the rounds in
Bellevue. The sick need to touch a success."

"How can you enjoy such a gruesome public duty?"

"They give me more than I give them. Touching me gives the
sick illusions while the sick give me reality."

TWENTY-SIX

*T*homas Nast's reputation was secure. He was one of the highest paid cartoonists of his day. Nast had illustrated books for the popular humorist Petroleum V. Nasby. He was raised as an immigrant boy in the German section of Greenwich Village. There he saw the tiger's-head emblem of Tweed's Big Six pumper racing by. He forgot nothing.

Nast was a natural artist-in-the-street as a young man. At nineteen he was earning the heady weekly salary of forty dollars as a magazine illustrator. He illustrated the series *Backgrounds of Civilization*, revealing poverty and its vices. He covered John Brown's hanging. He went to England for the most famous international sporting event of his time: Heenan vs. Sayers. A barbarous fight of two hours and twenty minutes was stopped by the police. Nast became a friend of the generous giant Heenan.

He followed the romantic Garibaldi's Red Brigade for Liberty in Sicily and Naples. At twenty-eight Nast was a worldly artist who had kept his original sympathy. His eyes glowed with that marvelous strength that is unassuming. He saw his own quest for fame with private dedication and public good humor.

Nast gave the world the *jolly* Santa Claus. A devoted Republican, he gave his party the symbol of the slow elephant. He also bestowed the symbol of the donkey or, more to the point, the domesticated ass on the Democrats. What an ornery beast! It turns its backside on friend and foe alike and kicks. Nast had the witty idea of putting the Tammany Indian on wheels so that it could go down its one-track mind. His symbol of communism was to be imitated thousands of times but never equaled, a grim-reaper skeleton in a high hat with the power of death in its bony fingers.

Nast was so popular, he was voted onto the board of a bank. When the board would not share its profits with the people who saved with them, Nast resigned. His popularity was in small towns, farms, big cities, everywhere Americans were trying to educate themselves and improve their conditions. With this diverse audience he fought for some of the most unpopular causes: the blacks, Chinese and Indians.

But though Tom Nast was successful beyond his dreams as an immigrant boy growing up in Greenwich Village, he was unfulfilled.

At the 1868 presidential convention in the brand-new Tammany Hall on Fourteenth Street east of Union Square, Tom Nast's instinctive eye, his passion against tyranny, his well-read background discovered the men and events for his own grand fulfillment as an artist. Unbeknownst to the peacocks onstage, they were about to gloriously fulfill Nast's life.

Harper's Weekly came out with a Nast cartoon showing Governor Seymour as the blood-haunted Lady Macbeth. A terrified Seymour is trying to rub his hands clean of the Draft Riots: "Out, damned spot! Out, I say!"

The Democrats' choice for president had barely recovered when Nast struck again. The inspiring Tweed Ring turned Nast into an artist exulting in his own powers. He was an artist living in his original fire. The fierce concentration of the cartoons possessed the open enjoyment of an artist coming into his own.

When he desired, Nast could be a draftsman to remind readers of the memorable illustrators of the great nineteenth-century novels. He did not rely on a rapier line, though he could capture the comedy of a man with such a line, or a teeny buckshot circle as he did with Tweed's eyes. His fatal thrust grew out of an accumulation of ever-darkening shadings that a patient spider might have spun out after walking across an ink pad. Tammany crooks were not crushed by caricature alone. Nast destroyed them under the weight of humanity remembered.

Tammany had no escape from the relentless Nast. He returned

to similar events from so many different angles that each time the event was alive with fresh passion. Nast contrasted two events of July 1863. The left panel displays victorious Grant at Vicksburg, the American flag flying behind Grant. The right panel shows Governor Seymour on a bloodstained platform with a dead child at his feet. His wisps of hair throw a shadow of devil horns behind him. In the background New York is burning as Seymour addresses the draft rioters as "my friends."

Loud and belligerent Tammany was trapped by Nast into silence. Protests would highlight a riot Tammany was anxious for the country to forget.

Grant was to say that two things elected him president: the sword of Sheridan and the pencil of Tom Nast.

TWENTY-SEVEN

$\mathcal{T}$he go-between with O'Brien was the city auditor, also the keeper of the city books and the collector for Tweed's
Ring, natty Jim Watson. Watson was at home in the white-collar
world as he was in jail. In both worlds he was without the albatross
of self-scrutiny. He knew which window paid off and threw away
the rest—a simple life that somehow caused his guts to leak out.
He needed his whiskey to heal the way a wounded man needs
water.

Watson arrived punctually at Berholf's Hotel on the outskirts of
town on Harlem Lane. Berholf's was far enough to serve as a resort
and near enough for horsemen to use as a watering hole. Fast
trotters up wide Third Avenue might stop at Wintergreen's. Berholf's was a darker tale. Sporting gents going to seed gave Berholf's
the luster Watson was most at home in. In the winter the landscape
froze along with business. No one was loitering, not even a whore.

Watson ordered a bottle of champagne and watched the snowfall
and sleigh races outside. He had no will to nurse a bottle, especially
alone in deserted Berholf's. Watson downed glass after glass without a warning valve going off. Then he gulped from the bottle
while waiting for the tardy O'Brien.

Watson finally sensed he was in no condition to negotiate an
important and dangerous deal for the Boss. He hied out of Ber-

holf's in his alcoholic glide, taking the stiff, unsure steps of a man getting used to stronger eyeglasses. Tottering to his sleigh, he ordered his driver to move over and snatched the reins for a quick getaway before O'Brien showed up.

Watson and O'Brien unknowingly passed each other in the snowfall. At Berholf's, O'Brien was told Watson had just left. He flew out cursing Watson for not waiting. Though O'Brien was late, his face clouded with distrust at not being met.

Snow-covered streets are dangerous because they lose their sound. O'Brien drove toward a narrow stretch in front of the St. Charles Hotel known as The Pass. Peering through the snowfall, he saw a reckless sleigh wobbling in and out of the icy ruts ahead, threatening to overturn as it entered the dangerous pass. Just as the sleigh was losing control, it was challenged by an aggressive sleigh racing unheeded into The Pass from the opposite direction.

O'Brien winced at the sickening collision. A shaft ran through the oncoming horse, which was instantly killed. The second horse, terrified and out of control, reared back to fall on its reckless driver. The helpless hooves stamping in the air struck its master on the forehead.

O'Brien whipped his horse to the rescue. He jumped out, slid and stumbled over ice and snow to the pitiful moaning. A face awash with blood was crying out, "Help me, help me." O'Brien pulled the dying man free of the struggling horse. When the bleeding head fell back into O'Brien's arms, he recognized the unconscious Watson. Immediately he dropped Watson, who sank back into the snowbank that was reddening with his blood.

O'Brien leapt into his own sleigh and drove deep into the shadows to watch unseen. His eyes were ablaze with his stroke of good luck. The accident was a once-in-a-lifetime opportunity that ran a feral energy through him.

To his amazement Watson's driver staggered up and dragged Watson through the snow and into the hotel.

Hours later a limp Watson was carried to his sleigh and propped up. The driver's breath smoked in the cold air. Before Watson's bandaged head there was darkness.

An excited O'Brien trailed behind. Watson's sleigh stopped before his new house on Forty-second Street—a house he had bought with Ring money for driving out property owners along the Hudson for a real-estate killing to be named Riverside Drive.

O'Brien couldn't believe what he was seeing! Watson was walking up the stoop of his house unaided. Each game step Watson took turned a knife in O'Brien.

He whipped his horse downtown, bumping, rocking, pitching out of and into icy ruts down dark streets. Stopping before a battered dwelling, he booted the rickety door open and barged into the sleeping house. A growling bulldog leapt from a dark corner at his throat.

O'Brien caught the bull around the neck and squeezed, shaking the bull until spittle leaked, and flung the beast against the wall where it slumped into a hunchback and whined piteously.

Leaping up the creaking stairs, the first door he banged open revealed an attic room chocked with kids sleeping pell-mell on shelf beds and cots. He crashed through to the large bedroom and yanked a sleeping man from under the covers as his startled wife screamed. The husband wrestled in the dark with his attacker as the children wailed and his wife cried for help.

"Shut them up," O'Brien warned the man he was choking.

The husband relieved their fears. "It's the sheriff."

"The next mayor." O'Brien banged the husband's head on the bare floor as the terrified wife listened intently.

"I'm making you rich, Copeland." The sheriff banged Copeland's head for luck. "You must act fast. Watson's horse kicked him in the head. He'll be out of the office for days." O'Brien's heated breath scared Copeland. "I want a copy of Tweed's books."

The wife shut the door and went to quiet the children.

Copeland's hoarseness expressed the impossible. "No one sees the books. No one's trusted near them."

"I hate crybabies." O'Brien could burn Copeland alive in his oily sweat. "Where are the vouchers kept?"

"In Watson's office."

"Jimmy it."

"The door is guarded."

"I'll find a way to get you thirty seconds."

"I'll be killed if found out."

"Forty-five seconds."

"I wouldn't know what to copy. There's hundreds, thousands of vouchers."

"Eighteen sixty-nine, 1870 will do nicely." O'Brien threw Copeland away with the contempt he showed his dog. "Two juicy Tweed years. That damn high-hat Brains will deal with me now. No go-betweens. I'm going to scramble eggs."

At the mention of Sweeny, Copeland was desperate to get out. "The steal can't be done."

"Tonight."

"Impossible."

"Work overtime."

"Let this wait. Let me think. Maybe I can come up—"

"Watson's skull is too thick. He could return tomorrow."

"Who'll protect my family?"

"I'm making you rich. What more protection you want?" O'Brien belched as he ran out of the house with the bull whining.

The next morning a messenger from the comptroller's office found Tweed leaving his new Fifth Avenue mansion and told him Watson had died. Tweed, stepping into his sleigh piled high with furs, wanted to know if Watson's office was tightly guarded. The messenger relayed Connolly's assurance that a reliable man, who worked his pants off night and day, was on the books. His name was Copeland.

TWENTY-EIGHT

A Nast cartoon could have no more art than a kid's drawing on a sidewalk, yet caught the same spontaneity to be seen.

On a quiet Sunday morning a banker visited Nast's studio. He was no stereotype of a banker. His intelligence showed he had sweetened a practical life with art. He entered the art world as he did his club, cherishing the familiar and willing to pay artists who saw no more than he did. He knew Nast's work thoroughly, yet he was not prepared for the visual onslaught of Nast's studio.

Without the thoughtful spacing of a museum or the weekly interval of publication, the studio was charged with the concentrated force of Nast's work, the crowded walls an inferno of gross and pompous circus figures with their helpless victims underfoot.

The impact was of a simple man standing against the demons of a Republic's night with only his pen. His drawings gave the faint of heart their faith against corruption, the timid saw bravery at work and the illiterate received an education in how free men think.

Nast did not excel solely as a visual artist. He had a keen scent for comedy. Before the banker's uncomfortable eyes was a splendid example of Nast's humor on the language of public relations in the service of politics. A larger-than-life, beer-barrel Tweed is pondering the widening of Broadway. Tweed loftily explains away the exorbitant and scandalous profits as "gross irregularity but not fraudulent." This remark is made not defensively, nor with a shadow of guilt, but with a sunny optimism that all is well.

The banker smiled, though he could not smile off the next cartoon on the traditional Fourth of July speech: the first of twenty-two panels, taking apart the speech sentence by sentence by lifting the veil on false words to expose their true meaning, began with Humpty Dumpty Tweed delivering the hallowed oratory with the word *friends.* The *F* was illustrated as a hangman's tree with the body of Suffrage hanging from it. ". . . keeping alive the patriotic fires . . ." was illustrated by Tweed and his cronies dancing around Justice burned at the stake.

Nast drew faces of villains on bodies of beasts. This political zoology startled his readers, but the marvel of Nast was his own growth. Nast educated himself in the public eye. At first he mistook Sweeny for the leader of the Ring and had him carry around the nameplate "Brains." Tweed was but a spear carrier in a Roman carnival of thievery. But when Nast honed in on his true target, Tweed, his exuberant and rich imagination caught fire. Tweed becomes a commanding belly-body nightmare in the shape of a bulging bag of money, his facial features compressed into a dollar sign. When Tweed was drawn realistically, his vulture eyes have no more conscience than burnt cigarette holes.

Tweed was also the Roman emperor in battle dress and sword, his girth overflowing his throne at the Colosseum, a Caligula who dares to make his horse a senator, and down on the arena floor maniacal beasts are about to devour the maiden body of the Republic thrown to the voracious Tammany tiger. Illustrating the Biblical contrast of the rich getting richer and the poor getting poorer, Tweed was shown at an idyllic picnic raising a toast to the voters. In "Wholesale and Retail," the panel on "Wholesale" shows a bloated Tweed emerging from the city treasury saluted by the police on guard, while in "Retail" a starving father caught stealing a loaf of bread is clubbed by the police as his hungry family looks on.

The banker was glad to turn from the moral outrage of the drawings to the friendly Nast. Nast was not physically imposing, though his being an artist in his oats created that impression. He possessed a quality rare in celebrities. The insights from his art shone with sympathy on his face. His quiet dedication was in his eloquent eyes.

Turning to Nast's easel, where the next cartoon was coming alive before his eyes, the banker was forced to wince. Human vultures in the shape of Tweed, Sweeny, Connolly and "Mayor Haul"—as Nast nicknamed elegant Oakey—viewed a thunderstorm from the safety of their cliff. The vultures built a comfortable nest on the bones of the city treasury, justice, taxpayers and rent payers. Nast titled this scene high on the mountain fastness, "Let Us Prey."

The banker tried to hide his revulsion while appreciating Nast's art. He brought up what was closest to Nast's heart. "Tom, your home was always a jolly place with music and readings from the classics. Now it's silent."

"Children are the music of my life. I sorely miss my wife Sarah, who used to read to me as I drew."

"No man looks lonelier than you without your family. Where have they gone?"

"Morristown, New Jersey." Nast continued to draw as he dragged the words out of himself.

"It's not the season," said the puzzled banker.

"Look out the window," Nast suggested.

The banker saw threatening roughs loitering on an empty street and was sincerely embarrassed. "I'm sorry, Tom." A personal injury was in the banker's voice.

"You wouldn't want to read the hate mail I receive threatening my life."

"Did you call the police?"

"Of course."

"I'll get those thugs removed at once."

"There's nothing you can do," Nast told the impressive banker as he worked away at his easel. "I appreciate your concern."

"Maybe not me, but I've friends who can do it."

"Your most powerful friends can't help. The police captain of this precinct is my good friend. He protected my family at all times and chased the roughs whenever they appeared. Tweed had the captain transferred." *You understand what we're up against?* was on Nast's face.

"My coming here is a stroke of luck." The banker was sincere. "I bring a grant from private donors who wish to honor your work. It will allow you to study abroad and advance your art."

Without glancing away from his drawing board Nast said that he was thankful.

"You will reach the rank of Hogarth."

"You're most kind." Nast darkened the storm in the drawing.

"You can be another Goya."

Nast shook off this compliment.

"Would you consider going?"

"Oh, yes." Nast concentrated on inking in a boulder struck by lightning. "I only need to find time."

Nast's visitor was sincerely cordial. "Your honorarium will keep you from worrying about time. I believe it is a hundred thousand dollars."

"Education comes high." Nast watched his drawing take final shape. "Do you imagine I could receive two hundred thousand?"

"From the praise I've heard of you that should be no trouble."

"An investment in my future?" Nast drew in zero eyes.

"Your future is assured."

"How can one refuse patrons when they are so rare?" Nast drew in the lightning bolt striking a menacing boulder over the heads of the Tweed Ring vultures.

"You couldn't ask for more discreet patrons."

"You sound acquainted with the salons."

"I know business better than art. In art I do business only with what I like."

Nast enjoyed the banker's frankness as he stroked in the talons of the vultures.

"Do you think you need study?"

"No end of it," Nast was quick to agree.

The banker said helpfully, "The Ring business will get you into trouble. The Ring owns judges who can throw you in prison for libel."

"The Ring gives me a healthy respect for the law. With your honorarium Sarah and the children could live fashionably instead of in hiding." He drew fear in the eyes of the vultures. "Do you think I could get five hundred thousand dollars?"

"A possibility."

Nast said good-humoredly, "Do you know how much *Harper's Weekly* pays me for an entire year of my drawings?"

"You are worth whatever extraordinary amount you receive."

"I have tripled *Harper's Weekly* circulation."

"I'm not surprised, Tom. You have struck a chord in this nation that honest men and women have long wanted to hear."

"My annual pay is five thousand dollars." Nast smiled, pleased.

That's all? was on the banker's face. "There you are, Tom. You are a young man, barely in his thirties. Think of what a good life you will have ahead of you."

"I do think. That's my trouble. I've made up my mind." Nast finished off the Tweed vulture with a shrunken planet diamond on his feathered chest. "I want the Tweed Ring behind bars. And I'm going to put them there."

The banker was honestly concerned. "Be careful, for your family's sake, Tom, that you don't put yourself away first."

TWENTY-NINE

$\mathcal{S}$weeny did not enter his new courthouse office every morning as much as he invaded it as enemy land to be conquered and civilized. Seeing the sheriff's muddy shoes propped on his polished desk, the cool Sweeny was an eyelash away from strangling. "I won't step on you because I'll have to throw away my shoes." Sweeny went back to the circular corridor above the lobby, which was empty as usual this early in the morning.

The sheriff cheerfully warned, "Don't make it worse on yourself by calling a guard." He tossed the copied ledgers across the desk like a winning hand.

The redoubtable Sweeny was a match for anyone. "Stealing gets you in jail."

"This is copying and it'll get me my price."

"Your claim for services was made under the old charter. The new Board of Audit has no power to honor it."

"The power to honor me is in these ledgers." O'Brien glazed over happily, as an Easter egg. "I don't hear you calling the guard." O'Brien couldn't keep from taunting Sweeny, though he knew he was tempting fate.

Sweeny calmly replied, "Because I know you're not getting the money."

O'Brien tapped the ledger. "Refresh your memory."

Sweeny emitted a smile that on the face of any other man would be cause to call a doctor.

"I don't understand your reputation." O'Brien was feeling strangely off-base, which was the feeling Sweeny gave people. "Here's the figures. You have to come across. No education can get you out of this."

Sweeny was certain. "The newspapers will."

O'Brien thought Sweeny had a screw loose. "The newspapers will be down on your neck. Zip!"

Sweeny honed himself on the sheriff's greed. "But they won't pay you three hundred and fifty thousand dollars."

O'Brien paused and it was fatal. He floundered. He saw he couldn't outthink Sweeny. To regain his confidence he had to explode. "I'll give the ledgers away free to the newspapers. That's my duty." Caught in this stance, the sheriff unfortunately swung his feet off the desk for emphasis. "Bringing down the Boss will make me a hero. I'll be mayor, Governor."

"Vomit-bag inspector."

O'Brien bounded up with the snappy finality of a man who has cut off his nose and has to believe he's improved his looks. "I gave you your chance to save yourself."

"That's altruistic." Sweeny emitted his smile that wished the beholder bad luck. "Do you know what *altruistic* means?"

"High-hat garbage."

Sweeny knew he had a mouse under his paw. "It's not enough to know who holds the cards. You have to know how they'll be played. Altruism means doing good for others without expecting a favor in return."

O'Brien's jarred teeth showed in his gesture to compromise. "I'm open to understanding. Only a quarter of a million dollars and the ledgers are yours. Everyone lives happily ever after."

"I'm living happily now."

"You better." O'Brien angrily colored. "All the millions these ledgers showed you stole."

"Reformers will take your story and not give you a cent."

"Money lost now will be found a thousand times over when I'm mayor."

"I wouldn't travel so far on so little hope."

O'Brien felt betrayed, not the usual betrayal between friends but a change taking place in the larger world. He expected an educated man to have a sense of honor. A college man should see the light quicker. These were the men of the future. They were arriving in growing numbers to build the well-oiled machine in every profession. For the first time he was afraid of the educated man. A Tweed handshake was more efficient.

O'Brien let Sweeny have it. His fear made him eloquent and aggressive. "You're refusing my offer out of spite. You can't see giving in to an unschooled man who doesn't have your advantages. Goes against your pride. Pride is dead weight in a politician. If you'd rather hang than do business with a man who came up from the streets, then I say your fancy education taught you nothing. If that's what comes of miles of reading, then I say education, law books, living on Easy Street didn't civilize you. You'd be smarter in the gutter where you wouldn't make the mistake of false pride. There's your ignorance." O'Brien scooped up his ledger and fled the office with his honor intact.

Sweeny clawed at his palms, wrist, knuckles while muttering that Connolly was too dumb to protect his office.

He drove to a new, popular-style hotel where young married couples didn't have to set up housekeeping or attend to a houseful of servants and could have more leisure. Here Sweeny kept his mistress and their baby.

A husky woman, the kind who worked in a bathhouse for gentlemen, threw on her wrap to answer the loud knocking that woke her child too. "What're you doing back so early?"

Sweeny backed rudely against the door to slam it shut, and this wasn't his usual careful manner. "Get dressed."

"Where are we going?" She was worried.

"You're going to my brother, who can be trusted."

"He hasn't spoken to me since the baby." She smelled danger.

"Tell him—liquefy."

"Liquefy?" She picked up the crying child.

"My brother will understand."

"I don't."

"You pack."

She became scared. "Where am I going?"

"No place." He wanted her to drop the baby and start.

"Then why am I packing?"

"To get ready."

"What's wrong?" She held the baby closer.

"Must something be wrong to be ready when I want you?"

She wanted a positive sign that all was right between them. "Pete, you didn't even kiss our baby."

Sweeny pecked the child on its cheesy-tasting lips and rubbed his own lips clean.

She wanted further proof of his attachment. "I want our baby baptized."

"You know what they'll call you and the child?"

"Not if you marry me."

"You want to ruin me? Is that how you're going to help? Go to my brother. Liquefy everything."

She begged for crumbs. "Why can't you tell your brother?"

"I want you to be ready, in case. And I have to race off to see Tweed."

Tweed's Fifth Avenue mansion was perfumed by banks of flowers. A footman ushered Sweeny into the library. Tweed hove into view in a morning robe of gold silk. A monogrammed linen hung from his bull neck. A Schiller's Curl was in one hand and a cup of coffee in the other. "Pastry?" Tweed reached for the velvet cord to call the butler.

"Your idiot comptroller!"

Tweed finished his cream-filled horn of blond crust with a gargantuan bite, munching and sniffing, groaning ecstatically as he swallowed.

"O'Brien had our books copied under Connolly's nose."

Tweed remained Olympian. "How much does the runt want?"

"That's not the point." Sweeny's injured pride made him furious.

"I didn't ask for the point. I asked for the price."

"The price is madness. A quarter of a million."

"He's come down." Tweed was pleased. "Pay him."

"He's nothing. If not for you, he'd be nothing today."

Tweed patiently suggested, "If I can turn the other cheek?"

"Arrrggghhh." Sweeny hated to be at cross-purposes with Tweed. "The maggot has no place to go."

"*Harper's Weekly,* the *Times,* the *Nation* is not no place to go."

"The bastard doesn't want to be famous. He wants money. The numskull knows only one word, and he'll bring us down with it: money. Is that all we amount to? Is it an open secret? We are bound by money? Does anybody appreciate our endless meetings, haggling, fighting, twists and turns to endure in office? To accommodate every variety of people, even our enemies? You gave that loudmouth reformer Nat Sands a job as tax commissioner. Henry was appointed dock commissioner. Daley became a judge. That's the trouble with buying out your critics. Half your jobs are filled with your enemies."

"Refuse to make him rich and you'll make him a hero. He'll spill our books to the *Times* for nothing and run for office on the popularity it'll give him."

"The slime will lose money on that deal."

"He'll make it up in office."

"That's the plan he used on me. He'll go from blackmail to public hero without changing his convictions."

Tweed assured Sweeny, "We got him where we want. He knows the newspapers can't pay what we can pay."

A knock and the butler entered to whisper into Tweed's ear. Tweed told him to let the caller wait. The butler replied the man couldn't wait on pain of being stripped of his job. "Show the devil in," said Tweed.

A breathless heeler, impressed by his audience, not knowing how to begin, burst out, "Boss, I come from the *Sun*. O'Brien's peddling your books."

Tweed's cup and saucer rattled as he placed them on the gold-and-marble mantel. "What'd the *Sun* say?"

"The editor wasn't in. But they shouted it at him like chasing a dog off the lawn."

"Where'd the blackmailer go?"

"The *World*." The heeler tapped a pistol in his belt. "Want him wormed, Boss?"

"I never fight with my enemies," Tweed responded kindly. "I only buy them."

A knock and the butler let in another ruffian, who immediately announced, "I spit on the sneakin' barstid sewer rat."

"Where'd he go?"

"The *World* threw him out."

"Did he show them any papers?"

"They wouldn't look. He went out on his can."

"Thank you, boys." Tweed escorted them out and they basked in his company. When Tweed returned, he picked up his coffee with a steady hand. He was down on Sweeny and knew he had to avoid showing it. Anyone could turn these events into chaos. He had to plaster over it, and that's where you separate the leaders from the led. The trouble was that Sweeny was right, yet he had to go against him. "What O'Brien wants is going to look like peanuts if our books are printed."

"Blackmail is a bottomless pit."

Tweed inhaled uneasily and walked to the window. He knew he was troubled because more and more people appeared to be walking with an ease he envied. He turned to Sweeny, though he could just as well be talking to himself. "There must have been a time when people lived lives before they could sell them."

"There's no stopping the runt now."

"You should have settled with him. Anything is better than this hole."

"How can you settle with him? To hide he speaks with conviction."

Tweed didn't argue the description. Yet with all Sweeny's foresight they were in peril. "We must have unity, because divided we fall."

"You're right," Sweeny acknowledged the truth without accepting it. "I've put some chasers on him."

Tweed shook his head. "That'll only make him go quicker to every paper."

THIRTY

A harried O'Brien knew he was being shad-
owed. A Tammany rough spotted him at the *Sun*. A brutish thug
spied him at the *World*. He dreaded these roughs. He had hired
them when he was sheriff. They'd do anything to get the Boss's
attention. Violence was their way of promoting themselves. Any
party that used them knew fear from without and within.

O'Brien slipped into a palatial barbershop with mirrors large as
department-store windows. He had to seek havens in high-class
surroundings where his pursuers stood out. He was washed,
shaved, hot-toweled, shorn, powdered and rummed. He was Satur-
day-night clean yet not refreshed. He couldn't break free of his
danger. He saw the eyes of brutes everywhere. Politeness became
as suspect as a snub. He hurried off to Tilden's. The peace and
quiet of Gramercy Park would do him good. Steady his nerves to
deal with Tilden.

A butler ushered O'Brien into Tilden's library. Men who resembled ax murderers magically became bird fanciers in the ethereal
light of the stained-glass windows. The white-suited Tilden entered on a string of his own pulling.

O'Brien was no fool. He knew he needed Tilden. He also knew
Tilden graciously put people in their place by the attention he
lavished on them. O'Brien had to escape that position. But how?

He was not to the manor born. He didn't know the art of polite destruction. He didn't even know basic manners—how to ask about a man's health in order to ignore his answer and so establish one's superiority. He knew he was too crude. Too emotional. A fist. All he knew about polite society was to be humble and you had a foot in the door. But being humble to Sammy Tilden was putting your life in his hands. Bowing to Silky meant the neck was bare.

Tilden sat O'Brien down with a tap dancer's precision, click click click. Tilden enjoyed such huge success as a public man and railroad lawyer that he could enter into most conversations bored.

O'Brien came to the mark fast. "Sam, I've proof to blow Tweed's Ring to smithereens."

"Why'd you come in broad daylight?"

O'Brien was stunned by the head reformer's response.

"You must be followed."

"No one followed me. I swear," O'Brien neatly lied. He pulled the ledgers from under his shirt and tossed them on Tilden's ornately carved table. "Two fat years of the Ring that stuck to their fingers."

Tilden pored over the pages without evincing any surprise. His silence unnerved O'Brien, who thought he would at least be loudly congratulated. "Are you dead sure the figures are accurate, Jim?"

"Copied from the original dot for dot." This questioning and lack of response made O'Brien suspect what he had.

When the silence had worn O'Brien down, Tilden asked from on high as if doing O'Brien a favor, "I'd like this copy, Jim."

"What for?" O'Brien was suspicious, even though he had come to offer the documents.

"We'll nail Tweed to the wall at the right time."

At the right time rang false in O'Brien's street ears. "I can't give the ledgers away."

Tilden saw O'Brien was answering shrewdly. "What's on your mind?"

"I know it's altruistic"—O'Brien puffed himself up—"but I don't want anyone making money out of my civic duty by selling this copy."

Tilden arched his back.

"Not you, Sam. Christ, I'd go to hell and back for you and you know it. Someone in your employ. The newspapers would pay a million for it."

"Yes." Tilden smoothed over their differences. "You want to get the most mileage out of these records." Tilden hungered for the copies while remaining aloof.

"True." O'Brien dog-paddled it through.

"Did you notice any entries for a check of five thousand dollars?" Tilden trolled.

"I can't remember the small ones," O'Brien joked uneasily. He unexpectedly had Tilden on the hook and he didn't want any part of it.

"Erie Railroad." Tilden lightly jogged his memory.

O'Brien responded slowly, knowing he was walking on eggs and not knowing how he got there. "No checks to Erie."

"Tweed was made a member of the Erie board by Mr. Gould. He made a check out to me for that amount."

O'Brien fell into himself and sweated. This was more information than he should have or want to know. He worried how it would cost him.

"The check was for legal services."

Having lost his chance at the big money for the ledgers, he didn't want to lose being a hero. A mayor. His priceless ledgers were melting before his eyes. "Never saw it. You can put that in the bank." He had to joke to clear his nerves.

Tilden sat down. He relaxed by crossing his legs and pointing the toe of his shoe upward as though taking aim at his guest. This was Tilden's idea of the carefree gentleman.

O'Brien knew he was far from being home-free. He had to address himself to Tilden's immaculate white suit while keeping an eagle eye on the honky-tonk it covered. Tilden in with Tweed? He could never have imagined that one.

"You're correct," said Tilden, "not to exploit these ledgers for personal profit. That would throw a cloud over your motives." A curious undertone in Tilden suggested he was surprised Tweed did not offer a fortune. Tilden was curling inside himself, not knowing what to make of this situation. Tweed always paid off vipers. It made no sense to let O'Brien run free. Was this a demonic trap of Tweed's to ruin reform? Were these records fake? Poisoned bait?

O'Brien sensed Tilden's suspicion. He couldn't bear to lose both money and fame. "I want to do the city a service, and I went to two newspapers and they threw me out. I was thinking of the *Times*. They keep firing at Tweed no matter how much advertising he can take away from them."

To Tilden this was more like the truth. He uncrossed his legs to get in the thick of it. "I don't care for George Jones, who owns the *Times*. I don't trust Louis Jennings, who runs the *Times*. They're holier-than-thou."

"Where can I go?" O'Brien knew where, but he couldn't go anywhere without Tilden's permission if he wanted to get ahead in the new political order to come.

"What a shame if Tweed was brought down only to benefit the circulation of the *Times*."

"I won't go near them." O'Brien waited to see how Tilden would bail him out. He wanted to hear of rewards sworn in blood.

"If you'll trust the ledgers to me, I'll see that the information is placed where it'll do the most good."

"Sam." O'Brien's heart was in his mouth. "I paid an enormous sum—as you can well imagine—and took great risks—as you can well imagine—to get these copies."

"I understand." Tilden thought he was coming around and bided his time.

"If you should do the broadcasting, I'd fade into the background."

"The Ring would think twice before attacking a lawyer like me, but they'd think nothing of attacking a defenseless person like you. If there's the slightest taint of libel in these records, Tweed could drag you through the courts for the rest of your life at your expense. He doesn't have to find you guilty to punish you. He merely has to trap you in his legal machinery. I'm trying to protect you from digging your own grave."

"Let me sleep on it, Sam." He trusted Tweed more than Tilden.

He left in a stew of indecision that was eating him alive. Maybe he should have asked for less money from Tweed. Hours ago he could do no wrong with the ledgers, and now he couldn't do anything right. His instincts told him to strike quickly, no matter what he did, before he was dropped down a drain. He headed for the *Times* and Louis Jennings.

Jennings was an Englishman seldom met in travel folders: no guide tells you to come to England to meet pugilistic, acrimonious, pushy Englishmen. Yet Louis Jennings's push was exactly what O'Brien needed.

Jennings was working alone in his office when his door quietly opened and closed. There stood O'Brien, confident about what he had to offer and quaking about offering it. He was not at peace, but he was determined. Jennings greeted him indifferently, and this encouraged O'Brien to surprise the editor.

"Is it true Tweed passed a law that could put an editor in jail for criticizing him?"

"He's banned *Harper's Weekly* from the schools."

"One day you'll be hounded, Jennings."

"And more."

"Sunk in the Tombs."

"For an appetizer."

O'Brien took a breath to steady him. "You and Nast have had a hard fight."

"Have still." The weariness rose in Jennings.

"I said you've *had* a hard fight." O'Brien boasted. He handed Jennings the thick sheaf of papers. "The proof against Tweed. Exact copies of Slippery's books. The boys will be trying to murder you, as they've tried with me."

The pugnacious Jennings became a kid in a candy shop as he riffled through the pages.

O'Brien said modestly, "All I want is credit."

Credit didn't sit well with Jennings. He smelled a trap and felt butterflies in his gut. To bring down Tweed he'd be raising up a minor thief. He knew what editors must do, and he ran with the story. The scales were in the paper's favor, and he jumped eagerly into the horse trade.

O'Brien was feeling naked without the ledgers. "Will your boss George Jones back you?"

"Haven't we been firing at Tweed without this ammunition?" He jolted O'Brien with a hard look. "Tweed would give you a fortune."

"Sweeny won't fork over a cent."

Jennings caught the picture, whole and deep. "That doesn't sound like the shrewd Sweeny, but it does sound like the arrogant one."

"Sweeny has pride. That goes before a fall. Now who's gonna get the education, eh, Jennings?"

"You'll stand by these figures?"

"I have to, if I want the office due me."

Jennings was joyous at the raw copy in his hands.

THIRTY-ONE

*Y*ou say those three words. That's all. The mountain will come to you."

Connolly nodded yes to Tweed in the Boss's courthouse office, though tension was eating out his stomach. "Why must I go?"

"You look the most imposing. The party is counting on you." Tweed scrutinized Connolly's overbearing tendency to look like a mortician, and it didn't fill him with confidence.

"It didn't work with Nast," grumbled Connolly.

"With Nast it was too little and too late. You're giving George Jones, the owner of the *Times,* a chance not to print lies."

Connolly didn't care to take the lightning. "You said you took advertising away from Jones and he still kept firing. You kept looking for flaws in his land title for his building, and Jones kept firing."

"I still say if every city and town had a publisher like George Jones and an editor like George Curtis at *Harper's Weekly,* Thomas Jefferson would rise up and start dancing. But you're going to give Jones everyman's magic wish."

Connolly feared the redoubtable Jones as a species from another world, and in many ways he was right as far as the comptroller's world went. "Jones will come down on me before I can open my mouth. He knows who I am. He knows what I want."

Tweed tried to allay his own fears by drilling Connolly. "How will you greet Jones?"

"Good day, sir."

"Piss on good day. This man hates you on sight."

"The no-good son of a bitch."

"Swallow. Greet Jones as we agreed."

"Mr. Jones, I have three words to say to you."

"Sir," Tweed added.

"That no-good son of a bitch."

"Swallow your pride and that's how you'll feel superior."

"I can't tell lies." Connolly puffed himself up.

Tweed encouraged him. "You're a statesman. You learn to live with lies until you can't tell the difference."

Connolly boiled. "Brains is a nincompoop. To make us climb from paying out a quarter of a million to millions."

"There's no time to point the finger of blame. Nast comes out once a week. The *Times* every day."

"I never met Jones. I don't know what he looks like."

Tweed shook off Connolly's moroseness by implying it was an advantage not to know Jones. "I've a mutual lawyer friend who'll arrange the meeting. You go to the lawyer's office and Jones will be there."

"If that dummy Brains had only listened to reason."

"Don't return until you have Jones in your pocket."

Connolly swallowed hard. "What if Jones won't talk to me?"

"He won't talk, but he'll listen. Just stagger him with the three words and don't give him a chance to get on his high horse or he'll ride away."

"Is that all?"

"The words will argue better than you can."

At the sight of the grave Connolly, Jones whirled away in the law office as he would from sludge. "I don't want to see that person!"

"For God's sake"—Connolly was rattled—"I've only three words to say to you."

"You'll say them as I'm going out." Jones was at the door.

Connolly relished his new power. "Two million dollars."

Jones was nailed to the floor.

Connolly delighted in the plan working as Tweed foresaw. This had his true juices running. Butter wouldn't melt in his mouth. "If you do not publish stolen documents."

An astonished Jones found his voice, his tone paying tribute to the offer. "I don't think the devil himself would pay that high a price for me."

Connolly kept Jones from mounting his high horse. This optimism showed in Connolly's benevolence. "You'll be able to do anything you wish for the rest of your life."

"Nothing I could do would give me more enjoyment than what I'm doing now, running a free press. A newspaper that's not above money is beneath contempt." The charge was in the law office long after Jones left. The lawyer himself was staggered by the amount. Connolly was left hanging in his own stupor.

"If we can't shut Jones up, what can we do?" Connolly was jumpy in the meeting held in the mayor's office with Tweed in the mayor's chair, Elegant sitting on the corner of his desk and Sweeny as far from the comptroller as possible.

Tweed understood that no profession provides the education to protect a person from his own shortcomings. Their troubles were bringing out the sores that good times polished over. What they needed most for their protection was to stay together. Tweed cheerfully answered Connolly's question of what to do: "Eat together in public. Every day Jones and Jennings run our ledgers, we dine at Delmonico's."

"You can't brazen this out," said an edgy Sweeny. "It's better to lay low until the series runs its course."

"Laying low is an admission of guilt," said Tweed. "We're no more guilty than some men who have streets, parks and monuments named after them."

"Defending yourself also looks guilty," Sweeny skewered Tweed.

"If you want to lay low," Mayor Hall said, "you'll stick out from the rest of us." Oakey made certain he directed his remark to Sweeny.

"I'll lay you low," Sweeny retorted.

Tweed raised an open palm for peace. "It's not enough to eat together, we must display our families in public."

"That's suspicious," remarked Sweeny coldly.

"That's exploiting our wives and children, when we usually

keep them in the dark," said Oakey, who was suddenly agreeing with Sweeny.

"That's all we need," Connolly scoffed, "to be seen with a whore and her bastard."

An alert Tweed jumped forward to hold Sweeny.

"No families," Tweed agreed. "Wear dark suits."

Connolly eyed the razzle-dazzle suit of the elegant mayor. "Oakey dresses like a fruitcake."

Tweed sharply reprimanded the comptroller to let him know his place. "You stick to giving out the religious statements."

"As long," hissed the mayor, "as it's not mea culpa."

They stiffened at the hawking newsboys outside. "Tweed Ring exposed!"

"Read about the biggest steal in history!"

"Names and amounts from Tweed's records!"

Tweed stood up without a cloud on his face. "Gentlemen, we go to dine."

"We'll ride in my carriage," said the cautious Sweeny.

"We'll walk," Tweed stressed.

On their way to Delmonico's, shouting newsboys startled people into buying the *Times*.

No one approached their table, which was unusual, but Tweed was confident he had enough markers out to draw an army to their table if he wanted.

"Don't look branded," Tweed coaxed confidence out of them. "Let's see if we can name streets, parks and monuments that honor crooks, cowards and bigots." Tweed raised his hand for the game to begin, and the men at the table took heart. "A street named after a crook?"

The cultured Oakey answered brightly, "Vanderbilt."

Tweed was sailing with the energy picking up at the table. "A park named after a coward?"

Sweeny was quick as a tiger. "Bryant."

"A statue to a bigot?"

"Samuel Morse." Connolly gladly got in his licks.

"Stuyvesant," said Elegant.

"Whoa." Tweed raised his palm to shut them off. "One bigot is all I want or we'd be here all night. There you are, gentlemen. Streets, parks and monuments named after crooks, cowards and bigots."

They could not be happier if they had won a landslide. Their geniality attracted diners who came over for a handshake and to deplore the negative reporting of the *Times* and the constant harping of the press and magazines and their refusal to cover the news in a positive light.

A tormented O'Brien plunged into Jennings's office at a loss. What had gone wrong? The city was not aroused, the people not up in arms to throw the thieves out.

Jennings was loath to admit the faintest hint of defeat, yet he admitted the public may be sick of attacks against the friendly Tweed, who walked among the people as if everyone were guilty but himself. So strong was this impression he gave that he aroused one's thoughts on a deeper level. The public was yawning at the factual revelations. *There was too much stealing!* Too many people in on it. Too many figures to read. This was also summer. The educated citizen was likely to be out of the city. No matter the apathy, the *Times* would keep running the series until they ran out of ammunition.

A shaken O'Brien felt the ground going out from under him. He changed rooms, hotels, ate alone, haunted that he had not made a cent. Only now did he fully understand Tweed's optimism. The giving and receiving of favors was pulling off his biggest miracle.

O'Brien felt trapped in the monstrous public lethargy he had been fattened on. There was no heart, no soul, no conscience to the city's apathy that was squashing him.

THIRTY-TWO

Tweed was raging in his courthouse office just when he should have been riding high with the *Times* exposure largely falling on deaf ears. Experience had schooled him to stay calm before unforeseen disasters, but the Orange Riot stemming from Old World feuds had his blood up. He twisted, turned and squashed into a ball the newspaper headlining the bloodiest riot on the streets since the Draft Riots.

He whistled for his guards on the run, and when he opened the door, they had formed a flying wedge. Heelers had taken cover. Shiny Hats had disappeared. Job seekers had vanished. The courthouse backyard was strangely empty, as if City Hall were braced for a storm. As soon as they entered, it was evident why he needed his guards. Reporters harangued him as the wedge bulled through halls and up stairways to the mayor's office where Tweed burst in, leaving his guards outside.

The elegant mayor jumped up from behind his desk as though caught in a crime. His pince-nez fell off his nose and swung from its black silk ribbon like a pendulum across his bright damask vest. His publicity-hound flair was nowhere to be seen. When Elegant Oakey Hall wasn't orchestrating the press as a bon vivant who made colorful copy, he skillfully put reporters on the defensive in subtler ways. His snappy, man-about-town wit and pungent quotes made it easy for reporters to cover City Hall without reporting it.

Tweed had murder in his eyes. "We had the *Times* beaten! The city was back in our hands!"

Oakey backed against a wall of trophies and ribbons, cautioned, "Reporters are outside."

"Let them hear," Tweed shouted, "what an idiot you are!"

"You wanted the parade. You said it would get us national attention."

"Don't weasel. Nobody cared about ledgers. Everyone will care about this, you imbecile."

"I had four regiments of national guard, three platoons of police to protect a hundred and sixty parading Orangemen. I had the heroes of 1863—Walling, Dilks and Kelso—nail shut block after block of houses with tenants inside to keep roughs off the roof. I had factory owners threaten to fire any workers taking time off. Every lesson we learned from the Draft Riots was used." Oakey's eyes appeared to sink below their waterline. "I don't know how a few roughs got on the roofs to bombard the Orangemen. No city could be better organized for a riot without having a crystal ball."

"Not only Orangemen were beaten up but Italians, too, and they had nothing to do with the parade and weren't anywhere near it."

Oakey was frying in his juices as he reached for an excuse. "Who could tell gangs of roughs would be roaming neighborhoods running down Orangemen and they found, instead, Italians."

"Your fly will always be open." Tweed left. Though he was protected by his guards, they couldn't cram him through the reporters fast enough.

The reporters were hornets, shouting, angry, impatient. "How many were killed in the Orange Riot?"

"None," Tweed calmly called over the heads of his guards.

"Why didn't you protect the Orangemen?"

"We had four regiments of soldiers and three platoons of police for a mere hundred and sixty paraders."

"Senator Tweed, do you believe in one group censoring everyone else?"

"Boys, you know me better than that." Tweed smiled easily.

"Senator, do you think everyone should have the right to parade on their holiday?"

"I fought for that right and I'll never stop fighting for it."

"Do you fear making the Know-Nothings popular again?"

"Me?" he joked. "I'm always doing good for someone."

"Doing good? Is that what you call stealing the city blind?"

Tweed could not stomach being on the defensive. He had to ride his own tide. He stopped. The reporters swarmed around him. He knew his candor was his badge of independence. He would not take water. He was on his hind legs and feeling good roaring. "What are you going to do about it?"

THIRTY-THREE

Shortly before midnight the Squire of Gramercy Park began pacing his ornate parlor. The windows facing the park were tightly covered. The door opening on his splashing indoor fountain providing a needed coolness. Morrissey and O'Brien watched the absorbed Tilden's every move. It was not like the Squire to await another person so keenly.

Morrissey broke the nervous silence: "Sam, why did you, of all people, not attend the great rally at Cooper Union against Tweed and his Ring? The meeting formed a Committee of Seventy to conduct criminal suits against Tweed, and they're going to back honest candidates no matter what their party."

Tilden's personality did not take to questioning. "I'm for unity." His voice was clear, but his thoughts were on whatever made him pace. "I didn't want the rally to have an aspect of party warfare. No matter how high a price I had to pay for being absent at such an illustrious rally, I had to sacrifice private gain for the good of the party."

Morrissey and O'Brien, up from the streets, did not know how to act cagily with Tilden, so they accepted his answer with excessive courtesy, which in the streets would imply they didn't believe him.

A hackney coach was heard pulling up in the darkness outside, and Tilden abruptly stopped pacing.

Morrissey and O'Brien stood as if expecting royalty; nothing less could command this attention from the Squire.

A tall, heavyset man, ponderously self-assured, his expensive greatcoat turned up over his face, was let in quickly by the footman. Though the visitor was left alone in the downstairs waiting room, he did not uncover himself.

The impatient Tilden was hurriedly informed of his arrival yet answered calmly, "Tell him to wait."

Morrissey and O'Brien believed they heard a suppliant tone and became more impressed by the unseen visitor.

"Our victory is waiting." Tilden's eyes brightened. "A courageous judge out of all the rotten bark Tweed has appointed. He will grant injunctions against Tweed and his Ring and choke off their money supply."

Morrissey and O'Brien were skeptical and Morrissey asked, "How can you be certain?"

Tilden pulled the bell rope. "I promised him the nomination for governor."

The door was opened by the unseen footman, who quickly departed. Moments later the imposing visitor stepped into the parlor. He snapped off his large hat, pulled down his collar and out came the judicious face that caused the admiring guests to see victory.

"Judge Barnard!"

THIRTY-FOUR

I'll pull the asslicker's tongue out!" Tweed was on fire.

A petrified Connolly was slumped in a chair in Tweed's courthouse office.

"An injunction?" Tweed loudly sniggered. "Barnard can't spell the word. Neither can his law clerk. I know. I hired them. I showed Barnard how to spell his name, where his fly was and what to hold. Now he shows off with injunctions!"

Connolly's paralysis gave him the appearance of calm. "We're broke. The injunctions stop us from raising money by taxes."

"We must call in our markers," Tweed spat.

Connolly rubbed his face in alarm. "Even our markers are taxed to the hilt."

A tap on the door they were too depressed to answer. The door brazenly opened without an invitation. Tweed rocketed his bulk from his chair and choked the astonished O'Brien.

"I've come as a friend," O'Brien said, horrified.

Tweed battered O'Brien against the wall.

"To help," O'Brien hoarsely whispered.

Connolly jumped in as the cooler head. "The barstid wants to help."

Tweed kneed O'Brien, who sunk to the floor uttering, "You gave me my first job."

"He's grateful." Connolly sandwiched between them.

"Water," croaked O'Brien.

"Always complaining," Tweed said of the request.

"I could get Tilden to lay off." O'Brien rubbed his neck.

Tweed yanked O'Brien off the floor and punched him into a chair.

"Bourbon," croaked O'Brien.

Connolly poured a spot from his own flask, which Tweed poured into a saucer. O'Brien refused the offer. When Tweed went to choke him again, O'Brien slurped the saucer clean and boasted, "I'm the hero of the reformers. Tilden is running me for state senator."

Connolly was ready to strangle or worship O'Brien, depending on his answer. "How much?"

O'Brien replied contritely, "Three hundred and fifty thousand dollars."

Tweed's blow missed the ducking O'Brien by a hair.

O'Brien felt put upon. "It's small enough."

"For what?" Tweed curled his hand into a fist.

"To keep from being jailed."

A chill went through Connolly, who stroked his right kidney as though it were the true seat of his soul.

O'Brien took out a cigar, and Tweed rammed the cigar against the sheriff's mug.

"Let him talk," Connolly pleaded.

"I heard him. Where can we get that money?"

"We'll split it," Connolly urged.

"I don't carry around a hundred and seventy-five thousand in cash," said Tweed.

O'Brien piped up. "You have land."

Connolly jumped in to save O'Brien's neck from Tweed. He appealed to the sheriff's conscience. "Be fair."

O'Brien cockily stood up to leave.

Tweed spoke as if to brain O'Brien. "I'll give you my stables on Fourteenth Street."

O'Brien faced up to the Boss. "Fourteenth Street is going to the dogs."

His helplessness brought Augusta to mind. He wasn't the shape of a man she ever wanted. He couldn't give in to his worse thoughts no matter how true they may be. "My property on Fifteenth Street."

"What number?" O'Brien probed.

The probing touched Tweed's nerve. "One-thirty-seven."

"The rent roll is next to nothing."

Tweed swallowed hard. "Fourteen lots on One Hundred Fifth Street."

"Too far out of the city."

"My property at 120 East Twenty-third Street."

O'Brien nodded, satisfied. "A hundred and fifty thousand to go." He made it sound like a favor.

"You want my new mansion at 511 Fifth Avenue?"

"Too heavily mortgaged." O'Brien turned up his nose, proud he had blocked that sneak play.

"Three-oh-four West Forty-second Street." Tweed wished to kill O'Brien.

"Too near Dutch Hill."

"Dutch Hill is disappearing with the progress of the city."

"I'll take it. That's a hundred and forty thousand to go."

Haggling would deeply mortify him, so he rattled off, "Ten-sixty-five, 1067 and 1069 Third Avenue."

"I'll take it. Come up with ninety thousand more."

Tweed was on the lip of exploding but slid into the bidding as he would his hangman's noose, wishing it was quickly over. "Nine-twenty-two Broadway."

"Good."

"One seventy-two Mercer Street."

"Passable but good."

"Three lots on Fifty-seventh Street."

"Where on Fifty-seventh?"

"Ninth Avenue."

"Passable but good."

"Three lots on West Fifty-eighth and Ninth Avenue."

"Over the top." O'Brien played the genial host. "And you, Connolly?"

Connolly burned. "I've cash."

"I was positive of that." O'Brien stepped to the door.

"Good-bye," Connolly said as a curse.

"I'm not going." O'Brien opened the door and whistled.

A bent man in a soiled suit shuffled up the stairs.

"The notary will make our bargain official."

The stained notary entered and directed the Tammany leaders where to sign the documents before pressing his seal on it.

What pained Tweed most after the loss of money was seeing in the notary's eyes that any fall was possible in this world.

When O'Brien left, Connolly became frightened and unsure about what they had bought. Tweed was white with humiliation and had to prove himself anew. "I'm going to hold the biggest rally this city has ever seen."

Connolly revived at hearing the old spirit that had pulled them through so many tight spots before.

THIRTY-FIVE

$\mathcal{N}$ear the heart of the Lower East Side is Tweed Plaza. Today it cannot contain the overflow of twenty thousand cheering, applauding faithful blocking avenues, filling side streets, bringing vigorous traffic to a halt. A roar shivers store windows and the people themselves as Tweed's buggy is seen. He waves his cap above the heads of the crowd and mounts the platform under the spellbinding cheers of followers crushed against doorways and shops, leaning out windows, waving from roofs. The cheers beat themselves out against the worn tenements.

Their idolatry is taking him over. Their breath pounding against him, unnerving him, blowing him out of himself, turning his insides out until he feels he has none except this shuddering that can't be called privacy yet strikes deep within him. Their roaring idolatry is hammering him into a different shape, draining him of speech as it fires him up.

He would be a fool if he didn't hear in the undertow of their emotional response that they were cheering for the best in themselves too. Shouting their lungs out for recognition. They were *somebody* through him: bigger, better, stronger than any outsiders could know. They were tribal, territorial, clannish. Though city neighborhoods were new, their rites went back to ancient times.

Shaking as he was, he raised his arms to embrace them all. Hats, caps, canes were flung high into the air to salute him back.

They did not want to hear anything about guilt or innocence, foul play or revenge, crying or complaints. He had to prove in a grand and sweeping way that the attacks had not changed him—indeed had made him stronger. This was the inner confidence they longed to wrap themselves in. He stepped forward, exuding energy, eyes twinkling, and said naturally what they were starved to hear.

"I am home again!"

A tidal roar crashed over him so that he trembled inwardly and was silenced, humbled, forced to step back as a courtier before a higher authority. He had to raise his arms for silence or be battered into losing his head.

His raised arms brought silence. The silence of a great city crowd, however, is but the eye of a hurricane.

"I was born on these streets!"

For sheer exuberant hell they sent up a tumultuous cheer with whistling and applause.

"Our streets! These streets, so alien to the men uptown at Cooper Union, are the streets of my childhood. The home of my boyhood where I ran errands on streets warm with our dear memories. I dared to race on them as chief of the volunteer Big Six Americus fire company while the men at Cooper Union were in their clubs drinking in their easy chairs and their conscience not moving an inch to save a mother, father, child, baby. I have walked our neighborhoods. I know them house by house, family by family, while the men uptown can't even spell your names. Don't want to spell it. Wish they had never heard it. Our crowded neighborhoods, so despised by those at Cooper Union, are the cherished streets of our lives where we learned to get on in their world."

The crowd was his.

He could not speak for minutes, though he implored with his embracing arms for silence. They would not be silent until certain they gave the best of themselves and more.

"I know I can place myself, my record, all I have performed as a public servant, plainly before your eyes."

A spontaneous cheer of agreement. Those packed into the back-water streets, who could not see or hear Tweed, wanted to be part of the demonstration and let out a roar moments later as an inspired echo that overwhelmed the original cheer.

"The manner in which I have been received has sent a throb to my heart."

Emotional coughing and sniffing.

"I would be unjust to myself—unjust to those who have seen fit to entrust me with office—if, at times like these, when to be a politician, when to hold public office, is to be condemned without a trial, if I did not have engraved on my heart the proud satisfaction that I can go into the streets of my childhood, into the scenes of my boyhood, to the friends of my manhood, take them by the hand, face them in the manner of lifelong friends, and say to them, 'Here is my record.' And finding it meets with their approval!"

The crowd went wild.

Up rose a vibrating chant: "Tweeeed! Tweeeed! Tweeeed!" The chant of devotion punctuated with blasting shouts: "Down with Cooper Union! Down with the Committee of Seventy!"

A reddened Tweed had difficulty continuing, and when he did, he spoke heatedly. "Reviled and maligned as a man has seldom been, I point proudly to my record, which is open to all. I court full and impartial investigation into all my official acts. I am able to face my accuser in the only manly way in which those who slander us can be met. I place myself in your hands!"

Victorious shouting.

"I accept your renomination of me as your state senator. I thank you for your magnificent trust. I will say only a few golden words: Go home early, work hard."

An engulfing roar begged him to stay.

Tweed waved his cap in salute. He was off the platform and into the crowd as though he could nest there for life.

THIRTY-SIX

$\mathcal{T}$he public wants to see moral outrage from us," Mayor Hall badgered Tweed. "We must show voters we have principles. Throw Connolly to the dogs."

"It's Sweeny's fault," Tweed said morosely, swatting away plaster peeling from the courthouse ceiling.

"Slippery, by his own admission, is responsible. He wants a bigger cut of my share."

Tweed quickly turned off this faucet. "Connolly is clean. He'd have paid O'Brien."

Elegant Oakey put on his superior rubber-band smile. A smile without excess. He used only what he needed. Snap! His smile disappeared. "Connolly is comptroller." Smile. "He handles the money." Smile. "He keeps the records." Crescendo smile. "We can't know everything that goes on behind our backs."

"Who's going to believe that?"

"No one has to believe it as long as they can be made to swallow it."

Tweed dismissed the idea. "You don't want to throw Connolly to the wolves. He has the vouchers."

"The *Times* printed some of them. The city yawned. The public doesn't want numbers. They want a head on a platter."

"Standing together is our strongest weapon." Tweed gloomily closed his eyes and found no rest in himself.

"Throw the public a body."

Tweed quietly assured him, "They won't stop with one."

"Didn't the *Herald* demand Slippery's resignation?"

Tweed was detached. "Because you put them up to it."

Elegant was embarrassed, not at what he'd done but that Tweed had found out.

They heard a new pitchman outside City Hall. He waved fistfuls of money to attract workers on the city payroll. He would pay them their wages on the spot. City workers had only to hand over their promissory notes the city gave them in place of their full salary, and the pitchman would pay them fifty percent of the amount. These notes would be paid in full by the city, but no one knew when this would be. Everyone knew the pitchman would sue the city for the money and was bound to get the full amount of the promissory notes on the grounds that judgments against the city had to be paid.

"Go out the front door to draw the reporters," said Tweed. "I'm going out the back."

Hall was accosted by the reporters, and one greeted him tartly, "Looking well today, Mr. Mayor."

Oakey bristled with cheek. "Juvenal, the poet of the great Roman empire, observed that the people's longings are limited to two things only: bread and the games of the circus." He briskly raised his chin. "My philosophy—"

"What's your practice?"

The mayor ignored the crack. "No administration has done more for the poor. The happy Scot Thomas Carlyle said that the only way we'll recognize the poor is when they infect us with their diseases."

"Mayor Hall, have you heard the Committee of Seventy is going to examine Connolly's vouchers?"

The mayor urged restraint, lest justice be trampled on. "How can you disparage without trial a man who has given his life to public works? I've the utmost faith in Comptroller Connolly."

"Will that stop you from asking him to resign?"

"I trust the man."

"But will you stick by him?"

"A hundred and ten percent." The mayor smiled. "And that ten percent is not commission."

The reporters grinned and one asked, "Have you checked the vouchers?"

"That's not the mayor's function. I run the largest city in the world. Duties must be delegated, or nothing will get done." Elegant went on his way, satisfied he had planted an alibi that would clear him of his plan to have the vouchers stolen and get Connolly in hot water.

After the mayor sauntered off with a hi-ho superiority, an ink-stained wretch of the press began to sing under his breath:

> *"Here's to His Honor the Mayor*
> *Whose word no one relies on;*
> *Who rarely does an honest act*
> *Yet always does a wise one."*

The next day headlines on the stolen vouchers covered Tweed's desk as the members of the Board of Audit filed in. The mayor sat in a corner with the injury of innocence. Sweeny sat bundled up, though the September sun shone through the shadeless windows. Connolly was the only one who sat back restfully.

Tweed glared at Connolly. "We're hanging ourselves."

"It's not my fault," Connolly insisted in a tone that made him sound like he had insisted on his innocence a thousand times before.

Tweed sought to stare the truth out of Connolly. "Just before the reformers examine the vouchers, they disappear?"

"Stolen!" Connolly had no doubt.

"Call it what you will." Tweed leaned as a statue wanting to topple over and crush a mindless viewer. "The public wants your scalp."

Sweeny counseled, "For the good of the party, resign."

"Over your dead body." Connolly bumped back in his chair from the vitality of his denial, then slid forward like the breech of a cannon. "I had most to lose. The finger was bound to point to me. Why on earth should I destroy vouchers the *Times* had, O'Brien had, and for all I know, peddlers are wrapping fish in?"

"We'll stick by you." Mayor Hall supported the comptroller.

"I'm not going to be a sacrificial lamb." Connolly stared the mayor down with the fright that was rising in him.

Sweeny came in on a positive note. "Resigning will make you a hero. You've seen the light. You won't take the fall for us. You'll be free and clear while the mud is flung at us. If we fall, you'll be a favorite for higher office because you separated from us."

Tweed and Elegant were in awe of Sweeny.

Connolly roared at Sweeny, like a coal chute opening up, "You didn't have the humility to work with O'Brien."

Sweeny replied, "I had tons of humility. I didn't have the gall."

Tweed broke in to warn, "Divided we'll fall."

"Tell them," Connolly scoffed. "Whoever stole the vouchers was out to get me so they could stay free. Make me the patsy whose head the papers are howling for. I'm not taking this fall alone. I go—everyone goes."

Sweeny pleasantly assured him, "Your desire to destroy us will never be greater than your love to keep what you have."

Tweed, Hall and even Connolly had to admire the jugular wisdom of Brains. Tweed nursed the bruised comptroller. "Connolly is right. We stand together or fall apart."

Oakey objected to buttering Connolly. "Sweeny's right. The comptroller threatens to get us, but only he collects the money."

Connolly was too confident to raise his voice. "Mayor, you're required by law to sign each voucher."

"And you illegally took the biggest bite."

Sweeny no longer had the smell of a killer, only the smile. He sweetened Connolly's pot. "Your resignation will give you markers to call in for the rest of your life."

Tweed came around to Sweeny's view. "There's a point for you."

"His point is that he wants my scalp and he'll happily give it to the public so he can stay in office." Connolly knew he had them dead to rights.

"You weren't listening," said Tweed to the surprise of Sweeny and the attentive mayor. "Sweeny said . . . wait, let me finish. You have leadership quality. The party comes first to you. Always has. Destroy us and you disgrace the party. You'll forever be cast out. Resign and you'll be recognized as the man who saved the party in New York."

Connolly was listening, disturbed. "How?" he shrewdly asked.

"How?" Tweed gave him the gift. "Tell the truth."

Sweeny and Hall almost fell off their chairs.

Tweed rolled on. "You hired the jailbird Watson to give him another chance in life. A first step out of the muck. This is just like your deeply religious character. You care. You go out on the limb for your fellow man. How does Watson repay you? He stabs you in the back. Now Watson is gone to his Maker. You're left the victim."

A satisfied glint surfaced in Connolly's eyes, which was dull compared to Sweeny's and Hall's.

"Watson was in control of your office. Everyone will testify to that because it's the truth. I'll testify. Sweeny and Oakey will testify." Tweed could feel the comptroller's pulse quicken. Just when he had Connolly nibbling, he shifted course to the consternation of Sweeny, Oakey and even Connolly. "But you don't see it that way."

Connolly was unhappy. "Why not?"

"Your integrity. You don't want to blame a dead man who can't answer back."

Connolly lost his zealous face that made him look like he was cursing a winner home.

Tweed rode this affirmative response. "You were in charge of the office and you'll take the blame on your shoulders."

Connolly's unhappy eyes took on shade.

Sweeny and Hall hung by their thumbs, hoping this would come out right.

Tweed was absolutely convincing. "It's your responsibility. You have to take your stand where lesser men would run and hide and thus admit their guilt. Your upbringing will not allow you to make ignorance an excuse. Your conscience is your guide. You'll show the national party how a leader acts."

Sweeny and Hall sat aglow.

"You'll win the biggest press you ever had. Out of the jaws of adversity," Tweed guaranteed, "you'll pluck your ticket to higher office."

Connolly sat back, pleased.

"You'll make your statement from the steps of City Hall. Flags. The press. A big crowd. The works."

They marveled at the thoughtful stupor Connolly was thrown into. They waited as a baker for a prized cake to emerge from the oven. Was the flour thoroughly kneaded? Was it a pinch too sweet or sour? Was the heat too high or too low or not even?

Connolly told Tweed with gratitude, "That's a fine idea. My relation with Watson was a trust. A bond."

"Letter-perfect," Tweed praised him.

"Without conscience there'd be chaos."

His conviction was more than they had dreamed.

"What I am to Watson, Oakey is to me," Connolly continued in the same tone. "How much nobler it would be if the responsibility I took for Watson's actions the mayor took for me, as he is legally bound by the new charter."

"You sanctimonious hooker!" Oakey raged.

"You hypocritical weasel. You stole the vouchers."

Tweed jumped in. "Let us meet when we're more charitable."

Connolly scourged Sweeny and Hall. "O'Brien is a baby to deal with compared to you two. He only had energy."

Sweeny icily eyed Connolly to let the shoe fit. "Energy has its own confidence, you pious baloney bender. That's why the poor need such little education to rise."

Tweed commanded. "We must part friends. Oakey, shake with Connolly."

The mayor was suspicious of this olive branch. "You and Connolly are against Sweeny and me."

What's this? Tweed's face flushed.

Sweeny was eager to hear more.

Tweed arrogantly rode over his mayor. "Have you been seeing Tilden to divide us?"

"I saw the notary." Oakey's face lined with disgust. "You and Connolly paid O'Brien to plead your cases with Tilden!"

Sweeny knocked over his chair, bolting up. "You paid that putrid maggot? Bought the promise of a hooker?"

Tweed felt squeezed into a corner and was forced to admit. "Money can do everything. It even does your thinking. You begin to rely on money instead of common sense."

Sweeny rang into their skulls. "To exploit stupidity you must indulge in it. You're blackmailed forever. You never buy principles. You only buy the man."

Tweed owned up so sincerely, he impressed them. "It was a mistake. Over and done with and won't happen again. Let's pledge to meet tomorrow and iron out our differences."

"I pledge," said Oakey.

"I'll be here," Sweeny swore.

"Count on me," Connolly said firmly.

"Shake," said Tweed.

They shook hands and parted with breezy confidence.

THIRTY-SEVEN

Connolly left with a cold drizzle inside him. How could this happen to him? All his life he had lived with the certainty that when things went wrong for others, they'd open an opportunity for him. No one was more optimistic than he with this outlook. Now Tweed, Sweeny, Oakey smelled that he would be their opportunity. How could this be when he was obsessed with touching all bases, crossing every *t*, dotting every *i* and keeping his backside covered? His touch-me-not manner was unassailable. Yet they threw him to the dogs like a human sacrifice. He was nothing more to them than a man to kick in the gutter. They reviled his strong personal qualities. How infernally smart must a man be? The chilling drizzle kept falling inside him, calling up his humiliation.

That night he dug from his backyard and the foundation of his house a million and a half dollars stuffed in Civil War cartridge cases and biscuit tins and rushed his unwilling wife to Washington to buy government bonds.

He entered his wife's dressing room where there were pumice stones for her feet, Vegetine for her complaints, cherry syrup for her spirits. Hanging off the wall was her prophylactic linen for sexual intercourse, now as dry as salted fish. He went to her little lined-up saucers with their darker and darker rings of evaporating black dyes. Taking her tiny dauber, he touched up his mustache and temples. Then he drove a covered landau through the evening to Gramercy Park.

Though the little green swatch of private park is always a delight when one is inside its gate, there is a special appreciation in the evening rush hour when the din of people released from work can be heard in the distance and the closed park provides a remoteness from the cares of the day.

At his approach the park gate was unlocked from inside by Tilden. When Connolly saw the white-haired, ramrod-stiff man sitting on the bench, he ignored Tilden, who held his life in his hands, to bow before the silent figure. "Judge O'Conor, Your Honor, I am Comptroller Connolly. I've always looked forward to meeting the legal genius of New York, sir."

Tilden gleamed at the stiff-necked Connolly being humbled.

Judge O'Conor was lean of meat, strong of bone and a mix of sorrow and determination. His slightly sour face had buried nothing. His eyes had seen the world and his nose found it wanting.

Connolly reverently took O'Conor's frail hand. The adulation embarrassed the stony old man, though a life of lawsuits made him appreciate uncontested moments.

Tilden knew exactly when to inform Connolly. "Judge O'Conor has come out of retirement to be the legal adviser of the Committee of Seventy. He will lead the court fight against Tweed and his Ring."

"Their cause is lost!" Connolly hastened to separate himself from the old man's target. He also silently noted the contrast between the selfless O'Conor and Tilden, grown vain with ambition.

O'Conor spoke to Connolly as a hangman after the final prayer. "Mr. Connolly?"

"Sir?" Connolly was honored to have his attention.

"You are a disgrace to the city and the Republic."

Connolly manfully bent to the lash. "I seek to redeem myself, Your Honor."

Tilden spoke with goodwill to Connolly. "I offer you immunity from arrest."

Connolly thanked him.

"You are to resign your office and install Andy Green as comptroller."

Connolly was appalled. "I'm to be sacrificed."

"A sacrifice would hardly be free from prosecution." Tilden's sarcastic hum hinted to Connolly to be grateful there was no mention of stolen money.

"Resign? That's bad enough." Connolly sought to save face. "But to install Andy Green? That's making me a traitor in the eyes of the loyal people who worked for me."

"The choice is yours alone to make." Tilden was so sure of his man, he let Connolly squirm.

Connolly blustered, "What you want can't be had. It's illegal."

Tilden deferred to O'Conor, who gave a succinct opinion. "Replacing yourself in office with Mr. Green is legal."

Connolly sat drunkenly. "I'll be handing you all our records. I'll be disgraced. Finished."

Tilden reminded him of the silver lining. "But free."

THIRTY-EIGHT

$\mathcal{S}$weeny felt his way along the rock basement of his brother's modest house, a chill fastening on his bones. Firefly glints from mica sparkled off his candle flame. The wall a shower of sparks resembling a knife against a whetstone as he descended the rickety slats. Scurrying through cramped aisles between dusty stacks of vintage wines and champagne, he paid no attention to the warped and yellowed labels, nor to the faded inventory cards with dates going back to Louis XIV. Sweeny worshiped the grape by hoarding it. A pulled cork was not a festive occasion but the dissipation of an investment no intoxication could rival. He crouched toward a door hacked into the rock. It took all of Sweeny's strength to throw the cranky lock, unwire the hasp, kick the bolt through and wrench open the floor-scraping door, thickly reinforced in back with split logs.

Sweeny ducked into the crawlspace, the clay ground holding the dampness of rains from other weeks. He pried out a wooden mallet from between the barrels and began tapping their bellies. He had no patience for the task, yet was driven to keep on, crouched low, breathing short. A hand spread across the barrel as though defining a pregnancy. The other hand kept up an obsessive beat with the mallet: tap, tap, tap.

The cork began to rise in the bunghole. His fingers weaned the cork out and poked into the hole. Ecstasy. His fingers came up, not stained with wine but pinching money. He swiftly stuck the money back, hammered the cork in with one smart blow, sealed the bunghole with wax. Sweeny stamped the seal with his Greek letters of academic excellence. He rolled these barrels out of the crawlspace and addressed the shipping labels for delivery to Montreal.

All was going well until he kicked the barrels standing in the corner one by one and discovered full barrels when he needed empty ones. He searched the crude cellar on hands and knees for a drain. There was none. Disgusted, he rapped his mallet on the ceiling beam. His kindly brother cracked open the basement door. Sweeny urged him in with the mallet.

"I need empties," Sweeny agonized.

His peaceful brother was baffled. "I saved them."

"Not enough."

"I'll buy more."

"There's no time. Empty these barrels in the river."

"Prize French wine?" The brother couldn't believe it.

"You don't drink."

The brother shook his head against it. "Rare French wine for the river? People are bound to be suspicious."

Sweeny gave in to humor his brother and get him on the way. "Give the wine. Let them come with buckets, bottles, cans."

"Who?" His brother stubbornly didn't see the light.

"The people," Sweeny said grandly.

His shaken brother didn't utter a word.

"We want the barrels back as fast as they're emptied."

"You paid a fortune for the wine."

Sweeny tried to be jubilant. "Wine for the people!"

"It's not even a holiday."

"No one will be the least suspicious if you make it festive." Sweeny nudged his brother out and crouched back into the crawlspace. He dug out tin boxes with bass-note fullness. He was overjoyed until he heard enthusiastic singing outside and went white with alarm. "For he's a jolly good fellow!"

His smiling brother returned with the empty barrel.

"Get those idiots to shut up."

He was offended by Sweeny's callousness. "They're thanking you."

"You told them I was here?"

"To avoid suspicion. They knew I wouldn't give wine away."

Sweeny bowed his head and sucked up his gut and came up calm. "I'm embarrassed being thanked." He helped his brother walk up another barrel and returned to fill the empty one, knocking off the top hoop and pouring in the money.

Outside, an unrestrained chorus sang his praise: "For he's a jolly good fellow. That no one can denyyyyyyyy!"

His grinning brother returned with another empty barrel.

"Can't you shut those nitwits up?"

His brother quit grinning as he stared through the candlelit darkness. The wine dregs had splattered Sweeny with its bloody stains. His brother kept the murderous image to himself.

The singing outside turned devotional. "For Sweeny is a jolly good fellow!"

"No more wine. They're getting out of control."

"Cutting off their supply won't hurt them now."

"What are they doing?"

"Resting."

"Where?" Sweeny was on eggs.

"In the gutter."

"In front of this house?" Sweeny was aghast.

"They can't budge."

Sweeny waved his bloody hands. "Make them." When his brother left, Sweeny poured tin boxes of money into the barrels while hearing himself being eulogized in song.

His brother returned, out of breath. "They won't leave until they can express their thanks to you in person."

The singing had reached a wild pitch of happiness.

"Say a few words to them." His brother believed in niceties.

Sweeny slapped on the shipping label. "Thank them for their loyalty."

THIRTY-NINE

$\mathcal{S}$heriff Matt Brennan never arrested a man he deemed a friend. He climbed the stairs, empty of Shiny Hats and favor seekers, to Tweed's Duane Street office, hangdog. He knocked apologetically.

"Let yourself in, Matt."

Matt entered, housebroken, politely inquiring if the papers burning in the fireplace were important. Tweed replied they had value only if read. The sheriff informed Tweed, whose broad back was to the fireplace, that pages had clumped together. Tweed thanked the sheriff. Brennan grabbed the poker to see that the papers burned, and Tweed accepted his dedication. The service done with pride, he then gently knighted Tweed with a hand on the shoulder. "Boss, you are my man." His look was of a faithful customer who found it difficult to believe a tavern had closing hours.

Tweed cheered up his sheriff. "Orders are orders."

The sheriff knew where the whisk broom hung behind the door and whisked the Boss down.

"Did they say how I'm charged?"

The sheriff was embarrassed. "Taking six million dollars. Can I get your coat?"

"I'm not going anyplace." He said it with an assurance that

unnerved the sheriff and had to make it up to him. "Matt, I'll not do anything to harm your reputation."

The sheriff reminded him of the impossible. "Your bail is set at a million."

"Is that a record?" Tweed hoped it was.

"Every cent." The sheriff nodded. "Did you hear the latest, Boss? Prince Garvey fled to Paris. Too much, too soon, eh, Boss?"

"Never hire a man who has no taste in women."

"Never bitter, only wiser, eh, Boss? Your collector, Elbert Woodward, flew the coop too."

"Elbe was a good collector. He looked like a murder weapon dropped in the street."

"I saved the best for last," Brennan said gleefully. "Silky Sammy arrested Slippery Dick Connolly."

A grinning Tweed applauded. "A present from Tilden!"

"Mrs. Connolly will not fetch bail."

A beaming Tweed threw her a kiss. "Bless her heart. What a grand old biddy."

"She's wailing she doesn't have the money. She knows old Slippery can't ask for it. His friends had to cough up the half million. Then Slippery jumped bail for Egypt."

"Slippery is fair. He ducks out on everyone. Is there word on Black Brains?"

"Montreal, Boss. The Brain is heading for Paris." Then the sheriff looked kindly on Tweed, saying that they must be going.

"Would you mind waiting, Matt? Bail is bound to show up."

The faithful sheriff was uneasy because he couldn't believe it.

"Jay Gould promised." Tweed let it drop.

The sheriff was impressed. "Have you hired lawyers, Boss?"

"They cost me an arm and leg. Dudley Field, Elihu Root, John Graham and a half dozen others."

"Is that why O'Conor is stalling?"

"We're both jockeying for delays. O'Conor doesn't want to try me before my judges and is waiting for a new term. The longer he waits, the better for him and me. He'll eventually get his kind of judge and I'll get time for people to forget."

"A good trade-off, Boss. They've shorn you of every position but not of every pull."

"I'm still state senator. There's enough powder in that office to blow Tilden to hell."

"The boys are saying it honored you not to run out on Jubilee Jim Fisk when he was lying in his own blood, shot by his whore's lover."

"What's a friend for? We sat on the Erie board together."

"Newspapermen connected you to the stink though you were clean."

"Newspapers say I'm wallowing among ambitious men. What's another spot if you're sending your suit out to be cleaned by the courts?"

A courteous knock at the door. Tweed motioned the sheriff to sit in his chair. Brennan refused out of respect. Tweed pushed him into his seat without formality and opened the door.

Liveried men were lined up down the stairs.

"Your million-dollar bail, sir. Compliments of Jay Gould."

The self-important butler stepped smartly to the desk and placed a suitcase before the sheriff. "One hundred thousand dollars, Your Honor."

The sheriff nervously unbuckled the leather straps and peeked in. A pond of money. He quickly shut the temptation from sight. No sooner had he shut the lid when another servant entered and placed a similar suitcase on the first. "One hundred thousand dollars, Your Honor."

"Thank you." He opened and shut the lid quicker than the first peek.

The servants paraded in one at a time. "One hundred thousand dollars, Your Honor." The suitcases stacked on top of another. The eighth suitcase blocked out the sheriff's face. The ninth hid his head. The tenth walled him off. The last liveried servant announced, "One million dollars, Your Honor. Mr. Tweed's bail." He marched out as the sheriff begged Tweed to keep the bail until he could round up deputies to cart it away.

When the frazzled sheriff left, in came Tweed's clean-cut son, Billy Junior, stout with confidence and alive with ability. That the father shined in the presence of his militantly grown-up son was obvious. He was transferring a million dollars in property and two million dollars in cash to his name. Billy Junior refused to hear this cautious move. Tweed told him it was for his mother's sake. She'd need the money, and the money had to be kept safe from the vultures who'd be after it with false claims.

Billy Junior, showing he knew the world, conveyed what almost everyone was thinking. O'Conor couldn't get a jury to convict. There was hardly a man who didn't have a friend or relative in debt to Tweed for a job or favor. The son refused the money.

Tweed, with a fatherly warmth, told his son there are countries where people live well without a Bill of Rights, but there's no country where people live well without money. Tweed was disheartened at seeing his son wasn't convinced.

Billy Junior put his arm around his father in a proud way and reminded him of the marvelous stories he told about Grandpa working at what he loved and Grandpa always giving encouragement. Now he was a bigger success than Grandpa, yet his advice to his son was getting darker and darker.

He couldn't evade a son the way he did the public. The truth was darker to him. Everyone should have bought Grandpa's dedicated craftsmanship, but they hunt for cheap bargains which are the most expensive ways to buy. Grandpa dissolved the ugliness of his world with his love of labor. After convincing his son he then ignored his son's growing up by forcing the bank receipts on him.

Billy Junior cavalierly stuck the receipts in his coat.

This offhand treatment did not escape Tweed, who watched part of the fortune he was going on trial for being carelessly stuffed in his son's pocket.

He walked Billy Junior to the door with faith in his son's integrity while gravely doubting his wisdom with wealth he hadn't earned. Would his enormous fortune go down the drain? The horror of this justice put a crimp in his optimism about the justice he was buying.

FORTY

ilden was close to becoming a national hero, and this strengthened his hand in everything he did. Now another scandal made it appear fate was on his side. This caused his unusual boasting in a secluded chamber with O'Brien at his heels. "I told you Tweed could be brought down, Senator." Tilden's sadistic respect was to address the newly elected State Senator O'Brien by his title to keep the upstart beholden, tempted for more and in place. "How do you like it falling in our laps?" Tilden spoke of fate. "Jubilee Jim Fisk murdered over his whore, Josie Mansfield, at the Broadway Central Hotel, and Tweed rushing over to comfort Jubilee's dying moments. I tell you, Fisk's murder over a whore, more than any revelation so far, has woke the public again."

The former sheriff, now riding high, retained his insecurity. He was not ashamed of his low beginnings and had the good sense not to live it down in politics. He even took pride in his saloon redness that brought out the startled whiteness of his eyes. He was rising in the world, yet every day he feared the roof was about to fall in on him. He was more his own man when he was an ass kisser. Being a rug underfoot, he could trip up people when he wanted. Now he was a state senator, and he walked on tiptoe because

Tilden made him edgy. He needed to ride on Tilden's coattails, and the price was slavery.

He spoke to Tilden as if the railroad lawyer were a tinderbox the most casual spark might set off with devastating consequences. "The Fisk scandal will only make Tweed work the jury twice as hard. Tweed leaves very little to chance, especially justice."

"Why are you worried?" Tilden was his confident self. "We have our judge sitting. Our district attorney prosecuting. We have Tweed's financial records, witnesses against him and the guilt of his cronies who escaped."

An aide knocking on the chamber door informed them Tweed was arriving and the court was preparing to go into session.

O'Brien asked about Tweed and was told he was creating a circus outside. Tilden scoffed that Tweed could no longer get away with that disguise. O'Brien hinted it may not be a disguise but Tweed's confidence in the jury. When they stepped into the hall, they heard the hullabaloo out on the street.

O'Brien said dryly and not without fear and admiration, "I wonder who is on trial?"

Perplexity flickered across Tilden's surface and was gone. "I wonder why these ignorant people hate us so?"

O'Brien said, drier than before, "It's all the good we do them."

They heard the leather-lunged shout of a booster: "Boss, you got a heart as big as a meetinghouse."

Tweed's eyes twinkled as he doffed his velour fedora of evening blue with wide brim raked sportily up one side. The faithful patting him on his broad back and shoulders for *their good luck.* His monumental bail became him, and it being paid in one fell swoop by the master Jay Gould was seen as homage.

Victory was on Tweed's face, relaxed, content, almost mindlessly happy in his hubris. Tweed's own wealth was a mockery to his followers grinding out their weary days, yet they celebrated him. Educated New Yorkers, observing this shameless idolatry with despair, failed to recognize that many of the poor share the same failings as some of the well-to-do. They do not shy away from a crook if he is their crook. Win or lose, the faithful would be vindicated. If Tweed lost, it justified their contempt for the law. If Tweed won, it proved the Boss could buy anyone.

In the courtroom Tweed encouraged a clubhouse informality. He turned his chair around to horse with friends and well-wishers,

shaking hands, winking, keeping his back to the judge. The courtroom bore a Tweed hallmark. He had the gallery.

When Dudley Field, an old lion of the New York courts and the
head of Tweed's team of lawyers, rose to set the stage in his opening remarks, the noisy gallery fell silent.

Dudley Field raised his head and recited from memory the many
victories inscribed on a future monument to his client. "His
Honor William M. Tweed. State Senator. United States Congressional Representative. Grand Sachem of Sachems and Chairman of
the General Committee of Saint Tammany. Attorney-at-law.
Temperance to the strictest degree, as was his father before him.
Won first elected office as a Democrat with the backing of a prominent member of the opposition Whig party who supported Mr.
Tweed for his character, devotion and honest labors to the people
of his crowded ward. In the Panic of 1857, when decent families
were found frozen to death in their flats, Senator Tweed delivered
wood, coal and food to the suffering, paid for out of his own pocket.

"His Honor William M. Tweed. Chairman of the Board of the
Broadway National Bank. President of the Guardian Bank for
Savings. Trustee of the Oriental Savings Bank. Commissioner of
Public Works. Commissioner of Public Schools. Deputy Commis-
sioner of Streets. Board Member of the Erie Railroad. President of
the New York Printing Company. President of the Sheffield Rock
Quarry Company. Founder and President with the much loved
Republican Henry Smith of the Indian Harbor Clubhouse, Green-
wich, Connecticut. Owner and President of the Metropolitan
Hotel. Chief of the Americus Volunteer Big Six Fire Company of
the fire-plagued Lower East Side. Honored by a plaza in his name,
Tweed Plaza, for his many good works."

This lofty roll of credentials made Tweed's enemies placid. His
faithful burst into applause that the Tilden judge quickly hammered down.

Nearing the end of his opening remarks, Mr. Field was in high
stride, strenuous and unstinting in praise of his client and the gross
injustice against him. "Others ran. Others hid. Others cannot be
found. Here he is like a noble Roman!"

A raucous eruption drowned out the judge's hammering.

Tweed sat in his chair, poised above the adulation yet privately
soaking it in.

When the outburst lowered to a continuous simmering buzz, the faithful found the prosecutor was equal to his task. After a moment of stillness the prosecutor's voice became the fire bell he so dramatically evoked. "Mr. Tweed has alarmed the city like a fire bell at midnight. Men awoke from their fancied security to discover that in the very heart of the commercial emporium of the Western world a series of systematic crimes had been perpetrated. Crimes of such colossal character they transcend in wickedness anything recorded in the history of crime in the civilized world from the morning of Creation. The clerk who embezzles twenty-five dollars goes to state prison. The man who robs the taxpayers' treasury of six million dollars can only be punished by a misdemeanor. Verdict or no verdict, you cannot, must not, whitewash the defendant so that men will boast of being his friend."

No matter how forcefully the prosecutor presented confessions of guilt, written records, sworn testimony of witnesses, he did not wipe the smiles off Tweed's followers.

The next witness did.

The prosecutor was now a cat playing with mice as he told the judge he wished to call a surprise witness. The courtroom buzzed. Tweed was curious without being worried. His gallery did not enjoy surprises and were on edge. Policemen entered in ranks and lined up as a solid wall on both sides of the aisle to protect the witness from the spectators. Then, of all things, a French dandy appeared. Was the prosecutor crazy? What kind of trick was this? The scoffing and hilarity turned to wrath when the witness walked out of the police protection to the judge's bench and the gallery recognized the creature.

"Prince Garvey!" Catcalls rained down on Garvey. When the dandy Prince passed Tweed, the Boss cranked out the sound of a neck cracking. Garvey stiffened as though poleaxed.

The judge threatened to clear the court. He was saved by the swearing-in of the witness. Tweed and his gallery wished to hear every word of the turncoat. The reception took the shine off Garvey's bay-rummed face. He was too scared to know the gallery's vehemence was also a substitute for their lowered confidence.

Tweed summoned an aide to find out how Garvey was slipped into the country when he had heelers planted at every pier. He was told that Garvey was brought in disguised as a woman.

In the witness chair, facing former friends and benefactors, Garvey fidgeted and squirmed in his Paris clothes. His face brightened with sweat. Worst of all, he was drawn like a victim to a cobra to look into Tweed's menacing eyes.

The prosecutor led Garvey through his paces. The Prince described in damaging details the routine of overbilling courthouse contractors. The astronomical profit in government waste. The many bipartisan contributors to the party that spawned waste. Waste was at the heart of power. Waste had to be protected at all costs for the greed of the Ring and the power of the party to spawn contributors to it.

The prosecutor's crutch could not keep the Prince from twitching. Tweed's counsel, seeing Garvey's mortification, sprang up and called to the jury to see a telltale sign of the guilt of the witness. "Watch Garvey's face as he looks at Senator Tweed!"

Indeed it was a look that revealed more true history than volumes. Garvey's cringing while in the protection of the court was terrifying to behold. Not that many sympathized with Garvey, but his condition threw a terrifying shadow over their own. Those loyal to Tweed exulted in Garvey's fear. Those against Tweed felt that dreaded moment when justice vanishes while law reigns and the weak or unprepared are at the mercy of brutes.

Judge Davis condescendingly sniffed at Tweed's lawyer. "Do you want me to appoint a clerk to watch Mr. Garvey's face?"

At recess Garvey was bathing in his own sweat. A police escort was provided for the few steps through the judge's door where he was allowed to rest in a heavily guarded anteroom off the court. Tweed's henchman found, as Garvey's sweating foretold, easy access to the guarded room.

Tweed loomed into the anteroom, and Garvey dropped to his knees for mercy. Tweed one-handed Garvey under the throat and yanked him to his trembling feet. "You piss-ass scum."

Garvey plunged to his expensively tailored knees again.

Tweed one-handed him around the back of his neck, as he would a dog, and raised the choking Garvey.

Garvey was drowning in his French clothes.

"You were a beggar and I took you out of the gutter and made you rich."

"Boss, my gratitude stops me from crying out for help."

Tweed knocked the Prince's head against the wall, and Garvey's greased hair slid over his shiny forehead.

"They gave me immunity from prosecution. No money to return. What could I do?"

"Give it back. Say a word about friendship. Say a word about being helped out of the muck. Learn to do something beside sticking a knife in your friend's back." Tweed went berserk banging Garvey's barbered head so loudly against the wall, the reporters heard. Tweed left before they barged in.

"What did Tweed say?"

The bulging-eyed Garvey rubbed his neck. It was moments before he could mutter, "It was blasphemous."

At the trial's end Judge Davis knew what was in the back of everyone's mind. He sternly charged the jury, "Discharge your duty in the light of *evidence*. Bear in mind there is no stain more deep and damning that a juror may bring upon his character than by being false to his oath and bringing in a false verdict."

Day after day the jury had heard eyewitnesses confirm names, places, dates of fraudulent transactions spreading into every nook and cranny of the city's multimillion-dollar business. The evidence was completely against Tweed. A former Tweed bookkeeper named O'Rourke estimated the stealing at two hundred million dollars!

Tweed's confidence in the face of the evidence chilled observers who were against him.

When the jury filed in, spectators rose to hear the verdict. One juror flicked lint off his sleeve. Tweed caught the high sign, turned his back on the court, yawned, a smile waiting in the corners of his mouth.

Judge Davis started with displeasure at the foreman. "I understand you have not agreed?"

The foreman resisted being chastised. "We've not, Your Honor."

"If the jury had more time, do you think you might agree?" The judge's question was a demand.

"No, Your Honor. We're hopelessly apart."

Tweed's opposition sat appalled, mourning for the law, their city, themselves, that a crook as gigantic as Tweed was going free. Tweed's faithful held in their exhilaration.

Judge Davis reminded the jurors of their sacred oath. He stared at their faces to browbeat the truth out of them.

He was forced to announce what he dare not think. He couldn't believe he was going to make official this foul miscarriage of justice. His stern face denounced the jury. Then he dropped into thought as in a deep sleep to heal a wound.

Of all the exposures in this trial of lofty and low men, the most painful to absorb was the lonely judge resisting a false verdict he had to hand down to uphold the law. His heartsickness transcended the man. He couldn't find his voice. Tweed was escaping the enormity of his crime with another unspeakable crime of bribing jurors. The burdened judge appeared also to be stained by this act, his power eroded. The mountainous facts against Tweed were nought compared to his show of power in court.

Slowly Judge David addressed the jury as if casting them out of civilization. "The jury is discharged!"

Amid the cheering and hat waving, Tweed eyed the depressed judge and stung him vengefully with a cheap and nasty pose of superior knowledge. In this moment of victory Tweed knew he had been poisoned too. In happier days he'd have made the sporting gesture, not the vengeful one. The thug Morrissey was able to honor Heenan's courage by kissing the shapeless fists that had punched him out. Tweed wanted victories to raise him up to his better self as they had in his younger days. Now he felt an internal justice working against him even in his hour of triumph.

He had not lost his original zest for one ritual. He faced the reporters ganging around him with his old bravura.

"Senator Tweed, do you know how the jury voted?"

"Eleven to two for conviction," replied Tweed with a heave-ho.

"That's thirteen. There's only twelve jurors."

"The judge," said Tweed, "was against me too."

Their laughter gave him the sensation he was on top again.

FORTY-ONE

A colossus rising out of the East River loomed over the city, never out of sight, rarely out of mind, standing against the sky as a daily sign of better times ahead. This dream coming into reality was the tower of the Brooklyn Bridge, eighty-five feet above low tidewater. No more dangerous winter ferry rides with life and limb at stake, less ferry traffic in the perilous fogs, a faster open road to the flat farmlands of Brooklyn and Long Island. While this prosperous future was rising out of the river, another Panic was shaping New York as nothing else since the potato blights in the Old World.

The New York Stock Exchange closed.

The Bank of Commonwealth was ruined.

The National Trust Company went bankrupt.

Decent, hardworking people raising themselves up plunged back into the poverty from whence they came. Merchants of long standing went to the wall. City factories and country mills closed. Railroads halted construction. Banks remaining open certified large checks but did not cash them. Helpless people swarmed outside closed banks and at the steps of the Treasury at Broad and Wall Streets and were worked over by pickpockets.

At the free ice-water barrel in Printing House Square headlines were hawked over popular music played by little violin girls dressed in their Sunday best. The violin girls playing for tips replaced the muddy, barefoot, crossing sweeper girls. New war money stepped up the pace, and the city became too dangerous for sweeper girls to brave the mad traffic.

Newsboys shouted to their captive audience in front of failed banks: "Delaware, Lackawanna and Western Railroad goes under! Fond du Lac Railroad done for!"

Boys also hawked handbills or "Penny a piece!" Up-to-the-minute lists of fallen firms rushed off tiny private presses. The boys moved quickly through a crowd. Anyone wanting to become important for a penny bought a handbill to announce the latest failures, and a crowd formed around him. "Delauney, Iselin and Clarke, brokers, suspended. E. A. Benedict, broker, suspended. L. V. Kirby and Company, dry goods, closed, debt of half million dollars."

Another band of boys swooped down upon the suddenly destitute peddling the thickest list of bankruptcies and bank failures, claiming to have names seen nowhere else. It was true that while some of their failures were correct, others were rumors. Men lacking imagination and daring thrived on this news. Panics stamped their plodding, marginal existence as well done.

This Panic was the third in less than four decades of boiling optimism. Many feared this Panic would burn through the seventies. It was fueled by the rampant speculation of the postwar sixties. Stocks could be bought on margin for as little as ten percent. Banks needed imposing architecture, for their foundations rested on the phantom shoulders of credit.

The Tweed Ring robberies went off the front page to be replaced by unspeakable scandals. A money scandal out of Washington dwarfed Tweed. This robbery took the name of the corporation Crédit Mobilier. Oakes Ames, a New England congressman, swore, "I never gave a share of stock, directly or indirectly, to any member of Congress." Two friendly congressional committees found they could not avoid his guilt. When confronted, Ames confessed buying congressmen to promote a railroad as a patriotic act.

The juiciest scandal was sexual. The man accused of epic sex? An unbelievable figure. He was white-haired, venerated, a member of an illustrious family, and a clergyman hero to the solid middle class: Reverend Henry Ward Beecher. Beecher's daring accuser was herself a grand cake of scandal. Her name spoke volumes: Victoria Woodhull. Her sister also preached and practiced—favoring the latter—free love, she was mistress to old Commodore Vanderbilt; pioneer woman Wall Street broker; and the first American publisher of the *Communist Manifesto*. Victoria was more scandalous than her sister, and chased from more hotels.

Victoria Woodhull was intelligent, independent, infernally ahead of her time, and she abhorred cant. She acted as if respectable men sat on the lid of disorder with their own disorders.

She was the first woman to run for President of the United States. Frederick Douglass, the famed black abolitionist, accepted second place on her ticket. She chose Douglass because they both represented the repressed peoples of the earth, he through his race, she through her sex. Her scandal lay in calling for the same standard of morality for both sexes. If that didn't enlighten the guardians of morality, she declared that she could sleep with a hundred men and still be as virtuous as their Aunt Bess baking apple pies. Her ideas were shocking enough, but they became incendiary coming from a woman of undeniable beauty.

Victoria, of all people, accused the venerable Beecher of sexual energy on a satanic scale. Her accusations in the popular and sensational weekly she published with her sister read like a circus poster: twenty mistresses! Each mistress a devout church-goer! This revelation of demonic lubricity among churchwomen tapped a dark root in the public's vivid imagination. A parishioner paramour of Victoria sued Beecher for alleged adultery with *his* wife. Poor Beecher unburdened himself by confessing to "unusual intimacy" with her, whereas if he had confessed to the usual kind he might not have haunted the nation's curiosity so powerfully.

The trial ended in a hung jury, but not before a hungry public gorged themselves on backstairs clerical life and purple gossip that put the borough of churches, Brooklyn, for once and for all on the national popular map.

In this postwar climate the valiant O'Conor searched for twelve untainted jurors for the second Tweed trial. Day after day potential jurors were weighed by O'Conor's sharp questions. Each day O'Conor returned to his office with little to show for his diligence.

The dogged old man converted his office into a war room. In his safe a detailed map of Manhattan had a red dot before a juror's address. O'Conor distrusted city detectives and assigned his own detective to follow each juror to see that no one tampered with him.

A ward police chief was a political appointee. If his party lost the ward elections, the police chief lost his job. The veteran Sergeant Walling of the Draft Riots was transferred after his party lost his ward. A tide of immigrants was giving ward after ward to the Tammany Democrats, who appointed their own chiefs.

One day O'Conor's map had the full quota of twelve untainted jurors. He was locking up the map for the last time when a detective informed him that Police Captain Walsh had contacted juror number eight.

O'Conor went through his daily detective reports. Juror number eight, Edward Lubry, had absolutely no discernible connection with Tweed or his machine. Once more O'Conor sent out his own detectives, this time to fine-comb number eight's background.

When O'Conor retired from his honorable public life, he had absorbed more knowledge than most men are capable of digesting. Now he was frightened about the law. Tweed was a crook of unbelievable magnitude whose reach went through every layer of society: respectable and disreputable, press and church, courts and police, reform and conservative, poor and wealthy. Tweed had mined that richest vein of self-interest above his neighbor's interest. Men who desired their own security are driven by their greed to make their society insecure.

An O'Conor detective uncovered that juror number eight was a barber to one of Tweed's army of cronies. Juror number eight was censured and excused.

The uneasy senators Tilden and O'Brien came down from Albany. They worried—for shrewd and good reasons—why Tweed did not escape with his millions as Sweeny, Connolly and the rest. They worried why Tweed chose to stand trial a second time. They knew their worrying held more than a grain of truth. With the help of Tweed's upstate Republican friends, in his everlasting debt for spoils connected with rebuilding Albany, Tweed could crucify Tilden and O'Brien. Tweed could throw a roadblock across Tilden's drive for the White House. The facts told Tilden and O'Brien that Tweed was trapped. Their experience told them that this was when Tweed was most dangerous.

What galled Tweed's enemies was his walking around full-sail, as if not he but his amateur, ignorant accusers were on trial.

O'Conor, knowing how formidable Tweed was, asked O'Brien if there was anyone to *trust* who knew Tweed's friends and would be courageous enough to work with them. Finding such an invaluable person would go a long way toward insuring an untainted jury. For Tweed to go free again was unthinkable. O'Brien suggested Shamus, an honest young man who had quietly left the organization though he was in high favor with the Boss.

When O'Conor saw Shamus, who was still young enough to glow with the openness of calf love, he was certain he had the assistant he sought and invited him to join his staff. Shamus replied to an offer others would jump at: "It matters what I do."

"I need you to advise me about a jury, fortunately or unfortunately, that's been selected. You know the web of Tweed's connections."

"No one, sir, can know them all. His friends are legion. They include his foes, if you know what I mean. Fear."

O'Conor's eyebrows raised at this sad prospect, which confirmed his knowledge. He was impressed with Shamus. The respect was mutual, as Shamus idolized O'Conor. "That's why I need any information you can give me."

"I beg your pardon, sir. I can't take the offer."

O'Conor was used to people bending their knee. "You'll be well paid."

"I was so by Tweed and I left."

"Any profession you wish to enter will be easier with my recommendation."

"I will not inform, sir."

O'Conor smiled down from his experience at the innocence of Shamus. "There's nothing to do with informing. You'll simply advise me if the selected juror has the remotest connection with Tweed. If surprise witnesses are sprung on us, I'll need to know their background."

"Sir, I wish you the best of luck."

Confrontations had formed O'Conor to quickly suspect motives. "Have you seen Tweed lately?"

"I've not seen him since I left."

"Why is that?" O'Conor was suspicious. "You didn't argue?"

"After working in Tweed's office and seeing the frailty of men, I'd rather face war where there's chance of seeing bravery."

The adversarial stripe in O'Conor vanished. The idea of an idealistic lad working in Tweed's office! "Then you believe Tweed fixes juries?"

"Absolutely. He doesn't take justice lightly."

"That he'd fix the jury on his second trial?"

"Positively."

O'Conor raised a forbidding finger for Shamus to be certain. "Can he fix a jury where every precaution has been taken?"

"He can. He would. He will."

O'Conor slumped. "And you don't mean to help us?"

"No one can help you, sir, unless you stop letting yourself be used."

"Damn you!" O'Conor exploded. "Used by whom? You are preposterous."

"I hope not, sir."

"You hope not?" You malign a man *and you hope not?*"

"Is it true you're letting Black Brains return to this country if he refunds four hundred thousand dollars from his dead brother's estate?"

"We're working on it."

"Brains stole millions."

"You miss the point."

"Connolly escaped with at least five million dollars. One and a half million in government bonds."

"I said, lad, you miss the point."

"Mayor Oakey Hall has been set free."

"After inconclusive trials."

"Inconclusive? His signatures are on the vouchers."

"You don't know the rules of evidence."

"Rules of evidence don't know crooks."

O'Conor was not used to taking medicine. He sniffed loudly.

"Sheriff O'Brien should be impeached. Instead he's endorsed for higher office and elected state senator. Ingersol, Keyser, Woodward, the old Board of Supervisors stole millions, and they're free with their boodle. This justice favors a life of crime. Have you seen how despairing Tom Nast's cartoons have become? Nast should be celebrating his brave fight to expose Tweed and his Ring, but he is heartsick. Sir, the way justice works is as demoralizing as Tweed's stealing."

"The point is that Tweed is the thief we want. The Boss. We need witnesses against him. Your innocence in legal matters, no matter how laudable, is useless."

"Innocence is useless"—Shamus stuck up for his point—"yet to live without it is to live without the sun."

O'Conor's manful quality was revealed in his apology. "I regret so much of my career is based upon being accusatory. The form before you was shaped from the best of intentions."

Shamus was embarrassed O'Conor felt he had to apologize to him. "Tilden knows the public fight is to get Tweed. The private fight is to get control of Tweed's political machine."

"You must join my staff. I'll get you through the quotas of the finest colleges."

Shamus would not be put off. "You can't put only Tweed on trial without Vanderbilt, Gould, Astor, Brains, Slippery, Haul and the rest of the army who profited. Is justice blind because she's impartial or because she fears to look on power?"

"You know better," O'Conor snapped.

"I don't see better. The city's biggest slumlord is a church. Trinity on Wall Street is a landlord of whorehouses. Wait, wait, let me finish. Trinity is the landlord of an entire red-light district named in its honor, Heavenly Acres."

O'Conor smiled, and the smile was wiped off his face.

"What does your impartial law say about that? Just what Tweed says. It's easier to succeed if you take things as you find them. The comptroller has to open his books to the public by law every three months. Connolly didn't open his books for three years. No bank loaning the city money protested. What does your law say about that? Just what Tweed says. You take things as you find them. A dozen newspapers collapsed around the state after Tweed couldn't support them. There's no law against that. Sir, you can't save the city by pulling up a poisonous plant and leaving unchanged the soil from which the poison grew."

"I'm not unmoved by what you say," O'Conor remarked sadly.

"Freeing the Ring to get at Tweed is just what the wards see is wrong. Justice becomes a private club."

A thoughtful shade fell over O'Conor. "You know me better than that."

"Yes, sir. Your family was friends with the sainted Robert Emmett. That's why I can speak to you about the helpless. Especially those who perform as cheerleaders to their own selves being robbed."

O'Conor was sympathetic. "You are dealing with human nature. I must deal with law."

"The men who knew the law did so little to relieve the hunger Kathleen went through. Children with death whispering in their windpipes. Arms too weak to beg. Every morning hungry families on the road searching for food and smelling their own death soon to come. Hunger gave children the voice of crows. Mothers and fathers lying down to die and all their care and love couldn't keep them from turning into bundles of rags across the blighted fields."

"Would you have me jail an entire society?" O'Conor became defensive.

"I'd be certain, sir, I wasn't being used for Tilden's ambitions. He wants that great political machine Tweed has built."

"I'm not immune to your argument. The private use of public law. That's why I'll get an untainted jury if it takes a generation until Tweed's influence dies out."

"Tweed holds the last trump. If you convict him, his confession will block Tilden's road to the White House. Tweed can name names of reformers he bought and sold, like the soap-fat man. Tilden must be tempted to allow Tweed to escape."

"If that can be proved, I'll resign and accuse Tilden."

"Then someday, sir, when Tweed escapes, you'll resign."

"Join my staff to see if an honest lad can improve an old lawyer?" O'Conor enjoyed the strange elation of being outdone by untrained honesty.

"Kathleen made me see Tweed in his true light."

"Who is Kathleen?"

His face became more expressive than any words he could find.

A smiling O'Conor saw his opening. "Tell Kathleen you are working for Judge O'Conor."

"First I must get her to talk to me again."

"I cannot assure your future with Kathleen, but I can with the law where your quality is needed."

A smiling Shamus shook the master lawyer's hand.

O'Conor was more content than he had been in months. "I do believe we're at last going to have Tweed on the ropes."

FORTY-TWO

*T*weed was scrutinizing O'Conor's list of jurors as though it were a death threat wherein he had to find good news.

He sat behind an imperial desk as president of the Broadway National Bank. His pince-nez with dangling black ribbon perched precariously on his grand nose. He appeared every bit the book-keeper-scholar. This was Elijah Purdy's office overlooking the busy marketplace. The walls remained decorated with badges, scrolls and framed tributes. When Billy Junior entered, Tweed knew he brought bad news by the concern on his son's face.

Billy Junior was unable to sell their property at a fair price and felt he had let his father down.

On the eve of the second trial Tweed needed to raise money, but the word was out on O'Conor's handpicked jury. The vultures were on the fence waiting, knowing Tweed had to sell at their price. Tweed was riled at their foul tactics, which he never used. The Tweed price was known for generosity. He rubbed the disappointment from his face in an offhand manner to disguise his emotion from his son. After all these years he had to learn that the markers you give out are best called in when you've got power.

Realistic news also came from Jay Gould, and Tweed couldn't blame him. Gould couldn't spoil his chances with Tilden, the next governor and future candidate for the White House.

Tweed's melancholy meeting with his son was interrupted by the kindhearted Sheriff Brennan, who entered jubilantly. "O'Conor is dying."

Tweed sprang alive. He sent Billy Junior to Fort Washington where O'Conor's estate sat high on the windy and scenic plateau opposite the Palisades. Shiny lacquered carriages lined O'Conor's country driveway. In the hall of the mansion servants wept. Upstairs, a wall of doctors stood around the dying man's bed.

By the time Billy Junior returned to report, his father was reading O'Conor's obituary in the latest edition. Several city courts had adjourned in honor of O'Conor. One paper ran an article on the prospect of Tweed eventually going free.

Courtrooms belong to the sporting scene. A judge's record is sometimes better known than a horse's. The most entertaining judges are those who make up with prejudice what they lack in judicial knowledge.

The first witness was the former corporation counsel Richard O'Gorman, a workhorse and drudge used by his Tammany superiors like butter on a plate. The lowliest spectators felt above O'Gorman, though once he'd been high up the ladder. Today Tweed's gallery was on the verge of revelry.

A curious murmuring broke out in the rear of the court and was ignored. No one had seen the courtroom door open, nor the feeble, winter-bundled man enter. When the police did not stop him—but stood at attention!—spectators buzzed.

The trial proceeded, unaware of the coming disturbance. The tall man wore a heavy greatcoat buttoned to his throat. His collar was pulled up above his neck, hiding all but his rawboned face. The cold was intolerable to him though the courtroom was warm. His parched lips were cracked by fever. He held one hand inside his greatcoat, between the buttons on his chest. His other hand hung down his side, gripping the stiff brim of his high hat. Borrowed time was melting his eyes. The murmuring was in awe even from his enemies: "O'Conor has risen from the grave to get Tweed!"

The judge's attention turned away from the trial to the mounting simmer in the courtroom. The trial stopped. Spectators began to stand in tribute to the old man as he passed. The prosecutor was overjoyed. Tweed's lawyer, Dudley Field, hastened to the fragile O'Conor to congratulate him on his heroic recovery. The judge himself stepped down from the bench to extend his hand in greeting. A grinding rose in Tweed's throat.

The outcome of the trial was now a foregone conclusion, and the jury did not take long to deliberate. The jurors filed in with overcoats and hats, signifying they had reached a verdict.

"Gentlemen," asked the chief clerk, "have you agreed upon a verdict?"

"We have," answered the foreman.

"What say you? Is William M. Tweed guilty or not?"

"Guilty."

Groaning protests amid the applause.

The foreman continued. "Guilty on two hundred and four counts in the indictment."

The momentous verdict silenced the court.

"Prisoner at the bar," asked the judge, "have you anything to say why sentence should not be pronounced on you?"

Tweed's contempt for the proceedings made him stand mute.

The chief clerk requested the prisoner to rise and receive the sentence of the court.

Tweed rose as a balloon drifting, straightening up at the last second to his full height like a man who had no need to please anyone. His Christmas belly hung forward as an image of boodle. His planet diamond bore a mineral resemblance to him, sparkling out of a hidden life that had nothing to do with guilt or innocence.

In the midst of a victory for justice there was an unnameable fear in the courtroom as when a heaviness presses down before a storm, recalling unknown powers shaping us.

"William M. Tweed, you stand convicted by the verdict of an intelligent and honest jury of a large number of particular crimes. You are honored and respected by large classes of the community, holding high public office, and, I have no doubt, beloved by your associates. With all these trusts you saw fit to pervert the powers with which you were clothed. You became more infamous than any like character in the history of the civilized world. I sentence you to twelve years in the penitentiary on Blackwell's Island and to pay a fine of twelve and a half thousand dollars."

To prevent rioting, Tweed was run out the back by a flying wedge of police and detectives and raced to the Ludlow Street jail he had helped build. The warden gave up his suite to Tweed. Oysters from Delmonico's were brought in. The jailer who filled out forms asked Tweed his occupation, and he cheerfully responded, "Statesman!"

The laughter and smiles made him comfortable in these strange and forbidding surroundings. He was not in Ludlow long before three of his lawyers arrived to say they had his sentence reduced to one year. He requested a private ferry to Blackwell's Island penitentiary in the East River, and this was granted.

When only the early-morning river fog filled the streets, Tweed was taken under heavy guard to the docks. The reduced sentence for his years of criminal activity was proof he remained a force to be reckoned with even in jail and was not to be unduly provoked.

To be a convicted man was not in his blood. He bid his lawyers adieu, patted a police nag while recalling his own Thoroughbreds in Greenwich and gallantly headed for the pier as he might take leave of a party that had lasted through the night.

A sword through his gut could not have stopped him quicker.

A lawyer asked the haunted-eyed Tweed, "What is it, Senator?"

"I'll never go on that ferry."

"You ordered it, Bill." The lawyer was worried.

Tweed backed off the slip, his voice so distant, they didn't hear his undercurrent. "I'll take the regular ferry."

A detective said, "The regular prison ferry goes at an earlier hour, when the city is asleep."

Tweed was trapped between being unable to say what he wanted or being condemned—as no judge or jury could condemn him—by saying it. He took stompy, commanding steps back to his city but was gently turned around. Lawyers and detectives tried to break through to him that he had requested a private ferry. He burst out against their ignorance of the city as well as from his torment. "This is the charity commissioner's ferry that takes the dead tenement children!"

A lawyer saw a way out with the regular prison ferry returning. He called to the skipper that Senator Tweed was to be taken. The skipper shouted back that the ferry was reserved for another run. There was a heavy load of prisoners today. He pointed to the van drawing up and unloading. The Irish poor had become so dominant in the city's prisons, the police van was popularly nicknamed the Paddy wagon.

Tweed eyed the sad lot of ignorant lifers done up with the stink of bravado. Guards herded them with smart raps of the billy, the prisoners' tough muttering only thinly disguising how completely they accepted their fate. They were packed into the rusty hulk of a ferry but left a wide space for Tweed.

Tweed took one glance and knew he'd never melt in with the prison cattle. That he couldn't—not even for a moment!—be connected with these helpless men. Until this second he didn't know what it meant to be a convicted criminal. He pushed out his belly, turned and braved it to the empty charity commissioner's ferry he had sworn minutes ago he'd never ride. It was difficult to tell by his show of confidence whether he had tamed the image of children's coffins, or whether those coffins had broken something inside him that would never heal.

Fog on the river molted against the ferry's lanterns. He saw the city that was his cradle, his milk, vanish into the mist without a sound, and his soul drifted out of him as the fog penetrated in.

Ahead was the humpbacked outline of Blackwell's Island. Veiled in the haze was the neglected penitentiary, the ramshackle insane asylum, the haunted look of the charity hospital, workhouse and pauper's graveyard. The howls of the insane carried on the damp winds back to the city. New Yorkers kept Blackwell's out of mind. Here grave robbers dug up corpses for the medical schools. The sick without family or friends were doomed. The dead without money were buried. He could bear all this easily except for the warden coming out to welcome him with a wholeheartedness at having a celebrity, and this brought out Tweed's remorse.

When he coughed out the moist air, the attentive warden said, "That's a mighty bad cold you have, Boss."

"Bad or good," Tweed replied, "it's the best I have."

The grinning warden asked, "Have you heard there's now Boss Tweed restaurants? All you can eat."

After that Tweed willingly entered the dark and chilly penitentiary and was surprised at the hectic commotion inside the damp hall. In the gloomy light he heard a rattle of coughs, hawking, wheezing, blown noses and sniffles. The old and infirm so cold, they ate with their eyes closed. The warden told him these hungry people had never committed a crime, but the city jails were full of them. They were lodgers from the Panic and grateful for shelter. The warden escorted Tweed to a suite with a lit fireplace.

Tweed kept away from the bed, fearing sleep would be an act of surrender to his surroundings. The prison was cheek by jowl with the asylum, and the ravings that would not cease degraded him. By the middle of the night nothing could warm the chill in his sinking insides, not the fireplace nor the blankets wrapped around him. He climbed into bed with his clothes on and felt he was wetting himself with his life.

FORTY-THREE

*W*hen Billy Junior arrived the next morning, his father with mad energy was writing away in his neat bookkeeper's hand his confession to O'Conor: naming names, dates, places, amounts. He knew that if he confessed all, Tilden would not accept it. He had to walk a fine line of confessing only what he could get away with.

Billy Junior was sent to O'Conor to ask if he would reduce his father's sentence for a confession. O'Conor readily agreed that this was a possibility, depending on the quality of the confession; but even if this quality was foolproof, it would come to nought if Tilden refused. Yet O'Conor didn't see how Tilden could refuse a watertight confession.

When O'Conor read the confession and saw that it was valid, he passed it on to Tilden. In anticipation of being set free, Tweed was transferred back to Ludlow while Tilden went over the confession.

It was at Ludlow that Billy Junior came to tell his father the most extraordinary news since the trials started. Tilden had returned the confession for insufficient evidence. O'Conor had publicly dissented and resigned. Tweed didn't know whether to laugh or cry. He laughed when he said, "There's no mercy."

Billy Junior saw his father's situation was hopeless. When

Tweed felt his son's sympathetic pat on his back, he knew he had to reveal his plan now with the utmost dignity. He needed Billy Junior's help. His own father had asked him for help in selling his chairs, and that had turned him into a man with a realistic view of how the world worked. Now he was depending on his son's help but in a way that could be destructive to Billy Junior. "Billy"—he was walking on coals—"I'm going to escape."

Pain flushed Billy Junior's face. To keep his father's words from tearing him apart he hurriedly said, "Speak to Mom about it."

"I will," Tweed assured him. "I paid for home visits. The warden and his keeper will ride me to see your mother."

His loyal son turned into an embarrassed accuser. "Mother couldn't face an escape."

Tweed knew from his own father that trouble lies in wait for the very best and caring of parents. You raise children for a better world and they soon fall into the real one. If the best of parents can be contradicted by their children after so little experience, what hope is there? The hope is that his father lived a life—succeed or fail!—his child could take pride in.

Billy Junior thought he'd be praised for his generosity. "I'm giving you your money back. You'll be able to afford the best lawyers."

Tweed became deathly frightened. "Never! No children of mine are going to be poor. The poor are unconscious. The ignorance of people shapes their politicians." He was torturing himself by seeing so clearly and acting blindly.

"Mother holds up her head because you stood and fought and didn't run like the rest of them."

Tweed lowered his voice in a confidential way that conferred equality on the listener. His thick fingers uncurled to release the futility in himself. He never wanted a proud son to hear a troubled father. He desperately wanted to avoid joining that army of fathers who shovel their compromised guts over their children as pearls of wisdom. Without trimmings, he said, "A chalk mark on the top step of our house means I'll be escaping that night."

That confidence was not what his bewildered son wanted to hear. "How can you believe an escape will set you free?"

Seeing a son's despair at a father's shallow thinking, Tweed burned with sympathy for him. "When things go wrong, you don't want to remember your experience because that's what trapped you." He wanted the impossible. He wanted to make his son see without hurting him. "Defeat leaves you without experience for a time."

Billy Junior was defensively silent.

Tweed's inside crumbled into his curling and uncurling hands. If only he could catch his futility and crush it. What he was seeing of himself shocked him into saying, "How soft men must be to survive. Their nightmares disappear as soon as they turn on the lights."

A saddened Billy Junior surprised his father. "I'll help."

FORTY-FOUR

$\mathcal{A}$ few days later Warden Dunham and Keeper Hogan took Tweed on his daily ride to dine with Mary Jane. Tweed spotted an *X* chalked on the front step of his house.

He tried not to stiffen and give himself away.

Billy Junior greeted him with a courtesy that had long gone out of fashion except in the strictest families. He couldn't look his son in the eye to find out what was wrong. He feared the warden or keeper might read things there too. He felt the danger was from family rather than the police. Billy Junior's backing off shook Tweed.

His son invited the officials into the parlor for tea and cake while Tweed went upstairs to see Mary Jane. Tweed heard his son genially hosting his escort and was proud of him.

Mary Jane's greeting was simply noticing him. Her arms hung lifelessly from stiff shoulders, as if awaiting the unforeseen with little faith. He no longer knew how to kiss his wife. The longer the marriage, the deeper the kiss as it goes through years of joy and pain.

She didn't want an excuse. "I know what's on your mind."

"I'm sure you do." He added her name as if it were a bright part of his life to say it. "Mary Jane."

"You're going to stay here and vindicate yourself."

"Mary Jane." He tried to win her back, though he knew what he would say was going to repel her. "I'm . . . going."

She refused to dignify him with a response.

"I can't spend the rest of my life in jail."

"Escape and you admit your guilt."

What tied his tongue is that he could never take a superior stance to his wife's quality, no matter how innocent that quality may be.

"What made the family proud is that you stayed to fight and clear your name."

He wanted to reassure her, but he didn't know how to reply without disturbing her. "I'm leaving only until I can get a fair trial in the courts." He was pleased at how fair that sounded.

Her voice faded with the shame of having to tell him the obvious. "You're running away like any guilty man. The law protects the innocent."

He didn't want to tell her the torture of jail is knowing mediocrities walk outside. He told her what he knew from experience. "The law has a nervous hemline."

Mary Jane sickened at the thought of his escape. Her plain face, lit up by her innate goodness, became dull, drawn, lifeless.

"Nothing you say can excuse your escape." She tried to reach him.

He wanted her to see the light. "It's merely a legal maneuver."

"Your children won't believe it's legal."

What was killing him was what they were not saying. Their intimacies came from being parents and not as husband and wife. He begged Mary Jane, "Take the children to Paris. Tell them they're going on vacation."

She didn't want to look on the alien shape he had become. She asked him as she would a stranger, "When are you going?"

"Soon as I leave here."

Mary Jane turned to stone. "You're immune to being called a crook. Nothing bothers you. No court of law can shame you. You've become your father's worst fears. You've killed the man to fit the office." She hated saying it.

He was compelled to speak into her resistance, balance himself in her eyes, tell her that what was wrong with him was more terrifying than what she believed. He could barely tell it to himself, so how could he tell it to her?—but he did. "I have my father's blindness." It was killing him. "I can't escape from that!"

Frightened, she shook her head against where he was heading. "Don't ruin everything."

He wanted her to see he was vastly improved over the man who went on trial; tougher, surer, truer. His voice, like his news, was disconnected and conveyed how cut off he had become. "My father's kindness left me unprepared for life. The care he took on a piece of wood would be misplaced with most people."

"Don't destroy what's best about you and think you're improving yourself." Her plea not to go on was also a warning he had already gone too far. "When you succeeded, you praised yourself; and when you failed, you blamed others."

He couldn't stop. Like a caught bird, he had another voice as victim. A grating call. Pebbles and grist. His harsh fate unmasked. His end on top of him before he knew it. "I had to forget my father's way or I'd never get anywhere."

Tears ran down her face. "He gave you the marvelous confidence that attracted me. Don't destroy memories of your father."

His voice came from a long way off. The exploding husband. The husband she had known vanished before her eyes. "I want to burn my past. The ignorance we receive as a trust. You and my father don't know how anything works. I wish I could have lived your ignorant lives. Then my past would've made me happy, and I'd be honoring it."

She didn't want to hear how little was left of him, yet she was driven to listen.

"My past that was so happy keeps returning darker and darker."

"Don't let what happened destroy the memory of your father. Bill, you'll have nothing left."

His hands wanted to explain what speech couldn't, fingers touching, tapping cheek, chest, bull neck. What appeared to be disorder was his trying to identify himself. He accidentally reached out and touched her, and though she was sympathetic she couldn't help wincing inside herself. Now he saw she was still the intimate woman she had always been, but his work over the years had made him untouchable to her. He suddenly became afraid of himself, especially his isolation. "Do you know, Mary Jane, I couldn't dream happier memories than I had. My memories gave me strength."

Her eyes swelled with tears.

He was on a bizarre test of strength to see how much of himself he could stand. "All my push and energy!" He sniffed contemptuously. "I wasn't *murderous* enough."

Mary Jane pleaded with him to see. "We loved you the way you were."

"No, no!" He waved Mary Jane off because her saying *love* painfully injured him. She could never say that word routinely or as a substitute for what couldn't be felt. "Thank God there's one law that doesn't go through politics. A law inside me that's incorruptible."

Mary Jane reddened with understanding.

He was drowning. "The only justice is what we find out about ourselves." He wiped his mouth with his knuckles. Each wipe left him unsatisfied. "I was an ignoramus when I succeeded. I failed with a bellyful of knowledge."

She desperately wanted to stop his frenzied feeding on himself. She shook her head at being married to him and blind to him at the same time. "You should have married a more tolerant woman."

"Are you crazy?" He roughly grabbed her hand and kissed her fingers. "When I bought and sold people, I was admired. When I ceased to care, I was honored. This house was a different world to me."

Mary Jane felt strangely at rest without being at peace. "Why didn't you tell me this before?"

His head nodded on a string. "I needed you to stand up for me."

Instead of his unexpected humility being a relief, she missed the strange attraction of standing against a storm. When he was humble, she found him out of his skin and difficult to recognize. Emotional worms surfaced to his once pleasant face. "You should have left politics long ago." She couldn't help feeling repulsed. "You've become so destructive."

He answered as a man curled inside himself. "My destructive self has become my strength."

She didn't want to understand, and she understood only too well. "Your power made you powerless to see yourself. You're so distorted."

A nightmare heat was on him. He wanted her to see justice through his eyes. "That's how I succeeded."

Feeling his energy beating against her gave her the courage for a last appeal. "No matter how corrupt the world is, you have a chance as a father to be a decent human being. Stay here for your children."

He fell into a staring silence, as though a dark chasm had opened at his feet. She had brought him back to those who were closest to him and loved him. Mary Jane was about to smile her radiant, tearful congratulations to him for coming around at last, when Billy Junior tapped rapidly on the door. "It's time to leave."

"I'm not ready," came his hurried reply. He had to convince Mary Jane of the rightness of his cause.

"You'll miss your *chance,*" Billy Junior said harshly, "to escape."

"I'm talking to your mother."

"We can hear it," he warned his father.

"Leave off and I'll be down faster."

Mary Jane quietly asked, "Where're you going?"

"I can't tell you. That way nobody will be obliged to lie."

Mary Jane retorted, "Don't protect us in that way!"

Billy Junior rushed him, "What's taking you so long to say good-bye?"

Tweed wished he had not opened the door. Having degraded his father's memory, he saw he had now degraded himself in his son's eyes. He so wanted his son to have the conviction he could prevail against the longest odds. After all the comforts, servants, riches and gifts of city and country living, he was leaving his son with an experience of running away under a cloud. This would always weigh heavily and weaken a son he wanted to make strong.

Billy Junior took away his voice by not looking at him. What could he draw up from himself to say in his defense? The good a father does must remain unspoken lest the selfless good is lost, and all is lost. He couldn't imagine not wanting to look at *his* father. He finally found his respectful voice. "I'll be down soon."

His son abruptly turned away. "You don't have time to waste."

Mary Jane saw a blow had aged her husband and knew from whence it came.

He tried to regain himself and end on a sane note. "You don't know what politics has rotted in you until you try to have personal relations."

Their eyes exchanged permission for him to gently place his arm on her shoulder as he left. How gentle he was; his touch stiffened her. But he felt her inner apology. The draining of her tension against him was as warm as lovemaking. This was her original warmth when she first allowed him through her shyness.

He didn't want to leave her when they hadn't been this close in years, but Mary Jane quickly left him alone and disappeared behind a closed door. Out on the landing by himself he heard the chatty voices downstairs. He needed to encourage his son, but in the rush he had lost his chance to say good-bye.

His weight hindered him from stepping quietly down the stairs. He had to stop on every other step to listen until he reached the bottom. He plucked his coat and hat off the wall, opened and closed the front door swiftly to keep the cold air from hinting he had left. A raw wind hurled the winter against him. He foolishly stopped to glance at his watch. Taking his time brought back his needed dignity.

He was late.

Rushing heartsick around the corner, he was met by a roar of exuberance containing outbursts of joy and sorrow. The shouting and wailing came up from the Battery.

He stopped in his tracks.

The nervous driver, scared out of his wits, waved him into a new ice wagon of wooden sides and canvas roof carrying coal in the winter.

"What is that?" Tweed climbed, huffing and puffing, over the tailgate to hide on a bench among the coal.

"I don't know." He feigned ignorance to get away.

"I must see what's happening." Tweed's excitement was up. He climbed toward the protesting driver and slid in alongside him.

"You must sit back there," said the edgy driver, "or you'll be seen."

Tweed pulled down the leather hood to shade them.

"The ship captain passing Barnegat Light won't wait for you. The bay is open where anyone can see you climb aboard."

"Then hurry to the Battery and let me see what's going on," he bullied the driver.

They passed Gosling's, that storm center of eating, emptying out with patrons bursting in their skins like the wurst they devoured. They left mountains of food so freshly gnashed, their appetites hovered over the tables. A grand opera could be staged at lunch in Gosling's and not be heard. Now these patrons were swept along with carriages and wagons by the thickening crowds heading down Broadway.

"Immigrants!" came the cries from those up ahead. "Ships as far as you can see! Millions of immigrants are here!"

The homeless uncurled from doorways to sneak down quieter streets.

"Finns, Danes, Norwegians, Swedes, Poles, Hungarians, Ukrainians, Lithuanians, Russians, Scotch, English, Italians, Jews, French, Germans and Irish. A hundred times more, a thousand times more than before!"

The driver was scared. "Let's get out of here."

Tweed was on fire. "They've been driven out by the panic in Europe." He wasn't easily startled, but he was startled now. "We haven't absorbed the immigrants from the potato blights. This human migration could go on for another twenty, thirty, forty years."

The crowd at the foot of Broadway was roaring at the sight they had come upon.

Then Tweed saw it too.

A forest in the water. Ship masts clogging the bay. Kissing, hugging, weeping immigrants spreading onto the Battery from their landing at Castle Garden. Bundles, satchels, chests strapped to their backs, held in their arms, carried on their heads. Children hoisted on shoulders to see the United States. Men, women, children kissing the sidewalks of New York. Foreign languages spraying over everyone with kinship.

Tweed glowed at the open emotions of the immigrants. "They're getting off the boats today, and all their lives they'll be telling their children and grandchildren how New York began with their arrival. But they're pouring into molds made by Boss Tweed."

He ordered the driver to fly down a side street toward the Hudson River. The night ferry was ready to take him across. He looked back at the worn streets where old and new buildings appeared to have conquered nature. He knew better. Streets and buildings hold on to people the way seashells keep the hum of the sea. People coming together and parting like the tides going in and out around their island. Men and women retaining their origins, salt-licked like the sea.

EPILOGUE

Mulberry was a madhouse.

Police were everywhere, combing the wards, tracking down leads, putting the screws to their informers, guarding terminals, fencing off piers, searching the swamps of Staten Island. Every enterprise tied to the police for survival—opium dens, flash houses, sporting pits—went on the alert for information.

Tweed's escape revived the horrendous Tweed Ring scandals. The "biggest thief in the history of civilization" ballooned over the public, an eclipse that wouldn't go away.

The escape did not remind the public that Tilden had helped put the Boss away. The escape reminded intelligent New Yorkers that Jones of the *Times* and his tenacious editor, Jennings; Nast and his gifted and uncompromising editor, Curtis, of *Harper's Weekly;* and Godkin of *The Nation* were fighting Tilden for hemming and hawing on the Tweed scandals—always to his ambitious advantage. The escape reminded the public how little money had been recovered. The biggest crooks got away. Yet Tilden was running for president.

The public bought newspapers like money at a sale. The Panic was forgotten as newsboys outshouted each other: "Tweed Escapes! The Boss Vanishes into Thin Air! Ten-thousand-dollar Reward! Tweed in Georgia! Tweed Escapes to Ontario! Tweed Seen in North Carolina!

A disguised Tweed with a different name was on a small boat to Barcelona. On the long voyage he lost his appetite, half his weight, his legs bloated painfully, clothes hung off him. Yet when the bark *Carmen* docked at Vigo in the Canary Islands, he was readily recognized by a custom official from a Nast cartoon, and returned to the United States.

Soon after returning, sick, worn and grizzled, Tweed died in the Ludlow Street jail that he had helped build. His funeral was sparsely attended and little noticed. None of his family attended.

ABOUT THE AUTHOR

MORRIS RENEK's previous novels include *Las Vegas Strip, Heck, The Big Hello* and the bestselling *Siam Miami*.